THE HADRA

THE HADRA

Book 57, Part 2, of the Hadra Archives,
as recorded by Tazzil of Zelindar
for Alyeeta the Witch

by Diana Rivers

Boston ♦ Lace Publications

ACKNOWLEDGMENTS

I would like to thank all of the women of my family and tribe who have listened to these stories over the years and given me support and encouragement, especially Path and Bea and Cedar and Judy and Marilyn and Chris, as well as my Sisters from WomanWrites and from the Midwest Women's Festival. This book is dedicated to Wanda and Brenda and Cheri and Pam and all the other brave women of Camp Sister Spirit who, with vision and tenacity, are creating Zelindar right here in Mississippi.

Typeset and printed in the United States of America.

This is a paperback original from Lace Publications,
an imprint of Alyson Publications, Inc.,
40 Plympton St., Boston, Massachusetts 02118.

This book is printed on acid-free, recycled paper.

First edition, first printing: June 1995

2 4 5 3 1

ISBN 1-55583-319-5

PROLOGUE

O Mother, Great Goddess, was I ever so young and innocent? Who could believe it now? But I have these pages here before me as proof. I never thought to see it again, this account Alyeeta made me keep of my early life and that first part of our journey. Yet Zheran has just this morning laid it in my hands. (How that came about, of course, is a whole other story.) The entire packet was lost during that winter we spent in the caves. At the time I did not miss it. If I had, I would not have cared. I myself was lost that winter, wandering in some icy blizzard of the spirit where nothing mattered. After that, so much happened so fast that writing was altogether forgotten.

Before we left the Wanderer camp, I had carefully wrapped my account in oiled cloth and placed it in the bottom of my pack for safekeeping. I never wrote another word in it. How it came into another's possession ... Well, I will tell of that later. It has been almost ten years since we rode out of that valley and I last looked at these pages. Now it all comes flooding back to me: our finding each other and gathering together, our flight from the Zarn's army, all the hardships and adventures of that time. How strange it seems to read these words, written so long ago by that young woman whose memories I share, who is myself and yet not myself, who is, indeed, in many ways a stranger. Since that time, no matter what I have witnessed or what has befallen me, I have never again felt the same raging bitterness that possessed me then. And never, though I live to be a hundred, will I be able to regain the loving innocence that was my birth-gift. That grieves me still, though I accept it now. Of all the gifts the Goddess bestowed on me, and I can now acknowledge that they were many, that loving innocence was the sweetest gift of all. Ah well, I am as I am. *As it must be,* as the Witches taught us to say. I cannot live my life backward and I would not live another's, so I must accept who I have become. All that happened back then helped to shape the person I am now.

My family named me Tazmirrel, for the One the farm folk ask for water when their wells run dry. I was also named for my mother's mother, whom I never knew. My family called me Tazzia, and later my Hadra sisters called me Tazzi. None of those names fits the young woman who came out of the caves that spring, the one who had gone alone to meet with the old Asharan. I became Tazzil, which suited well enough who I grew to be, the councilor I became. Those who know me best still call me Tazzi, but it is Tazzil who will write the remainder of this account, as I have this day decided to finish the task Alyeeta set for me those many years ago.

★

Looking back, that whole first year seems a wild blur. What I recall most vividly is great tongues of fire blazing against the night, horses whinnying, people shouting and running, the smell of smoke, and, above all, the fear, that terrible new feeling that came so suddenly into my life. Of our departure from the Wanderer valley I remember little. The Witches' belling out, the trip to the Asharan asking place, and all the turmoil that preceded it had sapped my strength, not only of body but of mind and spirit as well. I had been left so depleted, I was scarcely among the living. Pell tells me that when we left they set me on my horse and rode one on either side of me for a ways, to keep me safe. Clearly, I was of no use then to myself or any other. That journey to the caves is all hazy to me now, like peering through deep water for what lies beneath. But, for the sake of the story that follows, I will say some words here about the caves themselves and how we knew of them.

It was Hereschell who led us there, in one of his many acts of kindness on our behalf: Hereschell the Wanderer, who, in spite of our rudeness and poor manners, had become our good friend. I sometimes thought he saw us as his family, the one he never had, though when I said that to him once, he coughed and spluttered and shook his head. "Do you think me some great fool, Tazzi? Why would I choose a family that would cause me nothing but heartache and trouble?" *Why indeed?* I thought to myself.

On the way to those caves, we had to ride through deep woods for several days. It was during this part of our journey that we crossed the invisible boundary that lay between Garmishair and Yarmald. There was nothing to mark the place: no rock stacks, no banners, no line on the road, not even any notches in the trees. Had I not been riding next to Hereschell, I would have been quite unaware of any change, but he stopped his horse and said, with something like awe in his voice, "Now we are leaving Garmishair and entering Yarmald. This is a magic place where Wanderers, Witches, and Kourmairi have more power, and the Zarns have less." To my amazement he slid off his horse, knelt on the road, and kissed the ground.

"How can you tell?" I asked crossly after he had remounted. "One tree, one rock, one clump of moss looks much like any other to me." I thought perhaps he was jesting with us, and I was in no mood for his jokes.

He answered very seriously, "I know because I can feel it. I have ridden this road so many times that my heart pulls at me when we get close. But if you go into the woods two hundred feet to either side of the road, you will find a group of three standing stones that marks the place."

"What is this Yarmald?" Pell asked with some impatience. "I thought Garmishair went all the way to the sea."

"That is what the Zarns would like you to think. The Shokarn of Eezore call everything Garmishair that lies between the Rhonathrin Mountains and the sea. They feel they should have dominion over all of it. But the people of Yarmald do not agree. They fight back in their own ways to keep themselves free. Yarmald is a peninsula, with ocean protecting it on three sides. If you go far north or far south, you will come to the spot where water makes a deep cut into the land. Yarmald is also a place of will and spirit. It is a state of mind." I knew from the reverence in Hereschell's voice that there was something of importance here. As I had neither the wits nor the energy to pursue it at that moment, I stored it away to look at later.

Finally, after several more days, the woods opened up. Suddenly we emerged onto wide, gently rolling headlands, covered with grass, all golden yellow from the frost. The caves themselves were not visible from the headlands. Though they had several entrances, all save one were hidden in the steep face of the sea cliff, and were accessible only by a series of hand- and footholds carved into the rock itself. Those entrances led to several large central chambers and to the hot springs that gave the caves their warmth.

Aside from those carefully cut hand- and footholds, there were other signs of former habitation that made me think these caves might once have been an Asharan sanctuary: some carved symbols on the cave walls near the hot springs, a large stone at the top of the slope that must once have been an altar, and another that might have been a sentry stone. Whether this was now a Wanderer place or something Hereschell had discovered on his own and was sharing with us, I had no way of knowing. When I asked him, he shrugged, shook his head, and turned away, acting like the mute he sometimes pretended to be. Alyeeta, who obviously had some prior knowledge of this place, was no more informative.

We made our winter home in the central chambers of those caves. It was dark, damp, stuffy, and crowded there, but also far from the Zarn's roads and, we hoped, out of reach of his army; a place of relative safety where we could rest and heal — and, above all, stop running. With Hereschell's help, almost all the money and valuables we had gathered, including my cache of gold coins, had been traded to the Thieves Guild in exchange for food and provisions. Jhemar, Zenoria, Zari, Daijar, and some of the other horsewomen had taken most of our horses south into hiding, since we could feed and shelter only a few with us there at the caves.

Of that winter I remember little. No doubt many stories could be written of our time in the caves and all that happened there. If so, others will have to write them. As for myself, I moved will-less and witless through those days, doing only those tasks that were thrust into my hands and stopping only when someone relieved me of them.

One thing I do recall from that winter is Alyeeta's gentleness, her unfailing kindness to me. I suppose she understood just how fragile my hold on sanity had become. Besides, as Telakeet so often said, she probably loved me more than was wise. For that while, at least, she put aside her sharp tongue and let me see into the sweetness under her hard crust, a sweetness that was like clear water flowing under ice and gravel. I grew to love and trust her in a whole new way. She became my refuge: the mother, sister, lover I had lost; the teacher I had longed for, yet never thought to find. For a while, Alyeeta the Witch became my village, my family, and my home.

Another thing I remember from that time in the caves is Pell's face in front of me, Pell's eyes looking intently into mine, Pell saying with concern, "Tazzi, where are you? Tazzi, come back, we need you here. Where are you wandering, Terrazen?" She would say such things over and over until Alyeeta would come and pull her away. But not even for Pell could I bring myself back. The terrible rage was gone, but nothing had come to take its place. The well was empty to the bottom.

I was not the only one whose mind was bent or wandering that winter. The worst killer among us was not the Zarn's guards, for they never found us, or even the terrible cold and the short rations, but a thing we came to call the gibbering madness. Sometimes a young woman's powers came on her all at once and crushed her. Those that had the madness could not be made to eat or drink or care for themselves in any way, and their words made little sense. Sometimes, when none of us was watching, they ran out naked into the ice and snow, often dying of exposure or lack of food. If they managed to survive, the madness left them after a time.

Had it been a gentler place, or had there been enough of us who were well in body and strong of mind, we might have been able to care for the ones who were not. Then, most of the women who died that winter might have been saved. But even for those of us who kept our bodies whole, it was hard to keep our sanity. The crowding and the closeness of the caves took their toll on our minds, and in that harsh, winter-gripped land, any who ventured out had to have all her wits about her. In the end, I think most of us were more than a little mad by the time winter was over, even the Witches themselves.

1

Not even the coming of spring seemed to lift my spirits or bring much change in my condition. When the ground thawed enough, we buried our dead from the winter. I knew none of them well, or perhaps grief could have reached through my numbness. Instead, as I helped dig and carry, I felt as cold as the ground itself. Chanting the words for the dead, I could not find it in my heart to grieve. Indeed, I almost envied them. They looked so peaceful in their frozen sleep. To me, living seemed too much effort, for too little gain. In spite of our new freedom, I remained as heavyhearted as if we were still imprisoned in the caves by winter's cold.

One morning I went to sit watch at the entrance to the upper cave. That, at least, was something I could do. This entrance was one that had been blocked and hidden all winter for safety. It was the only one that opened onto the upper plateau and faced south. From where I sat on my rock in the sun, leaning against the entrance wall, I could look west to the ocean, where the sun glinted off the waves; south along the long, curving headlands now greening with spring; and east to the far fringe of trees. I was sharing the watch with Lhiri, who was at the top of the slope facing north. For that moment we were the eyes of the camp. Between us, we could see in all directions.

All around me, new spring grass was thrusting up out of the dark soil in a blaze of green, gray-white patches of snow were melting in silver-blue rivulets, and the trees that were so stark in winter were beginning to show the first soft bloom of buds. It was a sight that should have gladdened my heart after the privations of that long winter. Instead, I gazed at all that brilliance with dead eyes. Though my mind knew better, my heart saw endless shades of gray. Finally, lulled by the warmth of the sun, my head began to nod. In spite of being on watch, I shut my eyes to doze a little, trusting that all was well and promising myself that it would be for no more than a moment or so.

I woke with a start, the hair rising on the back of my neck. Frightened, I looked around quickly, sure I had betrayed us to some danger by my carelessness. Instead, I saw that some of the Witches had gathered nearby. They were speaking softly, nodding and gesturing in my direction. Obviously, I was the subject of their intense discussion. When they saw that I was awake and had noticed them, they spoke a little louder, but it was still in the ancient language the Witches used for rituals and secrets. I could understand little of what they said, though clearly it concerned me.

A chill like cold fingers crept up my back. There was no enemy advancing after all. But for me, facing the Witches might be almost as dangerous. The last time they had concerned themselves with me, the Witches had done a belling out, and I had almost died of it. I felt a momentary rush of anger and wanted to shout at them to speak Kourmairi so that I could understand and take some part in my own fate. Then, that utter weariness came over me again, that carelessness for my own life. I thought, *What does it matter after all? Why should I care what they do with me?* Even if it was dangerous and painful, I would bear it gladly if only it would help free me from that horrifying pit of emptiness into which I had sunk. Two words I heard repeated over and over. The first, *yhagarth,* I knew meant death of the soul or spirit, a very serious matter from the way they said it. The second, *Koyani,* I discovered the meaning of soon enough.

Alyeeta seemed to be arguing some point with the others. At last she stepped forward and made a slight bow in front of me. She spoke so formally it chilled my blood. It was as if we had no personal connection, as if we had never been friends or lovers. "I have been sent to ask if you will meet with us before the altar rock at the turning of the night. Someone will come to fetch you and help make you ready." This was phrased as a request, but I understood it to be an order. Even in my numbed state, I felt little tremors of terror rush up my body. When I tried to question Alyeeta, she raised a hand for silence and turned away.

I spent the rest of the day alone with my fears, for I was reluctant to share them with anyone. Occupying myself away from the others, I did little jobs of sorting and clearing down in the caves. Pell, however, stopped me in passing. With a look of concern she stared into my face. "What ails you, Tazzi? You are sending out waves of fear." I could not shut down my thoughts quickly enough. Suddenly she was grinning and nodding. "Ah, so the Witches have some plan for you. Let us hope it works better than all my poor attempts." With a growl of annoyance, I shook off her hand and hurried away.

That night I slept fitfully until Olna came to rouse me. She was trying to look very solemn, but by the light of her candle, I glimpsed a little edge of amusement, a secret smile she could not quite conceal. Though I tried hard, I could read nothing from her mind. When I sought to question her in words, she raised her hand for silence, as Alyeeta had done. Then, holding out that hand to me, she led me to one of the hot springs. There, with embarrassing attention to details, she helped me bathe. Afterward, she rubbed me down with sweet-oil, set out some sandals for me to put on, and helped me into a long, loose robe made of dark cloth. It looked like a piece of Witchwork, all heavily embroidered with an intricate design of symbols in brightly colored threads. When Olna was finished with this work, all done in silence, she beckoned me to follow. Full of apprehension, I went with her.

As the half-moon gave off enough light to see by, we took no torch or lamp. The silence of the night pressed in around us. With no word spoken between us, Olna's dark, robed figure moved always just a step ahead of me. My fear increased as we went. At each turn of the path I told myself that I could stop right there, that I did not need to take another step, that the Witches could not really compel me against my will. Yet, each time, I took the next step. My curiosity seemed to outweigh my fears and draw me on. There was a little voice in my head that said, *Think what you may miss if you turn back now.* Somehow I trusted Alyeeta and her love for me to keep me safe. The last time, she had warned me over and over of the harm that would come if I did not change my ways. This time there had been no warnings, so I told myself there could be no harm. That did nothing to lessen my fear, but it did keep me walking forward, following after Olna's always retreating back. From the direction of our path, I suspected that the altar was our destination.

I was familiar with the altar place, but had never ventured there at night. Even on those nights when I had the upper watch, I had avoided it. It felt as if there was too much power present there. But in daylight, before the winter cold had forced us into the caves, I had often gone to sit alone in that place. From there I could look out at the ocean and think on the mysterious Ashara, the first people, the ones who most likely had used the caves before us and made that altar. The altar stone was set in a shallow bowl of earth near the top of the slope above the cave entrance. Only the sentry rock itself was higher. Both rocks must have been brought there by human hand — or at least by human intent. There were few other rocks above the cliff face, and none was of that size.

The altar rock itself was flat on top, its dark surface so smoothly polished by use that one could see a slight reflection there. It was more than four hands in thickness and wide enough so that a person could lie on it in any direction. The sides of it were carved with various signs and symbols. Some of them were familiar. Many were strange to my eyes but resembled symbols the Witches used. Though the windswept headlands were mostly treeless, there was a grove of trees around the altar, clearly planted there in some far past time. They were not tall, but looked ancient, all bent and twisted, leaning inland as if shaped by the force of the ocean wind. Two of them grew together at the top, forming an archway, an entrance to the grove and to the altar.

Now, as we approached the place, even Olna slowed her steps. I had to force myself to put one foot in front of the other. Even from a distance, I could see the fire blazing in a pit in front of the altar and a ring of standing torches among the trees. As we came closer, I noticed a gate between the arched trees that had not been there before. It flickered in the torchlight, seeming to appear and disappear before my eyes. On the altar itself there were a number of lit candles that formed a triangle within a circle, but I could neither see nor sense any other sign of human presence. Olna and I seemed to be utterly alone there.

Suddenly, out of the silence, a strange sound started. It began almost as a whisper, then quickly rose to a chant or some sort of singing. It sounded like the wind blowing, like the rush of water, like the wail of wild animals at night, like the keening cry of Kourmairi women mourning a death — and yet like none of these. In truth, it sounded like nothing I had ever heard before. Terror shook me. It was as if those strange, twisted trees themselves had voices, as if the night itself had decided to sing. Ready to run, I grabbed for Olna's hand to hold me steady. At that moment, several figures stepped suddenly from behind the trees. They were darkly robed and hooded, and all wore masks. It might have been the spirit of each tree that suddenly stepped forth. I gave a cry of fright, ready to bolt and run. Olna gripped my hand tightly. "Wait, you know them all. Let them work their magic. There is no harm here — only power."

The figure closest to me took another step and tipped up her mask. It was Alyeeta, and yet not Alyeeta. It was Alyeeta charged with some other presence. When she spoke, however, it was with her ordinary voice. "Listen before you run, Tazzi. This is the Koyani ritual we are about to perform for your sake, but we do this only if you are willing, only with your consent. It is the ritual we do for Witches who have overused their powers and whose spirits are floating, not anchored in their bodies. Such a state may be desirable for the casting of spells, but only for a short while. You have been wandering all winter far from yourself, mind and spirit and body separated. For that long it is dangerous, very dangerous. I was so afraid you would never come back to yourself that I persuaded the others to do this. Think on it, Tazzia. We have never done this before for any who is not a Witch. There is much power in it. You must decide if you will trust yourself into our hands. None should come to this circle against her will, or the ritual will fail and the power will be wrongly bent." Behind her careful, formal words, I sensed Alyeeta pleading with me. She was afraid for me and had set her will against the other Witches to make this happen.

So it was mine to decide. I felt a lifting of my fears and almost laughed aloud. I was to have a choice in this after all and would not be forced or compelled, as I had first feared. It was more as if the other Witches were being compelled by Alyeeta for my sake. If so, perhaps they were not so terrible or so frightening after all. Suddenly I felt more alive, more present in my body than I had in months. *Why not?* I thought. *Let them do what they please with me. What does it matter anyhow?*

Alyeeta held up her hand. "No," she said quickly, before I had spoken those words aloud. "You cannot do this as you have been doing with your life, thinking it does not matter and throwing yourself away as if you were throwing garbage to the seabirds. You must mean it. You must bring your whole self to this thing. And you must trust the Witches as you never have before."

"But will they hurt me?" I asked quickly. My voice came out sounding small, humble, and frightened.

"No one will hurt you here, you have Alyeeta's pledge on that. There is no harm in this place, though at moments you may be frightened. There will be times when the Mother's power will move through us and through you as well." Alyeeta still spoke in her ordinary voice, but I heard a pledge there to match the most solemn oath.

Suddenly I wanted very much to come back from that dead place where my spirit had been wandering. I wanted it as much as I had ever wanted anything in my whole life. "I am here," I whispered. "I am ready. What must I do?"

"Before you can step through the gateway into that other realm, you must say three times, 'I do this thing of my own free will. No one compels me here.' If you cannot say those words from your heart, then this should not be done. And say it loudly, so that all may hear, even the Goddess."

I was trembling again, and my voice would not come. When it broke through, it cracked and wavered. "I do this thing of my own free will. No one compels me here." The second time I spoke louder and the words came with more ease. "I do this thing of my own free will. No one compels me here." The third time my voice boomed out, startling me with its strength. "I do this thing of my own free will! No one compels me here!"

The gate between the trees vanished like smoke. Some sort of force seemed to shift and realign itself. "Welcome to the sacred circle," Alyeeta said, holding out her hand. Olna came on the other side and took my arm. Between them, I stepped through the archway of guardian trees. We stopped before the altar. The other Witches all took a step forward and the strange singing began again, only this time it was more like chanting and had less wildness in it. Alyeeta said some words, then bent to blow out the candles. With care, she gathered them all in a little basket that had been sitting next to the altar. Then she took several handfuls of herbs out of that basket and scattered them in the fire. Sparks flared and thick smoke roiled up, almost purple in color. She said more words I could not understand. The odor was so pungent it dizzied my senses, making me sway on my feet. "Stand here," Alyeeta said with some impatience, taking my arm and moving me right next to the altar.

As Alyeeta stepped back, each of the other figures stepped forward in turn, tossed a handful of those strong-smelling herbs on the fire, and said some ritual words. The fire flared up brightly. In that leaping light, their frightening and mysterious masks seemed to come to life, grotesque and beautiful by turn. Then, standing on either side of me, Alyeeta and Olna reached out, slipped off the robe I was wearing, and laid it over the stone.

Now I was naked among all those robed figures. A tremor went through me as the warmth of the fire and the cool night air touched me at the same moment: fingers of hot and cold running up and down my body. Soon I was trembling in earnest. I thought again of fleeing, but Olna whispered in my ear, "Have courage. There is more pleasure here than you have ever experienced. There is not much in this world that I, Olna the Witch, find to envy about anyone, but I have to admit that I envy you this night, Tazzi. Lie down now on the altar so we may all find a place for our hands."

With these words, I understood that it was through sex they meant to call me back into my body. Now my trembling had a very different source, but it was too late to leave. I had already given my word. Besides, I was in a fever of curiosity. I lay back as I had been told, expecting cold to seep through the robe. To my surprise, the rock was warm. Whether this had been done with coals or magic or hot water from the springs, I had no time to ask. While the other dark, robed figures gathered around the altar, Alyeeta and Olna put a small pillow under my head, fanned my hair out around it, stretched my arms out to the sides, and gently opened and spread my hands. Then, very slowly, they both ran their hands down either side of my body and spread my legs wide, leaving my sex open and unprotected. Quickly, I tried to close my legs again but found I could not move.

Alyeeta bent down on one side of me and whispered, "You have willed yourself here and pledged yourself to this. Now let yourself go." Olna leaned over from the other side and kissed me gently on the mouth. "Much pleasure on your journey, Tazzi. Alyeeta and I will keep you safe." I looked up at Olna and gave a slight nod. Then Alyeeta said, "As it must be," and pulled down her mask. With that, the other Witches closed their circle around the altar, and Olna disappeared among them.

The chant had fallen to a murmur. Now it rose in volume again. Soon I could feel the sound of it resonating deep in my body. The shapes around me started moving in time to the chant, slowly at first and then faster and faster, until they were weaving and bobbing in a constant motion. Next they began moving their hands toward me and then away again, never quite touching, though I could feel energy pulsing from their fingertips and sometimes even see lines of light. They were all dark silhouettes against the blaze of the torches. Only at moments now could I distinguish the masks that loomed over me out of the darkness. They were larger than life, animal and human combined, frightening and ancient and divine and oddly comforting; beautiful or horrifying depending on how the light caught them.

This went on for so long that I wondered if it was all they planned to do, if, in fact, they did not mean to touch me at all. After a while my body began yearning toward their hands, though I could no more move toward them than I had been able to move away before. The yearning grew into a pleasurable pain. Then it became a hunger that I felt in my hardening nipples and the swelling between my legs and finally all over my body. *Touch me, please touch me!* my body cried silently. I was wide open to their hands, to the sound of the chant, to the night, to the universe itself. I wanted to beg, to plead, to shout — but I could not find my voice. I could only nod my head.

Though it was as light as a feather, that first touch was a shock that ran along my nerve ends and set off a shower of sparks. Soon there were more featherlight touches. After a while I could feel hands on me everywhere, moving soft and insistent, while my whole body quivered in response. Suddenly it seemed as if my ears had been unplugged, for I could understand the words of their chant. "Through the body we come to the spirit. Through the spirit we come to the body." They sang this over and over while their touch became stronger and deeper. Their hands seemed to move in circles, following the rhythm of their chant. "Through the body we come to the spirit. Through the spirit we come to the body."

Then the chant shifted. Some of the voices took up new words, weaving them in with the old ones. "The Mother gives us both to be one, one to be both. All mystery and power lies in that union." This too was sung over and over, till a third set of voices began chanting, "Sex is Her gift to bind us to the magic of creation. Sex is Her gift to remember the spirit dwelling in the body." Then all the voices joined, chanting together, "Honor the body, honor the spirit, honor the mind."

Body and spirit seemed to be doing very well, but mind was almost forgotten as their touch deepened and grew more forceful. Indeed, for a long while, mind seemed to have left me altogether. When their chanting turned to sound again, a drone that rose and fell like wind in the trees, I finally found my own voice. I could hear it weaving in with their chant, singing, humming, laughing, moaning, crying out. My body felt as if it were rising, opening, growing to meet their hands. There were hands everywhere on me, hands touching, stroking, pinching, caressing; fingers entering my most private places, plunging deeply and bringing shudders of pleasure.

Then, suddenly, though I never saw them remove their masks, I felt mouths on me as well as hands: mouths and tongues and teeth on my cheeks, my neck, the palms of my hands, my breasts, my nipples, and between my legs. At the same time, fingers were thrusting fiercely into me and my own body was thrusting back just as fiercely against them. The sensations came from every part of my body. Now I was truly moving through body into spirit and back again. Colors were bursting in the darkness. At moments the hands had faces. Sometimes I seemed to see Pell and sometimes Rishka. Sometimes it was Kara, Kara as we had been as children, and for that moment I was back on the banks of the river with her, shuddering with pleasure in the hot sun. A myriad of scenes flashed before me from places I knew, as well as glimpses of places I had never seen that must have come from the minds of the Witches.

All this while, my body was responding to every touch. Suddenly, I could feel power rising up from between my legs, rising into my belly, where my will had lain dormant for so long; rising into my chest, where my heart had been frozen; rising into my throat, where silence had lived all winter. Finally, pain, pleasure, rage, anguish, and joy all burst out in a great wailing scream that shook me to the core. This was followed with a silence so profound it seemed as if every living thing had been swallowed by that explosion of sound.

After a while I heard my own sobbing, and the world came spinning back into place. The fire and the torches had burned down. The grove was full of gentle moonlight. The Witches had taken up their chant again, "Through the body we come to the spirit. Through the spirit we come to the body." Their strange masks were gone and I could see each of their faces quite clearly. Some of them were playing drums or little pipes to accompany the singing. The sound of the chant was like a lullaby now. I felt soothed and rocked by it, as I had when I was little and my mother sang to me. Just as I was about to drift away on that river of sound, Telakeet said something, the chanting stopped, and they all set down their instruments. Then each of them stepped forward in turn to touch me gently with a hand and kiss me on the forehead, even Telakeet. Shalamith was last. Her face was glowing golden in the moonlight. After she kissed me, she put her hands on either side of my face and intoned softly, "Remember always that you are Her daughter, that you are both human and divine, that you are a child of this time and a child of all time." I could make little sense of these words. The tone of this speech was so unlike Shalamith that I took it to be a part of the ritual that she had been chosen to say. As she straightened, she said in her own familiar voice, "Welcome back among us, Tazzia. May the Goddess bless you and hold you always in Her hands. Do not cast aside Her gifts so lightly in the future." I nodded wordlessly.

Afterward, they covered me and I slept, or rather dozed, right there on the altar, my head filled with music and bright colors and a sense of other places. It was Olna who came for me again, gently shaking me awake in the gray light of dawn. She wrapped me in the altar robe and led me, again in silence, to the cave entrance where I had sat the morning before. At a nod from Olna, Josleen, who was sitting watch that morning, rose and moved farther up the slope. With great care, Olna helped me to sit on the rock, making sure I was well covered by the robe, treating me almost as if I were an invalid. Then she sat down beside me, took my hand between hers, and held it in her lap. I sensed her taking slow deep breaths and followed her example.

As the gray of the morning mist lifted, I felt as if I were watching someone paint the world with colors of aching brilliance right before my astonished eyes. There was a sparkle of silver on the surface of the sea. Beneath that, there were endless shades of blue and green, with purple in the shadows and long bands of blazing white that marked the foam lines. The grass was so green it hurt my eyes. Sprinkled through it were tiny white and blue flowers tossing in the wind. I could almost swear they had not been blooming the day before. The tree line glowed red with the still-unseen rising sun. Buds on the branches were opening in a haze of pale green and yellow and pink and lavender. I wanted to jump up and shout with the joy of seeing again. I turned to tell Olna of the wonder of it all. She shook her head. "This is not the time to talk. Just look and drink it in, and remember what it means to be alive when you next think to throw it all away." This was as close to a reproach as Olna could manage. I thought to say, *Next time I will remember what Witches can do, and that will be enough to keep me in this world,* but I resisted. Instead, keeping my mouth shut and my eyes open, I fell for a while into a sort of trance of seeing.

I had been watching a flower that seemed to be opening right in front of me when I felt a sudden, strong pull on my mind. Turning, I looked down to the farthest reaches of the plateau, for that was where the signal had come from. At first everything seemed unchanged. Then, as I stared, I saw tiny black dots of motion coming this way. Horses! I leapt to my feet with a shout. From behind me, Josleen blew a loud blast on the signal shell. The sentry from the top of the hill answered with the warning bell, and I heard drums start up from within the caves. Soon women were pouring out of the entrance beside me or struggling up the steep paths from the lower caves. In minutes, most of the encampment was milling about outside, full of excitement and loud talk, yawning, stretching, and pointing.

The specks quickly grew into horses, clearly ours, running at full speed and accompanied by a few riders. Our horses, coming back! I threw off the encumbrance of the robe. Naked, wearing only the sandals Olna had lent me, I ran out with the others. Shouting and waving, we poured down the slope to greet the riders, while they shouted and waved back. Now I could make out Zenoria, Jhemar, Zari, and some of the others. We gathered to meet them, and soon the horses were milling around us. Before the riders even had a chance to dismount, Pell, Renaise, and Kazouri were already calling out questions. Not seeing Dancer, I had a moment of fear, wondering if something had befallen her during the hard winter, or if she would even remember me. As I was turning, looking hopefully in all directions, I was hit in the back by something large and hairy that almost sent me sprawling. I turned to see Dancer standing behind me with her sides heaving. Her head was lowered as if making ready to nudge me again.

With a shout, I threw my arms around her neck and pressed my face against her sweaty hide, breathing in that sweet, familiar smell. Then I kicked off the sandals. Without thought, I was on her back and we were flying up the slope. From there we galloped in a great curve out to the edge of the trees. The wind whipped her mane and my hair. Colors blurred and bled together in my tears. As we covered the earth in great bounding leaps, I felt a rush of sexual pleasure from the surging power of her muscles pressing up between my bare legs. Just before we reached the trees, she turned back with no signal from me. Suddenly we were riding full speed toward the caves. We came to a panting halt in front of the mass of women.

Shaking, I slid from Dancer's back. I would have crumpled to the ground if Pell had not caught me. Rishka was instantly on the other side of me, with Kara beside her. They were all holding and supporting me while I caught my breath. Kara was laughing and crying at the same time, but Pell said in her usual mocking way, "So, Tazzi, you have returned to the land of the living. I see you love your horse more than your sisters. It is for Dancer that you came back."

I was shaking my head. "No! No! Not true! It is the Witches who—"

"No matter," Kara said quickly. "You are back among us. That is what counts." Then she turned angrily to Pell. "Why do you always have to be so mocking?"

"Because I find it so hard to cry." Pell made a little bow before me, half-mocking and half-serious. When she spoke, however, her words were all serious. "Tazzi, I am truly glad to see you back among us by whatever road you had to take. I feared for you all this winter, but nothing that I said or did could reach you. If the Witches have accomplished this miracle with their magic, then I will have to go and thank them all."

I blushed, suddenly remembering how that miracle had been accomplished. Images of what had happened on the altar last night rushed into my head, and I was unable to shield my thoughts in time. Pell gave a roar of laughter. "So that is how they do their magic. If only I had known..." Before I could protest, she caught me in a bone-crushing embrace. "However it happened, I hope you are back with us for good. Now let us go join the others." They all three helped me up on Dancer's back, for I had no strength left. Then, with Rishka mounted behind me, and Pell and Kara walking on either side of me, we went, together with the mass of women, back up the slope to greet one another and circle and talk and make our plans for the future, while the horses went off to graze.

★

2

For me, life had stood still that winter. Time had been suspended, frozen in place. Now, with the spring thaw, everything was moving and flowing again: my own spirit, the women around me, the horses, the land herself. The rains came, melting the last of the snow, turning every crevice into a torrent of water and every path into a stream. The grass grew tall, flowers bloomed in great shifting patches of color, and leaves began to open. With their masses of white blooms, the flowering-lodi trees shone like snow against the new green of the hills.

We all longed to be out of the caves, but each time we moved our cookfires outside during a few days of fine weather, the rain and mud returned to drive us back into the cave entrances. It was particularly hard for the Muinyairin, who were used to the freedom and open spaces of the desert. Rishka had turned moody and short-tempered, almost as bristly as when she first came to us. Hayika avoided the rest of us whenever she could, saying with her usual rudeness, "What a fool I was for bringing the horses back. I should have just kept riding south when I had the chance."

In reality, we had no wish to make a new camp in that place. We were all restless, quarrelsome, and impatient; wanting to be gone from there, to be on the move again. Our provisions were low, the food monotonous, our clothes and bedding smelled of rot and mildew, and our tempers were short. We made our plans to leave, though we still had to wait for the horses to rest and fatten on the new grass. In the meantime, we set to work clearing out the caves, drying our things as best we could on sunny days, and packing everything in readiness for departure. I envied the horses, who had none of this bother. They slept on their feet, carried their coats on their backs, and found food right under their noses.

In the midst of all this, I had my own personal journey to make. I was not the same Tazzi who had gone into the caves that winter. That Tazzi had died. She had been nothing but a walking ghost for months. The young woman the Witches had called back to life with the magic of flesh and passion was a new person. As such, she was in need of a new name. I went to consult with Alyeeta, thinking that the Witches, of course, would have a ritual for such a thing. She looked me up and down as if I were an intruder and answered tartly, "The Witches have done enough for you already, girl, more than enough. You must not expect our help for every little thing in your life. Go ask the Mother for whatever help you need, or look into your own heart for what lies there. That should be quite enough."

Startled, I took a step back. Her response was as unexpected as a slap. Clearly, Alyeeta had resharpened her tongue. I was no longer the favored child under her loving protection. At some earlier time, I would have been crushed by hurt or seething with anger or both. And I would surely have nursed those feelings for future use. Instead, I found myself laughing in a great burst of good humor. The sun had come out, and Alyeeta's scowling face looked very comical on that bright, clear spring morning. "Well, I can see that the sweet Alyeeta of the winter is gone. She must have melted away in the spring rains. Thank you, however, for your good advice. I will do as you say. I will go and ask the Mother for Her help, as the Witches have no more to give." Then I leaned forward, gave Alyeeta a quick kiss on the mouth, and went running off in search of Dancer. Just once, I glanced back to see her staring after me, shaking her head, looking both pleased and puzzled.

I sent out a call from my mind and Dancer came galloping up, clods of dirt flying from her hooves. She stopped just inches away, close enough for me to feel the heat of her breath. I jumped on her back, leaned forward, and whispered in her ear, "Take me to some wonderful place full of power and magic and beauty." I had no idea what a horse could make of such words, but she set off with no hesitancy.

For a while, we went north along the edge of the sea cliffs. It was a glorious day. Spring and joy were bubbling in my blood. If I had been with a lover at that moment, no doubt we would soon have been off our horses and rolling together in the soft new grass. I felt just an instant of regret for my lost lovers and for the aloneness in my life at that time. Then, in the next instant, that mood lifted, carried away on an ocean breeze, and I felt myself rising with the seabirds and soaring out over the sea.

I must explain here that during our long sojourn in the caves, I had never once been down to the ocean. From our place of caves, there was no way down the dangerous high cliffs that rose straight out of the water. The only ways I had heard spoken of were farther north or farther south than I had cared to go in my gray mood — or on a borrowed horse. Besides, first there had been winter's cold and ice and then the rains of spring. Now, with a mix of fear and curiosity, I wondered if Dancer would help me find my own way down to the *Cherbonaishi*, "the wild waters," as Rishka called the sea. Calling out with their strange, sharp cry, the kiri soared and swooped, flying always just in front, as if to lure us on.

Riding on Dancer was always an adventure. She tossed her head so that her mane rose in the wind while she danced sideways, first to one side and then to the other, a creature so full of life it seemed as if she might take wing at any moment. When she finally tired of running, I let her stop and graze as she wished. I had no notion of where we were going and was in no hurry to get there. At last the grassy headlands narrowed and we neared the woods to the right of us. There, the land grew steeper and steeper, until it turned into the base of a hill.

Long before we came to it, I could hear the rush of water. All along the way, we had been crossing little rivulets that flowed down through the woods and rushed or meandered across the headlands before plunging over the cliffs into the sea. Dancer had made her way through these with ease. This torrent of water was different. It blocked our way. There was no question of crossing it, either on foot or on horseback. Fierce and wild, it had hollowed a deep gouge out of the headlands. The water in it frothed brown with spring flooding. I could hear boulders rumbling against each other from the power of its flow. Clearly, we were meant to stop here.

Slipping from Dancer's back, I went to look over the edge of the cliff. The sight made me suck in my breath. Fierce as these waters were now, they must have been much fiercer at some earlier time, for they had cut a deep hollow, making a natural stairway that plunged straight down to the sea. It was not an easy way to go, but it was at least a possible one. Below, the ocean frothed and foamed, rushing in and drawing back in long lines of waves. Instantly I felt the lure of Cherbonaishi, calling me, drawing me to her. When I looked back, I saw that Dancer had already gone to graze. I hesitated for just a moment longer, feeling very small and alone in the face of all that power. Then, as if the decision had been made for me, I felt my feet beginning to move.

Almost immediately, it became clear that my clothes were a hindrance on this journey — or at least that I did not want them. Quickly and impatiently I stripped them off. There was a sharp, restless breeze blowing, so I tied them for safekeeping to a little sapling whose roots went deep into the crevice of the rock face. The rest of this little tree hung perilously out over space with my clothes waving from its branches. Like flags in the wind, they marked the place of my descent.

The climb down was hard and perilous, far more difficult than it had appeared from above. Sometimes I had to make several tries before I found a purchase for my feet. Occasionally rocks broke away in my hands and went clattering down with a terrible echoing sound. Once, my foot slipped. With a gasp, I felt my whole body begin to slide until that foot came to rest on a little ledge.

In spite of my fear, I never once thought to go back. After a while, I even began to adapt to the task. I felt myself becoming a lizard or a snake, slithering down the rock surface with all of my body pressed against it, clinging to the crevices with my toes and fingers. Soon I lost myself in the pleasure of the climb. The rock was deliciously warm after the long chill of winter, and the sun was hot on my skin. Sometimes water, cold with snowmelt, would splash up from the cascade next to me, making me shiver with delight. At some moment I was amazed to look down and see how close the waves had come, how far I had already climbed.

As I neared the bottom, I could see that the rush of water next to me ended in a long waterfall. My little stone stairway brought me out at the base of it. I was even able to slip behind it and look out through a shimmering, shivering curtain of water at the blue-green, restless ocean. Then, with a shout, I climbed down the rest of the way until I found myself standing in front of the ocean herself, with her great waves towering up and rushing in at me.

Cold! Cold! Cold! That first touch of my foot told me all I needed to know. I would look with my eyes, not with my body. Still, that moment began my long, passionate love affair with Cherbonaishi. But that is not what I want to write of here. I had come to find a new name for myself. I felt as if I needed to put my body in water for this very private ritual to be sacred. The ocean and the waterfall were both too cold and too violent. I found myself being drawn to walk along the rocks at the edge of the sea, just out of reach of the waves. It was there that I found a little pool hollowed in the smooth rock, full of sun-warmed water. This was clearly an invitation. With a sigh, I lowered myself into the pool and groaned with pleasure. "Thank you, Mother," I said aloud.

I felt as if all of me were melting into that seductive warmth, all the aches and bruises from the hard climb down, all the cold and pain of that endless winter. With sudden gratitude I thought, *Whatever else happens to me in my life, I will always have this moment.* I could feel my breasts floating, softly buoyant in the water. I could see my body's reflection, wonderfully distorted by the quivering blue-green. This little piece of the ocean was just for me. I had not felt so loved or blessed since I had been a girl in my village and shared love with Kara down by the river. That memory stirred in me, pleasure this time instead of pain. I opened my legs slightly, letting in the sun-warmed water. Then I ran my fingers slowly several times over my hardening nipples. Finally my hands came to rest between my legs. I began to seek my pleasure there, with the warm water surrounding me, the waves crashing in front of me, and the dome of blue sky arching above. The kiri were soaring overhead. My cry, when it came, mingled with theirs. Afterward, I sank down to doze with my head against the rock and my chin just touching the water.

I sat up with a start, amazed to hear a voice so close. *In the world and for the needs of the world you will be Tazzil, close to your old name but with more power. Here and in your secret heart you will be Cherbonaishim, child of the sea.* I looked all around. No one was there, of course. I listened intently for more words, some further message, but already the voice had faded. Shivering, I stood up, not sure if it all came from my own mind or from another or from some distortion in the sounds of the sea. Clouds had covered the sun and the day was growing late. "Tazzil," I said aloud to try it out. "Tazzil! Tazzil! Tazzil!" I shouted to the ocean. The kiri answered me again. "Cherbonaishim," I whispered, making a pledge in my heart that I would find us a place to live and that it would be near the sea. It mattered little whose voice I had heard or where it had come from. I had found what I came for. Later I would thank Alyeeta for her good advice, but I was not sure if I would share with her my new names as yet.

As I rode toward the caves, I was much relieved to see our campfires burning like beacons ahead of me. When Dancer and I reached the camp, it was already dusk. I was just exchanging a few words with Tzaneel, who was standing watch that evening, when suddenly Alyeeta appeared beside me. She must have been watching for my return. She drew me away quickly, without even speaking to Tzaneel. "Well, what happened?" she asked impatiently. "Did you find what you went for? Do you have a new name?"

I was not going to give her that satisfaction. "You are the one who sent me off, Alyeeta, and for that I am grateful. The rest is between me and the Mother."

★

When I came back, I kept my new name in my heart and only gradually began to tell other women. They did not press me for it. Goddess knows, they had other matters on their minds, such as when we would leave and where we would end our journey. We would go south, that much we all agreed on, south in search of some unoccupied place along the coast where we could settle safely with our horses, build a settlement, and find some peace far away from the affairs of men and armies. The Khal Hadera Lossien would not spend another winter in the northland, that was clear. The question was Where we would go, and by what route? Pell was drawing maps again, asking advice of any who knew the coast and the south. Now that I had returned to myself, she had made me her second-in-command again. I was reluctant, but she said she needed me.

We consulted often with Jhemar and Zenoria and the others who had gone south with the horses. It was from them that we heard the rumors of unrest, or perhaps even rebellion, in the south; rebellion in the city of Mishghall or in some of the coastal settlements. The rumors made for exciting talk, but none of them was clear enough for making plans. Pell began to speak of sending scouts to Mishghall, such as Josleen and Megyair, or even of going there herself. The same fears attacked me as when the talk was of going to Eezore, but this time I already knew I would go wherever Pell went and do whatever she asked of me.

Now that I was able to look around me again and had some awareness of others, I could see how much we had changed during our time in the caves. Before, we had all been "green girls," as Alyeeta liked to say, confused and mistrustful of one another, unsure of ourselves and our powers. Now, with the help of the Witches, we were becoming a people, more secure in our powers, more united in spite of our differences and our quarrels, proud and confident in a way we had never been before. I could hear it all around me in the way women talked, see it in the way we moved, almost feel it in the air.

One result was that we were both more united and less so. Pell was no longer the undisputed leader. Many of us were finding our own voices.

Each little group seemed to be creating its own leaders. There were also women who spoke for the larger groups and were more listened to among them: Murghanth and Teko among the Sheezerti; Kilghari and Daijar among the Muinyairin; Lhiri for the former slaves of Eezore, and Ashai for the former Shokarn of that city; Maireth for the women of the Circle; Vestri for the Potters; and Johalla among the Wanderers. Mouraine, Permeeth, and Shartel, who had been leaders of the other encampments, still had a following here. In spite of being Pell's second-in-command, I found myself, along with Renaise and Kazouri, being pressed to speak on behalf of the Kourmairi. With all these different factions, there was constant tension and confusion in the camp. The impatience to be gone was rising among us, but so was the conflict over whether to mix into the affairs of Mishghall. If we did, it might be possible to save the city and secure the coast; if we didn't, we might be able to skirt around the city and remain invisible to the Zarn's guards.

One warm, sunny morning, after days of cold rain, I was taking my turn at standing watch by the cave entrance. The glint of the sun on something shiny caught my attention. I turned and was amazed to see an elegantly dressed man, apparently a stranger, riding in from the edge of the woods. Illyati and Johalla rode on either side of him, talking intently. Quickly, I raised the shell to blow a warning — but then I lowered it again. From the way they all rode together, those two seemed to know him, so instead, I watched and waited with curiosity. This man was dressed in the manner of a Shokarn Highborn, yet there was something oddly familiar about him, especially as he rode closer. Suddenly I felt Hereschell's presence in my head. *Do you know someone only by their clothes, Tazzi?*

"Hereschell!" I shouted as I set down the shell and ran to meet him. While we were exchanging greetings, several others ran up, Murghanth and Teko among them, along with some of the other Sheezerti. Murghanth cocked her head to one side and said in her most derisive manner, "So, you left here a Wanderer-beggar and have come back as a prince of Eezore. There must be a fine story in that, one worth hearing and retelling." Then her voice shifted. With both eagerness and sadness she asked, "Tell us of Eezore? How does it fare? Is the Zarn still in power? Are there any Sheezerti that you know of, still in hiding?"

Just at that moment, Pell joined us. She whistled in surprise, then began walking round and round, examining him. "Tell me, Hereschell, have you joined the Thieves Guild and become their chief? Or has some Shokarn lord discovered in you his long-lost relative?"

By then, others had gathered and were clamoring with questions of their own about where he had been and what he knew and whether, indeed, there was a rebellion raging in Mishghall. Lhiri, Nunyair, and Ashai wanted news of Eezore. Kazouri and Pell wanted to know about troop movements. Renaise asked about the possibility of more provisions. Murghanth continued her insistent questions about both Eezore and Mishghall. In this she was echoed by the other Sheezerti. I knew how desperately they missed city life, and thought that perhaps they had their own plans for Mishghall. Meanwhile, Illyati and Johalla were plainly angered by our rudeness. Trying to make herself heard over the commotion, Johalla shouted several times, "That is enough now!"

Hereschell, however, seemed to take no offense. He grinned down at us, plainly pleased with himself and the effect he was having. "Well, I see the Hadera Lossi have no better manners than when I saw them last. Wanderers would never think of questioning weary travelers in this way until they had been fed and rested and their horses watered and cared for."

In spite of his reproof, this was followed by another burst of questions. Clearly, Hereschell had no intention of answering at that moment. Finally Renaise called out loudly, "Come to my fire pit, Hereschell. There we will make you a traveler's welcome. I will find you soup and bread and a place to sit." In a quieter voice that had a little mockery in it, she added, "It may not be suitable for such a fine gentleman, but it is the best we can do in this poor place. The winter has been hard and our supplies are almost gone."

Hereschell made a slight bow from his horse. "A true gentleman accepts graciously whatever is offered." At that moment, Kazouri let out a roar for attention. With Daijar's help, she pushed through the crowd to make a path. Hereschell dismounted and handed the reins to her. He followed Renaise, with the rest of us trailing after them.

Though Hereschell smiled and laughed and joked with us and talked of the weather and horses and exchanged some gossip with Alyeeta about their shared past, it was not till after he had finished his second bowl of soup and cleaned the bowl with yet another piece of bread, lit a jol pipe, and taken several puffs that he at last consented to answer our questions.

"So you want to know how I came by these clothes? In the simplest way possible. They were given to me. And no, Pell, I did not join the Thieves Guild. I came by them honestly. I spent this last winter in Eezore as assistant gardener in a Great-House, playing dumb, being silent, and learning all manner of useful and amazing things, such as how they grow plants all winter in glass houses and where the Zarn's guards are moving next. These clothes were given to me by the young master of the house. As oldest son, he has been called to be captain of the guards and will probably be in uniform for some time. He is being sent to Mishghall to reinforce the Zarn's forces. They are being hard pressed there."

Hereschell shook his head, and I saw a look of grief cross his face. Then he said with some anger, "Lorren is no more suited to be a soldier and fight for the Zarn than I am, but as the oldest son he will do as he is ordered by his father and the Zarn. It is expected of the sons of the Highborn. I must say, I am glad to be a Wanderer, able to move as I please and answer to no one but myself. And yes, there is a hard-fought rebellion being waged in Mishghall. At this moment, the Kourmairi appear to be winning. The Zarn is worried enough to send reinforcements and that is what my young captain will lead.

"If he gets there in time, he will probably be able to secure the city and bring all those people under the heel of the Zarns again. If not, Mishghall will be free and, with it, all the settlements along this part of the coast. Perhaps in time, all of Yarmald can free itself again from the power of the Zarns. But not if Lorren succeeds in his mission. First, of course, he must get his men across the river in spring flood time, not an easy thing to do if all the bridges are gone. I am planning to ride south tomorrow with word that the Zarn is sending more men."

He shook his head again, and I could feel his pain almost as if it were in my own heart. "And so I betray the one Ganja in all of Eezore whom I trusted with my friendship and my voice, the one Ganja in that whole city who knew my true self and both loved and trusted me. With Lorren, I did not play at being dumb and mindless. We sat up many nights, he and I, by the light of just one candle, talking of everything you can imagine. I know my friendship mattered to him, too, for whom can a Shokarn lord really trust and share his heart with? Even so, I cannot betray the people of Mishghall to certain slaughter for the sake of one friend."

As he spoke, I had been looking about hopefully. When he finished, I asked him, almost in a whisper, "Where is Soneeshi the wolf? Is she hiding in the woods? I cannot sense her anywhere."

Hereschell shook his head a third time, and I felt my heart sink. "Gone back to the wild things when I left for Eezore," he said sadly. "But perhaps we shall meet again in Yarmald." Alyeeta was watching me intently. I turned away to hide my tears.

There followed a day of questions and maps and strategy disputes that went on into the evening. Arguments broke out among us along the old lines. The Kourmairi, the Sheezerti, and even some of the Wanderers among us spoke for helping the people of Mishghall in whatever way we were able. Pell, especially, had strong words to say in that direction, and I felt the chill of fate as I listened to her. The Muinyairin, on the other hand, were used to the wild desert and had no wish to go into the city. Many of the Shokarn, more afraid than the rest of us of the Shokarn guards, sided with them in a strange alliance. Suddenly we were separate peoples again, and not Khal Hadera Lossien together, or even "Hadera Lossi," as Hereschell said we were being called now in the world out there.

In the midst of this clamor, Pell called out, "What of us? Is the Zarn still hunting us?"

"The talk is that he thinks you have vanished mysteriously, witched away, perhaps. He still wants to find you. I am sure he would sleep better at night knowing that the matter was finished. But you are not his greatest worry at this moment. Right now, Mishghall, with its great port on the sea, is what draws most of his attention. And he is fearful of losing all of Yarmald as well. It is truly amazing how much the great and powerful can find to worry on."

Immediately, the argument flared up again. Hayika leapt to her feet, shouting, "Then we should slip by and vanish forever. What better time than when he is occupied elsewhere? Why let him know that we still exist? Or where we are? I, for one, am ready to ride as far away from men as possible. They mean nothing but trouble for us." Several Muinyairin shouted their accord.

"How do you expect to slip by?" Mouraine roared back. When she stood up to be better heard, I could see the sun flashing from her startling golden hair that was such a contrast to her dark skin. With her hands on her hips she was a formidable-looking woman. "The whole area, from the coast to the Escuro River, will be swarming with guards. How do you think we can vanish once we are out of the caves and on the move again?" There were mutterings of agreement from the women around her, women who had been part of her camp.

"What have we to do with the city of Mishghall? It is no affair of ours," Nunyair called back loudly.

At that, Murghanth began waving her thin, dark arms and stamping her feet in excitement. "Should we leave them trapped there just when they have almost won and there is a chance to free that whole part of the coast? What if we had left you to your fate in Eezore? Where would you be now? All you care about is your own, white, Shokarn skin and keeping it safe."

"Not so...," Nunyair shouted back, but Daijar interrupted her: "And what do you expect us to do? Fight like an army? You know we cannot do that. I say we take this opportunity while the Zarn is busy with Mishghall to disappear forever and find our own safe place far from them all."

"And I say that is a coward's choice!" Kazouri roared out over all the other voices.

"Yes! Yes! Yes! A coward's choice," Murghanth echoed, leaping up and down with her words.

"And I say you are fools who would sacrifice the rest of us, because some of you are still more loyal to the Kourmairi than to this Khal Hadera Lossien you all pretend to be." Hayika turned abruptly to look at Rishka. "What of you, Rishka?" she challenged suddenly. "You are unusually quiet. Will you ride with your Muinyairin sisters? This is all more dangerous than the shifting sands. Will you ride with us out of this trap?"

There was a moment of silence as all eyes turned toward Rishka. She drew herself up very straight and said loudly, "At this moment I will follow where Pell leads." This was instantly followed by cheers of approval and hoots of derision. Then the argument broke out louder than before. It grew so heated, I felt as if we were back at Alyeeta's clearing with peace among us to be made all over again or, worse yet, perhaps not even possible. Pell, who had already said her piece, kept strangely quiet through all this. It was as if she were observing it all from some great distance. Kilghari, Arnella, and Dorca, with their gentler ways, tried to keep some civility between us, but it was hopeless. Patience had been frayed by our long winter of enforced confinement, and tempers flared like fires in the wind. If our powers had not prevented it, I think we might well have been rolling on the ground, beating on each other with our fists.

My fear was that Alyeeta would suddenly turn one of her silencings on us. I was very aware of the Witches. They had moved away when our argument broke out and were gathered off to one side, watching us and talking among themselves. Finally I saw Olna nod. As Alyeeta took some steps in our direction, I felt the hair on the back of my neck go up. Just then Pell jumped up on a log and banged two pot lids together for silence. All heads turned toward her. For that moment, at least, the uproar abated and she had our attention.

As I have already said, Pell was no longer undisputed leader. Still, she had some authority among us, though I think it was her fairness that made others listen when she spoke. "There is no one course that will please us all," she called out. "That much, at least, is clear in this rain of mud. Perhaps that is as it should be. But even if we have different roads to travel, from this far away it is hard to know how to proceed. I propose that we all ride south together. Those who wish to skirt the city and continue south should separate from us after we reach the first of the Kourmairi settlements and go on with the extra horses and provisions. Perhaps from there, with more knowledge, you can discover how to pass unnoticed. The rest of us can continue toward the city to see how we can be of use there. From that closer vantage point, we can better plan what to do, after we see what is safe and what is even possible, since we are certainly not an army that can gather to fight another army. That way, if things go badly, we have not all committed to one course. And we must agree on a place to meet again afterward and a plan for summoning aid if we are in trouble."

Pell paused for a moment to catch her breath. When the noise level rose, she banged the pot lids again for silence. "Whether or not we encounter the Zarn's army, we must still move south as soon as possible and find a place to settle. If the Zarn's men retake Mishghall and go all the way to the coast, they will have us pinned here in the northland. I say enough of this arguing. The horses are fed and rested. Let us pack and leave. Sisters, let us ride south together in two days' time." She waved her arms to show that she was finished and jumped down. What she said had all been very simple, but women cheered and clapped. There was no more dissent. Voices called out, "Yes, let us move on." "Time to be gone from here." "Southward together." "On to Mishghall." "On to a new home." Pell had stopped our quarreling with one another, at least for the moment.

By the morning of the third day, we were mounted and on the road, moving south. Hereschell had already left to warn Mishghall of the coming of the Zarn's reinforcements. Mud and rain had slowed our departure, but now a new, bright sun was shining on the sodden landscape, making the world sparkle. Every little stream had turned into a rushing torrent, and the road itself was like a shallow river, but for that moment, the sky was blue and our hopes were high. After all our arguing, we were united again and glad to be riding together, even if we were soon to part.

34

This time we rode openly. There was no way to hide so many. Let the army of the Zarn of Eezore see us. Let all the Zarns of Garmishair hear of us. This time, let them be the ones to be afraid. The pleasure of it was intoxicating. We made no pretense of being men. We let our hair show, dressed as we pleased, wore bright clothes, raised our banners, sang loudly, and remembered again that we loved each other. The Hadera Lossi were on the move. Let others deal with us as they could. This time we were a force to be reckoned with.

As I had nothing festive of my own, I had borrowed something bright from both Rishka and Lhiri and, in the end, felt very splendid. I looked around at us all and thought how fine we looked on that bright day, all color and courage. Somehow, out of the mixtures of all our cultures, we had made a style of our own. *The Hadera Lossi.* Hereschell had said that is what they called us now. Would we simply be called Hadra someday, as I had seen in my vision from the hill above the Wanderer camp? I wondered if the place I saw that day lay somewhere in our future.

Full of joy at being alive in the world and glad to be on the road again, I turned to Pell. "After all this with Mishghall is over, where will we go?" Pell answered immediately, "Wherever you lead us, Tazzi. After Mishghall, I am ready to put down this load." I shivered and the day seemed a little less bright. Though there was this momentary break in the rain, from far off in the distance I could hear the sound of thunder again.

During this part of our journey, it was really Alyeeta who led us. She knew of a settlement near Mishghall where she said we would find welcome. "The headman is a good friend of mine. He will be very glad to see me again." I could not imagine how anyone could be glad to see such a mob of women, but for that moment I was willing to just follow wherever she led.

3

In spite of its great size, the meeting house in the Kourmairi settlement of Darthill was dark, noisy, smoky, and overcrowded; the air rank with the odor of unwashed bodies and damp clothing. I was feeling as confined and closed in as if I were trapped in the caves again. The worst of it was being surrounded by men. Their loud, rough voices grated on my ears. I had forgotten how crude and coarse Kourmairi men could be and how badly they treated their women. To me, men in large numbers meant danger, even Kourmairi men, though, for that moment, they called themselves our brothers and our friends. They seemed affable enough, but they bumped against me in passing or trampled on my feet with no thought or apology.

As I listened to the voices droning on and on, I pictured myself leaving that night with those of us who were traveling south. Goddess knows, I longed to be out of that crowded room, riding through the darkness and breathing deeply of the cool night air. Instead, I would probably be sleeping in some equally crowded and stuffy place. After that, I would likely be following Pell into Mishghall.

This meeting had been in progress since shortly past noon. We, ourselves, had just arrived in the settlement late that morning, after four days of riding — weary, short-tempered, and very wet. After that first brief moment of sun at the start of our journey, it had rained most of the way, finally slowing to a drizzle by dawn.

Before we had even come within sight of the village, we were met by a sizable group of Kourmairi men on horseback. This was not exactly the welcome Alyeeta had promised. They were all carrying crude spears or lances and were obviously very agitated and confused by our large numbers. We stopped at Pell's signal, and she called out to them, "We are Hadera Lossi, here to help you against the Shokarn." When that did not seem to reassure them, Alyeeta quickly volunteered to speak with them herself. She rode forward alone, showing no fear at all of their weapons. I heard the name Nhokosos mentioned several times. Soon they were all nodding and smiling like old friends.

Suddenly, one of the riders left their group and rode straight at us. After a moment of alarm, I was surprised to see that it was actually a young woman of near my age. Immediately there were angry protests from the men. One of them began calling out to her, "Ozzet, come back! Ozzet, you promised to stay with us!"

The man next to him, a man with a big, bristly mustache, said angrily, "I told you not to let her ride out with us today. This is what comes of giving her such freedom. If she were a decent woman, she would be at home with the others."

Without turning back, Ozzet answered, "First I must see these Hadera Lossi for myself. Then I will return." She rode down the line looking into each of our faces. When she got close to me, I could see there were tears running down her cheeks. "I knew there were others like us," she said in a choked voice. "All my life I have waited for this day. Why did it take so long?"

"Ozzet! Ozzet! Come back!" the first man continued in a pleading tone. "It is not safe. You know nothing of these women. They may be dangerous."

"We do not harm women," Pell replied angrily. "We are not—"

"Pay no attention," Ozzet interrupted. "That is my father. He is always afraid for me." Then she spun her horse around to face the men. "I am safe enough here. These are my people. They will not hurt me." With that, she turned back and continued down the line, only now she reached out a hand to touch us as she passed. We, in turn, reached out our hands to her. "All my life," she kept saying. "All my life, and now the waiting is over." Many of us were crying, even Pell, who leaned from her horse to give Ozzet a hug. "Welcome, Ozzet," I said to her as she passed me and our hands touched. "Be welcome among us, Ozzet," I heard Arnella say in back of me. I turned to watch as this stranger who was not a stranger slipped her horse in among ours.

After that, we drew aside for a quick discussion among ourselves, while one man rode back to the settlement with the news of our arrival.

With few words, it was decided that we would ride into Darthill together. Once there, we would part ways. Some of us would head south that very night, with the Kourmairi guide that had been offered. The rest of us would make a short stay in Darthill and go on from there to help in the defense of Mishghall. As soon as this was agreed upon, we rode on with our anxious escort of Kourmairi men.

Alyeeta's friend, Nhokosos, met us at the edge of the settlement with a small group of villagers. He, at least, made us feel welcome. Indeed, he seemed as delighted to see us as Alyeeta had promised — or perhaps it was Alyeeta herself he was delighted to see. There was something in his hearty manner that made me like him instantly and even feel some trust.

As headman of Darthill, it was Nhokosos who had called this meeting, but it was Ozzet who had insisted that we be present before she would say her part. The rest of the Star-Born seemed to feel as uncomfortable as I did in that place. Though we had tried our best to stay together, eventually the press of people grew too great. Those of us who had come in did so only at Pell's or Alyeeta's insistence. Many of the Star-Born were still outside. Even the Witches kept to the dark fringes of the room, all, that is, except Alyeeta, who appeared to be totally at ease, smoking a jol pipe and trading insults with Nhokosos while the room filled up. From the familiarity of their banter, I concluded that they knew each other very well, better than Alyeeta had suggested. Perhaps they had even been lovers at some time, though Alyeeta certainly had said nothing of the sort to me.

At last, when the room was packed to capacity, Nhokosos stepped up on the platform and struck a gong for silence. He had to strike it twice more before he could be heard over the din. "Our little village of Darthill, which has always been a place of peace, is about to be caught in the jaws of war, trapped between the guards and the city of Mishghall. Right now, all that stands between us and the Zarn's army are the floodwaters of the Escuro. Indeed, if Hereschell the Wanderer had not warned us in time so that we could destroy the bridges, we would already have been overrun. And now my friend, Alyeeta the Witch, has come with her women to give us some aid." This was met with hoots and whistles, a strange mixture of approval and derision. He had to strike the gong twice more before he could continue. "But first, we must ask Ozzet to tell us what she has seen while spying on the Zarn's men."

There were some angry mutterings from the men about a woman addressing the meeting. Then the one with the mustache called out,

"Shame on you, old man. How could you send a child on such an errand, and a girl-child at that?"

Nhokosos scowled at him. "Because she seemed to be the best one for the job. Because she is quick and clever and small and much less likely to be discovered than you would be, Rhomar. Also, she has some powers to keep her safe. Besides, at seventeen years of age, she is hardly a child." Once again, noise erupted from the crowd. Nhokosos had to call several more times for silence.

Ozzet had stepped up on the platform beside Nhokosos and was staring straight at Rhomar. Seeing her off her horse, I realized how small she was, almost as small as Cruzia. In size she might well have been a child, but when she spoke, shouting to be heard above the tumult, her voice was full of power. "No one sent me, Rhomar. I thought we should know what we are facing. I asked Grandfather, and he agreed to let me go." There was a moment of silence as Ozzet and Rhomar glared at each other. Then she turned to address the meeting. "As you all know, there is just one bridge left, our swinging rope bridge that spans Thunder Gorge and can be crossed only on foot. It is being well guarded. If the Shokarn try to cross it from the other side, it will be cut in an instant. One of the watchers is my cousin, and he let me pass. That is how I was able to cross the river and observe the guards. They have gathered on a rise just above the floodwaters, three or four hundred strong, with the best armor and weapons and many fine horses."

Ozzet continued with a detailed description of their camp. She ended by saying, "As soon as the river goes down, they will gather and camp on the shore. From there, they will be able to cross the next day, or perhaps the day after. They will crush us on their way to Mishghall. Once they join forces with what is left of the Zarn's army in the city, Mishghall will probably fall under their control again. Then we may not have a chance to rid ourselves of Zarns for another hundred years."

Suddenly men were shouting and stamping, roaring loudly, "No!" and, "Never!" and, "We will not let them cross!" These Koormir of Yarmald, with their fierceness and determination, were certainly very different from the cowed, submissive Koormir I had known from my childhood in Nemanthi. There, the worst weapon they might brandish was a pitchfork or a farmknife; carrying real weapons was forbidden by the Zarn's orders. Here, they carried swords and pikes and seemed both able and willing to use them.

Nhokosos signaled again for silence. "Then we must try to delay their crossing and block their way by whatever means we have. We must harry and harass them to slow their march."

Alyeeta made a rude noise that sounded like something between a cough and a laugh. She called out loudly, "Well, old friend, what good would that do? How long do you think you can hold off the Zarn's armed and disciplined guards with a troop of untrained and poorly armed farmboys? You have just heard what Ozzet said of their weapons and horses. They will crush you like bugs. We will need some better plan than that if we are going to save ourselves, and Mishghall as well."

"Well, what do you propose, Alyeeta? If these girls of yours would fight alongside us, we might stand a chance. Their numbers are far greater than the guards'."

"And I have already explained to you, more than once, I believe, that they cannot be used as a fighting force."

Rhomar pushed his way forward. "And I have already said that women are of no use in this matter. Witch, why did you bring this pack of cowards with you if they cannot do the work of men? What are they doing here if they are not willing to stand with us and fight?"

Alyeeta shook her head. "This has nothing to do with courage or cowardice. These young women cannot fight the way you want them to. Their powers will not allow it. Some of them would be only too glad to oblige."

Though I could not see Murghanth, I could hear her gravelly voice clearly enough. "If they are all such brave men, with no need of women, let them do without us. Let us go on to Mishghall, where we are needed."

Pell called back, "Wait, Murghanth, have a little patience. Let this work itself out."

The meeting droned on. One man called out, "If the guards cross tomorrow, the water will still be high and they will be forced to swim their horses partway. We can pick them off as they come."

And another answered, "And if they wait? You heard what Ozzet said of their numbers and their armor."

"What if we fight and these women stand along the banks and block their way, since they cannot be harmed with weapons?"

"A possible plan," Pell answered. "But who knows if our powers can be used that way, to help in killing?"

"You cannot do this, you cannot do that. What good are these so-called powers, anyhow? What kind of help is this? I say it is cowardice disguised with fancy talk. You women come riding out of the north, defying the Zarn's edict as if you were in possession of some great power, and now you refuse to help us fight his soldiers. What is this but cowardice?" Rhomar was shaking with anger.

Rishka jumped up on the platform. "I am tired of all this talk of cowardice. I, for one, would be only too happy to put my sword at your service if I could. If any wish to challenge me, they may do so now."

"We have no time to waste fighting with each other!" Pell called out. "What if the Zarn's army rides farther up or down the river and crosses in some other place? Once they are across, we are no match for them."

"This is by far the shallowest part of the river. Other places will not be passable for several days. They need to be in Mishghall as soon as possible."

Words flew back and forth. In all this madness, I found myself longing for Hereschell's clarity. More plans, ideas, and possibilities were talked of and argued about in those next few hours than I can possibly remember. Many questions were asked of Ozzet. Alyeeta, in particular, seemed to want details. I had nothing to add to any of this. All I wanted was to be out of there before I fainted. Finally, I grew dizzy from the lack of air and the loud voices. I was just looking for someplace to sit, or at least to lean against the wall, when I saw Alyeeta pushing vigorously through the crush, making her way in my direction. Ozzet was following close behind her.

"Out," Alyeeta said brusquely, grabbing my wrist and heading for the door. "Out of this place. Let them make whatever plans they wish. Alyeeta the Witch has her own plans. Sometimes trickery is more useful than bloodshed — and this is a good season for trickery." She spoke in that mysterious way she sometimes had. Clearly, she had something caught in her web. But she was not telling, and I could read nothing from her mind.

Suddenly we were outside in the sunshine. It was the first sun I had seen in days, but I felt fear instead of joy. I knew what it meant. Our time was fast running out.

"The Escuro will drop quickly now," Ozzet said anxiously. "There has been more drizzle than rain these last few days. And now with the sun and wind..."

"Good, it is just right. It will be perfect," Alyeeta declared joyfully, rubbing her hands together with pleasure. "Will you come with me, Tazzia? I need some help for this little venture."

"Only if you tell me what you are planning."

"No, I need to keep silent on it a little longer. If you will not come, then I must ask another." She glanced meaningfully toward Ozzet.

"Alyeeta!" I shouted in exasperation.

"Good, that is settled then. We will have to dress you for the part. Now, Ozzet, will you be our guide to the bridge? We must get across this evening, just at dusk."

"Not safe," Ozzet said quickly, shaking her head. "I cannot risk your lives that way."

"You risked your own this morning. Besides, is it not better to risk just two of us? If my little scheme does not work, then tomorrow everyone will be at risk. Now, if you will not help us, we will have to find it on our own."

"No, no, that is even more dangerous. I will help you."

"Good. First, go and gather for me three or four of the best, or at least the fastest, cooks in the village. I need stacks of fresh-cooked parmi-cakes." I could not imagine why Alyeeta seemed so jolly or how parmi-cakes could possibly save us. I certainly could read nothing from her well-blocked mind.

While the men were holding their meeting, most of the Kourmairi women were outside, doing all the "unimportant" work of the village: hanging clothes and bedding in the sun, drying grain, cooking food, and tending children. Ozzet quickly gathered some of them together. They were only too glad to assist us when Alyeeta said they might help defeat the Zarn's men by their own efforts. "We need some parmi-fruit sweet-cakes, as many as you can make, two or three hundred at least, even more if you can manage. And you must lend us two good, stout carrying baskets, strong but not too heavy. We will also need several gourds of parmi-syrup gone to quillof, for adding water to make a potent brew."

"Will you tell us what you plan?"

"Nothing more! You already know too much. Witches need secrecy to work with, unlike some young things who are born with the curse of honesty." She gestured in my direction.

After that, Alyeeta turned me over to an old woman named Domiri, saying, "Make her look much older, sixty or so, a little misshapen, not very bright, and none too clean. When you are done, I will put a haze over her so they cannot see her clearly, but the better your disguise, the easier it will be to hold that illusion steady." Then Alyeeta went off to supervise the fires and the cooking, while Domiri set to aging me. It turned out that she was Nhokosos's wife. While she worked, she entertained me with stories of both Alyeeta and the settlement in former times.

Well before dusk, Alyeeta and I were both dressed in our disguises. We had two large baskets packed and ready, one filled with hot parmi-cakes and the other with syrup and parmi-flavored quillof. With her kerchief and her gray wig, Alyeeta looked once again like the crazy or crafty old woman I had first met at the Hamishair market.

As Ozzet went to fetch the horses, a loud hum of noise rose from the meeting house entrance. The meeting was over, and people were pouring out into the late-afternoon sun. Suddenly, the village square thronged with Kourmairi men and Hadera Lossi. They immediately began questioning Alyeeta and me about her plans. I shook my head and stayed silent. Alyeeta seemed to take delight in answering rudely. "Just make sure you have your plans in readiness for tomorrow, and let me tend to my own affairs. And yes, we will cross the river. But that is all I will say."

No one could persuade Alyeeta to say one more word of what she intended to do, not even Nhokosos, who tried his best to block her way. "I cannot let two women go alone among all those rough and violent men," he protested.

"And have I ever in my life asked your permission for anything I did? Believe me, I have no plans to start now. Besides, do you think you could protect us if you came? They would cut up your old carcass in a minute and roast you over the fire." Alyeeta had a good audience and was clearly enjoying herself. She threw her arm over my shoulder. "I love this young woman more than life itself. Would I take her with me if I did not think to bring her back safely? Anyhow, think what the choices are here, old man. Tomorrow you will either stand down there on the shore and fight against an army and likely die, or else you will run away, in which case your village will be burned to the ground, your crops and animals will be destroyed, and your city will be overthrown once again. After that the guards will likely hunt you down one by one. Not a very pretty picture. I go to try some different way that will bring no harm, and perhaps do some good. But if you bother me enough, I will forget all about it and go to bed now, for I am very tired."

With a groan, Nhokosos threw up his hands, saying, "As you wish, Alyeeta. I put my trust in you. May it all go well."

"Thank you. Much better. Think on it, Nhokosos, in all the long years I have known you, has Alyeeta ever failed to do a thing she set herself to do?" With those words, she grabbed the arm of a passing Kourmairi.

"Give us a hand with these baskets, man. Time is wasting. The ewee will soon be out."

The man gave a rough laugh. "Witch, do you think the flood toads will frighten away four hundred Shokarn guards?"

"Perhaps as well as you could," she answered tartly.

Then Pell was standing in front of us. "Before you leave, Alyeeta, I need to know something more of your plans." Her serious tone cut through Alyeeta's banter.

Alyeeta answered with the same seriousness. "Have your women ready to stand at the river with the people of Darthill, if it comes to that, but give us this night and most of the morning to see what we can do. The Shokarn troops cannot begin crossing before noon, at the very earliest. Trust me, Pell. Ask me no more questions. I will do the best I can. Perhaps there still is a way to avoid all this bloodshed." Pell was silent a moment, staring into Alyeeta's eyes. Then she gave a nod, put her hand on my arm for one brief moment, and stepped back to let us pass.

Soon we were ready to go. We went on two horses: myself and Ozzet mounted on the first, and Alyeeta following on the second horse, which was laden with the baskets. The Hadera Lossi pressed in to say their good-byes. Kourmairi women crowded around to wish us well, while their men hung back, making rude comments to one another that were meant for our ears, comments on what would likely happen to two women challenging the Zarn's army, all of them bloody, ugly, and not very reassuring. I leaned forward and whispered to Ozzet, "I do not think any of them expect to see us again." We found ourselves trapped in this press of people until Alyeeta shouted, "OUT OF OUR WAY!" With that, everyone backed away in haste, and a path opened before us.

Relieved to finally be under way and free of the noise of the village, we rode in silence for a while, but I could sense the turmoil in Ozzet's mind. Finally, she turned and said, "There is so much I want to ask you, Tazzi, I hardly know where to begin. But now is not the time. If we live through this coming day, then perhaps we can sit together in some quiet place and you can tell me the story of how you all came together and of your journey here."

"Granted," I said, nodding. "And in exchange, you can tell me how you have survived this past year despite the Zarn's edict." She nodded in return.

Before long we turned toward the river, and the pathway steepened sharply. I could hear the rush of water off to the right, almost like the sound of a waterfall. Soon Ozzet stopped her horse. She made a signal like the triple call of a night bird to the Kourmairi sentry. Almost instantly, a young man was at our side. Silent as a wolf, he had moved quickly through the darkening woods. Ozzet bent and said some words in his ear. He nodded and waved us on. At a sign from Ozzet, we slipped off our horses and turned them over to the sentry. Ozzet took one pack and I took the other. On foot, Alyeeta and I followed Ozzet up ground that grew steeper with each step. I could sense other watchers, but none came out of hiding to challenge us. Soon we came to a stop at the edge of a gorge.

I sucked in my breath. The sight, even at dusk, was both glorious and terrifying. Below us, the ground dropped away into a deep chasm, cut through solid rock by the force of the water. The wide Escuro, trapped in this narrow way, was roaring and raging, booming with a sound like thunder. Water, white with froth and foam, sprayed up in huge geysers when it collided with great jagged rocks that had tumbled into the riverbed. In the dimming light, the wet walls of the gorge gleamed like dull silver. Crossing this gorge, and bound to a stout tree on either side, was a fine little spiderweb of a bridge, made of ropes and vines. The narrow slats that formed the walkway were wet with spray. The bridge itself was swaying slightly in the breeze that rushed up from below.

Even Alyeeta seemed impressed. There was a slight tremor in her voice when she asked, "Is that really the bridge we are to cross?" I had to smile when I thought of Alyeeta saying boldly that we would find our own way to this place.

"There is no other," Ozzet said jauntily. "I will take the packs now, and you both hold tight to the ropes." I wanted to protest that our pack baskets would be too much for one person and that we should each carry our own share, but peering down through the slats of the bridge had rendered me speechless with fear. When I turned to look at Alyeeta, her eyes were wide and her face was a strange shade of gray. I had never seen her afraid before, but all she said was "I hope the Goddess sees fit to send us back by a different way."

"Follow me," Ozzet said with authority. "Watch my back, look straight ahead, and whatever happens, do not look down. You will get accustomed to it after a while." She slung the packs on her shoulders, one on each side, and stepped onto that aerial spiderweb with what seemed to be perfect confidence. It swayed sickeningly over the chasm, and my stomach clenched. I had an attack of absolute cowardice. Neither foot would move. At that moment I would gladly have turned back, only all the alternatives I could think of were even worse.

"Go," Alyeeta said sharply. "You are holding us up." I noticed that for all her impatience, Alyeeta did not try passing me.

"Come on," Ozzet called out cheerfully. "It gets better. You just have to put one foot in front of the other."

Gripping the side ropes with sweaty hands, I took one timid step onto the bridge. Instantly the whole world lurched and swayed as my stomach jumped up into my throat.

"Move! Move!" Alyeeta hissed from in back of me. Terrified, I took one more step and then another. The world did not end. I was on the bridge, following Ozzet's back, one step after the other.

It never got easy, but after a while it was not so bad, though the one time I looked down persuaded me never to do that again. I could hear Alyeeta in back of me, gasping with fear. Ozzet went before us, balancing both baskets like an acrobat. Indeed, she had such fine balance she might have been a Sheezerti performer in the streets of Eezore. I think I held my breath the whole way across and did not let it out again until I felt solid, unmoving ground under my feet. I took a few more steps to be sure of my safety. Then, with no pride whatsoever, I threw myself down on the ground. With a groan, Alyeeta collapsed beside me. Ozzet patted me on the back. "You see, just as I said, not so bad after all." I could not find the voice to answer. For that moment, even Alyeeta was speechless.

4

As soon as we could catch our breath, Ozzet said urgently, "We must go quickly, while there is still some light. Stay close and pay attention. The way here is well hidden, which is why the Shokarn guards have not yet found the bridge. This path is also very difficult." We followed her silently through the gloom. The path was indeed narrow and twisting; very rocky and treacherous underfoot. It was as steep going down on this side as it had been steep going up on the other, but after the terrors of that bridge crossing, everything else seemed easy.

At last we reached the level of the river. The noise of the water was deafening. The ground under our feet shook from the impact of rolling rocks colliding with one another. Nonetheless, it was evident from the high-water marks that the river was already drawing back. Ozzet shook her head. "We have so little time left. Whatever you plan to do, I wish you luck. Just follow the river down, and you will come to their camp."

Alyeeta took a little silver whistle from her pouch and dangled it in front of Ozzet. "Listen for the sound of this whistle. Three times and then three more when it is over. One long single sound if we have trouble."

Ozzet nodded, looking very serious. "May the Mother keep you and guard you. May we meet again among the living." She set down our pack baskets, kissed me on both cheeks, hugged Alyeeta, and vanished silently into the dusk.

"As long as we do not have to go back over that bridge, all is well," Alyeeta muttered. "Better to take on a hundred armed guards, single-handed, than to repeat that ordeal." She picked up one of the packs. I slung the other onto my back and followed after her. Darkness was quickly closing in. Long before we came upon the Zarn's men, I could feel their presence and had to struggle to control my fear. Finally, after rounding a sharp bend in the riverbank, we spotted the first of their fires and heard the distant sound of voices. Alyeeta put out a hand to stop me, then quietly pulled me back out of sight. Evidently, we had not been seen by their sentries.

She signaled for silence and set down her pack. Then she squatted down, took some things from her pouch, laid them out in a pattern, and drew figures around them in the sand. At the same time, she began motioning with her other hand, while chanting in a harsh whisper, using words I could not understand. I sat down quietly, leaned back against my pack, and said nothing, having learned not to question or interrupt at such times. As I watched her intoning, I let my vision blur and my mind go blank. She always seemed very far away when the magic was on her, so different from the loving Alyeeta I had shared a bed with or the sharp-tongued Alyeeta of our daily lives.

Suddenly she came back to herself, gave me a shake, and put away all her treasures. "Now, remember, let me do most of the talking. Stay silent, act stupid, be watchful in all directions, but do not give an appearance of watchfulness. Remember to be old and dumb, two things which will make them feel superior and dull their suspicions." As I hefted my basket again, she pushed my head forward and shoved one shoulder down, so that I was hunched and crooked. "Stay calm and unafraid at the center, no matter what I do. Sometimes I may seem quite mad and sometimes a great fool. Stay calm even if I am raving, but remember to look properly frightened yourself at those times. Hold my skirt if at any moment they close in on us or seek to separate us."

"Alyeeta, whatever happens, I would rather be here with you than be waiting anxiously for your safe return."

"Is that why you consented to come with me?"

"That and my curiosity."

"Well, well, imagine that. It was certainly not your courage that drove you to it." She said this in her most derisive tone, then with a sudden change of mood, she added, "Oh, Tazzia, you have trusted your life to me. I hope I am not as much an old fool as the Kourmairi seem to think." She gave me a sudden hug. Just as suddenly, she let me go, picked up a walking stick from the driftwood piled up by the flood, bent herself over it, and set off. "Come, my poor, simple sister, we go to sweeten the night for these soldiers and make a little money." Right before my eyes, I saw

Alyeeta transform herself into a mindless old woman. As she hobbled along, she began to chant loudly, "We are bringing fine food and drink for you, parmi sweet-cakes and good quillof too."

We heard a loud shout, and then many other shouts echoing down the shore. A horn was blown. More torches were lit. First we were met by a sentry and then by several soldiers. Soon many more guards crowded around us. The sentry wanted to block our way. He threatened us with his sword, but one of the soldiers had raised the cloth on Alyeeta's pack. The aroma of fresh parmi-cakes floated on the damp night air. Instead of being attacked on the spot, we were escorted into camp by a pack of hungry soldiers.

Alyeeta was describing in detail the tastiness of her cakes and about to gather some coins for them when we heard a thunder of hoofbeats coming up the shore. The men parted. A young captain rode up in haste and threw himself from his horse. He grabbed Alyeeta's arm, shouting to his men at the same time, "Fools, how do you know this is not poison she wants to feed you?" I had to restrain myself from throwing my body between them.

Alyeeta instantly bowed and groveled. Her voice cracked and quavered as she pleaded, "Please, Captain, release me. You will break my old bones and frighten my sister, who has not much wits to start with. If you suspect poison, then feed us some of our own cakes, whichever ones you choose, and watch us for the results. But, truly, the cakes are good and hot and fresh, made of the best parmi-fruit. And the quillof is not strong, but very sweet, more like syrup than liquor."

"Set down your basket, old woman, and tell the brainless one to do the same." He took two cakes, handed one to each of us, and said sternly, "Eat these while we watch and wait. And drink some of your own brew as well." We sank down on the ground. There we ate and drank, surrounded by a large circle of curious men. By now this little drama had drawn most of the soldiers of the camp. Putting my witlessness on display, I ate slowly, allowing a little food to dribble down my tunic while I stared blankly into and through their faces. The tangy smell of parmi was strong in the air, for the cakes had been well covered and were still warm. The men began to grumble impatiently. The captain, meanwhile, was watching Alyeeta intently. "Where are you from, old woman?"

"We are Wanderers from the far north, above Pellor, but we just passed through the settlement of Kornfell. They thought you might be pleased to have some refreshments more interesting than camp food." The settlement she mentioned was one that had remained nominally loyal to the Zarns.

When it was clear we were not going to die, the captain said grudgingly to his men, "Eat what you please, but keep a close eye on them both." As he rode off, a brisk trade in cakes and quillof syrup began. More and more men came to clamor for their share. Our baskets were soon empty and our little pouches full of jangling coins. Those who had gone without could be heard grumbling and complaining to the others. A few good-natured and halfhearted arguments broke out.

Finally, Alyeeta held up her hands for peace. "We will come back tomorrow and bring more. Those who were cheated this day can be first tomorrow."

"We will not be here tomorrow," several of them said, and another added, "Tomorrow we cross the river and march for Mishghall. First we will crush that settlement of vermin on the other side. They have destroyed all the bridges and forced us to ford the river in flood time."

During this swirl of activity, I tried to keep my eyes sharp, as Alyeeta had told me, without betraying my wits. Sometimes, when the men came too close, my palms sweated and the hair on the back of my neck went up. Alyeeta, on the other hand, seemed relaxed and easy, totally who she appeared to be. She even took out her jol pipe and begged some jol from the nearest soldier as a way of striking up a conversation. He was soon telling her how, sometime the next day, the guards were going to cross the river and go on to subdue the rebellious city of Mishghall. As his tongue loosened with quillof, he talked quite freely of their intention to massacre all the Kourmairi men and even bragged of what body parts they would cut off for trophies. After that, he said, they intended to set fire to the city, but not before raping the women and carrying some off for later pleasure. In spite of his bloody words, he seemed a rather foolish and good-natured young man, with a frank, open face — kind enough in his own way. Alyeeta gave him every encouragement to talk, even a little free quillof from our stock. From his loose mouth, she soon had most of the strategy of the Zarn's army — or at least as much of it as he knew. At last, more than a little drunk, he fell asleep against a tree.

Meanwhile, games of chance had broken out. Alyeeta went to watch some dice throwing, with me trailing after her. She took several swigs from our one remaining jug of quillof — or at least appeared to do so. Soon she began to cough and laugh and make disparaging remarks about the players and their plays. At last, in exasperation, one of the men growled, "Throw the dice yourself, old woman, if you think you can do better."

Alyeeta immediately stepped back, protesting, "No, no, this is not my money. Much of it belongs to the women of Kornfell who helped to make the cakes. I cannot wager another's money in a game of chance. It would not be right." She continued, however, to make a show of drinking and went on with her insulting comments.

"But some of it must be yours. Put up a little and let us see what you can do. After all, you have more than enough to say about our skills."

"No, no, it would not be right." She was vehemently shaking her head. This banter went on for some time while more and more soldiers gathered, drawn by the commotion. Soon we had a circle around us, jeering at her or cheering her on. At last one man called out in exasperation, "Put up your money, woman, or shut your mouth and let us play in peace." Several others shouted their agreement. Finally, with a great show of reluctance, Alyeeta took out a small pile of coins. "I will wager this much and no more," she said, stacking them in front of her on the blanket.

Plainly showing the effects of drink, she was quickly losing her little sum. Turning quarrelsome and bad-tempered, she kept challenging them all to more throws. Still more of the men had come to watch. I heard shouts from all sides: "The Witch is betting." "The Witch is losing again." "Come watch the Witch!" While she cursed and grumbled and lost more money and then still more, I tried hard to remember Alyeeta's words about keeping calm and clear, no matter what madness she displayed. At last, almost in tears, she shook out her empty purse. Then she turned to me. "Sister, I must borrow a few coins from you. I cannot let these men best me this way. Surely my luck will turn."

I shook my head vigorously, fluttering my hands in helpless protest as she took some coins from my little pouch. The soldiers were all shouting mocking encouragement. On her next turn she won a little, and after that a little more, until she was winning more often than she was losing. Soon there was a pile of coins in front of her again. After a while she had gained back all she had lost. She started to gather up her coins, saying, "Well, we are even now and I have learned my lesson. I will not leave myself open to chance again." Some of the men barred her way, yelling and clapping and shouting, "Just one more turn, grandmother, just one more."

"Only one more," she agreed with drunken affability. Again she won, and again made as if to gather up her winnings. Again she was reluctantly persuaded to play one last time. Soon there was a large pile of coins before her. Determined not to be bested by an old Witch, the soldiers were borrowing from one another just to stay in the game. Wagers kept growing larger and more desperate. The frenzy around us was building. Then I clearly saw Alyeeta tap a die with her finger and roll it over after it fell. Again she won. My stomach clenched in a knot. If I had seen it, surely others would too. The next time she tapped a die, the young man who was losing most recklessly and desperately saw it and shouted, "Cheat, cheat, I saw her move the dice. She has been cheating us this whole time."

Now I was sure they would all be on us with drawn swords, but I had not counted on Alyeeta's power of drama. She leapt to her feet, a frightening sight with the firelight flashing madness in her eyes. In the wildest way she began screaming and shouting, "Never! Never! I have never cheated anyone in my whole life. Never in all my sixty years has anyone called me a cheat. Take back those ugly words, young man. You are the cheat. You tell such monstrous lies because you are losing."

The soldier was also on his feet, trying to shout her down, his face red with anger. "I saw you tap that die with your finger. I saw it clear as could be with my own eyes."

"You see, you are lying. No one else saw it. You are trying to taint my good name. You have dishonored my family. I swear by my mother and my mother's mother that I play an honest game."

"No doubt! You probably come from a whole family of liars and cheats!"

At that, Alyeeta began screaming and tearing her hair, dancing up and down in a circle, and shouting, "Liar, that man is a liar!" At the same time, the soldier was shouting, "That Witch is a cheat!"

I sensed the captain advancing through his men and so was able to warn Alyeeta before his hand fell on her arm with a tight grip. She whirled on him, saying between her teeth, "He called me a cheat because he is losing, but in truth, he is the liar." Then she turned to the soldier and yelled even louder, "Take back your lies, or I will cast a spell on you. The spell of the green snakes or the spell of the red dogs or the ... No, it will be the spell of the black toads! Yes, that is the very one. Recant, or I will rain black toads down on your lying head. If a single one of them touches you, your manhood will shrivel to the size of a thumb. Then it will turn purple and drop off." Alyeeta was waving her free arm about wildly. She seemed both comic and frightening. She certainly seemed mad.

By now, the other soldiers had begun shouting raucous mockery at both Alyeeta and their comrade. They called her names and taunted her to do her worst. As the captain attempted to restore order, some even reached out to poke at her with sticks and fingers.

Breaking free of the captain's grip, Alyeeta suddenly stood up to her full height. Her appearance was truly terrifying. In her deepest voice, the one she used for casting spells, she thundered, "A curse on all who mock me. Yes, by the Goddess, I shall rain down black toads on all who mock me. They will cover this beach by the thousands. Any man they touch will have his manhood shrivel up and fall off. That man shall be of no use to his wife or to any other woman — ever again!" Raising her arms to the heavens, she intoned, "With the help of the Goddess, I shall bring this curse down on all these laughing fools."

Now all was in an uproar. The captain had to shout for silence several times before he could make himself heard. "Old woman, you have caused more trouble in this camp than a herd of goats. You must be out of here now, this night. And take your idiot sister with you, before she comes to some harm. I am tempted to run you through with my sword for the disturbance you have made in my camp."

"Wait, Captain, I have only told the truth. For the sake of my honor, tie me to that tree for the night." She was pointing to a giant silverleaf at the top of the bank. "If I cannot cover this beach with black toads by morning, then you can all run me through with your swords. You, Captain, can have the pleasure of being first. Then the rest of you can bloody your weapons in my old body. Before you go hack the Kourmairi of Mishghall to bits, you can practice on me. Chop me up and throw the pieces to the fish if it pleases you. By evening I will be nothing but bones on the bottom of the Escuro, never to bother you again."

The captain shook his head in disgust, but his men had already gathered enough rope to tie up four horses. "My money," screamed Alyeeta as they started pulling her toward the tree. "Do not let him take my money. That is what he wants, that liar over there. He only wants my money. If my curse comes true, it shows that my heart is pure in the sight of the Goddess. Then my winnings are honorable, and that one is the liar and the cheat." She was pointing at her accuser.

The man lunged at her in a fury, but the captain blocked his way, saying, "Man, you will get your vengeance by morning light." Then he turned to me. "Here," he said sharply. "Gather up all this money." To Alyeeta he added, "Your sister will be holding your money safe for you. If you win this wager, it is all yours. If you lose, it is forfeited, along with your lives. Now, Witch, no more shouting. Enough commotion. Do not tempt me to run you through right now. We must have some peace in this camp tonight. We have much work to do tomorrow." As I scuttled sideways to gather up the money, I kept my eye on the captain, drooling a little for effect.

They tied Alyeeta to the giant silverleaf, the one she had pointed to. I followed after her, sniveling and hobbling and clinging to her skirts, yet ready in an instant to defend her — with my body if need be. The rope was wound many times around Alyeeta and the tree trunk, binding her securely to it. Silverleaf trees are sacred to the Witches, and I thought Alyeeta had chosen this one for her own purposes. It seemed like an ancient being as it towered over the other trees on the bank, rising tall and straight out of a great tangled nest of roots. In the flicker of torchlight, those roots looked like snakes, writhing from the shore out into the water. Its branches spread wide, and its broad, flat leaves gleamed like huge silver coins as they turned slowly in the breeze.

The captain set a guard on us, saying, "Old woman, if this is any sort of trick or if you seek to escape in the night, this soldier has orders to dispatch you instantly, you and your sister both. Now, we will have no more shouting and screeching and spellmaking, or I will end your life right now, is that understood? We will see in the morning what your spells can do. I trust my sleep will be better than yours."

Even all bound with ropes, Alyeeta drew herself up to her full height. With great passion and sudden seriousness, she declared, "My Goddess will not fail me. She will protect me from all harm. I will sleep as well as anyone here." Listening to her words, I wished I could feel half so confident.

"We shall see what the morning brings," the captain repeated as he turned away and went striding up the shore.

As I crouched beside Alyeeta, I asked in her head, *What if the toads do not come? What will we do then?*

She answered in whispered Kourmairi, "Do not fear, Little One. I will think of something else. They are easily played, these men. But the toads will come, Tazzia. I can already feel them gathering under our feet."

I sensed a young guardsman eyeing me hungrily, no doubt thinking that with my sister tied and helpless, I would be easy prey to his lust. Picking my nose diligently, I turned to stare straight at him with vacant innocence. When I knew I had his full attention, I let a little spittle run from the corners of my mouth. Then, for good measure, I began to scratch vigorously, first my head and then my crotch. I could feel his skin crawl with revulsion. He turned away in disgust and said to the man standing watch, "And to think we bought food from those two." I thought to have no trouble with him that night.

The camp began to quiet, as the captain had forbidden any further exchanges with the Witches or any more games of chance. When all was still, I felt Alyeeta tapping at the edges of my mind. *Reach for the horses and make a strong contact with them all. They must run free when the time comes and not let these soldiers mount.* I sent my mind out among the horses, gathering them in a net of thought that I could come back to later. I also kept watch on the soldiers so that none could sneak up, thinking to stab or rob us. I expected to keep watch on the whole camp, but I must have dozed, for I was awakened by Alyeeta's voice in my head. *I have tranced the guard, and I think the others sleep. Untie me quickly, for I cannot hold him long. But leave the ropes in place, so nothing will be noticed till the time comes for action. Especially free my hands. I will need them for the proper effect.*

Moving as cautiously as possible so as not to draw attention, I did as she told me. The fires had burned low and there was little light, save for some ground-glow. Untying was not so easily done. They had wound her round many times; also, that tangle of roots at the base of the tree was slippery and treacherous underfoot. As I worked, I could feel Alyeeta's presence in my head, impatiently urging me on. At last it was done and I could breathe again. This time I was determined to stay awake, though Alyeeta assured me that it was safe to sleep. "You will be wakened soon enough," she whispered gleefully.

5

In spite of my best intentions, I must have dozed again. I was jolted awake in the gray dawn by a terrible, loud trilling. This was instantly followed by shouts and screams. Toads! Toads everywhere! Alyeeta was right! The ewee had really come, just as she said they would. There were toads all along the river's edge. Whichever way I looked, there were little black toads: toads bursting through the sand, toads leaping about, toads making that ear-splitting sound. There were more toads than I had ever seen before at flood time, toads in such quantities, I could almost believe Alyeeta had spelled them into existence.

I shook my head in amazement. The whole shore had suddenly erupted into a scene of wild confusion. Shouting in terror, the Zarn's guards were fleeing in all directions, many with toads clinging to their clothes. They were leaving behind a chaos of belongings that littered the ground: food, clothes, tents, armor, weapons, and equipment. To goad them on, Alyeeta began waving her arms about wildly and screaming like one possessed, "You see, I told you, the curse has come true, the curse of the black toads has come down on your heads!" Our own guard had disappeared, without even a backward glance.

Frightened by all the noise, the horses were already skittish and ready to run. It took only a little push from me to make them afraid of the soldiers. Fully awake now, I threw myself into mind-speech with the horses and saw them rear up and leap away from their riders, throwing off those few who had succeeded in mounting. Some of the horses went thundering past us down the shore, while others dashed off into the woods. The frightened whinnying of horses and the curses of men were added to the maddening trilling of the toads.

Alyeeta, meanwhile, had thrown off her ropes. She was standing atop the high, gnarled roots of the silverleaf, arms raised, calling out to the Goddess and screeching at the men. Cursing, raving, and threatening, her madness seemed to be the central core of the turmoil that was swirling around us. "I told you I could do it!" she screamed at the fleeing soldiers. "I told you what would happen! I told you that I, Alyeeta the Witch, could bring down the curse of the black toads on your heads! Cheats! Liars! Fools! A curse on you all! Your manhood will shrivel up and fall away!"

In a matter of minutes, the shore was cleared of men and horses. As soon as I could release my mind-touch from the horses, I turned to Alyeeta. "Come down from there," I yelled at her. "Come down quickly, before one of them turns back and thinks to finish you off." She shook her head and triumphantly shouted more nonsense. Plainly, she was enjoying this sham of power. Annoyed, I grabbed her arm for a hard tug. She pulled back, but I was stronger. I succeeded in moving her from her perch so suddenly that she almost fell on top of me. We were none too soon. She was just starting to scold me for my interference when suddenly one of the men, raving madly, ran at her with his sword straight out before him. "Alyeeta!" I shouted in warning. Just in time, she rolled out of harm's way. Howling in rage, the man plunged on past her. Unable to stop in time, he dashed straight into the swollen Escuro and, with a scream, went swirling away. Almost instantly, he was out of sight, carried off in the rush of the floodwaters.

It seemed no time at all before the guards were all gone. Soon, even their shouts were distant. Alyeeta picked herself up and brushed off her clothes. "Now that all this rubbish has cleared itself away, we can signal the Kourmairi," she said with satisfaction. Clearly she was very pleased with herself. In fact, she seemed almost smug. That smugness could easily have been her undoing. It could even have cost her her life. As she threw back her head to laugh, I looked up just in time to see the captain bearing down on her, riding fast with his sword drawn. He was aiming straight at Alyeeta, shouting, "Death to you, Witch!"

Without a thought, I threw myself in front of her, directly between Alyeeta's body and the captain's sword. The impact of that force was as violent as a blow. It threw me to my knees, but it was force only, not sword and flesh. The horse had reared up before the captain could strike me. At that moment, his own sword seemed to turn against him. Then, as he lurched forward in the saddle, it was wrenched from his hold. For an instant, it appeared to be suspended in the air in front of me. Then it fell with a clatter on the gravel at my feet. The captain himself lay sprawled on the ground, with blood spurting from his side.

Much to my surprise, he struggled to his feet again almost instantly. He was clutching his side. Blood was oozing through his fingers. He was staring at me in amazement. "So, Witchling, you are not at all what you seem."

Throwing aside all semblance of age or witlessness, I held up my hands in front of me and said forcefully, "Not again, Captain. Your next try will likely kill you."

He made a slight bow, some mixture of mockery and respect. There was a strange smile on his face. "Khal Hadera Lossien! I have been sent often enough to hunt you down. Somehow you always managed to disappear before me like smoke or mist. I never really expected to see one of you at work. Your skills are most impressive. I suppose I should be grateful not to be wearing my sword through my innards." His anger seemed to have melted away. Toads were leaping all about him, landing here and there. Some were even hanging from his clothes, but he ignored them.

Somehow, his praise made me feel foolish as well as a little angry. "If your aim had been better, you would probably be dead now, and through no skill of mine," I answered gruffly. With a slight bow of my own, I added, "Hadera Lossi, I hear that is what they call us now." Then, just to try out the name, I said, "Lorren."

His eyes flew wide with surprise. "How did you know?"

"I picked it out of your head," I said quickly, afraid I might have betrayed Hereschell's trust.

"Well, you will certainly be something to watch in times to come."

Bothered by the sight of his blood, I reached into one of our baskets for a cloth, watching him carefully all the while. I tore the cloth in half and reached the pieces to him warily. "Fold one over to make a pad and bind it on with the other. I would help you, but I cannot trust you."

"I will do well enough for myself," he said, watching me intently. "I cannot say that I have much trust for you, either. Who knows what you might do next." Never taking his eyes from us, he pulled up his shirt, and with hands made awkward by pain, he bound his side. The wound was bloody but did not look vital.

"Lucky for you, your aim was not true. I would have warned you of the danger, but I had no chance."

"You would have warned me and so saved my life? You fight a strange battle, Hadera Lossi."

"I fight no battles at all," I said with annoyance. "We did not choose to fight this battle or any other. If we could, the Hadera Lossi would choose to live in peace far from your cities. Instead, we are hunted by the soldiers of the Zarn, all across Garmishair and into Yarmald. We are burned alive if you catch us. In spite of that, I take no pleasure in turning your blade back on you. It is nothing I can wish or unwish. And I certainly take no pleasure in your pain. I feel it almost as my own."

"She has the curse of empathy," Alyeeta said tartly. "It is one of the gifts, or one of the curses, of their powers. Personally, I am not nearly so kind to people who try to kill me."

He was shaking his head in amazement. "Well, this is a fair day's work. Two women have beaten the Zarn's army, with no blood shed but my own and no help but tiny black toads. I salute you, Daughter of the Great Star. And you, old Witch mother, I suppose you are also not what you seem. What else can you call down out of the sky besides black toads?"

"Red dogs, green snakes, and a great black bird-of-death the size of your horse, with a beak longer than your sword. Take care with your tongue and do not tempt me, soldier."

"I will consider myself warned. As you can see, I am trembling in my boots. Having seen the spell of the black toads, I have no wish to provoke you into calling down dogs or snakes." He looked up and down the shore that had been so quickly emptied of men and was now strewn with their leavings. "I think Mishghall is lost this day, but it is not likely to be the last battle fought for that city. The Zarn of Eezore has set his mind on it, and he is very determined."

Alyeeta turned a wolfish grin on him. "Do not count on winning the next time either, Captain. There is something new in this land that the Zarns have never dealt with before."

Ignoring her, he turned and looked me straight in the eye. "And what of the toads, Hadera Lossi, what are they really?"

"Only toads. They are the ewee, the flood toads of the Escuro." I said this without thought. He had drawn the truth out of me through no will of my own. Quickly, I shut my mouth before any more words could leap out.

He picked up one of those little black creatures and held it in his bare hands, not seeming the least bit afraid. Then he bent to peer at it closely.

"They do indeed appear to be real toads, and very small ones at that. I have never seen anything like them. Clearly, the Shokarn know nothing of them. There is nothing like this in Garmishair. Do they come out only at flood time?"

"They come every year when the water recedes."

"Watch out, you fool!" Alyeeta shouted. "These are not ordinary toads. This is a spell I learned from my old grandmother, and they will..."

"I heard you well enough when you were screeching at my men. They will unman me if they touch me. Spare me the nonsense, woman. I have made some study of nature and am not as gullible as my men. I may well be unmanned by this day, but not likely from the touch of black toads."

Alyeeta shrugged. "Ah well, you must admit that those little black creatures did as well as any spell — or for that matter any army — to route your men. What a sight, all those men scattering in all directions..." She began to laugh again.

I saw a look of rage cross Lorren's face. Then it was gone as quickly as it came, and suddenly he was laughing too. "The Zarn's army, routed by little black toads ... I can already tell you that it will not go well for me when I return to Eezore. There is no way I can reassemble those men of mine. Already I can hear the Kourmairi, coming to clear away our leavings." He held the toad up at eye level, saying, "Well, small beastie, you have no doubt destroyed my military career this day. I will probably go down in the history of Eezore as the only man ever to lose a battle to toads." He placed the toad carefully in his pocket. Then he stared straight at me. "Good luck, Hadera Lossi. I hope you stay free of the Zarn's reach. It would please me to see more displays of this power of yours, but now is not the time." With a nod to Alyeeta, he added, "Teach her well and keep her safe, old Witch, or whatever you are. She and her kind are something new in this tired old world." Then he turned to me again and said, "Woman, let me have my horse." His words were something between a plea and a demand.

"The horse is yours. You have a bond with it that I cannot bend with my will. Only do not ride at us again. It could be dangerous for you both."

He mounted awkwardly, holding his arm against his hurt side. As he turned to ride up the slope, he said, "Hadera Lossi, I think we shall meet again on some very different path."

"I have no doubt we shall." I wanted to speak his name again. Instead, I said quickly, "My name is Tazzil."

"Fool!" Alyeeta hissed.

"Well, Tazzil, I must be going, before your Kourmairi friends decide to revenge themselves on me for the Zarn's bad manners." As he rode up the rise, away from the riverbank, I could already hear voices from the opposite side.

When he had gone, Alyeeta shook me roughly. "Fool, you told him the truth. Truth is valuable, not something you owe to a soldier. I swear, all you star-brats have the disease of honesty, a dreadful case of truth-of-the-tongue."

I shrugged myself free of her grip. "I told him nothing he did not already know. He has knowledge, Alyeeta. Not as you have, or yet as I have, but he has knowledge nonetheless. Besides, as you have so often said yourself, some men are meant to be lied to, and some are not."

As soon as the captain had ridden away, Alyeeta took the little whistle from her pouch. She blew on it three times and then three more, a sound so shrill and piercing it could be heard even over the clamor of the ewee. I winced and had to cover my ears. A wild cheer went up from the other side. Soon Hadera Lossi and Kourmairi were massing on the opposite bank; strange gray shapes lurching about in the gray light.

After knotting together the cut pieces of the rope that had bound Alyeeta, I left one end fastened to the tree and tied the other to an abandoned spear. That done, I shouted across to the other side for them to make room for my throw. I could hear Pell and Rishka yelling their encouragement. My first two throws fell pitifully short. Soon I was hauling back endless lengths of wet rope, to the jeers of the Kourmairi men. Stung by their mockery, I was determined to succeed on my third try. I backed up the bank, then ran full force to the edge of the water and threw with a great shout, using all my powers and all Kazouri's teaching. My shout was answered by a shout from the other side, and I saw several figures wading out into the water. Then the rope was pulled taut and there were more cheers, shouts, and whistles.

It seemed as if some sort of argument was in progress over who would go first, but it was impossible to hear the words clearly over the turbulence of the water. That first crossing was a slow one, as the water was still treacherous and deep. I held my breath as I watched the rope swaying wildly. Then Pell appeared out of the gloom, with water pouring from her clothes. She was closely followed by Rishka, Zenoria, and several Kourmairi men. I grabbed Pell's hand and hauled her up the bank. She fell on me in a great wet hug, and soon we were rolling in the sand, laughing and shouting as the toads shrilled all around us.

"Gone, all gone, the whole lot of them," I yelled. "Oh, Pell, I wish you could have seen it. The camp was cleared in minutes. And it was all because of the toads."

"What do you mean, the toads? How is that possible?" she shouted back. But when I began to tell her, hardly able to make myself heard over the uproar, she said quickly, "Later. Tell me all of it later. Right now we must clear this place of their leavings as quickly as we can." As she spoke, she was already struggling to her feet and brushing off the wet sand.

Pell was satisfied to wait for the story, but those first Kourmairi men were full of questions. "Where is the Zarn's army?" "What happened here?" "How did two women do all this?" "Who helped you?"

Alyeeta drew herself up very tall. "Gone!" she said grandly. "The Shokarn army is all scattered. Those men are horseless, weaponless, near naked, and afraid for their manhood." As she spoke, she made a broad gesture with her hands, as if she had personally scattered the guards far and wide like bread crumbs, thrown to the birds.

"You did all that with toads?"

"Just as I said we would."

"...but how...?"

Alyeeta shrugged and turned her back. The men looked inquiringly at me, but I shook my head. I was already in enough trouble for my loose tongue. I had no wish to make it worse. Besides, a little mystery would add to their respect for us. And in truth, they had no power to draw words from me as Lorren had.

Those who crossed first brought three more lengths of rope with them. They tied one end of the ropes to trees, and used bows and arrows to send the other end back. This was far more effective than my feeble spear throw. As soon as the new ropes were in place, more gray figures began swarming across. Soon Alyeeta and I were surrounded by a circle of Hadera Lossi and Kourmairi, hugging and kissing us, rejoicing in our safety, praising us for our courage and cleverness, and asking endless questions. I was somewhat abashed by all this outpouring of praise, since I felt my own part in the matter had been very small. Alyeeta, of course, suffered from no such troubling modesty. She relished the attention and happily fabricated several different stories of how we, two lone women, had routed the Zarn's army. I made no attempt to contradict her.

When they had enough ropes in place, some of the Kourmairi men started crossing in boats, using a system of hooks and pulleys. Soon only the very young and the very old were left on the far shore, where they stood waving and calling encouragement. Even most of the Kourmairi women crossed the river, actively helped and encouraged by the Hadera Lossi. Once they were safely onshore, they began chattering wildly among themselves, at once frightened, excited, and a little scandalized by their own daring.

As the Kourmairi began gathering up the armor and weapons, arguments broke out among the men over the ownership of these spoils. Some of these arguments grew dangerously heated. All seemed about to erupt in violence when Nhokosos stepped from a boat, helped by two younger men and leaning heavily on his staff.

The headman shouted for silence. His voice was drowned out by the noisy wrangling of the men, mixed with the roar of the river and the incessant shrilling of the toads. When his shout did not bring silence, he blew on a shell-whistle that he wore on a thong around his neck. That sound, as loud as all the toads combined, got immediate attention. Then Nhokosos climbed up on a log, waved his arms, and roared in a voice of command, "Shame on you all. Is this how you show your gratitude, by quarreling over spoils, by making war on each other for loot? You would make the Zarn proud. His army has been routed, but you could still win this battle for him. You have been saved this day by these two women. Rightfully, all this belongs to them, since it was they, not you, who set the army to flight. Now you have swarmed across the river like scavengers, to fight over the remains. Have you no pride? What must they think of you?"

"No, no," Alyeeta called out to him. "Nhokosos, we have no use for weapons or armor. Let them do as they please with that. Leave us the horse packs, tents, food, some clothing, and most of the horses. Add some food from your own stores and we will be even. You can trade us winter grain and spring seeds for what you keep."

As the turmoil threatened to resume, Nhokosos pounded on the log with his staff. "Everything is to be taken back to the other side. What these women do not want will be sorted into piles. These will be assigned by drawn lots. If you do not like your lot, you may trade with another but you may not fight. There will be no Kourmairi blood shed over Shokarn loot."

After that, all was done with better will and less rivalry. The Kourmairi, as they gathered up those mounds of spoils, moved as fast and efficiently as beetles on a carcass. I am sure it took much less time to clear that camp than it had to set it up. More and more boats were being pulled across and loaded up, though after one turned over, losing its precious cargo to the hungry river, more care was taken not to overload them.

While the Kourmairi were occupied moving and sorting the loot, Alyeeta drew me aside, away from the bustle. After looking in all directions to make sure we were not being observed, she gave me her sly old woman look and held out her hand. "My pouch, Tazzia. I want all my winnings in my own hand. I do not trust you with them. You would just turn them over to Pell; she would add them to your common purse, to be used for that mob of star-brats. But this is mine, for my own use. I risked my life for it."

In the press of events, I had totally forgotten that I had stashed her little sack of money in my pouch. Hastily, I handed it back to her. As she cradled it in both hands, a look of naked greed crossed her face. "Good thing I relieved the soldiers of this last night, before those fools decided to run off. Otherwise, this money would have been scattered all over the shore, and the Koormir would already have made off with whatever was not trampled in the dirt." After looking all around again, Alyeeta sat down abruptly on a fallen tree and dumped the coins out into her skirt. I was amazed at the size of her stash. Crooning with delight, she began pouring the shining coins from hand to hand. "A good night's work. There is enough here to furnish a whole Witch convent, or at least, a very grand house in the style of Eezore." At just that moment, I heard Zari calling my name. I turned to look. When I turned back, Alyeeta was already standing, brushing out her skirt. The coins had vanished from sight. "Mention this to no one," she said quickly. There was a little edge of menace in her voice. Then, in a very different tone, she went on. "This is a busy moment for you, Tazzia. Go where you are needed. You have better things to do than stand here gossiping with an old woman."

It was time to think of gathering together the abandoned horses. Before we had been able to stop them, a group of Kourmairi men had caught some the loose ones and ridden off in pursuit of the fleeing soldiers. I went with Zari and Zenoria to bring back the rest. Putting all my mind-reach into it, I called to those horses in my head. They had been badly frightened, and when they reappeared, a few at a time, they were timid and hesitant. Snorting and rolling their eyes, they danced a step or so sideways for every few steps forward they took. When some of them were finally willing to come up to me, I talked to them and petted them, trying to gentle them as best I could. They rubbed against me in gratitude, snuffling softly and lipping my hand. Suddenly, in the midst of all that chaos, I slipped into a deep sense of creature connection, the kind of peace I so seldom feel with my own kind. For a while I stood there, tranced among the horses, until Zenoria's voice called me back.

The sun was beginning to break through the mist. Steam was rising from the sodden shore. The river, though still fierce and dangerous, was clearly receding. As the Kourmairi were anxious to be back on their own side, we began moving the horses across the river. Rishka took charge of this. She and Zenoria rode the lead horses, and soon there was a whole troupe crossing, swimming frantically in the middle and then struggling up the bank on the other side. After Alyeeta had watched this activity for a while, she informed me, with an expression of extreme distaste on her face, that she would not think of crossing on horseback.

"Then why not wait till later in the day, when the water has receded more?" I asked. That seemed to me like a reasonable idea.

She gave me a scathing look and answered contemptuously, "Would you have me wait until summer? That is when I would feel comfortable crossing this river on a horse." Quickly I went back to my work. This was not a problem I could solve at that moment. Later, as I was busy with some loading, I heard my name called. I looked up to see Alyeeta seated in the bow of a boat like some grand lady. There were Kourmairi on either side of her, with many hands to hold her steady and keep her safe.

Soon the place was cleared of everything that could be carried. Nothing was left to signify the presence of an army, save for the still-smoldering fires. In the distance I could hear the shouts of the Kourmairi and sometimes the screams of the Shokarn. Somehow I was a part of this killing. I felt a sickness all through my body and leaned against the giant silverleaf for strength and comfort.

The others beckoned and called to me, urging me into a boat or onto a horse that was part of the crossing. Each time, I shook my head. Finally, I was the last one left. The morning mist had lifted and the sun was shining through. The river's edge was deeply trampled and covered with the bodies of tiny black toads, some crushed, and some mating and dying in the sun, as was their way. As I picked one up and bent to examine it, I thought of the man, Lorren, putting a toad in his pocket. He had said our paths would cross again. Somehow I had no doubt of it. I wondered what his fate in Eezore would be if he succeeded in making his way home. When I heard more screams from in back of me, I shivered and retched. I might have just stayed there, leaning against the tree, if Rishka had not come back for me. "Come on, Tazzi, it is over and done. Time to come back to the other side now."

"They are killing Shokarn soldiers, most of whom are naked and unarmed."

Rishka shrugged. "That is not our affair. That is the risk of being a soldier. Besides, it would be now or later. How could they survive across all that Kourmairi territory without food or clothes or horses? And if, somehow, they did get back to Eezore, they would either be executed by the Zarn for their defeat or be issued new clothes and weapons to come after us again. They are not really men — they are only machines for killing."

I looked back one last time at the shore. A single fire had leapt into flame from the breeze. After I kissed the rough bark of the silverleaf for luck, Rishka bound me against her with a strap. Together we stepped into the Escuro, holding tight to the ropes. The pull of the river was terrible. Brown water surged against me with a fury, sometimes splashing over my head and filling my mouth and nose. Fierce and deadly, it sucked at my spirit as well as my body, trying to tear me loose and carry me off. My palms were soon torn from holding the rope. At some moment it was ripped out of my hands. It was only Rishka's strong grip that kept me from being swept away down the river. When we both stumbled up the bank on the other side, many hands reached out to help. I was staggering and spitting out water. When Rishka untied us, I fell flat on the sand.

When I was finally able to sit up again, I could see that the Kourmairi women were already dividing the spoils into stacks. Meanwhile, their men were lounging against logs, smoking jol, saying which armor they wanted, and making wagers on the outcome of the lot drawing. There were far more goods than were needed by the people of Darthill. Deals settled on that day would make their wealth through trade with other tribes or even with the city of Mishghall.

I surveyed the scene with disgust, feeling distant and apart from it. Were these Kourmairi quarreling over spoils really my people? What did I care for any of them, or for that matter, what did they care for me? I only wanted to be gone from there. When I saw Alyeeta talking with Nhokosos, I knew she would strike us a good bargain in grain and spring seeds. It would not be another hungry winter, of that I was sure, but where would we be come winter? Would we have found a home? Goddess knows, I was sick of fleeing for our lives from place to place, always finding ourselves once more where we were not wanted.

By now the sun had broken through in earnest. It was blazing over everything, with the flood retreating before it. The sky had turned to blue, and the remaining clouds were being drawn west like a curtain being pulled by a giant hand. On this side, too, the flood toads were hopping and mating and dying, but their trills were no longer so loud and shrill. Probably by the middle of the next day, the guards would have been able to ride across without having to swim their horses. It was hard to believe that less than a day had passed since we stood in the Kourmairi meeting house and listened to Ozzet speak.

From where I sat, I could see some of the Hadera Lossi gathered around a pile of goods. I knew we had no need to draw lots. We would simply talk of who needed what and distribute the goods accordingly. We might be quarrelsome in some ways, but we would never fight each other for possessions. Just as I stood up to join them, I felt the hair prickle along my back as if I had been called. Something drew me to look up. At the top of a far hill, on the other side of the Escuro, sat a lone figure on horseback, a dark outline against the bright blue of the sky. From some impulse, I raised my hand in salute. The figure did the same, then turned and was gone. No one else had seen this exchange. They were all too busy.

The new horses had been gathered in a loose group. They were just beginning to graze. As I came toward them, I noticed a Kourmairi man edging in that direction as if he meant to take charge of them. It was Rhomar, the same man who had argued with Ozzet's father and then challenged Ozzet at the meeting. He had a hard, determined look on his face.

At just that same moment, Alyeeta stepped up to block his way. I paused to watch, ready to move forward if needed. "Man, those horses are ours, that was the agreement," Alyeeta said loudly. "Do not meddle with them."

A look of anger swept across the man's face at being thwarted in this way. He put his hand on his sword in a threatening gesture. "Well, Witch, that was no agreement of mine. I did not lend my name to it. In fact, I never heard of it." He was speaking insolently, looking at her to see what kind of challenge she might present.

Alyeeta took another step toward him and smiled. I knew that smile only too well. There was no humor in it. The hair went up on the back of my neck. In a friendly voice that belied the intent of her words, she said, "I had hoped that this day would make a seal of peace and friendship between the Kourmairi and the Khal Hadera Lossien. I would never wish to have any cause to send our Kourmairi friends fleeing before us like our Shokarn enemies. Surely you can see what good uses can be made of peace. You may keep all that is fancy and has worth: the tack, the bridles, the armor, the swords. We lay claim to the grain, the foodstuffs, the tents, the horses, and whatever else will help us survive. Let us make a good bargain and shake hands on it, for it profits us both."

She reached out her hand as if in friendship, ignoring his intended hostility, and took a step toward him. Rhomar coughed and muttered. He took his hand from his sword and twisted his mustache. When she took another step toward him, he thrust out his hand abruptly. "Friends," he muttered, "friends in peace." Scuffing his boots in the sand, he pressed her hand in his own, but he would not look her in the eye. Then he turned without another word, and suddenly walked away.

"It would not be good to have it said that a Kourmairi went back on the word of his headman," Alyeeta shouted after him.

At the same moment, I heard a string of curses from in back of me in Murghanth's deep, rough voice, curses clearly meant for Rhomar. She ended with "...your father's father should have been a lover of men," and then spit on the ground. As I looked around, I saw that this little exchange over the horses had gathered quite an audience. Several Kourmairi were keeping their distance, but obviously watching for the outcome. Teko was standing by Murghanth, with some of the Sheezerti behind them. Zenoria and Kazouri and Zari had moved in and were standing protectively by the horses.

Just as Rhomar was leaving, Pell came striding in our direction so that they passed quite close. "Puntyar!" he snarled at her with venomous hatred. "Just a bunch of filthy Puntyar!"

Pell stopped and looked after him, nodding her head. Then she called out loudly, "Yes, indeed, Puntyar, a very big bunch of Puntyar, more than *you* have ever seen before. And there are likely twice this many and more waiting to join up with us, so remember our numbers and learn to say that word with respect. Puntyar. As to filthy, it is very hard to stay clean on the road, but we will soon remedy that by finding a place to settle. Then we will bathe every day and be the cleanest Puntyar in all Yarmald. Yes, by the Mother, a very large bunch of very clean Puntyar. And do not think to come and borrow our horses again, man of Darthill, for we are also very watchful Puntyar."

Nhokosos had come up from the other side. "Are you having some trouble, Alyeeta?"

Alyeeta whirled around to face him. "By the Mother, I see little difference between the Shokarn and the Kourmairi, save that the Shokarn are even worse. That young fool there with the mustache thought to take the horses and perhaps even to make me dance on the end of his sword. Speak to him, will you please, Nhokosos? And remember to tell your people in Mishghall who it was that drove away the Shokarn army. When the Kourmairi march through the streets of their freed city, we, the Witches and the Khal Hadera Lossien, will be there in that march." Then she swung her hand around at the rest of us. "What are you all gawking at? Did you come to help? Do you think a Witch is not able to handle one Kourmairi? He is lucky he left before I thought to raise a spell. Be careful or I will turn the lot of you into little black toads!"

All the others, even Pell, moved away quickly, as if they had urgent business elsewhere, all but Murghanth, that is. Murghanth stood her ground, staring at Alyeeta. "Yes, I was curious," she said boldly. "I wanted to see what Witches can do." Then she gave a wild trill, as she might have for a street performance, and did a series of back flips that took her quickly out of range. Alyeeta's scowl was replaced by a broad grin. I was about to make my own hasty retreat when she said, "Wait, Tazzia." She came and put her arm through mine. "We have just saved this village, you and I, and we have probably saved the city of Mishghall as well. Let us walk around the settlement and show ourselves off. Let them see the two who saved their lives."

"It was you, Alyeeta. You thought of it. You did it all."

"And you came with me and saved my life. If not for you, I would have saved Darthill, but you might very well have had to add my funeral to the celebration. I like it much better this way. Let us enjoy this moment while we can." So, arm in arm, we walked about the settlement in the warming sun, while others counted swords and saddles and sacks of grain.

6 Riders had quickly been sent to Mishghall with word of the outcome of the battle, if indeed such a farce could really be called a battle. And those of us who were headed south had already left. In the meanwhile, the rest of us spent most of the day and well into the evening bargaining with the Kourmairi of Darthill, settling our affairs among them, and being properly feasted and thanked. We had to arrange for the safekeeping of our new possessions, smoke jol at this one or that one's fire, join the feasting in the village square, eat a ceremonial meal in the headman's house, be praised, be toasted, be stared at, and answer the same questions over and over and over again.

We even had to listen politely to widely exaggerated versions of what had just occurred, some already set to music. It seems we were part of the making of a legend. At first I had little patience for it, and Pell had even less. Alyeeta, on the other hand, seemed to glory in it all. It was Alyeeta who guided us through, reminding us that the goodwill of these people might stand us in good stead at some future time. In truth, I think she got great pleasure from being the center of all that attention. And this was the same Alyeeta who spoke so contemptuously of *humans*.

Surprisingly, it was Rishka who was the most affable among us. I think the people of Darthill reminded her of the Muinyairin she had grown up among. Though she often cursed her own people, I know she also missed them. To me, these Koormir certainly seemed very different from the timid farm folk of my village; wilder, ruder, and much fiercer. Rishka went about freely among them, linking arms with the younger women; speaking politely to the older ones and calling them "Mother." With the men, she talked and joked in their own rough style. She even drank some brew when it was offered. I watched all this with surprise. Except for that one time after our escape from Hamishair, I had never even tasted liquor. There had been none in my father's house. Though others in our village drank, sometimes to excess, he would not allow it in our home. He said it addled men's wits and made fools of them. I had no interest before, but now, watching Rishka become jollier and more lighthearted each time she raised her glass, I grew curious. I was well aware that Pell was trying to dissuade her, but it looked to me like a great temptation.

For a while, Alyeeta and I were led about by an eager crowd and obliged to tell our story again and again. Alyeeta, never one to be closely bound by the truth, took great pleasure in elaborating, until the tale became like a fancy weaving with only a few drab threads of truth running through it. Meanwhile, we were offered jol and brew everywhere we went. Alyeeta accepted a little here and there for politeness' sake. Each time I refused, I felt the pull of curiosity. Why should I obey my father in this when I had obeyed him in so little else? Besides, he was no longer in my life, maybe no longer in this world.

When we reached the feast in the square, there were huge pitchers of brew on the tables and many glasses already poured and waiting. On sudden impulse, I picked up a glass and downed the contents. The men roared and cheered with approval and raised their glasses to me. A warm glow went through me, followed by a sudden flash of heat that almost jolted my stomach up into my throat. I coughed violently and my eyes stung with tears. For a moment I swayed on my feet, very aware that the Kourmairi men were now laughing at me. Then I steadied myself, and the heat settled back into a warm glow. A strange sense of power filled me, very different from the powers I had lived with all my life. I took another glass and drank more slowly, ready this time for the heat. When I looked up, I saw Rishka watching me from across the table and raised my glass to her as I had seen other drinkers do. She seemed to give a slight shake of her head — or perhaps I only imagined it. The warm glow and the feeling of power had increased. As I was about to heft a third glass, Renaise came up beside me and said in my ear, "Take a care with that, Tazzi. If you are not used to that brew, it can make you both very sick and very foolish."

"You are not my mother!" I answered sharply, annoyed that my pleasure was being interfered with. Had I not helped to save this settlement and with it the city of Mishghall? How could anyone deny me a glass or two of brew? Surely I was entitled.

"I have no wish to be your mother, but you have already drunk too much to have your wits about you."

"I am a Khal Hadera Lossien," I said proudly, drawing myself up to my full height. "I am not one of those men in that tavern where you worked as a serving-wench."

"At this moment there is little difference. A drunk is a drunk. If you were in my uncle's tavern, I would call someone to toss you out into the street and throw a bucket of cold water over your head." She said this contemptuously as she turned to leave.

Renaise and I had long since made peace after our first bad beginnings, but some residue of ill feeling must have remained. I was gathering myself up for a scathing response when Pell tapped me on the shoulder. "Tazzi, the brew men drink is like poison for our senses. It will silence your mind-speech and dull your powers."

"Another mother!" I shouted angrily. "Well, let me tell you, it gives me pleasure, and it fills me with another kind of power which I much enjoy."

Pell shrugged. "Suit yourself. Later you will have cause to remember my words, of that you may be sure." Before I could make my clever answer, she was gone. Quickly I finished the glass I had been holding. For the rest of the day, I smoked and ate and drank, listening to no one's advice and doing exactly as I pleased. I was, no doubt, making a great fool of myself, but at least I was having a fine time.

Actually, that is not altogether true. I was not near so carefree as I pretended to be. Mostly I was in a strange kind of pain, a pain liquor could dull, but not erase. Perhaps I was trying to drown my feelings. All that day and into the evening, even over the noise and the music, even through the fog of the brew, I could hear occasional distant shouts and screams. No doubt it was the Zarn's soldiers, near naked, unhorsed, and unarmed, being hunted down and dispatched by the Kourmairi. The Kourmairi had every right to their rage, and after all, as Rishka so often reminded me, death is what soldiers are made for. Yet I felt the reverberations of those killings deep within me. I knew I had my part in this. And in my heart, I wished safety for the wounded captain with the tiny black toad in his pocket. I could not bear the thought of his being pulled from his horse and hacked to pieces.

Later that afternoon I heard shouts and blows from much closer, and then the sound of a woman screaming. I ran in that direction, pushing my way past Kourmairi, who seemed to be paying scant attention to the commotion. Kazouri was there before me, along with Maireth and Thalyisi. Rhomar, the man who had challenged Alyeeta for the horses, had evidently been beating his wife. He had his hand raised to hit her again. Kazouri stepped between them so that her huge bulk blocked the blow. From the shelter of Kazouri's back, the woman called to him, "This is my one chance, Rhomar. Who knows when it will come again. I must go to Mishghall with them, no matter what you say!" The woman had a bloody lip, and a purple bruise rising quickly under her left eye. Nonetheless, she seemed ready to hold her own.

Rhomar, in a rage at being robbed of his quarry, roared back, "Never! No wife of mine will ride with those filthy Puntyar. How could you think to disgrace me so? I will break both your legs before I will agree to let you go." With that, he tried to lunge around Kazouri and reach his wife.

Kazouri moved again to block his way, saying, "Then you must break mine first."

At that moment, Alyeeta suddenly appeared. She was closely followed by Nhokosos, who arrived very out of breath. When he rushed up beside her, she turned and said to him, loudly enough for all to hear, "This man seems to be a lover of trouble. Perhaps you should have sent him alone to meet with the Zarn's guards and show his courage there. Since he has such skill with his hands, he might have been able to stop them all on his own." Her tone was taunting and full of malice.

"Witch!" Rhomar yelled, whirling to face her. In his rage, he seemed ready to leap at Alyeeta in place of his wife. Nhokosos shouted, "Rhomar! Stop!" and put his hand on the man's arm. Rhomar raised his other arm as if he meant to strike his own headman, then dropped it with a groan. "Look what you have brought us to by inviting these women here. Soon our own women will all turn wild and be out of control. And what good is a man who cannot control his woman? After all, she is my wife. I do have some rights in the matter. I tell her, with good reason, that she cannot go to Mishghall, and she shouts back in my face as if she had turned into one of these cursed Hadera Lossi right before my eyes. As her husband, all I was doing was trying to bring her back to her senses. And then this walking mountain interfered between us."

"No matter what you thought to do, you cannot beat your wife, not now, not ever again," Kazouri said, with a voice like quiet thunder. "All that has changed. Remember that, man, when you think to raise your hand again."

Rhomar turned a look of pure hatred on Kazouri. If he could have killed her at that moment, I am sure he would have, with no mercy and no hesitation and likely much pleasure.

Meanwhile, Alyeeta was going on as if she had not been interrupted: "Of course, it is much easier to beat unarmed women than well-armed men, but I suppose that is the way of it."

At the same time, Nhokosos was saying firmly, "Rhomar, open your eyes. It was either these women or the Zarn's guards. Either way, things would have changed. If it had been the Zarn's guards, you might not be so fortunate as to be having this argument with your wife. The guards would be on their way, at this very moment, to retake Mishghall. First, they would have destroyed Darthill. You and Zheran would most likely be dead. Everything we love would have been torn down, burned, killed: our children, our houses, our animals, our land. The Escuro that nurtures our lives would be full of bodies and running red with blood. We have been spared all that. It seems a small price to forgo beating your wife."

"You are an old fool. This fall, when the choosing is done, I will stand against you for headman. You will see, there are others here who think as I do." With that, he took two steps back and said to Kazouri, "Stand aside. I will not touch her, but I must speak to that woman." Kazouri took one step aside, keeping a careful eye on him. Rhomar said, in a voice that could have cut stone, "Zheran, listen carefully. If you go to Mishghall, do not come back. You will no longer be my wife. There will be no place for you here. You will be considered as dead, at my hearth and in this village as well. Our sons will stay here with me. You would not be fit to be their mother."

I saw her lip quiver and her eyes go wide. She looked stricken, plainly more frightened than she had been when he raised his hand for the next blow. For a moment, I thought she was going to change her mind and throw herself on his mercy. Then she took several deep breaths. When she answered, it was quietly and from some place of power deep inside herself. "I will go to Mishghall tomorrow. I have made my choice and you must make yours, though I must tell you, Rhomar, this is not how I would have chosen to end our life together."

"Done!" he shouted, with no pause for thought. Then he turned and strode away without a backward glance.

"As it must be," Alyeeta said softly, while Kazouri muttered, "I think we have not seen the last of that man." The woman, Zheran, was looking bereft, as if she might cry at any moment.

"If you do not wish to stay in Mishghall, you are very welcome among us in our new settlement." I spoke on impulse, but of course there was no new settlement for any of us yet.

At my words, she turned to look at us, as if seeing us all for the first time. We were part of a choice she had made without intending to. Her life had been changed forever, blown apart by those few words. The pieces were still falling into place. Her lip was trembling again, ever so slightly, but when she spoke it was with great calm and dignity: "This is all very sudden and unexpected. I had no thought to leave forever, only to go and visit with my sister in Mishghall. We have not seen each other in many years. Each time before, when I asked to go, Rhomar found some new reason to deny me. This time I was determined. My children are old enough. I am not getting any younger. And now, who knows..." She shook her head. "My name is Zheran. I will ride out with you tomorrow. Later, after Mishghall, we shall see what the future brings." She was trying to sound strong and confident, but I noticed that for the rest of our time in Darthill she stayed close by Kazouri's side.

It was clear that Pell was in a fret to leave, but the matter was out of her hands. By evening, the Kourmairi, no doubt under the influence of brew, were making us pledges of undying friendship and guaranteeing safety for our possessions and our lives. I was sick of it all and wanted to crawl away to some private place, but the Sheezerti were in their glory.

As soon as the tables had been cleared away, they announced their performance with drums and cymbals. When all eyes were on them, Noya gave a sharp cry and they whirled into the circle in a series of wild leaps and flips. Next came a brilliant performance of juggling and tumbling, punctuated by rhythmic claps and shouts. They ended with a near miraculous balancing act that involved the whole troop. This was followed by a thunder of applause and a shower of coins. The Muinyairin, not to be outdone, leapt into the circle the moment the Sheezerti had bowed out. They did their sword dance to the loud encouragement of the Kourmairi men, some of whom, clumsily, tried to join in.

I was just wondering how we were going to stop this madness from going on all night, when riders came from Mishghall with the message that there would be a grand victory march through the city the day after the morrow, led by those notables who had survived the siege. With them was a young woman named Dhashoti, who was clearly one of ours. She said she was to be our guide into the city. Immediately, we sent riders south to catch up with Hayika and the others and ask if they wanted to march with us through the streets of Mishghall, since there was no longer any need to hide from the Zarn's army.

Suddenly all this motion was too much for me. It seemed as if the messengers and Dhashoti and the leaping, twirling Sheezerti and the Muinyairin with their flashing swords and the grinning Kourmairi men and the flirting Kourmairi women were all whirling around together. There was no still place in all the world and no solid spot to stand. I began swaying on my feet. My stomach was rising up into my throat. Hands came and firmly took hold of my arms. Voices on each side of me said, "Come over to the edge of the clearing, Tazzi," and, "Lean on us, Tazzi." I did as I was told, hardly aware of my feet touching the ground. The voices told me to bend my head over and open my mouth. As I did so, everything I had consumed that day came gushing out in a great shower of vomit.

My throat burned and tears ran down my face. One of those hands passed me a damp rag to wipe my face and mouth, while the others supported me. After a few more retches, I was able to stand on my own and look about. The owner of one set of hands was Rishka, and the other, Pell. Renaise was holding out another clean cloth to me. With the drink out of my system, a sudden embarrassed sanity returned. I was about to make my craven apologies and admissions, but Pell shook her head. "We have all done it at some time in our lives. You just waited longer than the rest of us. Now perhaps you will remember that drink is not our friend."

I was shaking my head to clear it. "Well, Renaise, do you have your bucket of water ready?" I asked ruefully.

"No, you will have to find your own. It will help the ache in your head."

"Rishka, how is it that you are not suffering in the same way? Surely you had enough drink this day to fell a bull."

"I know how to give the appearance of being deep in my cups and quite jolly, while actually drinking very little. After my first time, I knew it was nothing I wanted to do again." They took me back between them, unrolled my mat, and laid me down on it. Renaise brought me a large wet cloth for my head. Then Olna came with her healing presence. She sat by me patiently, holding my hand in hers and murmuring softly to me until I fell asleep.

★

I was being roughly shaken awake. I opened my eyes a slit and saw Murghanth's long, skinny arm. Quickly I shut my eyes again and groaned. My head throbbed. My mouth was dry and tasted foul. I wanted to be left alone for another hour at least — or maybe a year. Or better yet, forever. The shaking became more urgent and Murghanth's grating voice was added to it. "Hurry, Tazzi! We let you sleep until last, but now it is time. We must be gone before the Kourmairi awaken and impede our departure."

"And we must reach the city tonight if we are to march with them tomorrow." That was Teko's voice. She was standing just behind Murghanth, peering down at me. I groaned again and struggled to sit up. Murghanth was saying excitedly, "Think of it, we are going to march openly together through a free city, a city where Zarns have no more power. Free women in a free city! On your feet, Tazzi! It is time to go! You can sleep on Dancer's back on the way." With that, she gave a hard tug on my arm and I found myself standing. Instantly, Teko was rolling up my bedroll.

Something was wrong with me, very wrong, so wrong that at first I could not understand what it was. Then it came to me like a blow. Silence! My head was stuffed with silence, a silence louder and more persistent than any noise. I heard sounds that were outside and came in through my ears. But what had always been with me since I could first remember, my inner ear, that speechless knowing of another's thoughts and feelings, that was dead to me. A block of stone was in its place. I shook my head to clear it. Nothing changed. The powers I had cursed so often were gone. It felt as if some part of me had died or been cut away.

Pell was walking swiftly toward me, with Dancer following. "On your horse, Tazzi. It is time to go."

"Oh, Pell, it is all gone. What have I done? Will I ever...?" I asked in a panic, with my hands pressed around my head.

She was grinning and gave me a pat on the back. It may have been kindly meant, but it felt like a blow from the paw of an Oolanth cat. "Give it time, it will all come back. Only, next time, remember..."

"Never! I will never forget! I will never drink a drop of their brew again, not as long as I live. I pledge to the Mother to remember all my life, if only my powers will return." I said this fervently, little knowing I was echoing every sorry drunk who wakens in the morning, full of regret, with a thick and aching head.

Pell burst out laughing. "That is what they all say. On your horse now, so we can be on the road."

We made our escape easily enough. Except for Nhokosos and a few others who planned to go to Mishghall with us and were already mounted to ride, most of the Kourmairi men, including Rhomar, were sleeping off the celebration. With so few men about, the women of Darthill were suddenly much in evidence, packing extra food and bedding for us, showering us with kisses and attention. Ozzet and four other young women who were clearly star-brats had declared they were coming with us, though some of their mothers were pleading with them not to go.

Dhashoti planned to ride back with us in spite of her hard ride the day before. She had declared herself our guide and our key to the city. Besides Zheran, who had not left Kazouri's side, five or six other Kourmairi women had decided to accompany us and were all eager to be off before their men awakened.

Having traveled hard and slept little the past few nights, I quickly passed into a state beyond weariness. With the additional effects of hard brew, I was like a sleepwalker when I climbed on Dancer's back. As soon as we were clear of the settlement, I dozed off and stayed in that state for much of the ride.

It was evening and almost dark before we came within sight of the city walls. Well before we could see the flaring light of her torches or glimpse her walls, looming dark before us, we could hear the warning bells of Mishghall, ringing loudly to announce our presence. Soon many more torches were lit and people began pouring out of the city to greet us, clapping, cheering, shouting, staring, showering us with questions and praise, reaching out to touch us. Some were even hissing or booing. To a city that has just thrown off its invaders, several hundred women advancing on its walls must have been a daunting sight. In spite of that, the folk of Mishghall remained, for the most part, good-humored and kindly, offering us food and shelter and whatever else we needed.

After climbing on Kazouri's shoulders and beating on a Sheezerti drum for silence, Pell made a little speech for us. Bowing in all directions, she thanked the Kourmairi of Mishghall many times for their generosity, explaining that due to our great numbers, we preferred to camp where we were. She ended by saying, "Food, however, will be gladly accepted." Soon food was pouring into our hands from all sides. We did not have the bother of cooking on our own fires that night. It was left to Dhashoti to firmly and politely clear away the crowd of Kourmairi that pressed around us, explaining that we needed some rest after the great battle. Otherwise, we might have been forced to take part in still another all-night celebration.

When Nhokosos finally left, taking with him the folk of Darthill, Zheran decided to stay with us. She said she was not yet ready to go into the city. The woman seemed to crave our company. Many times during the evening I had noticed her watching us intently, as if studying our ways for future use. Meanwhile, Renaise, her cousin Thalyisi, and some of the Sheezerti struggled to make order out of the chaos of our temporary camp. At last all the Koormir of Mishghall had departed, all except for the Hadera Lossi of that city, those young women who had somehow evaded the Zarn's edict and army, and managed to stay safely hidden within the city's walls. They remained with us through that night.

Even now, as I write of this, remembering it fills my heart to breaking with both joy and sorrow. The Hadera Lossi of Mishghall were crying, laughing, looking into our faces, touching our hands, saying over and over with wonderment: "So many of you..." "You finally came..." "Who could believe after all this time that we would finally be free..." "That we could be safe..." "So many lost ... dead ... burned ... gone..." "Hunted like animals..." "How different we all are and yet..." They poured out their stories of death and courage and treachery and survival, and they eagerly asked for ours. If I told it all, everything I saw and heard that night, it would more than fill the biggest book on Alyeeta's shelves. Dhashoti's story alone could make a book.

As soon as there was a pause in their stories, many of us began questioning them about Mishghall. We knew, of course, that it was a port city, built around the curve of the bay, but there was so much else we wanted to learn. Soon Pell was down on her knees with Dhashoti, drawing lines in the dirt for the streets, the avenues, the largest buildings, the parks, plazas, docks, and wharves. The main street that went from north to south was called Shell Street, a grand avenue, really, Dhashoti said. It was down this avenue that the march would proceed. As we talked, I grew ever more eager to see this city built by the Koormir, by my own people. Growing up, I thought all the Koormir were farmers in little dirt villages like Nemanthi and only the Shokarn lived in cities. Clearly I had much to learn.

Suddenly Pell stood up, wiping her hands on her pants. She beckoned Kazouri over and climbed on her shoulders again so she could be seen over that mass of women. Kazouri bellowed for silence. When Pell had our attention she shouted, "Tomorrow, we, the Khal Hadera Lossien, need to go at the head of the march, in front of everyone."

"What do you mean?" Dhashoti cried, shocked and alarmed. "Even in front of the headman and the officials of Mishghall? Not possible! No! No! It would be too disrespectful."

At almost the same moment, Ozzet shouted, "Not in front of Nhokosos and his men. They would be most displeased."

"Yes, exactly that, however disrespectful or displeasing it might be," Pell answered instantly. "In front of all of them, so they never forget the sight of a thousand or more of us Puntyar marching in their streets. Listen, I have been on my own since my eleventh year, observing the ways of men and devising strategies to stay alive in spite of them. This has left me with a good nose for survival and a very small store of respect for men, except perhaps the Wanderers.

"The Koormir are nice enough now. They are glad to have us as allies to help win their battles against the Zarn. But how will they treat us in times of peace? Will we even be able to have peace with them? Rhomar is right, there are many others who think as he does. As soon as they are sure the weight of the Zarn is off their backs, their male pride will begin to chafe at the thought that women helped them gain their freedom. They may wish to be rid of us as well. Their pride may even make them thirst for vengeance. Respect? They are the ones who must have respect for us or we will never be safe among them.

"I think if they had their choice, these Kourmairi men would treat us much as they treat the Shokarn guards. Remember, to them we are just so many Puntyar, as they so often like to remind us. So I say we go at the head of the march tomorrow! Let us give them a show they will never forget!" Pell raised both her arms and shook her fists. There was a roar of shouts and cheers but also many voices raised in argument, mostly from the women of Darthill and Mishghall.

Pell swung off Kazouri's shoulders and said to Dhashoti, "Now it is yours to decide. Remember, if you do this with us, you go against a whole lifetime of training." Dhashoti looked troubled and confused, but Rishka was nodding her head and grinning widely. I could see her eyes sparkling with excitement in the firelight. The Sheezerti were already making their plans. Most the women who had ridden with us for a while were ready to follow Pell's lead in this. Even those Witches who had stayed with us, Alyeeta, Shalamith, and Telakeet, all agreed with Pell's plan, Alyeeta in particular. "That will give these *humans* something to think on," she said with relish. Meanwhile, I could see Dhashoti moving about among the Hadera Lossi of Mishghall and Darthill, talking intently and gesturing with her hands. Sooner than I expected, she came back and nodded to Pell.

"This is what they say. They will walk with you at the head of the march if you will promise not to go the whole way in that manner, but only part of it. Then we separate and make way for the headman and the rest of the procession. If the rest of you can agree to that, then we are with you."

"Done?" Pell asked, looking around at all of us.

"Done!" we shouted back, the word echoing through our ranks.

"Done," Pell said to Dhashoti, with a clasp of her hand. "But only if you will be our guide and give us our signals."

And so our agreements were made. There was another round of cheers. Then Noya of the Sheezerti said, "We must have a banner to march under. We should not go into the streets without our own banner to speak for us."

"Where would we get such a thing?" someone else shouted back.

"We should make it," Tama answered boldly. I had seldom heard her speak up in front of others in that way.

"When?" "How?" "With what?" "Who will make it?" "What words should it have?" asked a chorus of voices.

In the end, Tama cleared a space on the dirt to draw with Pell's stick, while Dhashoti and some of the others went into the city for fabric, thread, and scissors. "What should we put on this banner?" Tama called out.

"Horses," someone shouted. "Women on horses," someone else called back. Maireth stepped forward to say forcefully, "The symbols of the Circle: the circle, the triangle, the star, one inside the other. We have waited a long time to be able to show ourselves in public." Many voices called out, "Yes, the Circle, we have been silent too long." "The Great Star," someone else shouted, and there was a roar of approval. All this while, Tama was drawing rapidly and with considerable skill everything as it was suggested.

"We should write *Khal Hadera Lossien* across the top," Kazouri called out.

"No, they do not call us that anymore, and even for us it is too long. It should say *Hadera Lossi,* for that is what they call us now."

I had been sitting, watching Tama draw. At those last words, I jumped up and shouted, "No, not their name for us, our own. If we cannot be Khal Hadera Lossien, then let us be called Hadra, for that is what it will come to in the end." I felt a chill run down my back as I remembered looking down from the hill in the Wanderer encampment into a vision of a very different valley, perhaps in some future time. Quickly I turned to ask Alyeeta, "Is that a Witch word or an Asharan word?"

Before she could respond, Nunyair answered in a loud voice, "It is a Shokarn word. It means 'wild ones.'" At that, there was an uproar of shouts and cheers. I could hear "Hadra" echoing from all around me and felt again that shiver of foreknowing.

When the others returned, they brought with them a bright blue sheet to use for the banner and a pole to carry it on, as well as scissors, thread, needles, and many colorful scraps of fabric. Tama organized the work with the help of Lhiri of Eezore, Dhashoti of Mishghall, and the Sheezerti of the streets. Maireth lovingly cut the symbols of the Circle out of the brightest colors, and others of the Circle helped her sew them on. Rishka cut out the horses, following Tama's drawings, and Tama herself made the figures.

As there were more than enough eager hands to do the work, I drew back to watch. Pell stood next to me, looking at all this activity with a strange little smile on her face. Her expression was such a mix of pleasure and sorrow that it made me want to cry. Suddenly she turned that look on me. "All these years, Tazzi, all these years ... struggling, planning, enduring ... never knowing if this day would finally come. I am almost ready to let go of it, sister, almost ready. Right now I am weary to the bone, weary to my very soul." *And soon I will be handing it on to you.* She turned away quickly and disappeared into the crowd, but not before I saw tears sparkling on her cheeks. She had not said those last words aloud, but I trembled when I heard them in my head.

And so, again, we made a late night of it. But this time I was very wide awake. My powers had come back to me. Full of gratitude for that, I listened to everything with my inner senses as well as my outer ones. I also remembered to eat sparingly and to drink no brew at all. Together, that night, we made a huge, blue banner that had at its center three horses of different colors ridden by three women of different colors, all dressed in their brightest clothes, and carrying banners. Around them was a circle of symbols, brilliant-hued and intricate. Shining above everything was a giant star, the Great Star that had dominated all our lives. Across the top, written in large letters, were the words *The Hadra of Yarmald.*

7

Restless and eager to be moving, we woke early the next morning and quickly gathered our belongings. The finished banner had been carefully rolled up on its pole. Our plan was to drift into the city in small groups, each group accompanied by one of the women native to Mishghall. After assembling in parks and side streets near Shell Street, we would await Dhashoti's signal.

My heart was pounding with excitement as I followed Dhashoti's group through the carved and arched east gateway into the city of Mishghall. My first impression was of rippling colors everywhere. Flags and banners were flying from every building: from flagpoles, from windows, from balconies, from market stalls. Even that early in the morning, the streets were full of people. There was a feeling of eager anticipation in the crowd. We were sometimes greeted like heroes and cheered along and sometimes met with hostile stares or words, but no one tried to stop us or block our way.

I looked around me openmouthed. This city was so different from Eezore, which shows its power in huge buildings made of great blocks of gray stone. Here there was a profusion of balconies, courtyards, benches, fountains, parks, and gardens. Ornately carved bridges curved over wide streets or waterways, and cobbled alleys wound out of sight under arches covered with vines and flowers. Busy markets full of color and noise were already setting up for the day. Below the city, but visible from any rise, was the great curve of the harbor. Beyond that lay the aching blue of the sea herself, the Cherbonaishi, alive with boats whose bright sails were catching the morning light. And, of course, there were horses, dogs, donkeys, oxen, and people, people, people everywhere I looked, as well as throngs of little children darting about, fast as schools of fish. But even with all that bustle and motion, I felt none of the terror that had gripped me upon entering Eezore. Instead, I found myself looking about eagerly, filled with curiosity, pleasure, amazement, and even a rush of pride. The Kourmairi had built this wonderful city. We, their children, could do the same. I did not say any of this to my Muinyairin or Shokarn sisters but kept it in my heart, knowing I would never forget that first sight of Mishghall.

Not all was beauty, however. There were many signs of the long conflict: smashed and overturned statues, burnt-out buildings, some still smoldering, and, in a few places, entire blocks charred and destroyed. Everywhere I looked, I saw hastily erected rock piles topped with flowers in memory of the recent dead. And among those still living, I saw wounds and burns, scarred faces and missing limbs, even among the children. My heart ached for what had happened here. It made me very glad for my part in turning back the guards.

As we went through the markets, I noticed that it was mostly women who minded the booths. Smiling and reaching for our hands, they gave us fruit and sweet-breads and flowers for our hair and whatever else they had. We were not allowed to pay. Everything was free, as if we really had rescued their city.

Yet under all this friendliness, I could feel a thread of uneasiness, a vibration of suspicion and fear, especially from those men who lounged about, watching everything. I suppose, in their eyes, we were not really women, but had somehow usurped the place of men. How were they to know how to treat us? Would we stay on, a new weight on their city, now that they were rid of the Zarn's men? If so, how could they be rid of us? I could read their thoughts as clear as spoken words and remembered Pell's words from the night before. From some men I even felt hostility, anger that it was women who had saved their city, anger and a desire for vengeance, as if somehow we had unmanned them. Beautiful as this city was, it was no refuge for us. I heard the words *Hadera Lossi,* and sometimes *Hadra* or even *Puntyar* but never *Khal Hadera Lossien.*

The market was buzzing with talk of the great battle; each story was wilder than the last. One told of how we had stood on the line with the villagers of Darthill and driven back the Zarn's army bare-handed; another of how we had summoned the Oolanth cats down from the hills to help us scatter the soldiers; and still another of how we had crept into their camp, silent as night, and set fire to it while the guards slept. Some, of course, spoke of the ewee, the little black toads who come out each year when the river floods, but even those stories were twisted around. I could almost believe that Alyeeta had been at work, spreading tales. Who knows what these stories might turn into in a month's time — or even by the next day?

Zheran had stayed with us in the city. She had not been back to Mishghall since being married off at thirteen to Rhomar — the son of her father's friend — and going to live with him in Darthill. Almost as excited by the sights as we were, her reserve gave way to childlike pleasure at this sudden freedom. In the market she laughed and joked and teased just like any of us, saying over and over, "I almost feel like a girl again." Not till we crossed paths with Nhokosos and the other folk of Darthill did she speak again of seeing her sister. Asking them to wait, she hugged some of us in a tearful good-bye. That done, she stepped back and said in very formal Kourmairi, "Thank you for more than words can say and more than the heart can hold. Even after you are long gone from here and in a place of your own, I will think of you often. I will never forget you." Then she was gone, vanished, surrounded by that little troupe of riders. I felt a pang of loss and wondered what her life would be like among people who had so little place for independent women.

I had just remounted after strolling through the market for a while, with flowers in my hair and a sack of hot sweet-rolls in hand. Several of us were riding together toward our meeting place near Shell Street when we suddenly heard shouts, cries, screams, and the unmistakable sounds of blows coming from the direction of a small square. Rishka beckoned to me. With three or four others, we quickly turned aside and went to see. As we came on the scene, there was no mistaking the source of those sounds. One man was hitting a woman, while two others held her. The small crowd that had gathered seemed to be shouting encouragement to the man and urging him on. In spite of the hopeless odds, the woman was struggling fiercely, screeching obscenities at the crowd as well as her captors. Rishka rode forward and grabbed the man by his collar, so that for a moment he was suspended in the air. His last blow went far wide of its mark.

"Man, this is the time to be celebrating your freedom, not the time to be beating women," she said forcefully, giving him an angry shake.

"This woman is a whore. She was a tax collector for the Zarn. She deserves to die."

"Oh, really. And how would you have protected her, if she had refused that work?"

"The woman is a whore. Why should we have to protect her?"

"So you think she should have risked her life for you, but you would not do the same for her?"

"Are you deaf? I tell you the woman is a whore!"

At that moment, the woman tore herself free of the other two men. They had been neglecting their work to stare at us in amazement. Instantly, she whirled on Rishka and shouted, "I can defend myself well enough! I do not need some filthy Puntyar to speak for me!" With that, she set to straightening her clothes, pulling her torn dress together in an effort to cover herself. Her hair was in wild disarray and her face bruised and bloody, but her spirit blazed with defiance.

I saw Rishka's face cloud over and thought she might lash out with some of her old rage. Instead, she shook herself as if shaking off a chill. Then she threw back her head and laughed, much as Pell might have done. "You did not appear to be doing so well on your own before we came. There are none here who seem ready to step forward and save you from that man. Climb on behind me on my horse, and we will get you free of here." With that, Rishka pushed the man hard so that he lurched away. Then she reached out for the woman's arm.

The woman struck at her hand, shouting, "Do not touch me, filthy Puntyar. I would rather take my chances with these men."

The men, in turn, began pressing forward, making threatening gestures and shouting, "Give her to us!" "We will take care of her ourselves!" "Death to the whore!"

Pell, meanwhile, had ridden up. She leaned over and muttered to me with disgust, "Just as I said, they are dangerous fools." Then, loud enough for everyone in the square to hear, she called out with good-natured mockery, "Woman, is it ignorance or envy that makes you shout so loudly about the Puntyar? If it is ignorance, that is easily enough cured. There are those among us who would be pleased to help you make acquaintance with our skills. I could give you names. If it is envy, then I wish you half as much pleasure in your bed with such as these," she gestured at the men who had been taunting and jeering, "as we find in ours."

"She is the Zarn's piece," a man from the crowd called out eagerly. "Let us get hold of her and teach her a lesson."

"And what would be left alive at the end of your lesson? You are very brave against one woman, all three of you. Were you as brave against the Zarn's guards?" There were shouts and hoots and whistles and derisive laughter and some curses in response.

This woman now turned on Pell, no doubt about to let loose with another stream of curses. Pell held up her hand and said quickly, "What is your name, woman? If we are to continue this way, we need a name."

"Katchaira, queen of the whores," a man from the back yelled.

"Well, Katchaira, we cannot leave you here, no matter how it may wound your pride or soil your fine reputation to ride off with the Hadra on this glorious day."

As Katchaira was shouting, "Never...," Pell made a signal to Kazouri, who was now standing in back of the woman. Kazouri nodded and moved forward unseen. She swept Katchaira up in her huge arms as easily as if that one were a child or a doll, swung her horse about, and headed out of the square, with her captive under her arm. The rest of us hastily turned to ride after them. As soon as we were clear of the square, Kazouri swung the angry woman up in front of her on her horse and held her there firmly. Surprisingly, Katchaira's protests subsided as soon as we were out of the square. Kazouri was leaning forward, talking earnestly in the woman's ear. Whatever she said, it seemed to have a magical effect on Katchaira, or Katchia, as we later came to call her.

When we caught up with Dhashoti and she saw who was with us, she made no comment, but disgust was plainly written on her face. It did not take the skill of mind-speech to read her thoughts. To my surprise, instead of shouting defiant curses or making rude remarks, Katchia turned her face away and visibly shrank into herself.

As we reached the park, we were met by a small procession of Kourmairi women coming from the opposite direction. They were all brightly dressed, clearly in their festive clothes. Between them they carried a platform with a large statue of the Goddess at the center. The statue and the platform were all decked with ribbons, flowers, and shells and circled by lit candles. This procession went twice around the square, chanting and ringing bells. Then they stopped in the center, in front of a large, vacant, stone slab. Many rushed forward to help set the Goddess in place, and others, mostly women, quickly brought little offerings of fruit or flowers and stayed to join in the chanting.

The figure itself was most impressive. It looked to be carved of some highly polished dark wood and was much finer than any I had ever seen at home. In Nemanthi, where only women honored the Goddess, most statues of the Mother were no more than little clay figures, made by the women of the house and kept in a small niche in the kitchen to watch over hearth and home. Even the figures at the Essu were nothing like this one.

I could feel Dhashoti being pulled toward the chanters, could see the look of longing on her face. Though she did not abandon us, she was watching them intently. "I wonder how they have managed to keep her safely hidden away for more than two years," she said with awe in her voice. "Things must truly be changing if it is time to bring the Goddess out of hiding."

As we assembled in the park, more and more of the local populace came to stare, so that our numbers on both sides kept growing. While we were gathering in this way, some among us began dressing for the march, pulling from the bottom of our packs whatever finery we had managed to salvage from the disasters of our lives. I, of course, had nothing pretty to put on, as I had escaped wearing only my brother's clothes. But Zenoria lent me some bright yarn and shells for my newly grown hair, and Zari even offered to braid it Muinyairin style. Renaise added a sash, and, much to my surprise, Murghanth slipped some strings of beads around my neck. In the end, I felt as well decked out as any for the day. All around me, women were dressing; sharing and comparing what they had to wear. The Sheezerti, of course, dressed in the colorful costumes of their troupe, and the few Muinyairin who had stayed with us wore the bright clothes of their people, colors so intense one could almost think they were trying to make up for their small numbers by sheer visual brilliance. We were going to make a show of ourselves, a show we hoped the people of Mishghall would remember for years to come.

As we dressed, we made our plans for how and in what order we would enter the march. Soon after that, we separated to wait on opposite sides of the avenue and down many little alleys, while Dhashoti went to stand watch for us on a bridge that spanned Shell Street.

Now there was nothing to do but stay alert and listen for Dhashoti's signal. After being so sure, I was suddenly very afraid. This was a rude and daring thing we were about to do. The populace, gathering thickly around us and muttering about our large numbers, added greatly to my fears. I kept silent, trying to shield my thoughts so as not to frighten my companions or make them doubtful. Suddenly Pell, standing near me, said loudly, "This day we should remember that we are women. No more hiding, no more concealment, no more farmer-man disguises. I want to celebrate my womanself. Off with our shirts. Let them see our breasts. Let our breasts shine in the sun. We should go bare-breasted, to remind them that it was women who freed their city."

Instantly, a fierce argument broke out, or, rather, several arguments. "Not me!" I said quickly. "There is no way you could persuade me to do such a thing." I was horrified. I could not imagine riding bare-breasted through a city of men, especially with so much hostility all around. I did not even bother reminding Pell that it was not the Hadra who had rescued the city of Mishghall, but one Witch, one fool, and a million tiny black toads. Throughout the argument, I kept my arms crossed over my breasts as if for protection. When Pell finally said, "Well, I will go shirtless, even if no one else will," I knew my card had been played. There would be at least two of us. I would not let Pell do that alone.

As Pell began stripping off her shirt, I felt fear rising in my throat. Then Rishka, next to me, said, "I will do this thing if you will." And behind me Murghanth growled, "I will unlace my tunic and show my skinny little breasts if you think that will impress them, but I will not take off my good embroidered vest, for it was my grandmother's. She wore it for performing in the street and it is all I have left of her." Kazouri roared with laughter, and in one gesture pulled her tunic off over her head. Suddenly, with no more hesitation, I was unbuttoning my tunic and retying my bright borrowed sash around my waist. All around me, women were baring their breasts. The Hadra on the other side of the street had seen us and were doing the same. Maireth was swinging her shirt high over her head, shouting, "Let them see what the Zarns' fastfire has done to us. Let them look on that work." Now the men in our crowd of watchers were whistling, shouting, and pointing; some with derision, some with amazement, still others with admiration or approval.

Just then I heard Dhashoti's signal from the bridge. Soon she was running toward us, forcing her way through the swarm of people. Faintly, from the distance, came the sound of shouts, cries, music, and the thunder of marching feet. The procession was coming! It was time!

Over the commotion Kazouri roared, "Make way for the Hadra of Yarmald!" Suddenly we were moving forward through the crowd, pouring out of the side streets and into the main avenue to place ourselves at the head of the march. There was a howl of anger when the people saw what we meant to do. They might have moved to stop us, but we were too quick and too many and they were caught unprepared.

Murghanth blew shrilly on her little whistle. I saw Maireth and four of the other burned ones coming from the opposite side of the street, stripped to the waist, their scars terrible and beautiful in the morning light. Quickly Rishka crossed in front of them, followed by Dhashoti, Pell, and Ozzet.

Dhashoti and Ozzet carried our glorious banner with forked sticks propped under its pole, so that it seemed to float over Pell's head. I hurried to take my place as fifth on that front line, as we had agreed, and soon found myself clinging tightly to Dancer's back. Full of excitement, she was busy earning her name, weaving and prancing about, almost unseating me. I knew that the burned ones were falling into place behind us, and after them the Sheezerti: Murghanth, Teko, Noya, and the others. Next, I knew, were the Witches, and then some women of the Circle. Behind them, I hoped, the rest of us were falling into line, five or six abreast, as had been planned. The Sheezerti were playing loudly on their drums, the sound mixing strangely with the Kourmairi bands in back of us. As we started forward, the angry voices of the crowd grew loud and threatening. There were many shouts of "Puntyar," "Disgrace," and "Insult to our people." Some were even yelling, "Stop them!" and moving to block our way.

I leaned forward to catch Pell's attention and hissed at her, "Do something! Quickly! Before they mob us! This was your idea. You got us out here half-naked in front of them all, and now they are ready to eat us alive. Instead of marching through this city in triumph, we may soon be dragged through on our faces."

Dhashoti, riding between us, echoed my words. "Do something quickly, Pell. I cannot carry this banner proudly through waves of hate coming from my own people."

Even Pell looked worried. With a nod to both of us, she grabbed Torvir's mane and gave a quick push to get herself up on her knees. With another push she was standing precariously on his bony back. Balancing herself for a moment, she raised her arms high over her head and shouted, "Mishghall! Free today! Free tomorrow! Free forever!" Instantly the rest of us took up the cry. Then some of the watchers on the street forgot their hostility and joined us, shouting loudly, "Mishghall, Mishghall..."

Soon we could hear that cry echoing in back of us down the line of march, "Mishghall, free today, free tomorrow, free forever!" Finally, it was resounding around us like thunder and echoing from the rooftops, a roar so loud that I imagined it could be heard beyond the city walls, if any guards were still in hiding. Grinning, Pell slid down to safety on Torvir's back. "There, I have done my best," she said with another nod. "Now it is your turn to amaze and entertain."

Rishka, on the other side of Pell, quickly took up the challenge. She raised two swords and began twirling them high above her head, then slapping the blades together, Muinyairin style, when she caught them again, so that they rang out in time to the chant. This brought more loud cheers from these same watchers who only moments before had been ready to pull us from our horses and tear us limb from limb. From behind us I could hear the rapid and insistent beat of the Sheezerti drums. Now that the crowd was with us, not against us, I was wishing I had something of my own to add to the show. Just as I thought that, Dancer, with no signal from me, reared up, spun about, and came down dancing on her front feet. There were no more boos or hisses or shouts of "Puntyar," but many shouts for us to "do it again, do it again," which Dancer quickly obliged. This brought another storm of wild cheers and applause. Thus encouraged, Dancer went through a whole series of tricks: leaps, turns, bows, prances, and dancing steps that I had certainly never taught her. All I could do was cling desperately to her mane while people shouted for more. I knew our image of power would not be improved by a spectacular, half-naked fall in front of the line of march.

Rishka, seeing what we were up to, encouraged Lightfoot to do some fancy footwork of his own. Dancer, of course, had to match it. "Well done," Pell said, as she signaled Dhashoti and Ozzet to drop back a few steps. For a short while, Rishka and I rode alone at the front, with our horses rearing and dancing and springing about. Rishka was clearly enjoying herself, ignoring my desperate pleas to stop. I could barely hold on. Dancer was following some inner voice of her own. She was completely deaf to mine. Clearly, she had been in parades before and was doing exactly what she had been trained to do.

Just as I felt myself slipping precariously, I heard shouts from in back of us, "Make way for the Sheezerti of Eezore." Much to my relief, the Sheezerti swept around us and pushed their way up to the front. Dancer paused in her madness. I took advantage of the moment to slip safely from her back and stand unnoticed in the press of the crowd. Leaning against her, I struggled to catch my breath. I was dizzy and soaked with sweat, but Dancer was scarcely breathing hard. No doubt, had I been willing, she could have danced the whole way at the head of the march.

Already we had won the day by our audacity. The Koormir of Mishghall may not love Witches and star-brats, but they do love a good show, and we were certainly giving them that. The Sheezerti, who had never ridden horseback before leaving Eezore, had the natural balance of acrobats. They were not so much good riders as mounted tumblers who used their horses' backs as a platform for their tricks. While agilely leaping on and off, they were doing twists, turns, and flips, shaking their tambourines and making rushes into the crowd to collect money in their hats. I cheered as they passed, only too glad to let someone else go at the front for a while. With relief, I stayed to watch as the Witches passed, then the Circle, then Ozzet with the young women of Darthill. After that, many other Hadra rode by, among them Kazouri, with Katchaira of Mishghall mounted in front of her on Crusher's back. Katchia, bare-breasted like the rest of us, was waving and bowing in all directions, her face flushed with excitement and pride.

I had no desire to find a place again in the march and could happily have stood there all day watching my sisters pass. Suddenly, I felt a presence next to me and turned to see Zheran standing quietly at my side. "Did you find your sister?" I asked, shouting to be heard above the din. "Will you be staying with her?"

Zheran shook her head. She had a strange look on her face. "My sister says she cannot have me in her house. Her husband will not abide a woman who has left her man. She cannot go against his will. She is far more afraid of him than I ever was of Rhomar."

"Then what will you do?" I asked, dismayed.

"I will go with the Hadera Lossi — no, I mean the Hadra — to your new settlement. I do not think I can live with men anymore." She had said she would come, not even asking if we would have her.

"But we have no settlement," I said quickly. "We have nothing, only our horses and the road before us and the few possessions we have managed to salvage. Who knows how many miles lie between us and a settlement of our own, miles or perhaps years. Until then, we are like Wanderers. What kind of life is that for a woman who has had her own home and husband and children?"

"The one I choose," she said with quiet dignity. Then she gave a sudden little smile. "Or who knows, perhaps the one the Goddess chose for me. When you find this settlement, I will help you organize it. I have many skills, and this time no one will tell me not to use them because I am a woman." Her tone changed suddenly. "Unless, of course, you will not take me because I do not have your powers. Perhaps you only spoke before out of pity and because you thought I would not come. After all, I can never be a Hadra." There was pride in her tone and an unspoken plea behind her words.

I said quickly, "If you are willing to endure our hardships, Zheran, then come with us and be welcome wherever we go. Among us, you will be free to do whatever you have the skill and the will to do." I said all this earnestly enough, but in my head I heard the words *Trouble, this means trouble.* Some inexplicable fear clutched at my heart. At the same moment there was a loud signal. The Hadra in the march were pulling to the side so that I was suddenly surrounded by women, all talking excitedly. Zheran took my arm so as not to lose me in the press, and I felt her shiver. I was suddenly awed by her courage. At the same time, I felt very protective. "Would you ride next to me when we rejoin the march?"

She shook her head and said sadly, "I have no horse. I gave her back to Nhokosos thinking I would not need her in the city or be able to afford her care here."

"We will find you another or regain that one before he leaves. To come with us, you must have a horse. In the meantime, would you like to ride on Dancer with me?"

She nodded, saying, "I would be honored," and I felt her tremble again.

As we spoke, the last of the Hadra who had been in the march moved aside. Marching to the wild cheers of the crowd, the Koormir swept forward between us, rank after rank of them. They were mostly men, led by the headman, or, as he is called in Mishghall, the mayor, and his own personal troop of soldiers. There were flags and banners flying, horns blowing, and drums resounding loudly. It was very grand and glorious. We all bowed as they passed. Then Pell took up her chant again, which was soon echoing back from all around us. The switch went so smoothly, it looked as if it had been planned and agreed upon. And indeed, the mayor would have been a fool to act as if we had marched at the front in spite of him or against his will. For his part, he appeared to take it in good spirits and bowed to us in return, nodding from side to side as he passed our ranks. Watching all this, I thought to myself, *At least for a while the Koormir of Mishghall will remember the Hadra as we were this day. They will not forget how we rode bare-breasted at the front of their march with our swords flashing, our horses dancing, and our great banner flying overhead. Let that be imprinted on their memories.*

Soon after the mayor had passed, Nhokosos, with the folk of Darthill, rode by to more loud cheers. To my surprise, Alyeeta was riding next to him, waving and smiling to the crowd. After a while, there were even groups of Kourmairi women marching. Most of them had some representation of the Goddess with them, sometimes carried on a platform, sometimes raised high on a pole or stitched into a banner. I watched them all go by with an ache in my heart. These were my people, yet I was not one of them. I never could be and never truly had been. This was a Kourmairi city, but I could not live here, would not be welcome among them. I could not abide their ways, nor they mine. I wished them peace, I wished them strength against all the Zarns of Garmishair, but I knew my own home would have to be elsewhere. After a while, I grew weary of watching this endless flow of people. I was tired and hungry. My feet hurt and the day was growing late.

Aiyee! Aiyee! Aiyee! Suddenly, Hayika and the other women who had gone south with her surged in around us from both sides of the street. We shouted greetings and news to each other. Soon we found ourselves pushed into rejoining the march, no longer in our carefully planned ranks, but in a great flood of women, pressing forward like the Escuro. Other watchers from the street rushed pell-mell to join the march, wherever they could squeeze themselves in. It was in this way that we all, Kourmairi and Hadra together, flowed out of the city by the south gate and poured like a living river into a huge meadow, large enough to have been an Essu ground.

Exhausted, I eased Zheran down and then swung myself off Dancer's back with a deep sigh. Immediately I saw that I had put myself between Katchia and Dhashoti. I quickly stepped back out of their way. It was as if I had landed in a nest of knives. With great bitterness in her voice, Katchia was saying, "What right did you have to look at me that way? Am I some sort of trash in your eyes because you were born with the power to protect yourself and I was not?" Dhashoti was looking down at the ground and shaking her head. "Look at me!" Katchia raged. "Answer me! By what right?"

"None, no right," Dhashoti replied, almost in a whisper, without looking up. "That is how I was trained from childhood, to have contempt for whores. Every time I was nice to some boy, my mother would say, 'Take care, or you will grow up to be one of *them,*' meaning, of course, a whore. Little did she think I would grow up to be something much worse in her eyes. I already was, though she did not know it then. But in truth, I never met a whore face-to-face before this. Now I am ashamed of my own quick judgment and the pain it cost you. And how can I say that I am any better? All this winter, I paid for my safety with my body. Even now, my cousin lurks about as if he thinks to have me back in his power."

Suddenly, almost as if her words had summoned him, a young man slipped out of the horde of people and leaned over to say some words in her ear. Dhashoti whirled about with an angry cry. "No! Never again!"

she shouted. Immediately he found himself surrounded by a circle of Hadra, myself included.

"So now you show your true colors," he snarled. "After all I did to keep you safe, you are still a Puntyar and you consort with whores. I should have denounced you to the guards while I had the chance."

Furious, I shouted in his face, "Sometimes I wish my powers did not stop me from doing harm. If not for that, you would be lying on the ground from the force of my blow."

Katchia pushed past me roughly, saying, "I have no such powers to stay my hand." Before any of us could think to stop her, she had stepped up to him and swung her arm so the back of her fist connected with his jaw. He was caught completely by surprise, knocked off his feet from the force of the blow. Staring up at her wide-eyed, he lay on the ground with blood spurting from his cut lip. She leapt at him and began kicking him everywhere: in the head, the side, the stomach; wherever she could reach him. All the while she was shouting, "This is for every man who ever raped me, who beat me, who mocked me, who robbed me, who called me names..." She spit out a new phrase in time to each kick. It was clear she intended to finish his life. For a moment we all stared at her in shocked amazement, frozen in place. Then Kazouri broke the spell, shouting, "Stop her before she kills him! Tazzi, help me hold her!" This time, not even Kazouri's great strength was enough. It took myself and Murghanth as well to subdue her. Pell pulled the man to his feet. He spit out two teeth, and shrugged free of her hands, snarling, "You are all whores and murderers, all dirty Puntyar!"

Pell wiped the blood from her hands down the sides of her pants and said calmly, "And you are a fool. Times have changed. Look around you, Cousin. The time for owning women is over. The Zarn can no longer lord it over Mishghall, and men can no longer lord it over women. You forced yourself on Dhashoti all winter by threatening to denounce her to the guards. Do you expect her to be grateful? Would you be grateful for such a bargain?"

"I am not a woman," he said with contempt. "I would not make such a bargain." Katchia gave a roar of rage and tried to lunge at him again. Quickly two men came out of the crowd and led the cousin away, while Katchia shouted that she wanted to kill him, that in fact killing was too good for such scum.

Katchia was still struggling in our arms when Dhashoti came to stand in front of her with her head bowed. "Thank you, Katchaira, for doing what I could not do for myself, but wanted to so many times. I will never forget that." She reached out and put her hand on Katchia's arm.

Katchia quieted suddenly. She stood looking down at Dhashoti's hand for a long moment. All motion seemed stilled. No one spoke. Then, very slowly, she put her own hand over Dhashoti's. "To the end of the old and the beginning of the new. Never again will I collect taxes for any Zarn or lay my body down for any man to use against my will. Never again will your cousin be able to abuse you in that way. Never!" We eased our grip and she shook free of us. Fingers pointing, she swept the watchers with her hand. "Never again," she called out. When one man jeered, she took a step toward him, rage flashing from her eyes. He hastily stepped back and vanished into the throng.

Wanting to be away from Katchia's anger, I looked around and noticed a small grove of trees that formed a high spot in the field. Several Hadra were gathered there, along with a few Kourmairi, so I hurried eagerly in that direction. When I arrived, I was surprised to see Renaise standing in the center of a small crowd. Apparently, she was about to dance. Full of curiosity, I pushed my way toward the front of the crowd.

Some torches had already been lit. Noya was playing her drum, and Vestri her flute. Renaise had changed her clothes and was wearing a long, soft, gauzy skirt of bright blue, stitched with bursts of brilliant color. It hung low on her hips. Above it, she had on a richly embroidered vest that bared her belly and her full round breasts, as well as her arms. As torchlight played on her body, she began to move, slowly at first, rolling her hips and her belly. Seeing this, I was suddenly flooded with desire, not for Renaise herself, but for all women, for the part of us that is round and soft and full, the part that we, as Hadra, had been forced to hide for so long. Thalyisi, Renaise's cousin, was standing next to me. She winked and leaned toward me to whisper suggestively in my ear, "Nice to watch, eh? This is how we used to dance in our village for the man we were to marry — though not, of course, half-naked that way."

I had to admit to myself that Renaise danced very well and that I certainly enjoyed being witness to it. This was a side of her I could not have imagined. Dhashoti, who must have followed me there, was watching with rapt attention, her eyes shining, and her mouth slightly open. Renaise was answering her looks with heated glances. More drummers had joined in. The women around me, Hadra and Kourmairi both, began clapping out the rhythm, stamping their feet in time to the music and shouting encouragement. Some of the men were shouting too, though more crudely. Some of them were even tossing coins at her feet, to which Renaise responded by dancing faster, rapidly undulating her breasts, her hips, and her belly. She had a sensuous smile on her face, as if to encourage them. The men shouted louder and she quickly acquired quite a sizable pile of coins. Soon her body was glistening with sweat. Watching her, I could feel the heat rising between my legs, and with it that pleasurable tension, almost like pain.

With a sudden little cry, Renaise abruptly stopped her dance. She was breathing hard and seemed somewhat unsteady on her feet. Looking around at all those people, she appeared slightly dazed or surprised. When she caught sight of the pile of shiny coins, she shook her head in bewilderment. Dhashoti rushed forward to throw a shawl over her sweaty shoulders and help her to steady herself.

As soon as Renaise stepped out of the center, the Sheezerti rushed in to take her place, doing their tricks and their tumbling, collecting more coins, and calling for grain and tools and whatever else we might need for our new venture. By now, quite a large crowd had gathered, drawn by the music. It was getting dark and more torches had been lit. Tribute was beginning to pile up: clothing and bedding, a sack of grain, a plow, baskets of potatoes and eggs, more grain, some chairs that looked none too sturdy, shovels and hoes and other garden tools. The pile was growing dangerously high. I was somewhat uncomfortable with this, not sure if the Kourmairi saw themselves as thanking an ally or paying tribute to an invader or perhaps clearing out their storage bins.

When they were done performing, the Sheezerti slipped back into the crowd to make music for the rest of us. In time to their drums, some of the Hadra began to dance. After watching for a while, I finally joined the others. With the pleasure of movement, I could feel the fears and tensions of the day flowing out of my body. Soon, even some of the Kourmairi women were dancing with us, while others of them drummed and clapped. We women were all grinning at each other in delight, but from the glowers and mutters of their men, I could tell they were none too pleased at this turn of events.

One man, growing impatient, even reached out to grab his woman's arm. "Come away from here. These Witches will poison your mind," he snarled. The woman pulled free of his grasp. Telakeet leapt to her feet with a growl. The man reached out again, but before he could grab his wife a second time or Telakeet could do him any damage, Shalamith stood up and stepped between them with her glowing presence. She was in her shining aspect. She threw back her golden hair and arched her back so that her breasts gleamed in the torchlight. The man gasped and stepped back at once, almost colliding with me. The woman stepped back to the other side and raised her hands as if in reverence. By now, the dancing and drumming had come to a halt. We were all staring at this little drama.

Shalamith tossed her hair again, setting off sparks of light. Then, with a loud clap of her hands, she called out in that magically resonant voice of hers, "Come, let us have music again; let us dance wildly and boldly. This is the night we all celebrate the freeing of Mishghall: Kourmairi, and Hadra, and Witch together." Then she took up her little ferl and began to play. Soon Murghanth joined her on her whistle and Kara added her flute to Vestri's, while the others began drumming again. For a while, there was much music and many of us were dancing. Some of the Kourmairi men even joined us. Yet Shalamith was always the glowing center around which the scene swirled. It was her voice that set the tempo, her ferl that led the music. Finally, when the rest of us grew tired, Shalamith played and sang alone. All eyes were fixed on her. She charmed us all: men, women, children; Hadra and Kourmairi alike. In fact, she seemed to glory in it. The coins began to rain again, showering at her feet and making a little glowing mound.

When at last it grew late, Telakeet stood up, pulled her robe tight, and said with a hiss, "Enough, Witch. You are worse than the Zarn's army. You have already bewitched these people. Do you wish to pauperize them as well?"

Shalamith stopped abruptly. The golden haze vanished in an instant. She seemed to sink in on herself, looking suddenly old and gray. Telakeet slipped a cloak over her shoulders and put an arm around her. Sighing with exhaustion, Shalamith huddled into the shelter of that cloak. Then, leaning on Telakeet for support, she slowly walked away.

Pell instantly set to collecting the coins and organizing the goods. Renaise and Dhashoti came forward to help. To my surprise, Katchia joined them, making a careful count of everything that had been amassed. I was suddenly aware of the coolness of the night around me. The Kourmairi had already started to drift away.

8

The sun poured down on us, not with the fierceness of summer's heat but with the soft warmth of spring. It felt like a blessing after the endless winter cold and the long rains of early spring. With our horses ambling along at a leisurely pace, we rode between wide open lands that stretched on either side of the road, fields quivering with spring green and dotted with bright flowers.

I was riding with Pell, Jhemar, Dorca, Zheran, Murghanth, Teko, and a few others. We were only a small band at that moment. Though Vaiya from Mishghall had stayed behind to be our guide, most of the other Hadra had already gone on ahead to see a place Dhashoti knew of by the river, a place she thought would make a good settlement for us. Some had gone still further with Ozzet, to another possible place, and a few had remained in the city to store our goods and settle our affairs there.

We were still riding on the Zarn's straight paved way, part of the system of roads built into Koormir lands for the movement of Shokarn troops. It was easy enough to follow, but Vaiya had assured us we would soon be turning off onto a network of winding dirt roads that would require her knowledge.

To my surprise, Alyeeta had chosen to stay with us. She was chatting quite companionably with Pell. In fact, I had seldom seen them so friendly. Alyeeta's little pony, Gandolair, had to trot every few steps to keep up with Torvir, Pell's fast rangy horse, who seemed to move at a ground-eating pace even when he was only walking. Tama rode on Torvir's back, in front of Pell, with her head resting back against Pell's shoulder, while her own horse followed after them. It was the most affection I had ever seen between them in public. Pell had her arm around Tama's waist and leaned forward occasionally to kiss her neck or whisper in her ear. It pleased me to watch them being so open. At the same time, I felt a strange little twisting ache in my heart. It had certainly never been like that when Pell and I were lovers.

I rode relaxed and easy. For once there was no fear of the guards at my back to drive me on. I had even taken off my shirt and tied it around my waist. *If I can ride bare-breasted through the streets of Mishghall,* I thought, *why not on these near-deserted roads?* My hair hung loose on my bare shoulders, caressing me as it moved softly in the slight breeze.

We passed a few Kourmairi on the way. They were traveling slowly, their wagons overloaded with possessions, no doubt returning to reclaim their family farms after the struggle for Mishghall. Some greeted us with cheers and some with sullen, wary silence, but all moved aside respectfully to let us pass.

Though many Hadra had been eager to see what Dhashoti wished to show us, I, myself, had been lazy and in no hurry. I knew the place would still be waiting there, whenever I arrived. Also, somewhere in my heart, I was sure it would not be the place for me, so I was in no rush to be disappointed. Jhemar, riding next to me, was dozing from time to time, her head nodding forward. With her empath sensitivity, she was probably much relieved to be out of the press of crowds and all their noisy head-clamor.

Suddenly, Cruzia began to sing in her high, clear voice,

> *"All so green and all so fair,*
> *Mother bless this land today.*
> *Keep her safe in Your wide hands.*
> *No man's wars must pass this way."*

It was a familiar Kourmairi spring song, except she had changed the last line of the chorus. She sang verse after verse, softly at first and then louder and louder, till the rest of us were drawn into joining her, even Jhemar, who had no ear whatsoever for song; even Pell, who, if anything, had less. Pell threw back her head and let out her voice with no regard at all for the tune. I might have laughed. Instead, I felt strangely touched by the innocence of that gesture. That we could ride down the road singing together in the sun after all that had happened seemed like a miracle to me. Perhaps Yarmald was indeed different from the rest of Garmishair and would give us a home. I wove my deeper voice in with Cruzia's high one and heard Murghanth and Teko in back of me harmonizing, playing with the tune and words as they might have juggled balls and sticks for one of their performances.

As the song died down, Jhemar began to nod again. I felt as if I would soon be joining her. My head was becoming very heavy on my neck. Suddenly Jhemar sat bolt upright, fully alert. "Guards!" she said tensely. "We are being followed! They are far more than our small number." I dressed in haste. Then I looked in all directions. Of course, I could see nothing. There was no sound but the sound of our own horses, yet I could feel Jhemar straining to catch that hint of presence with her inner ear. Tama immediately jumped back on her own horse, and Pell beckoned Jhemar to ride up next to her. "How many? What do you sense?"

"Between twenty and thirty, riding hard and with hostile intent. Fast-fire!" Jhemar spat out, as if the word itself was something filthy. I did not think to doubt her. She had far more sensitive inner hearing than the rest of us. The very thing that caused her such pain in a crowd was at other times a great gift among us.

"What can we do? We are out in the open. There is no place to hide and nowhere to run." There was panic in Dorca's voice. Zheran, on the other side of me, was stiff with fear, but kept her silence on it.

"So, our small piece of good fortune has made us into careless fools." Murghanth's voice was full of bitterness. It was like an accusation to those of us who had ridden at our ease.

"No use worrying over that now," Pell said grimly. "Let us get out the permeagent and make ourselves ready. Lucky you were with us," she added to Jhemar. Now I could feel Dorca's terror on one side of me, Zheran's rigid fear on the other, and Murghanth's rage pounding in my head. Though, as yet, I could hear nothing of the guards, still I could feel the chill of presence going up my spine.

We formed a circle facing outward and waited. Faintly at first and then louder, I could hear the sound of hoofbeats coming fast. Soon I smelled the acrid stench of fastfire. Suddenly, two riders came rushing in, one on each side of us, bent low over their horses. They were scattering gray powder as they went. Two others followed fast after them, lighting that powder. When they met with each other, they had us enclosed in a circle of fire that, I knew, would soon start burning inward. Several other horsemen rode up, so that we were quickly surrounded by men as well as fire.

"Well, I see we have caught ourselves some Witches in our circle of fire, or some star-brats or Hadera Lossi or whatever it is these muirlla think to call themselves now." The captain appeared immensely pleased with his success.

Pell took a deep breath and drew herself up very straight. "Hadra, that is how we call ourselves. Hadra, make sure to remember that, Captain. And your little fire tricks will not work any longer."

At Pell's signal, Jhemar, Teko, and myself rode forward with Pell and threw the altered permeagent on the fire so as to make ourselves an opening. Roiling black smoke filled the air, making me cough and choke. With a hiss and a sickening stench, the fire died down where the permeagent reached it, but the captain quickly summoned his men to block the opening we had made in their deadly circle. "I am not such a fool as that young captain who lost all his men to little black toads. I have no intention of returning to Eezore empty-handed and in disgrace. I even plan to take back some trophies, to show that I am no sluggard and have worked hard for the Zarn. If I am not mistaken, I think we have caught some of the leaders of these star-brats in our net of fastfire. He will be well pleased."

Even as he spoke, the rest of the circle was burning inward, the flames licking hungrily toward us. It was easy to see where this would end. We did not have an unlimited store of permeagent with us, and there were too few of us to stand off this many men. Even Pell seemed to be at a loss for the moment. Then suddenly Alyeeta was pushing past us, saying, "Follow me. When they move, be ready to make your break." We massed in back of her. My skin was crawling. I was beginning to feel the heat from the fire. Sweat was running down my body.

Alyeeta raised her arms skyward and intoned some words in a terrible deep voice. She repeated them over and over, as if gathering her power. In spite of the heat, chills were running up my spine. With a sneer the captain said, "Too late, Witch. The circle of fire is already closed." But under his mocking tone, I could hear the fear in his voice. Suddenly Alyeeta spread her arms wide, as if forcefully pushing something out and away from herself. At that instant, the flames at the edge of the opening suddenly shot forward toward the guardsmen in two long tongues of fire. Their horses reared and leapt back in terror, while the guardsmen themselves shouted with surprise. "Now!" Pell yelled as we all pressed forward in back of her. Alyeeta had to actually kick Gandolair to force him past that wall of flame. The rest of us rushed out pell-mell after her.

There was little heat from the fire Alyeeta had created. Turning, I saw that it had died down quickly, leaving no burn marks on the grass. Alyeeta rode up next to me. "Illusion," she muttered with a grin of triumph. "It works as well as the real thing, if someone is suggestible. Those fools did half the work for me."

The guards, meanwhile, were reassembling on the road at some distance from us. I expected that they would either ride off and leave us be or ride back to the attack again. Instead, it was Pell who wheeled her horse around and galloped recklessly after them, shouting as she went, "Wait! Wait, I have to speak with you!" She seemed possessed and rode directly into the captain's path, with the rest of us tearing after her. "Not so fast! Man of Eezore, there is something you must hear from us. You just tried to burn us alive, and now you think to ride off that way? You must listen to me, not for our sake but for the lives of your men."

"Are you mad, woman? You should be grateful we did not roast you all. Do not be fool enough to set yourselves in our path again."

"You are the fool. And you are the one who should be grateful you did not succeed. Have you not heard the stories of what happens to the men who burn us? They go mad and then they die. Go home, look about, listen to the stories in the market and on the street. You will see that what I tell you is true. The Zarn will not tell you, but others will. Look for the men who went on last year's raids. You will see for yourself. Not a pretty sight, believe me."

I could feel her tearing at his mind, searching for an opening, trying to make him see. "Not a soldier's death, Captain," she went on grimly. "Not glory and honor, but a death of horror, no escape, no cure, no weapon you can use against it. First blisters that burn all over your body, then disfigurement, pain, rot, madness, and death. All inevitable and unstoppable, but with time enough to suffer much before the end. Think on it. You are lucky you did not succeed."

I rode up next to Pell. "Leave us alone!" I shouted at those men, suddenly feeling full of my own angry power. "We want nothing from the Zarn, nothing but to be left in peace. What does he want from us? We have gone as far away from him as we can."

"Nothing!? What do you mean, nothing!? You have stolen Mishghall from him. He will never forgive you for that."

"Mishghall!" I replied furiously. "Mishghall is a Kourmairi city built by the Koormir themselves. We did not take it from the Zarn. It never belonged to him. Besides, it was the Koormir who defeated the guards."

"With your help! Mishghall was his port to the sea. The Zarn has controlled that access for a very long time. No, he will never forgive you for that loss. And you can be sure he will grant you no peace here, not ever. That is a fool's wish."

Murghanth pushed in front of me. "Tell your master that if he will not leave us in peace at this far edge of Yarmald, then we will come back to Eezore, in force, all of us. We will tear down his city over his head, stone by stone, till not one building is left standing. His gates will never close again. His guardsmen will all go mad from what they have done. His people will flee. He will be left alone, a ragged wanderer with no wealth, no guard, and no city left at his command. Tell him that."

"Yes, tell him all of that!" Teko echoed furiously. "Surely he remembers the last time the Hadra had cause to visit Eezore. He could not have forgotten so soon. Tell him that if he does not leave us be, we will come back a hundred hundred strong."

Dorca had gathered her courage and come closer. Suddenly one of the men exclaimed in amazement, "Dorcalyshia, is that really you? Cousin, what are you doing among these vile women?"

"Ermand, Cousin, it has been so long. I can hardly believe it is you. What a terrible way to meet again. We were once so close. Just think, you might have burned me alive. I am here because I was driven out of my city by the Zarn's edict. And what are you doing here among these men who use fastfire, you who were once so gentle and so kind, more like a brother to me than my blood brothers ever were?"

"I am no longer that child. I am a guardsman now, and I obey the Zarn's orders. Star-brats are all enemies of the Zarn."

"How could I be his enemy? I have never met the man. I did nothing against him. And how could I be your enemy, Cousin, when I was always your friend and even defended you against the teasing of others? Have you forgotten how they called you a mother's boy because you were afraid of horses? Have you forgotten that I was the one who made them stop?"

"That is all childhood nonsense, put aside long ago. I am a man now, a guardsman who is proud to take orders from the Zarn. I am afraid of nothing now, not horses, not killing — certainly not a band of ragged women."

"Enough of this talk," the captain shouted angrily. "Regroup and ride out. We have already wasted too much time here. Surely we will find another trophy before we ride home."

At those words, he turned his horse to leave. With a shout, Pell moved to block his way again. This time all her mockery was gone. "Fool!" she screamed at him. "Do you still think to find other victims, when I have already told you what sort of death awaits you for burning us? Did you hear nothing of what I said? Nothing?!"

At that moment, Alyeeta leaned forward and said with fierce malice, "Captain, I would gladly paint a line across Yarmald with your blood and set a spell on it so no Zarn's man can ever cross here again. Now go! Get out of our sight."

At the same time, Tama rode up next to Pell and tugged on her sleeve, saying softly, "Come away, Pell, it is no use to talk to them. They must find their own fate."

Pell flashed a protective glance at Tama. Then I saw a look of grief and fear cross her face. When she turned back to the captain, she was suddenly pure rage. It was as if she had finally been pushed over the boundaries of sanity. "Enough! This is enough!" she screamed into his startled face. "This has gone on long enough! This is past bearing!" She was raving now, screeching with the voice of an Oolanth cat. The sound ripped at my nerves like sharp claws. "If my powers did not prevent me, I would tear out your eyes, tear out your bloody heart, rip off your arms like sticks, and leave you here for the birds-of-death to eat alive. Do you hear me, man? Leave us in peace or we will do as Murghanth says, come back to Eezore and tear it to pieces, stone from stone. Enough! The end! Get out of our lives! Enough! Enough! Enough!" She ended by shaking clenched fists over her head. Then her eyes rolled back in their sockets, and her whole body began shaking with anger. She threw back her head and started screaming with no words, screaming with raw, mindless fury.

The captain had pulled back. There was a look of horror on his face. "Now!" was all he said as he spun his horse around to flee. His men dashed after him with no semblance of order. Pell, in her demented state, was about to follow. "Hold her!" Jhemar shouted as she slipped off her horse and grabbed Torvir's reins. Pell was struggling with us. Madness had given her Kazouri's strength. Indeed, I wished at that moment that Kazouri were with us. We tried to unseat Pell, but our powers canceled each other's in the struggle. She thrashed and roared until Tama screamed her name loud enough for Pell to hear through her fog of madness. Then Pell stopped abruptly and said in a very different voice, "Have they gone?" She sounded almost like a plaintive child.

Tama rode up next to Pell, put an arm around her, and said gently, "Yes, Pell, yes, they have gone, all of them. It is over now."

Pell looked around, dazed and strange. "What happened to me? I feel as if I had been spelled." With those words, she slumped forward and slid from Torvir's back like a sack of grain.

Jhemar, who had the largest horse among us, carried Pell in front of her while the rest of us followed. We were very tense and watchful now, no longer full of the careless pleasure of that lovely spring day. It amazed me that the day itself had not changed after witnessing such ugliness. It was still as fair as before, only now there was no more joy in it for us. I rode with my hand on Tama's arm to comfort her. With a shake of her head she said sadly, "We thought to find a little peace and a little time together after all that awfulness. Now they have driven her mad. I only want to go as far from them as possible." The grief and bitterness in her voice tore at my heart.

Soon afterward, we turned off the Zarn's highway and began following Vaiya on a series of winding roads and tracks that would lead us to the Escuro River and to our meeting with Dhashoti and the others.

9

There was a loud outcry from among the women when we rode into the new camp with Pell's limp, unconscious body over the back of Jhemar's horse. Before we were even off our horses, many had rushed forward to carry her. They laid her down on a mat in a little brush shelter. Instantly, Tama came to kneel at her side. She took Pell's hand in hers and began crooning softly, as if to a sleeping child, "Sleep, beloved ... sleep, sweet one..." Alyeeta quickly gathered Olna, Arnella, Maireth, and others to consult together about Pell's healing. Feeling myself not needed there, I turned to leave.

Grieving women were fast gathering around Pell to give advice or look or touch or question us on what had happened. Though it was all from love and concern, still it frightened me. Soon there would be no space or air around her, no way for the healers to work. I was looking about for help when Kazouri grabbed my arm. Together, we organized a circle to keep the others back at a safe distance. This way, women could approach Pell only one at a time and with the consent of her healers.

Afterward, when things were calmer and Pell seemed to be resting peacefully, Kazouri stayed to stand watch over her while I went to look for Dhashoti. I found her deep in conversation with several Hadra I did not know. She looked up with a smile and tried to draw me into the circle. I shook my head. "I wanted to ask you to show me this place they are calling Ishlair and tell me how you found it. I will come back when you are not so busy."

"Wait, Tazzi, now is as good a time as any." She gave a quick nod to the others and slipped her arm through mine. Together we walked down the shore, following a deep curve of the Escuro. Here the river was bordered by willows and then by a broad sweep of grassland that rose gently into wooded hills. Dhashoti stopped and stared out across the swiftly moving water. "I knew of this place because I remembered it from childhood. When I was a girl, my father would come here every summer with a wagon-load of goods from Mishghall. We would camp by the river for a few weeks while he traded with folk from the south. It was at this very spot on the Escuro that I learned how to swim. Truly I had more freedom here in those few weeks of summer than in all my time in Mishghall. Oh, Tazzi, it is so wonderful to be back here again."

Dhashoti showed me everything while I followed her around, asking many questions. When we stopped to rest partway up the hillside, she made a broad gesture with her hand that took in the whole view below us. "I called it Ishlair in memory of a village the Shokarn burned to the ground. My grandmother escaped from there. Tell me, Tazzi, is it not beautiful? There is everything we need here for a settlement."

"Indeed, very beautiful," I answered with a nod, but I was shielding hard, trying not to let my thoughts leak through and spoil her joy. Yes, there was everything here that was needed for a settlement, but no room for the city I envisioned, the city that haunted me in my waking time as well as in my dreams.

When I came back, Kazouri was still standing guard. Tama was still kneeling just as I had left her, and Pell looked as if she had not moved. Everything was the same, except that Pell's face looked softer, fuller, more relaxed than I had ever seen it, even in sleep. She was so still, her breath so light, I had to touch her to know for sure that she lived. I drew Alyeeta aside. "How is she? What has happened? Is she mad? Is this the gibbering madness? Will she ever be herself again?"

"Yes, indeed, it is certainly madness. What else could it be? Only a madwoman would ride at the guards that way. But no, it is not the same madness that attacked your women in the caves last winter. This is the madness of exhaustion, an exhaustion so deep it is bottomless. She has carried the world on her back for too long. She has depleted everything she had; mind, body, spirit. That rage was her last reserve. We will do the best we can for her, but do not expect her to come back to her old self — to return unchanged. A price has been paid. That is the truth, Tazzi, though I wish I could tell you differently." I nodded silently and walked away with a terrible ache in my heart.

Pell came back to consciousness the next morning, opening her eyes and saying a few mumbled words before she slipped away again. For that day and part of the following one, she slept most of the time, hardly knowing where or who she was in her few waking moments. Tama stayed by her as much as she could, watching over her anxiously. Olna and I took our turns during those few moments when we could get Tama to leave. By the third day, Pell was conscious and more like herself, able to eat and talk and sit up for a short while. For the next day or so, I think she even gloried a little in being waited on. When I came to peer down at her anxiously, she was able to joke with me, saying, "Well, Tazzi, I told you I wanted to grow fat and lazy in the sun when we found our own place. Who would have expected it to be so soon?"

Before long, however, Pell grew restless. She became impatient with this enforced idleness and with us as well. "You all pretend to fuss over me, when in reality I am your prisoner here."

"You should be more grateful, then," Alyeeta answered sharply. "For a prisoner, you are being very well treated. Believe me, with all the special teas and herbs and tinctures your healing requires, I feel more like your slave than your jailer." Olna, Tama, Maireth, and Alyeeta all insisted that Pell needed more rest. Though she was sounding more like her old self, her eyes still had a haunted look, an emptiness that frightened me. I wondered if this was how I had seemed to her, all that past winter. Now I understood why she had worried so for me. When I tried to talk to Pell about her moment of rage and madness, she shrugged and quickly turned my words aside, saying, "No cause for worry. Only fatigue, nothing more, nothing to be alarmed about." I was not convinced. I knew Alyeeta shared my deep concern. But you cannot force talk with one who insists on silence.

Meanwhile, a new settlement was being established around us, and we were all learning to live with our new name. We were no longer Shokarn and Kourmairi and Muinyairin. We were now *The Hadra*, whatever that might mean. We held meetings, we made plans, we talked of the future as if we really believed we had one, and we worked hard to bring it about. Everywhere I looked, women were building shelters, laying paths and clearing for roads, digging cisterns and lining them with rocks, turning earth and planting gardens. As second-in-command, I tried to take Pell's place while she recuperated, but in truth there was very little place to take. Pell had been leader when we were moving and gathering. Now, with our settling, everything had changed. Other women came forward to do the work and take the leadership, especially Dhashoti, since she had found this place.

I was not the one who was needed. None of my skills seemed to matter, not even the reading and writing Alyeeta had taught me, for it was not yet time for that, nor the healing, for I had long since been replaced as a healer by Maireth, Arnella, and others. Besides, I had probably burned out my healing powers. Even my skills at peacemaking were not needed. Unaccountably, we had become more peaceful with each other. Perhaps we were really becoming the Hadra we called ourselves. As to organizing the camp, Renaise, Teko, Murghanth, and Thalyisi were far better at that than I could ever be.

I felt unsettled and out of sorts, as I had several times before among the Star-Born, an outcast among outcasts, unable to find my own place. Whatever it was of worth that Alyeeta and Pell had seen in me, I surely did not see it in myself at that moment. I alternated between trying unsuccessfully to take some sort of command and doing the humblest of work at the beck and call of Renaise or Murghanth or whoever else was organizing the camp. In short, I rushed about trying to do everything and in the end, did very little. Even that little, I did not do well. I worked hard, but only part of me was there. My heart was not in it, and that was the truth of the matter.

After a while, I became like a restless wind blowing through the settlement. However beautiful Ishlair might be, it was not the place for me. *Not the place. Not the place. Not the place.* I heard those words over and over in my head. In fact, I heard them everywhere I went: in the sighing of the wind, the rush of the water, the shurring of the grass. And yet, where was this place? What did I know of some other place? Ishlair seemed to me still within the Zarn's reach. Surely we had learned that much from our last encounter with the guards. And for me, we were still too close to the city of Mishghall — though others among us counted that an advantage.

I needed to leave for a while. I felt almost as poisonous there as I had been in the Wanderers' camp before the Witches had finally belled me out, something I certainly did not want repeated. I began to envy the horse that had a stall or a field, the dog that had a kennel, the cat that had a hearth to sleep beside. As for humans who had a place they could call home, no matter how small or humble, I could not imagine such luck. I felt like a leaf ripped from the tree and tossed in the wind. It was hard to help build a settlement I knew I could not live in. However beautiful it might be, it would never be my home. I felt it in my bones. It made my heart ache to see how happy the others were and not to share that happiness, to feel set apart one more time. I did not begrudge them their pleasure in this new place; I only wished I could feel the same.

I tried talking to Olna. In her kind, gentle way, she did her best to counsel me, but in the end I shrugged off her advice. It was as if I had a fever in me, a fever of agitation and an unreachable anguish. At last, even Alyeeta lost patience with me. "By the Goddess, Tazzi, you have what you wished for, peace and a place to make a home, but you are as restless as a bad wind and have no gratitude at all for your good fortune."

I agreed with her. Every day I prayed to the Goddess for some gratitude, and some humility as well, but my angry spirit was not soothed nor my restlessness abated. Each time I went to try and talk with Pell, I would find her laughing and talking in the sun with the others or taking her ease with Tama, happily doing small tasks, such as repairing a pack or binding a handle to a hoe. When I finally found her alone, she shook her head. "Not now, Tazzi, that is all too serious. Today the sun is shining and I am glad just to be alive. Come sit down and share this bowl of fruit and tarmar with me. They feed me much too much when all I do is lie around." I shook my head in turn and went away. It was a long time before I tried to talk to Pell again — on that or any other matter.

When Zari and Zenoria said they were taking a message to Ozzet's settlement, two days ride away, I decided to go with them, hoping that the ride would distract me or that maybe I could find whatever I was looking for. I got much encouragement from Pell and Alyeeta and some of the others. I think everyone was glad to see me leave and take my ill-humor with me.

As it was, Zari and Zenoria talked of horses the whole way, so I felt very much alone on that trip, even with the sound of their voices. When we reached the site of the settlement, I could see that this spot was, if anything, even more beautiful than the one I had left. But it was not the place, either. I knew that instantly. It was much the same for me there as it had been at Ishlair. Everyone seemed happy, hopeful, busy. Again I felt out of step. This settlement was also too close to Mishghall, and I could still feel the presence of the Zarn's men. Besides, something else was calling me, something that was not there, some other place, though I had no idea where it was and only a little notion of what it looked like.

As we were heading back to Ishlair, I noticed some steep bluffs on the other side of the river and what looked like a little footpath winding up a crevice between them. I felt pulled to climb to the top. I told Zari and Zenoria to leave me there and go on, that I had some thinking to do. Uneasy for my safety, they argued for a while, saying they would wait below or come with me. Finally, I was so insistent that in the end they had no choice but to go.

Dancer swam across the Escuro with me clinging to her back. Then I left her grazing while I climbed up the crevice. It was a fierce scramble the whole way to the top, but at least it kept my mind occupied. In the end, it was worth every hard step. When I finally hauled myself over the edge and struggled to my feet, the whole world lay spread out before me. I could see several bends of the river. Our settlement lay in the far distance in one direction, and what might have been smoke from Ozzet's camp was visible in the other. I could even see the tiny line of the Zarn's road far off in the misty distance, not a reassuring sight. I had no idea what I was looking for, only that I had been strongly drawn to that spot. The sun was warm, a light breeze was blowing, a soft carpet of moss covered the ground, and a beautiful view lay spread out below me. I took off my shirt and leaned back against a rock to watch a flock of kiri birds dipping and rising, gray-white against the bright blue of the sky. Far off, a hawk was soaring over the river.

After a while, the hawk began circling closer and closer, till it was spiraling directly overhead. Almost in a trance, I watched that circular motion as if nothing else existed in the world. I think I must have dozed and dreamt — or perhaps I had a vision such as Witches have. Suddenly, it was as if I had slipped into the mind of the hawk and could see through her eyes. The view that lay spread out below me was very different from the one my waking self had just been looking at. With my hawk eyes, I saw three hills, bordered by ocean on one side and a wide bend of the river on the other. A white, stone city covered those hills. One of the hills was topped by a big, round, stone building gleaming in the sun. Wanting to come closer, even to walk those streets, I tried to will myself down to that city. Instead, with a sudden jolt, I found myself back on the bluffs above the Escuro, precariously close to the edge.

It was all gone! I sat up with a gasp, feeling the knife-edge pain of loss, but I could not linger. The sun was low. It was getting cool. I still had a hard river crossing and a long ride ahead of me, so I scrambled down as quickly as safety would allow. As it was, I was not back in camp till long after nightfall. Kazouri was just making ready to come look for me, with Zari and Zenoria as guides.

★

For those next few weeks, I carried my vision with me. I did not share it with the other Hadra, as no one else seemed to share my discontent, but at last I was able to work with a good heart. I would not stay. I knew that now, though I did not know how or in what way I would be leaving or who would come with me. But while I was there, I would do my best. I began to pay some attention to the others, Dhashoti in particular, for now that I was accessible again, she shared her plans with me. With my experience, I was able to help and advise her. In some way, I may even have been — for that time at least — her second there, as I had once been Pell's.

Of the dozens of new women in the camp, there were two besides Dhashoti who particularly caught my attention. One of them was Zheran. What can I say about Zheran? That I had begun to notice her more and more, to really see her. In the beginning I did not think of her as someone like myself, but as someone much older, a wife, a mother, a woman of Darthill, a Kourmairi — someone of a different generation, like my mother, perhaps, though in truth she was nothing like my mother. At first, she was just some angry man's wife, possible trouble, and the first woman to come live among us who was not a Hadra or a Witch — though no doubt she would not be the last. Her courage touched me deeply, but our fates and lives seemed to me irrevocably different. She was even physically different: rounder, softer, more full-bodied, from having children — not hard and lean like so many of the Hadra from our hungry time on the road.

At first, I could not believe she would choose to stay with us. I half expected her to be drawn home by her children, by the life she had stepped out of so suddenly, or even by some longing for the man she had left. I thought she might go back and try to sue for peace with Rhomar, perhaps getting Nhokosos to intercede on her behalf. But when I asked, she shook her head, saying with sadness and a sort of weary resignation, "I love my sons, but they are more Rhomar's now than mine. They were born when I was very young, the first when I was only fourteen years of age, hard births both. The second tore me inside so that I almost bled to death. Rhomar is very proud of his sons. I think he had hoped to have an army of sons, but the midwife said I was to have no more children and gave me a potion of crushed jeezil seeds to prevent quickening.

"My boys were so sweet when they were young, but Rhomar quickly drove us apart, saying he did not want them infected with my womanly ways. According to him, it was not fit for sons to be close to their mothers. He said if I wanted a child to make my own, I should try for a daughter. How could he say such a thing when he knew it might kill me?

"It broke my heart to see how he set about training the boys for manhood, 'hardening' them, he called it. No weakness or tears were allowed. It grieves me to leave them, yet they are almost strangers to me now. I wonder if they will grieve for me. If so, they must never let their father know."

"And what of Rhomar? Do you think he will come after you?"

"Why should he? He is the one who told me to leave. No, I think he will find another woman to give him more sons. He is handsome and has a good piece of land. Some young woman will be glad enough to marry him. Why should he come after me? I am spoiled goods. O Mother! I wish I had birthed a daughter for myself while I could still have children."

Several times I had noticed Zheran watching me with a look of concern on her face. When I was weary and had not the sense to stop, she would try to lure me into sitting down and bring me a bowl of food. Then she would sit quietly by me, a steady, peaceful presence. Zheran had made herself busy in the new settlement, doing many of the things that needed doing in a quiet, dignified, determined way. Yet it was clear that she also did not fit here, this woman who had left everything to come with us, even though she could never be a Hadra. She did not even try. She insisted on wearing the blouses and long skirts of a married woman of the Koormir and steadfastly refused all our offers of trousers and tunics. "I am who I am," she would say, "and your clothes cannot make me otherwise." One day, when I caught her watching me in that intent way she had, she said, "This is not your place, Tazzil. You cannot settle here. There is something else you are meant to do."

"What do you know?" I answered angrily. "You scarcely know me at all." I was tired of being watched in that way.

She took no offense at my rudeness. Indeed, she hardly seemed to notice it. She just nodded and said quietly, "I know what I see, Tazzil."

While Zheran was reserved and distant among us, though very efficient at everything she did, Katchia — now that she was done cursing us and calling us dirty Puntyar — joined our lives with gusto. She took over organizing and distributing our goods, accounting for everything with her tax collector skill, so that we knew the exact nature and quantity of all our supplies, in the city of Mishghall as well as here in the settlement. She made fast friends with Renaise, Thalyisi, and the others who supervised the daily running of the camp. As she had somehow managed to escape with several packs of cards, she was constantly teaching us new games. Katchia was loud, bold, brazen, bristly, quick to anger, and equally quick to laugh loudly when her anger cooled. Each time I had to deal with her, I found myself caught between admiration, anger, and amusement. Pell enjoyed her spirit and responded to her boldness with good-humored banter. Rishka, on the other hand, had no patience with her at all and often felt insulted and angry. Katchia was like a burr in her boot. Rishka would say to me through her teeth, "We were too kind. We should have left her in the square in Mishghall for those men to deal with." For her part, Katchia took pleasure in baiting Rishka at every possible occasion.

It was Kazouri's response that was the most surprising. Kazouri was smitten. She took a fancy to Katchia in a most extraordinary way. I had never seen Kazouri take that kind of interest in another woman before. In fact, I had never thought of Kazouri in that way. I had always seen her as strong, steady, and good-humored; our rock, our shelter in the storm, our power and protection. Now I saw her reduced to helplessness, puzzled and magnetized. Her heart was plain-written on her face as she watched Katchia with her large, dark, pleading eyes. It was like seeing a big, good-natured, somewhat simple, loyal, loving dog enamored of a volatile, fast-moving, bright-colored bird. For her part, Katchia was glad enough to return Kazouri's love, though probably not in the same fashion as it was offered. Kazouri's love was useful and protective; it assured Katchia of safety and a place among us. At the same time, she flirted outrageously with the rest of us, whenever she was not fighting or arguing or causing some other commotion. Though this may have caused Kazouri pain, it certainly brought alive a side of her that had long been dormant.

At that time, it seemed to me as if everyone in camp had someone to love: Renaise continued to charm Dhashoti; Pell and Tama were finally free to be together; Rishka and Zari had resumed their old relationship; Murghanth and Teko were proudly open with their affection. I could go on and on with the naming. Sex and freedom and the warmth of early summer and the smell of new-turned earth and the sight of new little green shoots were a heady mix. Perhaps some part of me understood that Zheran looked on me in that way. But I, who had known so many lovers, had no room in my life for such things at that moment. Instead of feeling lonely, in truth I felt as if I had my own secret lover. I did not know her name and had barely glimpsed her face, yet she haunted my dreams and troubled my waking hours. I was filled with longing for her, this place I had seen only in my visions, a longing as passionate and painful as I have ever felt for any mortal woman. Each time we rode out, I searched for her on every route we went by. She always eluded me, though sometimes I thought I caught a glimpse of her, around some far bend of the road.

★

Spring had turned to high summer and soon summer would give way to fall. Finally, I sought Pell out, thinking she was well enough to hear me. Before I could get the words out, she pulled me down beside her. "Listen, Tazzi, I know what is in your mind. No need for a lot of words, but I must tell you clearly that I am quite content with being here, or if not content, at least too exhausted to try to move us on again, one more time. I see you have a bright, wonderful city in your head. You are full of fire for doing more, for keeping going, for finding the perfect place for this city of your dreams. You must understand that, for me, it is over. I said I would get us to safety, and I have done that. I have pushed as far as I can, pushed others and pushed myself. Nine years of struggle is long enough for anyone. I am weary to the bone. I am done with it, finished with this game of being leader. Now I am turning it over. Yours now, Tazzi, your turn, just as I warned you. You lead and I will follow. If you choose to stay here and build, I will be happy to stay too, for a month, a year, a lifetime, whatever you decide.

"If you are determined to go on and search elsewhere, I will be glad enough to go with you and help make that settlement. You have only to say. But for myself, I am done with leading: with guiding, planning, organizing, persuading, conferring, convincing, pushing, worrying, and especially with being responsible for everyone else's life. Gladly, I hand it over to you. You can be the chief of this new venture."

My heart was pounding with fear. Pell was right. She had warned me many times, yet I could hardly believe she was really saying this. I was so accustomed to leaning on her guidance. I had tried to pretend over the summer that she only needed a little rest. *Too soon!* I wanted to shout. *No, Pell, I am not ready yet!* Yet I knew that was not fair. Everything she had spoken was the truth.

As if I had said the words aloud, she asked with sarcasm, "And just when would you be ready, Tazzi? When would it be time? Can you not see that you will only be ready when I step back? When it is in your hands? Otherwise, it will never be time. You must stop leaning on me, for there is nothing left to lean on, nothing, only an empty shell. I have carried this burden long enough. If you want this city of the Hadra to come into existence, then you must be the one to make it happen. You cannot look to me for that. It would not be fair to ask. More than that, it would be utterly useless."

I shook myself as if shaking off a chill. "What about Tama?" I asked, wanting to shift the focus of our talk. "Is she willing to leave?"

"Tama has already told me this is not her chosen place. She said she would not be sorry to go on, though she would gladly stay here with me if that was what I wanted. I must tell you that if she chose to stay, then I would too. I have left her once, against my own wishes, certainly against hers. I will not do that again, not even for you, Tazzi, not even for all your dreams. Tama and I will have some happiness together out of all this, that is our right. Never again will I leave her standing at the gate."

Tears sprang up in my eyes. I was suddenly touched by the chill of old griefs. Pell and I had been lovers, but she never would have said that of me. She had used me for her body's needs, because I was there and Tama was not. Pell caught my thought and answered with thought, *All too true, Tazzi. Can you ever forgive me?* Aloud she said, "That is part of why I will no longer lead. I must be free now to be true to my heart as well as to my dreams. I am sorry for the hurt I caused you."

To my surprise, she reached out her arms and drew me into a gentle hug, quite unlike the Pell I had always known. Instead of pulling back with hurt pride and anger, I let her hold me close. Something softened in my heart; some old frozen place inside began to melt. Finally, Pell drew back a little and said with some of her old fire, "You know, Tazzi, I share your dream of a great Hadra city, a city as beautiful as Mishghall, but one that is our own, built by us for our needs. I see a library and an archive, where we will keep our books and records for ourselves and for all the Hadra of the future. I myself might even learn to read and write. I see a House of the Mother, with a fine statue of the Goddess made by our own hands. I see houses, streets, parks — a city that will take years to build, lifetimes maybe — only I have nothing left in me to make it happen."

As she spoke, I saw it in my mind again: three hills between the river and the ocean and a city shining there. For that moment, I knew we were sharing the same vision. But then she went on, "If it is to be, then you must be the one to pull us together, to inspire, drive, plot, plead, plan, argue, and push. Not me. Great Goddess, not me!" She shook her head and sighed with utter weariness.

"Oh, Pell, how could I command you after having followed you for so long?"

"Command? Command!" Pell burst out. Her face changed. For a moment, at least, the weariness lifted and she exploded with laughter. "Command? Probably as successfully as I commanded you. The few times I tried, you defied me to my face. You cannot command the Hadra. How can you command those who cannot be compelled by force? Out in the man's world, they follow commands on fear of death. Death is the final arbiter, the tune they all dance to. Think of it: if there were no such fear, then each would do as they thought best, and there would be no Zarns to lord it over others. Everyone out there is compelled by the fear of death. But they have all grown so accustomed to taking orders, they dare not even think of what they really want in their lives.

"The Hadra, of course, cannot be led by orders as the guards can. You cannot play captain to this unruly lot. But they will follow your passion and your vision if those are strong enough." She spoke so intently that, for a moment, she almost sounded like her old self. "That is what compels. Why else did you follow me? But first you must trust in yourself. You must trust in your own power. You must let it fill you. You must take it into your own hands. The passion and the vision are there, Tazzi. The power is there too. I have watched it grow all this summer, but it is you who must own it. Alyeeta and I have seen it in you for a long time now, and we are not fools. We have both tried to train you for this moment. Part of you has been sleepwalking ever since you were driven out of Nemanthi. Now it is time to wake up, Tazzi, and stop following in my footsteps. Wake up and take on your own fate!"

I looked into her eyes for a long time, holding her gaze without blinking. Something was stirring and shifting inside me. Finally I said, "Pass your power on to me, Pell, if you no longer want it."

She shook her head. "I doubt if I have anything left to pass on. I doubt if you would want it."

"Do it," I said forcefully. Hardly knowing what I was asking for, I shut my eyes and held out my hands, palms up. For a while nothing happened, nothing moved. Then I felt a tremendous force and energy radiating over my hands. Next, I felt the shock of Pell's touch as her palms settled to rest against mine, hot as fire. I had to clamp my jaw to hold steady. My arms were shaking. *Breathe together,* she whispered in my head. We sat there breathing together for a long time. After she had withdrawn her hands, I sat there even longer, holding mine open to the Goddess.

★

For several days after Pell and I talked, I did nothing. Something had happened that I scarcely understood. I had to let it all settle in my heart. Then, before I asked the others, I spoke to Dhashoti, seeking my release and needing to settle things honorably with her.

"This comes as no surprise, Tazzil. I knew from that first day you were not happy here. I have no wish to hold you against your will. Ask whomever else you want, but please leave me Renaise, unless she is absolutely determined to go with you. May the Mother bless your venture. May we meet again under a summer sky." She took my face between her hands and kissed me on the forehead. I felt blessed. That part had been easier than I had expected.

Very slowly, one by one, I began asking women if they would come with me to this new place that I did not even know. I could not bring myself to gather them all together and ask them as a group. What if no one said yes?

Thalyisi, Noya, Teko, and Murghanth all told me no, that they were very happy where they were. Renaise, though I did not ask her, sought me out to make it clear that she had no intention of leaving Dhashoti. Just as I was about to become totally discouraged, Jhemar told me she would be glad to leave and very glad to be riding down the coast with me. Zenoria came over while we were talking, as if drawn to the energy. To my surprise, she said she would leave anytime I was ready. None of the women who had come from Eezore wanted to go, not Lhiri, Nunyair, Ashai, or any of the others. They were glad to stay near Mishghall, as were most of the Sheezerti. Even though I had expected this, it still hurt to leave Lhiri, though it was not likely I would miss Nunyair, not even for one moment. Kazouri only asked me if Pell was coming and if Katchia could. Much to my surprise, Katchia herself was quite ready to go. Hayika would have ridden off right then. Rishka said she would go wherever I did, though she wished Katchia somewhere else. The hardest person to ask was Alyeeta. What if she said no? Would I still have the courage to leave or the heart to do so? I finally went and stood before her with my head bowed. "I am leaving here to look for a place where we can make a city. Will you come with us?"

"I thought you would never ask me, that you thought me too old. I saw you whispering to this one or that one, hatching your little plots. I thought you meant to leave me here or make me come and beg."

"Please, Alyeeta, it was because I was afraid to ask, afraid you would say no. Will you come with me?"

"Why not? There is nothing to bind me here, nothing here more than any other place. With you gone, there will be even less."

"Alyeeta, we will find a home."

"Oh, Tazzia, what a dream. Witches have no home. That is all in the past. But I will go with you out of love and out of curiosity. I will go to see what is there."

Rishka had already asked Zari. Kilghari came looking for me to say, "I am tired of being a Muinyairin. I am sick of wandering. No matter how small or humble, I want my own home, built with my own hands. I want to live in one place, go to sleep every night in the same bed, and wake every morning to the same view. I want to plant a garden I can harvest. I even want to plant fruit trees and see them bear fruit, year after year. Ishlair is too close to Mishghall for me to feel safe here. I want to go with you, hoping this is the last time I am ever forced to travel again." Josleen and Megyair told me they would come, too, at least for a while, to be the messengers between the new settlement and Ishlair. I was surprised one morning to see Ozzet, riding into camp with several Hadra. She came straight up to me and with hardly any greeting said, "I hear you are going south to make a new place, a Hadra city. If so, I want to go with you."

"But you are already making a settlement on the river, and you have family near here, a whole village."

"All the more reason to go. My father is a weak, fearful man, always afraid for me and easily influenced. Rhomar is his friend and now Rhomar hates me. Even before, the man had no great liking for me. He was always wanting to tame me, telling my father I was too wild for a Kourmairi woman. Now that Zheran has left, he will never forgive me; he will be glad to think it all my fault. No, I need to be gone from this part of the world. I will miss my grandparents, especially Nhokosos. He was the only one who really understood me and gave me my freedom, but I need to make my life far away, in another place. Chomar and Valdain want to come with me. The others will go back to the settlement."

As I thought about the women who had spoken to go with me, it seemed as if most of them were the wild ones, restless and adventuresome, the women least suited for city life. Those who were staying were the ones who most wanted to live in a city again. I could see trouble ahead from this. When I told Pell my fears, she laughed in my face. "Did you think this was going to be easy, Tazzi? Did you imagine you were going to be gifted with it, free of trouble or pain? Think what you are trying to do. Trust me, it will be nothing but trouble from now on. You are undertaking to move, not just a mountain, but the whole world. At least now you will no longer be making us miserable with your miseries. You are getting what you asked for. I say, take what you can get and be grateful. Thank the Goddess for every woman who wants to go with you. Things will happen as She wills it. You must put yourself in Her path and be ready to accept whatever comes."

As I was talking to Pell, Zheran came to say that she wished to go with me. I had not even thought to ask her. Pell answered thoughtlessly, "Would it not be better to stay here, where you are near Darthill and your children?"

I had never seen Zheran angry, but at Pell's words she flared up suddenly. "Hadra, tell me clearly if you do not want me to come, but do not try to tell me how to live my life or make my choices."

Rebuked, Pell took a step back, surprise written plainly on her face. "I see I have overstepped myself. Lady, I meant no disrespect. Indeed, I honor your choices and your courage, too. Besides, it is for Tazzi to say who will and will not come on this journey, not for me." Zheran's face softened, but I could see she was very set on going, quite ready to challenge Pell, or anyone else if she had to.

"Come with us, Zheran," I said quickly. "We will need you. I promise there will be a place for you there."

Now I had all the women I needed, or at least enough to make a start. Of the Hadra, there was myself, Pell, Tama, Rishka, Zari, Jhemar, Kara, Vestri, Mouraine, Shartel, Zenoria, Hayika, Kilghari, Maireth, Ozzet and her two friends, and Megyair and Josleen. Of the Witches, Alyeeta was coming, of course, as well as Olna and Telakeet. Shalamith had decided to stay in Ishlair and perhaps go back to Mishghall. Zheran was the only Kourmairi riding with us. We were a little more than twenty, a strange company, perhaps, each of us on that road for her own reason.

That next morning, Renaise and the other women from the cookfires helped us to pack supplies, while Rishka, Zari, Zenoria, and Jhemar went to gather the horses. Every woman in Ishlair was there to wave good-bye and wish us well. When I finally rode away from Dhashoti's little settlement with my small troupe, it was with no regret and no fear and a terrible, tearing hope in my heart.

It was our second day on the road. We had just sat down to a hasty breakfast when Josleen, our sentry for that morning, rode in to say that a group of Wanderers were asking permission to enter our camp. They had with them a man who said he had an urgent message for the woman Tazzil and would speak only to her. Full of curiosity, I gave my assent. Moments later, the Wanderers were in our camp and I was on my feet to greet them, very curious to see this man who would only speak to me and who called me Tazzil.

He rode in between four tall Wanderers, not quite a prisoner, yet not a free man either. His skin was bronzed from much sun, but his hair had that unmistakable Shokarn fairness and was bleached almost white. The eyes that looked out at me from his deeply tanned face were of a bright, clear blue. Clearly this was no Kourmairi. It was certainly no man of my village, yet what other man would seek me out this way, as if we had some business together? I found the fearless directness of his stare unsettling.

Though his clothes were ragged and dirty, they were not poor. Once they had been of fine cloth and careful make. He sat his horse proudly. I could not imagine who this man was or what he wanted of me; still, there was something oddly familiar about his face that gave my heart a strange little twist. I nodded to the Wanderers to show I was willing to hear him. He rode straight at me, clearly knowing who I was. When he was close enough, he made a slight bow from horseback, then continued staring at me. He seemed to be searching my soul, wanting to see if I might be worthy of some task I knew nothing of and certainly had not asked for.

"So, we meet again, Tazzil of the Star-Born; or should I say Hadra, for I hear that is what you call yourselves now? I see you do not recognize me, though we once shared a moment of life and death." He spoke a strangely formal and stilted Kourmairi.

Suddenly, from his mind, I saw again the scene on the shore; the river in flood and the black toads, the ewe, leaping everywhere. My face broke into a wide grin. "Lorren!" I exclaimed, unaccountably glad to see him again and to see him alive. "I must say I am very relieved the Kourmairi did not catch up with you. No, I did not recognize you. You look very different from the man I last saw, the one who tried to run me through with his sword."

He nodded, grinning. "Very different, I promise: wiser, less bloody, and a lot more worn. And you are also very different. You are not the Witch's feebleminded old sister, as you pretended to be that day, Tazzil of the toads."

"You saw me that day as Alyeeta wished you to see me. Today I am myself. Now, why have you sought me out?"

Quickly he evaded my question with another. "Tell me, was it my friend Hereschell who betrayed me and so spoiled my grand surprise victory? If not for Hereschell and you and your Witch friend here, I might have regained Mishghall for the Zarn and so earned enough glory and riches to last me all my life."

"Hereschell meant you no harm. He was only...," I stammered quickly, wanting to protect Hereschell, or perhaps protect Lorren from the pain of that betrayal.

"And been miserable all my life," Lorren added quickly, interrupting my protest. "No need for your loyal defense of Hereschell. I thank him. I am deeply grateful, more than I have words for. Tell him so when you see him next. He saved me as well as Mishghall. And I am grateful to you as well. Think of all the death and misery I would have caused. In the end, I myself would have become a prisoner of Eezore, trapped in a life I despised with the blood of Mishghall on my hands. I have already done enough harm; you saved me from doing more. Now I am a free man, my own man."

"What has happened to you since the battle of the toads?"

He threw back his head and laughed. "Yes, the toads ... Now that was a brilliant strategy."

"Mine," Alyeeta said, pushing her way up beside me. "If the Zarn ever wants to know who defeated him at the Escuro River and sent his troops fleeing in fear, tell him it was Alyeeta the Witch. Tell him I have not forgotten how his father burned my beautiful Witch convent to the ground. Tell him that soon I will send black toads into his palace, yes, even into his bed, to attack his manhood there."

Lorren's face turned serious. "I am not likely ever to tell the Zarn anything again, not if I value my life. He was not pleased with my defeat. I ended up in the dungeon of Eezore, likely to be hung or beheaded; at least that was the talk among my jailers. Men loyal to my father managed to sneak me out through the gates. Even so, it must have taken much work and planning and probably quite a bit of gold. No, I will not be talking to the Zarn again, not of my own free will."

Pell had been tugging at my arm for a while. Suddenly she sent me a blast of mind-touch that jolted my attention. "Who is this man, that you would trust him?" she asked in an accusing tone. "I gather from your speech together that he was captain of the Zarn's guards at Darthill. Why do you even think to speak to him here in our own camp? You endanger us all."

"Pell, you named me leader for this part of our journey. You must either trust me to make my own judgments or you must decide not to follow." I could scarcely believe that I had said those words to Pell. Instead of blasting me with anger, she stepped back with a slight nod of her head.

"Quite right. I see you are learning. I have something to learn too if I really mean to let go of this burden."

Almost at the same moment, Lorren said, "She has no reason to trust me. The last time I saw her, I did indeed try to kill her, and her Witch friend here as well. I would have done so gladly if not for her powers. But I am a different man now, much humbled and wisened by my circumstances, believe me. I only carry a sword to defend myself against other men, but if it makes it easier for you to hear me, I will lay it down here on the ground. You may use it against me if you need to; you may kill me if you wish. I will not harm you. In fact, in payment for harm done, I have pledged myself to your survival and well-being, a Wanderer pledge and one not taken lightly.

"Take up your sword, man," Pell said in disgust. "You know we cannot use a blade against you."

"But I can," Alyeeta said quickly. She stepped forward with a look of calculated malice on her face and hefted the sword.

At almost the same moment, Zheran came and said to the men, "There is korshi, fresh fruit, and tea ready by the fire. Would you all care to join us there?"

Deftly, Jhemar slipped between Alyeeta and Lorren, adding quickly, "Forgive us. In our excitement, we forgot Wanderer courtesy. This Wanderer is embarrassed for her poor manners." As she made a broad gesture of welcome with her hand, I remembered again that Jhemar had been taken in by the Wanderers long before she and Pell had joined together to find the Star-Born.

With a hiss, Alyeeta dropped her arm, and the sword fell clanking to the rocks. "Offering him food will not turn this Shokarn lordling into a Wanderer, nor will it make him any more trustworthy."

The Wanderers dismounted, Lorren among them. They followed Zheran to the fire, where she ladled out bowls of food and passed them around with a smile of welcome. Watching her, I thought with a combination of amusement and chagrin, *This outsider has better manners than any of us.*

Katchia, meanwhile, put out a very different kind of welcome, turning on all her charms. She particularly had her eye on Strathorn, the youngest of the Wanderers. She managed to be the one to bring him his bowl, touching his shoulder with her hand when he took it and leaning forward so that her breasts showed temptingly at the opening of her tunic. This was not lost on Strathorn. After that, he watched her hungrily as she moved about the camp with an occasional smile in his direction or a sway of her hips.

While we ate, Hayika watched Lorren relentlessly, barely eating her own food. Finally, in a voice full of hostility, she asked, "Man, what do you want with us? Now that you have failed to bloody your sword in our flesh, burn us alive, or end our lives in some other monstrous way, what are you doing here in our camp?"

Zheran looked chagrined, and even Pell seemed startled at the rudeness of her questions, but Rishka was nodding in agreement, as were several others, Mouraine, Vestri, and Shartel among them. Lorren, however, seemed to take no offense. He stared at Hayika for a long moment as if searching deep inside for the answer, then gave a slight nod. "Curiosity," he said thoughtfully. "Yes, curiosity. As a student of the natural world, I am looking for information and answers. I was never cut out to be a soldier, only I made the mistake of being born the oldest son in my father's house. If I had been given a choice, I would have spent my whole life in the library or in the fields and woods. No one asked me my preference. When I first heard of the Star-Born, I was full of excitement, thinking, *Here is something new and amazing in the world.* I wanted to meet these creatures I was being sent out to kill." Those words set off some angry mutterings. Lorren went on when he could be heard again. "Yes, *creatures.* That is how they taught us to think of you. Then, at the river, when Tazzil leapt in front of the Witch to protect her and turned my sword against me without even trying, I knew this was a natural force to be reckoned with and studied with care. I want to see how you will evolve and shape yourselves, what you will become. That is all I want from you. That is my secret. In return, I am willing to give you, Tazzil, what you most want in the world."

Hayika snarled, "So you want to study us like bugs pinned to a board. Will you report back to your master then?"

At the same moment I jumped to my feet in anger. "What do you know of me and what I want? There are toads and dead men and much blood between us, Captain — not 'secrets.'" Yet even as I said those words, I felt a tug on my mind.

Mouraine had jumped up to stand beside me, the morning sun flashing on her golden hair. She took a threatening step in his direction. "Man, you take advantage of our goodwill."

Hayika and Megyair were muttering to each other. Rishka was making rude remarks in Muinyairin. Kazouri was shifting from foot to foot as if ready to spring at any moment. Lorren ignored them all and kept his eyes fastened on my face. "The talk among the Wanderers is that Tazzil the Hadra goes south with a small band of women. They say she is in search of a settlement by the sea, a place large enough to make a city. Is that truth, or is it only talk?"

"Truth," I said softly, sinking back into my seat. "How did you know?"

"If I told you that, who would speak in my ear again? The Wanderers have their ways. I know of such a place, far south of here, three hills between the river and the sea. If you can bring yourself to trust me, I will take you there."

I shut my eyes with a groan. I could see it in my mind again: the green hills, the blue of the river, the deeper purple-blue of the ocean. "Show me the way and I will follow," I said, standing up again as if under a spell.

Now a storm of argument broke out, with only Pell, Kara, Vestri, Jhemar, and Kilghari speaking to go with Lorren. The others shouted a hundred reasons why we should not trust this man, most of them good ones. I listened for a while, not adding my voice. Then I clapped for silence. Much to my surprise, I got what I asked for. "I will not argue with any of you. I will only say that I am going with Lorren. Those who want to come with us are welcome. I have seen this place in my sleep and in my waking dreams as well. I am haunted by it. I have to go, even at the risk of my life."

Instantly Rishka was on her feet. "I will not let you go alone with that man. I will go with you and watch his every move."

To my surprise, Zheran rose on the other side of me, saying with concern, "I will come too and watch over you."

"A trap," Hayika said bitterly. "He may well be leading you into a trap — or rather us, for I can see that no matter what we say, we are all going to be foolish enough to follow."

Lorren stood up slowly, watching Hayika. "I have nothing to gain and much to lose by a betrayal. The Wanderers can vouch for me. I am as much under the Zarn's death edict as any of you and far less able to protect myself. I have no master anymore to report back to." Then he suddenly turned his smile on me. "Besides, if I could not kill Tazzil with a whole army at my back, how could I harm her now?"

I found myself charmed into smiling back. I did not remind him that his whole army had not been at his back at all, but rushing away in flight from little black toads. Strangely enough, I found myself trusting this man almost as I had trusted Pell when we first met in the tavern. "Alyeeta?" I asked, looking to her as if she might have some final answer.

Lorren turned to her too. "Well, Witch, I see you are not the old woman you appeared to be but someone still young and strong."

"Make no assumptions, soldier. I am old enough to remember the Zarn's father and his father before him. I have stayed alive by being watchful of tricks."

"If you are still afraid I mean Tazzil some harm, put your hands on my head to read my truth. I have no evil intent hidden there. You may read me to my soul. I leave myself open to your hands."

"Give me your sword."

Lorren turned it and laid the hilt in her hand. Instantly, she raised it over his head as if to strike. I wanted to shout, "No, Alyeeta!" but found I had no voice. Lorren looked straight ahead and did not flinch. There was a moment of frozen silence as all of us stared at those two figures. Then, with some strange creature sound — a growl and a shout combined — Alyeeta threw the sword down and put her hands on his head.

This seemed like some odd sort of blessing, and unaccountably, it brought tears to my eyes. Seeing him standing there, open and defenseless under Alyeeta's hands, I wondered, *Who is this man, this stranger who pretends to know me, who acts, in fact, as if we are bonded, as if we have some claim on each other's lives?* He seemed dangerous to me, and yet, in no way could I have resisted going with him. "Do you trust him?" I asked Alyeeta.

After a long silence she nodded. "I have read him to the best of my ability. Though there is some secret that he holds, I can find in him no will to harm."

Suddenly the camp was full of the noise and motion of departure.

11

Not since childhood had I felt such joy bubbling in my blood, such eagerness for each new day. It was as if I had reconnected with Tazzia, the little village girl who spoke with creatures, loved everyone, and thought life was filled with magic; the child who had not yet felt the hatred of her fellow villagers, nor seen her lover killed before her eyes. I felt Tazzia in my heart again, filling me with love. It was like meeting again with a long-lost and almost forgotten beloved friend. I woke every morning with a sense of freshness, eager to be on the road, no longer driven by fear of what pursued us, but drawn forward by what lay ahead.

Going home ... Going home ... Those words sang themselves in my head, over and over, like a tuneless song or a chanted prayer, though in truth I was going farther and farther from the only home I had ever known. At night, I dreamt of walking up steep cobbled streets, past parks and gardens and white stone buildings.

Sometimes the others grumbled at the pace I set, but more often they let me sweep them along with my fervor, glad, no doubt, not to have to contend with the Tazzi who had been so full of bitter rage or the more recent one who had prowled about, restless as an Oolanth cat trapped in a cage. The other Wanderers had left us before noon of the first day, though not without Strathorn turning back many times with longing glances. Now we were following Lorren uphill and down, through woods and fields and yet more woods, going south by narrow, almost secret roads and meeting few others.

Sometimes I rode with Kara, my first love, who had not died after all, and we were able to share memories of our common past, no longer poisoned by my bitterness. I could even watch her now with her lover, Vestri, and not feel the bite of jealousy — or at least not feel it so deeply. It was as if I had my own lover waiting for me somewhere ahead and I was going eagerly to meet with her. Sometimes I rode with Pell, asking advice or reminiscing on our adventures together, for that is what they seemed, now that we were no longer in mortal danger. Or I rode with Mouraine, wanting to get to know her better, or even with Katchia, whose outrageous stories kept me laughing and whose bawdy mouth could embarrass even this Hadra into blushing.

Alyeeta, when I kept company with her, said how different I seemed, almost like a child. Rather than being overjoyed, she sounded sour and resentful. "I think this man has turned your head with all his fancy talk of a settlement. Beware he does not make a fool of you. You have as little sense at the moment as a lovesick village girl."

This last she said with utter contempt, but I was too happy to feel anger. Instead, I burst out laughing. "Oh, Alyeeta, you look as if you just bit into a sour lemon." Then, more seriously, I asked, "Alyeeta, can I never do anything right in your eyes? Would you rather have me as I was, so full of anger it tarnished everything I looked at, poisoned every word I spoke? Be glad for me. This newfound happiness may not last."

"No doubt. Most likely it will not," she answered tartly. "It is fool's work to hinge all your happiness on some man."

Now I understood. I could hear the twist of jealousy in Alyeeta's voice. "It is not the man," I said quickly. "What would I need in my life with a man? It is the place that calls me like a lover." Yet that was not altogether true. Though I made sure to share my time equally with everyone in my little troupe, trying hard to bind us together and be a good leader, still, in truth, my preference was to ride by Lorren. I was filled with curiosity about this man who had so recently been our enemy. Besides, he had much knowledge of the world that I wanted for myself, or, rather, for the Hadra.

My companions all had their own very different responses to him. Pell, Jhemar, Kazouri, and Zenoria plied him with questions about the Zarn's armies and intentions. Maireth, Kara, Ozzet, and many of the others did their best to avoid him, keeping their distance and saying nothing at all to him. Katchia began by flirting outrageously, saying such things as "I wonder why is it that Shokarn men are so much handsomer than the Koormir," or "If you just let me have your clothes for a little while, I could wash and mend them and have them looking almost new again. I would be only too glad to be of service." When Lorren made polite, uninterested responses and finally fell to ignoring her altogether, she retaliated with insults and rude comments. Hayika quickly joined in, and even Alyeeta had to add some unkind words of her own. It grew so bad that I cringed with embarrassment and fervently wished myself elsewhere.

When we finally reached a widening in the trail, I rode up next to Lorren. "What has happened to you since our meeting at the river?" I asked, hoping to cover the rudeness of my companions. "You never had a chance to answer my question."

"Much. A very long story, longer to tell than this ride will take us, but at least I will tell you a part of it. After the battle of the black toads, I made my way home, trying to gather what men I could on the way and always hiding from the wrath of the Koormir, not an easy thing to do, believe me. When we reached Eezore, a few of my men were already there, spreading wild stories of toads and Witches and rumors of an army of star-brats massing for battle. I was not given a hero's welcome, I can tell you that. The Zarn had me stripped of everything: my rank, my uniform, all my possessions; even my horse, and that hurt most of all. As you know, we have a tight bond, Pharoth and I. The rest I could have left with no regret. They can have it all, with my blessings.

"The Zarn's councilors questioned me over and over, the same questions again and again and again, night and day, till I thought my head would crack with it. Even the Zarn himself questioned me a few times. He wants to understand your powers. He is convinced it is something that can be made for him.

"My poor father, he was publicly humbled and forced to denounce me in front of crowds in the streets, very hard for such a proud man. People shouted insults at me and then began to throw things. If not for the guards, they might have torn me apart on the spot. They saw me as being at fault for the loss of their sons and their brothers, a traitor who had sided with the enemy and lost the battle by intention. Also, they no doubt enjoyed this chance to revenge themselves on one of the Highborn, who usually have such power over their lives.

"I was to be banished, driven out of the city with only the clothes on my back. While I was in my father's house, my brother, Ebron, came to say good-bye to me. He wished me farewell and good-speed and told me that he loved me still, no matter what had happened. 'I will try to bring your horse tonight, if I can find a way with bribe or friendship to pass the gate. Stay out of sight, but listen for the owl call we used as boys on our late-night adventures.'

"I was deeply touched that he would risk himself that way for me when I had brought such disgrace on the family. My father, on the other hand, made sure to say many times how glad he was that my mother had not lived to see this, how my disgrace would likely have killed her. Not words to gladden my heart, you may be sure. My poor brother, now he must carry all that weight in my place, be both the older and the younger son. I do not envy him his fate." He shook his head sadly. "I doubt I will ever see him again in this world.

"I must say, in the end I was thoroughly weary of all the shame and disgrace being heaped on my head. I only wanted to be gone from there, out of that city and on to some new life, no matter what it might be. Even then I thought of trying to find you again, since, strange as it may seem, you were the only Hadra I could think to trust. I was full of curiosity about this new thing that could challenge the powers of all the Zarns of Garmishair and shake Eezore to its very foundations. Then, just as I was preparing to leave, I was arrested instead and thrown into the dungeon. They must have decided I was a danger as a free man, even as a horseless, ragged beggar. Truth be told, I was surprised they had not done it before.

"Now the talk among the guards was of torture and execution. I tried to make peace with my fate and find some acceptance in my heart, not an easy thing to do, as freedom had been so near. This banishment that is such a terror for others had looked to me like a new life and another chance. In truth, it had looked like freedom. Now they had snatched it away. They left me there for three days and three nights to think on my fate, with only a little food and water and no company but the rats.

"In the middle of the third night, I was awakened by footsteps and low voices in the passageway. By the light of their single torch, I could see several large, roughly dressed men in dark masks. Their clothes were dark as well, so that they seemed to be moving shadows, pieces of the night. They had keys to the cell. As they entered, the largest of them quickly grabbed me in a grip of iron and clamped his hand over my mouth, while another of them said in a low voice next to my ear, 'Make no outcry or we are all dead. Come with us quietly and we will have you out of here.' I had no way of knowing if this really meant my freedom or only a quicker end, but as I was already a dead man, it mattered little.

"How we got out of the city that night is a whole other story that I will not tell you now. I never learned who it was that saved me. Suffice to say that well before dawn I was on my own horse, riding fast away from Eezore. I tried to stay well hidden in the daytime, but two days out of the city, the Wanderers caught up with me and took me to their camp. Later I discovered they had been following me in secret the whole way, making sure the Zarn's men were not on my trail. No doubt Hereschell had some part in all that, and Ebron too. Since then, I myself have become a Wanderer, learning the lessons of the Cerroi and taking the Wanderer pledge. I have also tried to unlearn being a Shokarn — not an easy task, believe me.

"For most of the summer I traveled up and down the coast, going sometimes with the Wanderers and sometimes on my own, seeing many wondrous and amazing things. It was in one of my solitary wanderings that I found this place I speak of and met with the Koormir there."

I could read in Lorren's mind something tangled and troubled about this place, some difficulty with the Koormir, but no details came clear. When I tried to question him, he shook his head, saying, "Wait until you see it, then you can decide." It almost seemed as if he were intentionally blocking my powers in some way.

"How do I know we can trust you? How can I be sure this is not some trap we are riding into? I know you are hiding something."

"I have already stood open under Alyeeta's hands, and you know she would defend you with her life. Please wait, Tazzil, I beg of you. Afterward, I will answer all your questions."

Hearing that, Hayika rode up next to Lorren and said bitterly, "Afterward may be too late. How do we know there is any truth to your stories? How do we know you are not still working for the Zarn?" Katchia joined in with her acid tongue, "What good will answers do after we have ridden into a trap? I have seen many men like you before, all charm and lies." Then Rishka began shouting, "He betrayed the Zarn, he will betray us as well!" And even Maireth joined in, saying, "Why should we trust a man who had orders to burn us alive? Look what men like you have done." She pulled up her shirt. Lorren flinched with pain and turned away. Hayika growled, "We should give him a taste of his fastfire."

I was almost afraid for Lorren. The commotion around us had grown so loud that when we reached a wide space in the road, I called for a halt and spun my horse around to face them all. Kazouri roared for silence. I was glad to hear the angry voices lowered to a mumble. "Off your horses and gather in a half-circle so I can see you," I shouted to them. "I need to say something to all of you." I stayed mounted so they could see me.

Watching them dismount and find their places, I wondered what I would say. I was not Pell, full of witty or compelling words. I had no rousing speech ready. All I knew was that we could not go on this way. The tension was intolerable. Even when they had gathered and were looking at me expectantly, nothing came to mind, so I simply took a deep breath, opened my mouth, and began, letting the words come as they would. "Sisters, Hadra, when I asked who would come with me to make the beginnings of a city for our own people, you are the ones who spoke up. We left not knowing where we were going or what we would find, but you had the courage or the curiosity or the faith or the foolishness to come. I did not question your reasons, though now I think perhaps I should have.

"Now this man has offered to show us a place. This may be a trap, this may mean our death, but I think not. He is a friend of Hereschell's. The Wanderers trust him. Alyeeta finds no treachery in him. Our own powers detect none. Each of us must weigh this matter in her own heart. But I tell you this clearly; no matter what the risk, I am going with him. I need to see this place because it calls to me. I have dreams and visions of it that leave me no peace. I could not turn back now, not even if my life depended on it. How could I ever sleep again? How could I go back and help build the settlement of Ishlair with a good heart, never knowing what we might have had?

"So..." I swept them all with a look. "Now is the time to decide. Those of you who distrust this man and think he means some mischief, this is your chance to turn back and take some other course. Those who still wish to go on with me must do so in good spirit and with no further insult to Lorren. If you stay, let this be an end to your spiteful barbs."

Suddenly, I had also come to the end of my little speech. I could only stare silently at them, thinking they would soon be leaving. They were staring back at me without a word. I wondered if I would be going on alone or almost alone. Surely Pell would come with me, and that meant Tama too. Probably Kara and Vestri would stay with us, and likely Alyeeta as well. Not enough to start a settlement, much less a city. It was clear that Hayika would leave and take Rishka and Zari with her. Kazouri would surely go with Katchia.

It seemed like hours before Hayika stood up slowly, stretched, and said insolently into the silence, "I have never in my life turned back for fear and I do not plan to do so now. And yes, I will try to curb my tongue. I say let us go on and see this place. It had better be worth the ride." Somehow she managed to make even her agreement sound like a threat.

Rishka jumped to her feet with a shout and grabbed Hayika in a hug. Suddenly, the rest of them were on their feet shouting and cheering, as if in some strange way they had all been waiting for Hayika's words.

Pell was grinning widely. She came and clapped me on the leg. "Not bad," she said admiringly. "Not bad at all. Just as I said: they cannot be compelled, but they can be inspired, though they may often test you to the limit." Pell was amused and seemed to think it all good fun. I was dripping with sweat and shaking inside. It was hard work, this game of being leader. I slipped off Dancer's back and almost fell right into Kazouri's arms. She grabbed my arm to steady me. Katchia was standing in back of her, looking very anxious. "Please, Tazzil, do not send me back. I will try to watch my words. Not an easy thing for me to do after all these years, but I will try." She was actually pleading and seemed contrite, almost frightened, not at all like the brash, outrageous Katchia she usually displayed to us.

"Good enough," I said, with a curt nod to her. Then I walked straight up to Hayika and looked her in the eye. "Either accept me as your leader or find yourself another. If you have some game of power to play out, then go play it elsewhere. We have serious work to do." Without waiting for an answer, I walked over to Lorren, who was sitting in the shade, elbows on his knees and chin in his hands, staring dejectedly at the ground.

"I am sorry for that," I told him. "But now, perhaps, there will be some peace."

He shook his head. "Maybe this was all a mistake. I had hoped in this way to undo some of the harm I have done, but who knows if that can ever be. They are right to mistrust me, you know. When I see the burns on Maireth and the others, I..." With a shiver he turned away. "I never understood. I suppose I never really thought of you as people..."

I squatted beside him. "We cannot undo the past, no matter how we wish to. We can only go forward. I want to see this place. I cannot think you mean to betray us, or I would sense it. The others will accept you after a while, as they have accepted Hereschell, but it may take some time."

Since we had already stopped, we ate a quick meal of bread, cheese, and fruit. Afterward, Lorren showed us a path he knew of that led down to the ocean. The water was warmer there than along the northern coast, and we were sheltered from the biggest waves by a long curving spit of black rocks. Shouting and splashing, we all ran into the water, suddenly full of play. As a child in Nemanthi I had learned to swim in the river, but the buoyancy of the sea amazed me. Soon I found myself floating on my back, squinting up at the bright blue sky, and remembering that sometimes life could be very fine.

★

Just as we were something new and strange in Lorren's world, so he was something new and strange in mine; a man who was a scholar, whose head was full of all the facts that filled Alyeeta's books. He had much knowledge of the world, knowledge that I thirsted for. And yes, he charmed me. I had never met a man like him. Certainly none of the boys in my village had been anything like him. I have to admit that it filled me with excitement to ride next to him and hear him speak of far places and other times and even the movement of the stars. He had a vast knowledge of the natural world that he shared with me. As we rode, he told me the names of the birds and trees and plants we passed and little bits of information about each one.

Alyeeta was right, and at the same time she was very wrong. It was certainly not passion of the body, of the flesh, that moved through me. I think no man could have moved me in that way. It is not in my Hadra nature. Nor was it passion of the spirit, for we could not even speak head to head. But there is another kind of passion, a passion of the mind, and that is what we shared. For that moment, it seemed to me as fine a passion as any other. And yet there was a part of him I could not abide, a part that made me angry to the core. I could see it clearly when Hayika said that he would like to pin us to a board to study like bugs. Not knowing the beingness of things — of creatures, of plants, of other humans — he could only look from the outside and never enter the inner realm of another. He was locked forever alone in his own skin, learning, knowing, gathering knowledge, but never truly understanding.

Yet even as I write these words, I remember the charm of those days, of that ride, of that "time between." I knew that when we reached this place, if it was indeed to be our place, then the hard work would begin. Summer was already wasting, and even in this warmer climate, we would have to build some sort of shelters before winter. We would be driven again, though this time by need, not fear. As we traveled, there was this little gift of unclaimed time. Whenever I started to worry about the future, I would have to remind myself to enjoy these days of freedom. The future would come soon enough. So, while I rode forward eagerly into the southland, some little part of me did not want to get there too soon.

Much as I loved the day's ride, evening was my favorite time. After we had made camp and eaten, we often gathered by the fire. One night, drawn by the music and the sound of talk and laughter, I was on my way to join some of the Hadra there when I noticed Katchia among them. I hesitated. At that moment, she was not my favorite person, though she certainly looked very beautiful in the firelight. Wearing a borrowed tunic opened to the waist, she was sitting with her head thrown back, joking, laughing, and flirting with the others, especially Hayika, whom she liked to tease. Just as I was turning to leave, I saw that familiar look of hurt and puzzlement cross Kazouri's face. Suddenly I was angry, very angry. I felt driven to speak to Katchia right then, though likely none of it was mine to say.

Slipping quietly around the edge of the circle, I tapped her on the shoulder. When she looked up at me, her face closed instantly, turning suddenly guarded and sullen. "I need to speak with you," I whispered in her ear. She nodded and rose with a scowl. Though she followed me without open protest, still I could feel her reluctance, the resistance in every movement of her body. I chose a spot not far from the fire where I could still see her face by its light, but could not be easily be heard by the others over the music and the noise. "I need to speak with you," I said again.

"So, what is this about, Tazzil?" she asked mockingly, cocking her head to one side to look at me. None of this was easy to say. As I was trying to gather my words, she winked and nodded. "Ah, yes, I see. No doubt you are angry with me for that little business with the Wanderer. You probably disapprove. But you Hadra are not so pure yourselves, you know. You do all sorts of things decent people would never think of doing."

At those words, I felt the heat of anger rush up the back of my neck. No wonder Rishka found her so maddening. Trying to cool my temper, I asked quickly, "What little business do you mean?" Then I laughed with sudden understanding. "Ah, that business. You know Strathorn would not have paid you, if that is what you mean by business."

"What are you saying, not paid me? I thought Wanderers were supposed to be honest men."

"Wanderers are very honest men. You may trust them above all others. But they do not pay for love. Among Wanderers, love is freely given."

138

"Then their women must all be fools. Why would they give away a thing when someone would pay them for it?"

"They live by a different code, Katchia. They live by the Cerroi."

"And I say again, they are fools."

"No, it is just that they live by a different code. They do not buy love and they do not force it. There is no such thing as rape among them. It would go against the Cerroi to take someone's body against her will. They could not imagine doing such a thing. Where love is never forced or stolen it can more easily be freely given, so when a Wanderer man sees a woman turning on her charms for him, he will likely assume she is making a free choice, not bargaining in coins. And yes, in truth, if you are going to do a trade in men, a Hadra camp with a Hadra lover may not be the best place to carry on your business. But none of that matters enough for me to call you from the fire. It is for Kazouri's sake I wanted to speak with you."

"What has she to do with any of this?"

"She is my friend and I see her hurting. She loves you from her heart. She loves you for yourself, Katchia, not like someone who pays money for the night and only wants your body."

"Love! What is this love?" she asked, with a sudden blaze of anger. "It seems like a very dangerous game to me. The other I know well enough how to play. I know how much to charge, what to give, and what to hold back. But this game of love ... No one has ever loved me for myself before, not even my mother. She would have sold me to the soldiers as a serving-girl and whatever else they needed. Certainly not my father. He claimed he had father's rights and kept me home for his own use till I was old enough to fight him off. Then he turned me out into the streets. No love there, of that you may be sure. Certainly no man who ever put his hands on me has said he loved me for myself. Even if he did, it is not likely I would have believed him." She laughed, but there was no humor in it.

The terrible cutting bitterness in her voice had a familiar sound. It could have been my own voice a year back or Rishka's or even Maireth's. Perhaps she was not so different from us, after all. She was shaking her head. When she went on, she spoke in a more thoughtful tone. "Respect, that I can understand. I had a good head for numbers, and as a bright child, I also learned some of reading and writing letters while running errands in the market. Later, I got respect from the Zarn's men when they saw I had the mind for this sort of thing and could be useful to them. But love? I know nothing of this love. It frightens me. It asks me to put down my armor, to open all the doors. I see only danger there. Where are the boundaries? Where is the safety? You are Kazouri's friend, you speak for her, but who will speak for me? Who will speak for Katchaira the whore? I must defend and protect myself; no one else will. I have learned that much in this life, if I have learned nothing else."

"Katchia, Kazouri would protect you with her life if necessary."

Suddenly, inexplicably, Katchia was crying. She was choking and sobbing, her shoulders shaking and then her whole body. As angry as I had been just moments before, my heart went out to her. I stood awkward and constrained. I wanted to hold her or at least put out a hand for comfort, but I was afraid. With all her talk of Puntyar, how would she take such a gesture? Before I could make a move, she stopped as suddenly as she had started. A strange expression crossed her face, a look of suspicion and craftiness. "What is this love you speak of so reverently? Love this — love that? So much fuss about a word. It is really all a very simple bargain. Kazouri loves my body. In return I have a place among you, some safety and security. Nothing so complicated in that."

I groaned. "Oh, Katchia, you do not begin to understand."

"Really? Well, why not try to explain it to me then?"

I took a deep breath, trying to think how to even begin. Before I had a chance, she leaned forward, eyes glittering with malice, teeth showing in a cutting smile. "All this talk of love turns my stomach, but I can see it really just comes down to money, after all. You had Kazouri chase away my Wanderer just when it might have turned promising, while anyone can see how you keep that captain all to yourself and will not let other women near him. Even raggedy as he is, with his fine clothes, he is likely worth more than other Wanderers. Are you going to tell me you make no profitable bargain there?"

At those words, heat rushed up into my face. "Katchia!" I shouted, so loud that women by the fire turned to look at us. I whirled at her in a rage, my hands balled into fists. Never in my life had I hit anyone. From the time I was very little, I knew I could not do so, but at that moment my hands itched to strike flesh. I had to actually clasp one hand with the other to control them. Probably nothing would have pleased Katchia more than to see me strike myself in an effort to strike at her.

As it was, she was nodding her head, grinning widely. "Aha, so the Hadra get angry just like ordinary mortals." With that, she burst out laughing, very pleased to have gotten to me in that way. She had played me like a fish on a line, and I had bitten hard. Other women were watching. Kazouri was on her feet, about to come over. I saw that more anger on my part would just fuel Katchia's pleasure and perhaps lead to troublesome conflict among the rest of us. Taking a deep breath, I went down inside myself as Alyeeta had taught me, trying to find a calm center, a place beyond the anger.

When I turned back, I looked straight into her eyes and said quietly, "I can see that words between us serve no purpose, or perhaps only serve the wrong one. Better to teach me a new game of cards than to play at words."

Katchia looked back intently, eyes full of challenge, trying to stare me down. Suddenly she shrugged and drew a pack of cards from her sleeve. "Well, why not. It serves to pass the time. I will teach you the game Two Zarns and a Maid. You must watch closely and pay sharp attention. It is a fast-moving game with many swift changes. Come by a lamp so we can see."

We played three hands, and by the end I was just beginning to understand the strategy. She was right about the swift changes: all went by in a rush. After the third hand, my brain was tired of trying to learn and Katchia was tired of trying to teach me. With a nod and few words, we went our separate ways, myself to talk to Lorren and Katchia back to the fire.

I found Lorren sitting at the edge of a bluff that overlooked the vast, dark sea. Pell and Jhemar had just been talking with him. I had passed them on their way to the fire circle. "See if you can cheer him up," Jhemar had said to me with concern. "He is very melancholy tonight. There are heavy things preying on his mind."

Lorren mostly kept apart from the Hadra. Though he had begun to make friends with a few of us, still he no doubt felt the wariness or hostility of the others, the unkind way they shunned him. When he beckoned me to sit by him, I could sense the sadness of his mood, but it seemed that something far heavier than petty Hadra meanness was troubling him. Not wanting to intrude, I made sure to keep a shield between our minds and waited. We sat next to each other for a while, with Lorren brooding in silence as I watched the lovely shifting light reflecting in the water.

The moon was almost half-full. Clouds scudded across her face so that the reflection of her light on the sea shifted constantly, appearing and disappearing, gleaming suddenly and then darkening in the restless water. The soft, warm sea breeze smelled of salt and felt like a caress on my bare arms. It seemed too fine a night for so much trouble. When Lorren finally spoke, his words were so sudden in the silence that they startled me.

"Hereschell told me not to go, but what could I have done? How could I have imagined going against everything I had ever known on the word of one man, one man who was a deaf-mute Wanderer-beggar? Against everything, everything I had ever been taught: my class, my father, my city, my people, my Zarn. Everything! Do you understand, Tazzil? In our little secret talks, Hereschell argued, begged, and pleaded. He even cried, but I said I had to go or I would lose everything in my life. And now, in the end, it has all come to the same thing, but between here and there lie many terrible things, many deaths on my head. If I had known then what I do now ... Ah, but that is every fool's refrain after committing some great wrong. The villages we went through on our way to Mishghall ... The things that were done under my command because that is what men are taught to do ... If I could undo it now, no matter what the cost..."

Horrors from his mind filled my own. I recoiled and shielded hard. With great effort I shut out his thoughts. For just that moment, I truly understood what Jhemar felt in being subjected to the turmoil of other minds. I could think of no way to comfort him for what he had done. He went on, his voice ragged with pain, "I am trying in some small way to make amends, though I know that is not really possible. Most of these women hate me. How can I blame them? It is their right. I understand. Yet I am very glad that I am now a Wanderer, that I do not have to live my life among the Hadra."

I laughed suddenly. "Goddess forbid! That would not make either side very happy." A sudden wave of foreboding went through me. "The Zarn spent so much time in chasing us, when in truth we wanted nothing that was his. I had hoped we could slip away and disappear at this far edge of the world. Now I suppose it will be worse than ever. He will need revenge for Mishghall and for the black toads as well."

"Yes and no. In spite of what I told Pell, the Zarn's desire to be rid of you has little to do with Mishghall. All the Zarns need you gone because your very existence challenges theirs. Absolute power cannot exist in the face of any other power. How can one be a Zarn and rule by unquestioned force when people exist anywhere who cannot be ruled by force? The very fact that there are Hadra in the world throws the power of the Zarns into question. Already things have shifted. Because of you, the surface has cracked beyond repair; the old rules cannot hold. Something new has come into being, a new way, a new time. You do not have to be many or raise an army or march on their cities to frighten them. You have only to exist, nothing more. The very rumor of such creatures is enough to strike fear in their hearts, keep them awake at night, and make them thirst for vengeance."

Alyeeta had said much the same thing to me. I remembered Olna saying once, "Those who cannot be controlled are a great threat to those who must control." I shook my head. "How strange...," I said with wonder, looking down in the moonlight at my hands, my arms, my feet, my very ordinary and familiar self that I had lived with all my life. "How strange is the turning of fate..." I spread my fingers wide and wiggled my toes in the dirt. "How strange that someone I have never seen and am not likely to meet, should find me such a danger. How strange that because my mother and father came together at exactly that moment and no other, I am a threat to Zarns. What do I know of the stars? I am only Tazmirrel, the little Witch-healer from Nemanthi. How can I have such power in the world?" I held my hands up to the moonlight and spread my fingers wide, watching the shafts of moonlight come down between them. "How strange...," I said again, and suddenly a great rush of power moved through me. Without any thought, I said in a voice that did not sound at all like my own, "No matter what the Zarns think or decide or do, we will build our Hadra city."

Lorren stood up suddenly. "Well, then we must get some sleep. If we rise early and keep to a good pace, we will be there tomorrow."

Tomorrow! So soon! Now that the magic "time between" was about to end, I was full of both eagerness and fear. Long after my talk with Lorren, I lay in my bedroll trying for sleep while the moon shifted overhead. Suddenly I thought how, in a way, Katchia was right. Lorren and I had indeed made a profitable bargain, though it had nothing to do with coins passing between us or with the touch and needs of bodies. I wanted the key to understanding his knowledge. In trade, he wanted the key to understanding my being; a fair enough exchange as such things go in the world.

12

In the warm, red-orange glow of sunset, we stood at the very top of the highest of the three hills. An outcrop of bare rock crowned the summit and allowed us a view in all directions.

It was only Lorren and myself. At his insistence, and over many objections from the rest of the Hadra, we had come here alone. He had brought me by a little wooded path barely wide enough for one horse, a way that kept this view secret from my eyes. The path had ended right at the base of the rock. From there, Lorren had led me up the rest of the way on foot with my eyes shut, making me promise not to look until he gave the signal. It was not an easy promise to keep, considering the steepness and roughness of the way. Finally, I could feel flat rock underfoot. As he steadied me in place, he shouted, "Now!" in a voice so full of excitement it made me shiver.

I had opened my eyes and gasped in amazement. There it was in front of me, the very place I had seen so many times in my dreams and visions, wonderfully familiar and yet totally new and unexpected. I turned and turned and turned so I could see it all: the great sweeping curve of the bay; the hills and valleys, partly tree-covered and partly carpeted with fields of green and gold; the river flashing blue and silver below us; the vastness of the ocean, stretching across the horizon and gleaming like burnished copper with the last rays of the setting sun. I kept drinking it in with my eyes as I turned, struck dumb with wonder, silent for so long that Lorren finally asked, "Well, Tazzil, what do you think?" In truth, I had forgotten his existence at that moment.

"Oh, Lorren, it is even more beautiful than I imagined. My visions are like pale ghosts compared to this. This is the place. This is truly the place of my dreams. It must be ours! We must have it! I can see a Hadra city rising on these hills, with our boats in the harbor and our gardens and orchards spreading below us."

"It is not yours quite yet. I was very sure you would like this place, but I needed you to see it first. I needed you to tell me yourself. Now we must set about securing it for you." Under his pleasure there was anxiety, a kind of sadness in his voice that made me turn away from that glorious scene to peer into his face.

"Secure it for us? What is the problem here? What have you not said?" I felt the heat of anger rising in my blood at the very thought that someone might take away this treasure, snatch it out of my hands, that it might not be ours after all. "What do you mean, Lorren? Is there more trouble here than you have told us? What is it you are hiding?"

★

Before reaching our final destination, we had ridden hard all day, stopping no more than absolutely necessary. No matter how inviting the ocean looked for a midday swim or how the groves of trees called to us for an afternoon nap after eating in their shade, we had resisted and pushed on. Lorren and I had set a hard, driving pace. There were many muttered complaints, but no outright rebellion. Even so, it was late afternoon before we reached the formation of standing stones and Lorren raised his hand for a halt.

"No farther, this is close enough. Beyond this point, Tazzil comes alone with me. If she says it is the place, then we must make our bargains with the Koormir. If not, they may have it back and fight to the death over it, if that is what they feel compelled to do."

There was a storm of protest at this. Pell and Rishka each insisted that she be allowed to come with me for my protection, even if no one else could. Kazouri insisted that she should be the one because of her great size, and Alyeeta countered she was best able to guard me with the strength of her spells. She even drew Lorren aside, to speak with him in private or perhaps to threaten him, considering the look on her face.

To all this, Lorren shook his head, saying firmly, "Only Tazzil, no one else. If she says yes, then all of you, and many more, may come. If she says no, then that is an end to it, and you must look elsewhere for a new home." Hayika and Katchia tried to shout him down, talking loudly of trust and traps. Many others joined them. I thought I would never be able to make myself heard over their noise.

Finally, remembering Pell in the march, I stood up on Dancer's back so I could be seen. Then I clapped my hands for silence and shouted, "Stop all this! That is enough! I will go with Lorren this evening and be back with an answer by midday tomorrow. Wait for me here, and have a little trust in this man you have followed for days. Have a little trust in me, as well." Then I slipped back down on Dancer's back and turned to Lorren. "Not another word of argument with them, it is futile. Just ride hard and I will follow." With no more words, Lorren spun around and took off at a gallop, with me riding hard after him. Soon we were racing around the bend and down the road. From behind us I heard Alyeeta shouting, "Man, you had better remember my words. I meant every one of them."

When the road widened, I rode up alongside him. "What did Alyeeta say to you?"

"She threatened my life and my manhood and anything else that I value if you do not come back safely. Oh, yes, she also said she would track me to the ends of the earth if I tried to escape her. She has quite a way with words, that one. Is she as bad as she sounds?"

"Worse," I said with a laugh. "Much worse, so your intentions had better be pure." Then I turned serious. "Lorren, I trust you and I do not trust you. What are you hiding? What has happened in that place? What is this talk of fighting? I sense much trouble there."

"Trust me for a little while longer, Tazzil. Please! Only wait until you see it. Then I will tell you everything. Do not try to pry it from my mind."

I had little choice, since he would not answer and I was too pulled by curiosity not to follow. All I could read in his head was trouble, but none of it came clear.

★

Looking around me now at that wondrous view, I felt consumed with a fever of desire. I knew this was the place for us, the place of my dreams. I wanted it in a way I had never wanted anything in my life before. I felt ready to tear apart anyone who would block my way. When I could pull my eyes away from that sight, I turned to Lorren and said fiercely, "In some strange way, I can even understand why men might want to kill each other to possess this land. Myself, I almost wish I could fight for it with my own hands."

As I said those words, Lorren turned pale and took a step backward. I saw a look of horror cross his face. "Never wish for such a thing, Tazzil! Never! Never! Never wish for the ability to kill. You are lucky beyond compare to be free of the wheel of killing. If I had been like you, my father could never have forced me into the Zarn's army to make a soldier of me. In my work as captain, I have killed men, women, and, yes, even little children when they got in the way of my army. And what of the men under my command? What terrible things have they done that I did not even see but am still responsible for?" Shaking his head, he looked as if he were about to cry. The anguish in his voice went through me like a knife. "I will see their faces and hear their cries for the rest of my life. There is nothing I can do to change that, to bring back those lives, to undo that pain. You cannot know how lucky you are to be off the wheel of killing. You are too young to understand what luck you have."

"Luck!?" I shouted. Suddenly I was shaking with fury. "Is that what you call luck? To have every hand turned against us and a price called down on our heads? Is it luck to be hunted from one end of this land to the other? To be driven out of our homes? To be hated? To be burned alive? Is that what you call luck? What do you know of our lives? You have only been a fugitive these last few months. Before that, you had every privilege Eezore could bestow on you. We have been fugitives almost since birth, cursed by some disturbance of the stars, not of our making. We have been outcasts in our own villages, often in our own homes. Do you think any of us asked to be born under the Great Star? Do you think we asked for this so-called gift, this curse of luck? To you we are only some new toy, creatures to be observed with interest. But believe me, Lorren, we are just as real as you are, our lives are just as real as yours. What do you know of our luck?"

Lorren looked stricken. I felt his pain in my own heart, felt the impact of my words beating against him. He raised his hand, almost as if to protect himself. "But all that is over now, Tazzil. You can have a home, a safe space, and some promised peace, a place to flourish, to become whatever it is you are meant to be. You are young. Things will be better. Soon you will begin to forget all that."

I sighed and shook my head. More gently I said, "I am not a child, Lorren. I can no more forget my horrors than you can forget yours. We each carry our memories and our burdens. I saw my lover murdered before my eyes by the village mob, with even my brother's hand raised against her. I have lost mother, sister, brother, father, my whole village, my home, everything — all in one night. I have had young women die in my arms of burns inflicted by the Zarn's men. I have even killed some with my own hands while they screamed and begged for the mercy of death; these hands that had been healer's hands ... It will be a long, long time, if ever, before I can forget what I have seen."

He was nodding, staring out toward the ocean, silent for a long while. I could still feel his pain vibrating inside me. When he finally spoke again, the sound was so low I had to strain to hear him, but his voice shook with passion. "Tazzil, if you are ever to have peace in this place, you must bring peace to it. If you cannot do that, then for the sake of all that you love and care for, go far from this place to settle. If you cannot bring peace here, then you Hadra will do far more harm with only your feelings than the Koormir can do with all their clumsy weapons."

I came to stand in front of him. "Lorren, now is the time. No more evasions. Tell me what has happened here. You must answer my questions before I can truly answer yours. If you want me to bring peace to this place, then you must tell me what sort of war has been fought here. I can feel it. I can feel it in my bones, at the core of my being. It is as if there is some ancient power here, something strange that wants to force me to pick up a weapon, to strike out, to take what is 'mine,' to get vengeance for all the wrongs that have been done to 'my family,' going back generations. Something here moves my heart besides the beauty of this place. I think there is old bloodshed and anger still here in these rocks and in this soil. I feel the echo of it stirring itself in me."

He sat down on a rock and beckoned me to sit by him. For a while he said nothing. We watched together in silence as the last fiery edge of sun sank into the sea. Finally, he sighed deeply and began, "Yes, it is true, I have been less than honest with you. But I was afraid that if you knew the whole story, you would not even come to see this place. And yes, there is blood and anger here. How could I think you would not feel it, with your Hadra senses? The story is that this land has been fought over by two bands of Kourmairi for three generations or more. Legend has it that it started as a feud between two brothers over a woman, but who knows the truth of those old tales. And what does all that matter anymore?

"The side that won would try to settle the land. The other side, once they had recovered from their defeat, would come to raid and plunder and destroy until they had driven the new settlers out. Then they would settle in their place, and the cycle would begin again. So it has gone for years, back and forth between them, with young men growing up pledged to avenge their fathers and uncles and older brothers, with animals slaughtered, fields burned, houses burned and torn down, women raped, and little children trampled under the hooves of horses.

"Those fields you see are watered with blood. This is one of the fairest places in all of South Yarmald, yet neither side can allow the other to prosper here and there is too much old bitterness for them to even think of sharing it.

"The Wanderers have been trying to make peace here but have had little success. Right now there is an uneasy truce, with neither side living on the land. When I first saw this place, I remembered Hereschell's stories of the Star-Born. I thought in particular of that one Star-Born I had met with face-to-face, the one who gave me back my horse and waved to me and wished me safely gone. Strange as it may seem to you, considering our near-lethal first encounter, you were the only Hadra I could think to trust. When I heard you were looking for a place to settle and make a city, I decided to find you and bring you here. I know of no better place in all of Yarmald."

"Only that it is someone else's," I answered harshly. Anger, grief, and bitter disappointment filled my heart. "You are right, Lorren, I would not have come. It is too cruel to show me this when we cannot have it. The Hadra need peace. We do not need to settle in the midst of someone else's war. We have had more than enough of that already."

"Wait, Tazzil, hear me out. There is more. It is not so simple or so hopeless. The Koormir know they cannot live here, that it only means more death for them. That much they can agree on. We have talked to them of passing it on to the Hadra, if you wanted it. They are thinking on it, meeting among themselves. We have promised to bring their leaders together to meet if you came and wanted to settle here. If they can agree to it, they will make a temporary peace among themselves, at least long enough for both sides to pull back and settle farther up or down the coast.

"It is very likely they will leave you this place. But first you must find the peace in your own heart to make me an answer. And for that you must understand what you are, the power that you have. From you, even wishes to kill can cause harm and disturb the balance."

"Oh, Lorren, who is to teach us what we are and what we can do when not even the Witches know?"

"You will have to teach yourselves, but do it with much care. Great power is not a free gift. It is both wonderful and terrible. If not held with respect, it will destroy better than the sharpest sword."

"Enough! Goddess! Spare me your lectures!" I turned away and began pacing up and down the rocky headland. Lorren was telling me again what Alyeeta had tried so hard to make me understand. "O Mother! Sometimes I grow so weary of all this talk of powers and gifts. I think they are nothing but a burden. Sometimes I would rather be an ordinary mortal and..."

"But, Tazzil, think what..."

I threw up my hands. "Please, Lorren, no more speeches about my great good fortune. I am what I am and cannot be otherwise. You will, no doubt, get the pleasure of observing me along with the rest of these strange new creatures. I assume you plan to settle nearby, to see how we behave. That, I suppose, is to be your reward for this work. In some way we are to be your toys."

"My reward is to stop the bloodshed, to help make peace among the Koormir, and to find a place for the Hadra to settle. I am trying to make up, in some small way, for the great harm I have done; trying to help mend the tear in the Circle, the Cerroi. If I get a chance to watch how you shape yourselves, what you become, then that is a gift indeed, but it is not what I do this for."

After a moment or so I shrugged. "I suppose there are worse things than being bugs under the observation of a Shokarn captain turned Wanderer. It is much better than being roast meat for the Zarn's men. At least you are not trying to burn us alive with fastfire. I should be grateful for that. And we have already survived under the scrutiny of the Witches. You are certainly much kinder than they are."

Sitting down by him again, I put a hand on his arm and said intently, "Lorren, even seeing only this much, I already know I love this place, love it with as much passion as I have ever felt for any woman. I would answer you yes, yes, yes, and yes! We, the Hadra, will build our city here. Gladly would I live here all my life. But I understand there is some other sort of answer that is needed, something that is much harder to say. Leave me alone here for a while so I can give you that answer. Leave me for the night. Darkness is when the earth speaks most clearly to her children, when the Mother comes among us."

"Oh, no, Tazzil, I could not possibly leave you here alone. I have brought you here ... There are hostile men ... I am responsible ... Alyeeta said..."

I burst out laughing at his distress. "Come, Lorren, after all this talk of powers, do you think I am some ordinary girl that you must protect in that way? I will be far safer here alone than you will be wherever you choose to sleep tonight. And do you think this is the first night I have spent sitting by myself in some high place?"

"Forgive me, Tazzil, I meant no offense. I see I have many new things to learn and many old habits to unlearn if I am going to succeed at this new life. Until tomorrow, then." Though he spoke quite formally and even made a slight bow, I saw the corners of his mouth turn up with a little smile.

As he was walking away, I called out to him, "Lorren, if you think we need protection, remind me later to tell you some stories of our adventures on the road." Let him hear what sorts of things we had managed without his help. But, of course, that was for future nights around the fire, after this had all been settled. I shivered as I heard his steps crunching on the rocky ground, but I did not turn to watch him leave. Instead, I sat staring out to sea as if the answers could be found there.

Soon it grew dark, and that lovely land faded away. I sat very still, just where Lorren had left me, trying hard to find some peace in my heart. I sat for so long the moon rose behind me, lighting the water and revealing the shape of the hills. It was so bright that even the trees seemed to come alive; even the shape of my own hand before my face was clear to me.

All this time, instead of finding peace, my hunger for this place grew and grew, as if feeding on itself. That hunger was too full of violence. The longing for violence throbbed and burned in my heart. It barred my way. My spirit shook and ached. Thinking only made things worse. The more I sought to subdue my anger and control my desire, the angrier I became and the more my desire swelled. Yet I knew I must subdue it if I was ever to have what I wanted. No matter how I tried, it seemed I could bring nothing but more turmoil to that place. At last my pride failed me. I saw the riddle was too much for me. "Mother, Mother, help me! Please!" I called aloud to Her. Then I threw myself down on the ground.

Suddenly I was sobbing with my face in the dirt. All in a rush, scenes of the fighting came to me. The flood of feelings that surged through me then was not mine. Those feelings seemed to be coming up from the very ground itself; waves of hatred and the lust for vengeance. Sometimes I was the killer, hot with rage, clearing the way with my sword; the next moment I felt the terror of the dying and my blood was soaking the earth. Death and pain were all around me and nothing else existed. I felt as if years were passing in this way, with no end to the killing and no hope in sight. Everything was gone but this agony, this terrible struggle being fought out against the cold ground. For a long while I lay there thrashing about, caught in the throes of that horror.

At last, after what seemed like hours, the passion wore itself out. A strange calm entered my heart. With no will of my own, I found myself sitting again on my vigil rock. It was as if some large hand had lifted me there. The thinking of my mind had been turned inside out. My riddle was solved. It was not that I must calm the rage of my longing so as to possess that place. Instead, if I could not calm my rage, I must leave that place, so others could live there in peace. It was a simple enough truth, I suppose, and one that Lorren had already tried to tell me several times. I had not been ready to hear it then. Now I saw that I must be fully prepared to leave, for the sake of the land I loved and the Hadra who had followed me there. Otherwise, nothing but disaster would follow.

LEAVE!? Leave this place now that I had finally found it? The pain of loss went through me so sharply that I had to press my hands against my chest. I almost expected to see blood running out between my fingers. No crying came, none of the relief of tears. I pressed that knowledge to me, holding it between my breasts like a knife blade pressing into my flesh. I filled myself with that awareness and my acceptance of it, going so deep into pain that I was no longer conscious of the rock I was sitting on or the sound of the ocean or the light of the moon on everything. I kept going further and deeper into pain, not struggling against it or seeking the escape of tears or rage, when suddenly it released me, letting go of me completely. I could feel my heart again, beating under my hands; hear my breathing and the rush of the waves and the kiri crying; feel the wind against my face and in my hair. Finally, I could feel the wetness of tears on my cheek.

The moon was sinking into the ocean. The whole night had passed. Dawn light was filling the world. I stood up with a groan to stretch my cramped and aching body. I reached my arms up to the sky. Aloud I said, "In Your hands, Mother. I stay or leave at Your will. As it must be." Something had happened to me that night that would change my life. Something had been given and something taken away. It might take me years to fully understand, but at least I had an answer for Lorren.

★

Lorren rode up the hill by the first morning light, with Dancer following. He came by a different path than the one we had struggled up the night before. Some echo of pain from the past night's struggle still rode in me.

I did not rush to meet him or shout my answer but waited quietly on my rock till he came and sat by me. Gently he reached out and brushed the dirt from my face. "Well, you look to have had a hard night. Do you have an answer for me?"

I nodded. "Here is your answer, Lorren. I will never wish another's death, not for this place or any other. If it is the will of the Goddess, and the Kourmairi can peacefully let it go into our hands, then I will gladly live here in peace for the rest of my life. If, at any time, I cannot find that peace in my own heart, then I will go away and live elsewhere." I put my hand over his in the manner of a pledge.

With something like pity in his eyes, he said, "I think those words were not easily come by."

I sighed. "No, it was very hard. When I could not struggle anymore, I turned myself over to the Mother and begged for Her help."

He looked surprised. "I did not think to find you believing in those old superstitious ways. Do you really think some ancient woman the size of a mountain hovers in the sky, waiting to answer your pleas?"

Heated answers rose to my lips, then just as quickly faded away. I took a deep breath. What did it matter? In some things we would never see eye to eye. "I know what I know, Lorren. There is more to this life than can fit between the covers of a book. And what do you believe in — Rha-is, the god of war?"

"Certainly not." He jumped to his feet and began pacing about. "I do not believe in gods any more than I believe in the magic of little black toads. I believe in the natural world. There is enough mystery and wonder there for me, far more than I can learn in this lifetime. As for the rest, the heavens go on their glorious way, with or without our small presence. Some think to search there for signs and omens, portents of their future. If there are gods, I think they have else to do than writing large messages across the sky for us. All we can surely read in the heavens is the weather. Even that is not always clear. We are free to shape our own lives and free to give them meaning. All else is foolishness and self-deceit."

I felt myself losing patience with this speech. "I have found my answers in my own way," I said boldly. "And that will have to be good enough for you." In the realms of the mind, Lorren may have been right, but there were mysteries at the core of life not accounted for in his books, my own powers among them.

His face broke into a wide grin. Nodding, he reached out to clasp my hands. "Something wonderful will come of this, Tazzil, I can feel it."

"Well, whatever comes of this night, it has cost me much. I am worn out and must get some rest." I spoke with some of my old sourness, but it was more in jest. Even so, I had a hard time getting onto Dancer's back.

In silence, we rode slowly down the hill. At times, the mist from the river engulfed us. At other moments, sudden shafts of sun broke through. Each turn of the road brought some new wonder into sight. At first I was floating in a dream of the future, filled with excitement at the possibilities for a settlement and a city. The rocks in that place gleamed white in the morning light, very different from the brick red rocks of the northern coast. I pictured wonderful white buildings rising on the green hillsides, buildings shaped by our own hands with the aid of our powers.

Then, as we rode farther down, I began to see the ruins. Some were of stone, many were of charred wood, and a few looked very recent. There were even some bones scattered on the ground that appeared to be human. Near the bottom of the hill, overlooking the sea, we came on the ruins of a huge stone building that might once have been a meeting hall. Suddenly I noticed a half-buried skull staring back at me, and the reality of all that had happened there swept over me in a rush.

Before I saw them or even heard their voices, I could feel the angry presence of men somewhere on the road before us. I rode up by Lorren to warn him. He nodded and looked tense but did not seem surprised. Finally, we came around a bend in the road and could see ahead of us, blocking the way, a small band of heavily armed Kourmairi men. They were sending out waves of fear and anger.

"That is Garrell, one of their leaders. Let me go first and speak with him." Without waiting for a response from me, Lorren rode forward, calling out, "Good morning to you, Garrell. Remember me? I am Lorren the Wanderer. I come to you unarmed and in peace." He held up his hands to show they were empty. "I ask that you come forward and meet with me in the road." There was a tense moment while the Kourmairi conferred among themselves. Then a young man with a long red scar running down the side of his face rode forward to meet with Lorren. He did not unsheathe his sword, but his visage was surly and scowling. The look he sent in my direction was murderous. I did not trust him with Lorren, yet I had no choice but to sit and watch. To move forward at that moment might only have made things worse and endangered us both.

Garrell stopped a few feet from Lorren. "Why have you brought these Hadra here to occupy our land? You thought to hide them by the standing stones, but our sentries have spied them out. You said you would consult with us first. Now you have broken your word, just as I said you would. How could we have been such fools as to trust a Shokarn?"

"Garrell, I am no longer a Shokarn. The Shokarn want me as little as I want them. I am a Wanderer now, and I keep my word. It is a pledge of honor. No one will occupy this land without your full consent and that of the others. Tazzil is the one who needed to give her answer, and she was already traveling with those others. The Hadra would not let her come alone."

"Is that one Tazzil?" There was scathing contempt in his tone. Under it, I felt his fear pounding like the fast-beating heart of a rabbit. I also felt his anger at being forced to deal with Lorren and especially with me. Clearly, this was not his choice. Now it was time. I rode forward, dismounted several feet away, and walked to meet him with slow, steady steps, never taking my eyes from his face.

From close up the scar was much more obvious, a jagged red line that ran from his scalp down along the side of his face. It went all the way to his chin. The healer in me thought how it could be mended, or at least lessened, though it seemed unlikely I would ever have the chance. Garrell's appearance struck me as a strange mixture of carelessness and pride. His clothes were ragged and filthy but put together in some semblance of a uniform. He sat stiff and upright on his horse, staring straight ahead.

I made a slight nod of my head and said with as much quiet dignity as I could summon, "Good day to you, Garrell. Yes, I am Tazzil. I am a Hadra, one of the Star-Born. Lorren told me of this place and it is indeed very beautiful. I would gladly settle here, but only if there is acceptance from both sides. We will take nothing from another and want nothing that is not freely given. It is not the Hadra way to take from others."

As I spoke, I thought to thank the Goddess or whoever it was who had helped me that night in my struggle. I could not have answered Garrell that way the day before. All my rage would have flared up in his face; all my greedy desire that wanted to take up a sword to possess this place. Now I could answer quietly and feel calm in my heart, though this man might well be the one who stood between me and what I most desired in the world. I held out my hands, palms up. "As it must be," I said quietly and stepped back.

"See that you keep to your word then, Hadra. You may look at the land, but nothing more, not until we have met together and decided." With that, he wheeled his horse around and rode back toward the others. With a shout he rode past them and they all turned to follow, galloping off so fast that in seconds, all that was left was their dust.

"Well, not a very friendly sort. How have you managed to speak to him at all?"

"Not easily, and with a great deal of patience. His father and uncle were both killed in this conflict; you can see the mark of it on his face. He has very little trust for anyone. The Wanderers are the ones who began the process and arranged for this present truce. I could not have done any of that on my own. And perhaps, after all, I even had some help from the Goddess in holding my tongue. Clearly, you did." With that, he laughed and winked at me.

I had a moment of feeling indignant, thinking that he was laughing at me. Then suddenly I was laughing with him, bent low over Dancer's back, swaying back and forth, laughing as much from relief as from humor. I was very glad those men were not still blocking our way.

When we rode back to the place of standing stones, we were greeted by a great shout. The Hadra swarmed all over us with questions. I suppose they had not really trusted Lorren after all. I whispered in Alyeeta's ear that she could unspell him now. As the questions mounted, I made them all come sit around me in a circle. Then I told them, in words and mind pictures, everything I could of that place. I told them what it looked like and what had happened to me that night and in the end, with some reluctance, I even spoke of our encounter with Garrell and his men.

13 There seemed no sense or order to this meeting — and no goal. Men from the opposing camps wrangled on and on. They shouted at one another, made threats, and called out insults to each other's ancestry. The air was thick with menace, as if at any moment heated words might lead to blows or worse. I could not understand what was happening or why we Hadra were there at all. Lorren made no move to create order or to shape a plan. Nor did Conath or Turin, two of the Wanderers who had brought Lorren into our camp and had also helped in setting up this meeting. They simply stood off to the side and watched, nodding and conferring quietly with each other.

The only woman among the Wanderers was a tall, dark woman with a commanding presence named Bathrani. With a swath of bright fabric wound around her head and more of that same bright fabric as a robe, her appearance drew instant notice, even in that tumultuous scene. She must have been more than six feet tall and towered over some of the men. Going back and forth from one side to the other, saying a few words to this one or that one, she almost seemed to be a thread, weaving them together.

When Lorren had brought her to meet me, she had given me a quick, bright smile, her teeth flashing in her dark face. Her hands, when she gripped mine, were full of power. After we met and just before the meeting began, I saw her conferring with Lorren and Olna, heads bent together as they talked intently. At the end I heard Lorren say, "Yes, the women are the key. Go ask the women..." Then I watched as Olna and Bathrani went out among the women, but I had no idea what they hoped to accomplish. Among the Koormir it is clearly the men who have the power, not the women. When I asked Lorren, all he would say was, "Trust me a little longer, Tazzil."

Now, listening to these men go on and on, my small store of trust was fast running out. The day was growing hot, there was little shade, and the noise of angry male voices was scraping on my nerves. They sounded like wrathful bees whose hive had been broken open.

The Hadra around me were growing restless and casting accusing looks in my direction. The Witches, Alyeeta and Telakeet, were off to one side, muttering to each other. After some particularly loud exchange of insults between the Kourmairi, Telakeet raised her voice and spat out contemptuously, "Men! They are still just as I remember them, more quarrelsome than the Hadra at their worst and far more trouble than they are worth. If this is any example, then I thank the Goddess for keeping me clear of them most of my life."

With a grin full of malice, Alyeeta leaned forward and answered, "They do have their uses at moments, Telakeet, even you would have to admit that. Or have you forgotten?" Telakeet's furious reply was lost to me in the uproar. Personally, I could see no good outcome to this meeting.

As there were no buildings of any size left standing, we were meeting in a wide cleared space next to the river, a space big enough to have been an Essu ground. There were several hundred Koormir in that clearing, so if they had decided to attack us, we would have been hard put to defend ourselves. It seemed a lot to trust our safety to four Wanderers, though at the moment most of the Kourmairi's animosity was directed toward each other, with little attention left for us.

Lorren had gone ahead of us that morning, to meet with the other Wanderers and arrange for this gathering. A large circle of stones had been laid out in the center of the clearing with a line drawn through the middle of it. Norn's clan had gathered on one side of this circle and Garrell's on the other, with the men at the front and the women and children to the back. A space had been left at one end of the circle for us to sit between the warring parties. We were all there except for Olna, who was off with Bathrani on her own mysterious mission, and Zheran, who had jumped up with a sudden exclamation of surprise and vanished among the women of Norn's tribe.

It seemed that some agreements had been made, for the men appeared to be unarmed and they remained sitting — at least most of the time. The women, on the other hand, were free to move about at the back of the circle, tending to the children and the cookfires, as long as they stayed out of the opposing camp. They were not, however, above trading insults with each other across the line or shouting out their own litany of wrongs.

When this listing of grievances and shouting of threats and abuse had gone on for two hours or more and I was ready to faint from heat and thirst, Lorren called out loudly, over the turmoil, "Are the women ready?" I could hear Olna answering from the back like some distant echo, "No, the women are not ready yet." I had no idea what manner of thing was being planned. Though I was nominally leader there, it seemed no one had seen fit to tell me. Numb and despairing, I listened as the wrangling went on again, though with less force and energy. The men were beginning to repeat themselves. There was a kind of weariness in their voices, as if all that rage had taken its toll and could not be maintained at such a pitch. It made my head ache and my ears ring. The whole thing seemed pointless and useless, almost beyond endurance.

Suddenly, just as I was about to leap to my feet shouting, "STOP!" I felt a strange sense of presence in back of me. I looked up to see Bathrani standing there, tall, quiet, and very powerful. One by one, the men noticed her and stopped talking. When there was total silence in that place, she said in a commanding voice, "The women are ready to speak now."

Instantly, men leapt up to protest, and for that moment, at least, they were united. "Our women do not speak for us." "They cannot make the peace, since we are the ones who do the fighting." "Kourmairi women do not tell their men what to do." "Women have no place in the councils of men." Many other such things were said. There was amazing agreement between all those men, who only moments before had been ready to hack each other to pieces. At last, Turin beat on a pot that Olna had passed to him and shouted, "Sit down, all of you! That was our agreement, that you men would remain sitting."

Grumbling and muttering, the men sat down again, with obvious reluctance. When Lorren could make himself heard, he said in a voice full of mockery and challenge, "I think you are afraid of your women. You are afraid of what they will say, and so you shout them down. Is that how brave men act?"

There was more muttering to that, until Garrell spoke out angrily, "What are you saying? I have never been afraid of any woman's words." His jaw was clenched and his scar had turned an angry, throbbing red.

Norn, not to be outdone, said the same, adding, "Let them speak, what harm can it do? It is still our decision to make." There was a weight of weariness in his voice.

Then Olna called out to Bathrani, "Is it time now?" And Bathrani answered, "Yes, it is time."

The last time I had noticed the Kourmairi women they had been in opposite camps, glowering at each other, cursing, spitting, and jeering. Whatever had happened among them had certainly not caught my attention. Now they came into the meeting with Bathrani leading them, her head held high and her walk slow and solemn. The women came quietly, walking single file behind each other, every other one from the opposing clan. They walked down the dividing line itself, entering the circle from the side opposite ours. When they had entirely filled that space, they all sat down as if at a signal.

Now the men were in an uproar. Lorren raised his hand, taking some power in that meeting for the first time. "Quiet!" he shouted, trying to make himself heard. "You men have had your say and your say and your say all day long, for whatever it has amounted to. And what have you accomplished? Can you say you have made peace? We are no closer to any kind of agreement than when we started. Let the women speak. You have agreed to that, and you must honor your word or you disgrace yourselves before them." He turned to the women. "Are you ready?"

Tenairis of Zelandria rose with difficulty, aided by two other women. She was stooped and leaned on a stick. Her voice quavered with age, but she had the fierce visage of a hawk as she stared straight ahead. "We are ready," she said with a nod. "Each of us who needs to speak will stand in turn to say what she has to say. We will speak what is in our hearts as we are moved to do so. We have agreed that we will not interrupt each other's words. I have been asked by these others to begin, as I am the oldest here and have likely seen the most killing."

She looked all around the circle, then took a deep breath and began, "We say the fighting is over. This is the end of it! It has gone on long enough! Cede the Hadra this place, where so many of our people have died; let their bones rest at last. Perhaps these strange new women can make an island of peace between us, for clearly you men cannot. There is more land up and down the coast and unclaimed land down the river. We need a place where we can raise our children without fear, where our homes will not be burnt down over our heads. If you cannot make peace today and abide by it, then do not come back tonight to your beds. You will find no welcome there. You may beat us, you may even kill us in your anger, but we will not turn from that. You cannot do much worse than you have already done.

"As for me, I oppose any continuation of this fighting. If it goes on, I intend to get in the way however I can. You may break all my old bones if it pleases you, for your hands are certainly stronger than mine and you have weapons. Death might even be welcome, after all I have seen. How can you hurt me more than you have already hurt me with your war? My old husband is dead, my son is dead, my beautiful granddaughter wanders among us maimed and witless. I could go on and on, but let the other women speak. I say this is enough!" She banged the ground with her stick. "ENOUGH!"

"Enough!" "Enough!" "Enough!" The women around her echoed her words like a strange, rough chorus as Tenairis sat down again. I shivered and chills went up my back.

Next, Raylia of Indaran stood up and said, "I am with Tenairis in everything she says, but I will speak my own grief here. I saw my sister violated, raped and murdered before my eyes, by men who were my mother's cousin's sons, men who should have been her suitors, not her killers. We need an end to this, before we are all dead. Then who will care what clan we come from or what grievances we carry? The birds-of-death do not care, they feast."

Another woman stood up. She was gaunt and thin, with a strangely ravaged face. I could feel the tension among the men. They even seemed to draw together, in spite of their enmity. There was some muttering among them, and one even blurted out, "No, not again! I do not want to hear it again."

Bathrani said firmly, "Let her speak."

But this woman did not speak. Instead, in terrible silence, she looked around at the men, one by one, until all eyes were on her. Then, with no word spoken, she slowly raised the sleeve of her tunic with her left hand. There was no arm there. The man who had spoken before cried out, "No! Enough! Stop!" She turned a mirthless grin on him while she continued raising the sleeve till it reached her shoulder. There was a raw, red stump where her arm should have been. Slowly she raised that stump and pointed it all about, as if it spoke for her. Then, still moving slowly, she lowered her sleeve again, bowed to the men, and took her place. The man who had called out turned away and staggered off, retching.

After a moment of silence another woman rose and cleared her throat. "Few women marry for love. I was one of the lucky ones. Now, for this piece of ground, my man is dead. Warriors, what will you give me to ease that loss? Vengeance? Another killing? Another mother's son dead? Another woman's husband murdered? Will I rejoice in her grief? Will it heal mine? I do not want a dead man's body. I want my own man home in my arms. I want back the years of living together that we will never have. You have stolen them from us with your fighting. What can you give me with your bloody hands that has any worth in my life? STOP! STOP!" Screaming that word, she threw herself down on the ground and beat the earth with her fists. Women gathered around to comfort her as she wailed and thrashed about.

Then Garrell's young wife, Friana, leapt to her feet. She held a baby to her breast. "I say to the men of my clan: If you cannot make peace this day, then I will go to live in Sierran's house and be her sister there. If you come to kill her and her sister and her children and her man, I will stand in the doorway with my baby in my arms and you must kill me first, you who are my uncles and my brothers. You must kill me first, my husband." There was a gasp of horror from some of the listeners.

Now more women stood up quickly, one after the other, while other women echoed their words with cries and moans and wails. "Let the Hadra have it. I must have some peace in my home. What use is this place to us?" "This has become a killing ground and the Goddess has abandoned us." "What use is a war that cannot stay won?" "My old father died in my arms with blood bubbling on his lips. I ask you, what harm had he ever done to anyone? What had he ever done besides be a good man and a kind man and a wise voice in the village?" "Before this last round of fighting started, I had three children. Now two of them are dead and one is blind. Tell me, warriors, what kind of glory can I find in your war?" Now the moaning and keening were louder. Women were shouting, "Yes! Yes! Enough! No more!" Every time men tried to interrupt, Lorren or one of the other Wanderers would say, "Wait, they have not finished yet, and you are pledged to listen." When one man grabbed angrily for his wife, Bathrani stepped quickly between them and several women shouted, "Shame! Shame!"

Finally, there was a long moment of silence, as if this part were done. The women were looking at each other, waiting for a signal to end, when one last woman stood up. She was of startling appearance, very tall for a Kourmairi and with skin no darker than a Muinyairin. That in itself was not so strange, for though the Shokarn have contempt for us, they also mix with us, as is the way with men. It was her deep red hair — darker than potter red, a straight, bright, shimmering fall of bronze — that caught the eye and made her so noticeable. It was also her extraordinary beauty.

She stood up to her full height, with none of that slight stoop at the shoulders that so many Kourmairi women have. If someone had said this was the Goddess Herself in earthly form, I could easily have believed it. At that moment, I might even have been tempted to throw myself at her feet, begging for help and guidance. But in spite of her appearance, this woman was all too human. Though she was tightly controlled, still I could feel waves of pain and anger emanating from her. When she spoke, a quaver of passion resonated in her voice.

"I, Yolande, renounce the Koormir and will return to the Wanderers if they will have me. You have been my people since I was two years of age, but there is nothing left to hold me among you. My old foster mother is long dead. My daughter, Eirilyne, was killed in your fighting. Like Denairi, I had the rare luck to marry a man I loved and who loved me in return. He is dead now, a gentle, caring man who was killed trying to make peace among you. You called him a coward because he would not fight, but he was the bravest man I ever knew. Now he is gone, and for what? There is no man among you I could be with. You all have his blood on your hands. I say give this land to the Hadra. They cannot do worse than you have done."

Then she turned and fastened the intense stare of her gray-green eyes on Lorren. "I hope you, at least, are an honorable man with no blood on your hands. I need to find someone I can trust who is not a killer." Then I heard her inner words as clearly as if she had spoken aloud, *These Hadra are too strange for me.*

At the same moment, I saw Lorren's stricken face as he blushed deeply and turned away. *Would that it were so,* I heard him say in his head.

When Yolande sat down again, there was a loud groan from among the women and several voices called out, "Stay with us, Yolande." "Do not leave us." "We are your family, your sisters."

At last it seemed as if all who wished to had spoken. Not one woman had wanted to exact vengeance or to continue the fighting. Finally, after a tense silence, Olna stood up, saying, "If all the women have had their say, we should..."

"Wait!" One more woman stood up. There were gasps of surprise. She was Norn's wife, Segna, wrinkled and bent, almost as old as Tenairis.

"Those who know me know it is not my way to speak in public places, but now I feel I have no choice. Listen with care, for I will not say this again. If the fighting does not stop, I will turn my back on this place and on all of you. I will walk away into the desert, to live alone there or to die, but I will not live among you anymore. I will not be part of this killing one more day. Look around you, Kourmairi, those of Zelandria and Indaran both. If you can sit in a circle and talk with no sword raised, then you can sit in a circle and make peace. Now I have said what I need to say and I am done." She gave a nod to the circle and sat down abruptly. No other women rose to speak. There was a long, shocked silence, even among the men.

It was over. The women had been given their say. Finally, Friana stood up, still with her baby in her arms. As she rose she began to sing in a sweet, clear voice. It was an old lullaby my mother had sung to me:

Safe in your mother's arms,
Soft as a dove,
Sleep, my sweet baby,
In comfort and love.

One by one, the other women rose and joined in the singing. They did not go in single file this time but walked out together with the two clans intermixed, the old ones leaning on the younger ones, all singing that lovely lullaby. Gradually the Hadra joined in. Together our voices rose and fell, swelled and diminished, women's voices weaving over and through each other until it was one great sound like the sighing and moaning of the sea. The old stone walls of the ruined shelter above us seemed to echo with our song.

At last Norn stood up and said wearily, "Let it be as my woman says. I have never heard her speak before on such matters. Let it be as she says. She has shaken me to my soul." He was shaking his head as he sat back down. Almost as if to himself, he added, "I thought all the games had been played out long ago. Perhaps, after all, there is something new in this world."

With rage contorting his face, Garrell leapt to his feet, shouting, "You killed my father, old man! Do you expect me to forget that so easily?"

"And you killed my son, with all his bright shining life ahead of him. I will never forget it, not as long as I live. But will it bring him back if I kill you? Will your mother's tears ease my heart?" Norn was shaking his head again. "Oh, how I am weary of all this. Garrell, we are being offered an honorable way to end this feud between us. I say let us take it while we can. We may not get another chance. Besides, our women are rebelling. They are telling us that if we keep on fighting, we do so alone."

Garrell spit with contempt. "Will you let women's words lead you like some snot-nosed child?"

"I have already answered, let it be as my woman says. You had better heed your own wife's words before some greater sorrow comes to you from this."

Suddenly, Lorren's voice was heard above the others. "Tell us, Garrell, which will it be, peace this day or will you go on killing each other till none of you are left?"

At almost the same moment, Friana called out, "Garrell, please ... I meant every word I said."

Garrell was surrounded by a group of young men, the same ones we had encountered with him on the road the day before. Some of them were muttering angrily and one leaned toward him and said with contempt, "Will you let your will be bent by this cowardly Shokarn traitor in the guise of a Wanderer? He has lost his own battle and been disgraced, stripped of rank and uniform by his people. Now he has come crawling here to us with his plots and his plans. Why should we listen to him?"

Lorren did not flush with anger as I expected him to, but before Garrell could respond he asked quickly, "Garrell, if you have a better plan, say it now and we will all listen."

Garrell muttered and mumbled, looking down at his feet, shifting from one to the other. At last he said sullenly, "I am used to doing, not to speaking. No, I have no better plan. Let it be as the women say. Let the Hadra have this land. It is already soaked with our blood."

"Done," Norn answered instantly. "I will take my people north, to the next fork on the Escuro if you will take yours south to the next bay on the coast."

Then Lorren called out, "Is there any man here who speaks to continue this old war?" Though the young men around Garrell shifted about and glowered at Lorren, none stepped forward or spoke up. "Good," Lorren went on after a pause. "You should both shake hands on this and make a pledge besides. Then you, Garrell, need to take your hotheaded young men away with you. There must be no reprisals, no raids, no killings. You and Norn are each responsible for that on your honor and will have to punish any who break the pledge. Your men should not meet or mingle together in any way during this next year. Let messages be carried by your women or by the Hadra. Let any trading be done by them or by the Wanderers. Then, in a year, if there has been no killing and no breaking of the pledge, you can meet together, some trading can resume, and we can begin to see what can be mended out of all this horror."

The Wanderer Conath stepped forward to say, "Before we are done here, Garrell and Norn, you both must bring your swords before the Hadra and pledge your peace to them in the style of your people."

Looking solemn and very tired, Norn stepped up to retrieve his sword from the pile of weapons. When he stepped back, Garrell came forward with a scowl to hunt for his. After they were both armed, they stood there awkwardly, staring at each other. Suddenly Alyeeta emerged from the crowd. She swung her pointing fingers around at all the men, ending with Norn and Garrell. "You had best mean what you say and remember to abide by it, for there are strong spells here to bind you and much ill luck for any who does not keep his word." She had been so silent through all this that I had almost forgotten her presence and was amazed to hear her now. I felt a little shiver of fear go through the crowd like a sharp cold breeze passing over hot skin.

Norn turned toward her, bowed his head slightly, and held out his sword as if to lay it down before Alyeeta. "Lady, I would be only too glad to end..."

"Make no pledges to me, old man," Alyeeta said quickly, taking a step back. "I am a Witch, not a Hadra. If you wish to make pledges of peace, make them to the future, not the past. Pledge to her," she said, pointing at me. "She is the one who brought us here. This land speaks to her more than to any of the rest of us. It speaks to her even in her dreams. Pledge to her and through her, to the Hadra. And also pledge that peace to each other."

This seemed more weight than I could bear. I felt suddenly confused and uncertain and terribly young. Wanting to go look for Pell, I started to shake my head. Alyeeta gave me a look that fastened me to the spot. Then, in that commanding voice of hers, she said, "Step forward, Tazmirrel of Nemanthi. These men have serious business with you. All of us will be witness to their words." I stepped forward, trying to control my shaking knees. I told myself to stand tall, as I had seen Yolande do. I tried to keep in mind Bathrani's straight, proud form.

Norn hesitated. He might rather make obeisance to a woman grown old in wisdom than be forced to make it to such a young one. I watched him gather himself, all of his strength and all of his dignity. At last he bowed to me. "Khal Hadera Lossien," he intoned solemnly. His voice thundered out in the clearing. Perhaps it was easier for this proud old man to make his pledge of peace to what sounded like a great and powerful people rather than to a green girl of hardly nineteen years. For me, it was certainly easier to accept for the Khal Hadera Lossien than in my own name. "We Kourmairi pledge to fight no more in this place," Norn went on. "We promise you peace here, and we will help protect it. May these hills, this river, and this bay be your home from now on and become your city in the future. On this promise, I give you my hand and my sword." With those words, he held out his sword to me. I took it with trembling hands. Then he stepped back and looked expectantly toward Garrell.

Garrell stood staring off into the distance. He was silent for so long I thought he meant to withdraw his pledge. Then, not to be outdone, he suddenly held out his sword to me, saying quickly, "Hadra, I pledge you peace in this place, a peace we promise not to break, a peace we will help maintain even against the Zarns' armies, if need be. I and all my people pledge you this. Let there be no more Kourmairi blood shed in this place." The words themselves were fine, but I sensed his grudging consent, felt the bitterness in his heart. In his head I heard him say, *Only because I must. Only because I have no choices left to me.* At that moment, I could almost feel sorry for him.

As I stood looking down at those two swords in my hands, swords that had taken many lives, I tried to think what this meant for me and for my people and for our future. Suddenly there were tears running down my face. Without even giving it thought, I said, "And in return we pledge you our help in keeping this land safe from the Zarns." It was not for myself or in my own name that I accepted those swords, nor even for the Hadra who were with me that day, but for others in the future, for what would be built here, for what we could not yet see or know. For that I accepted their pledges.

Somehow I trusted Norn, with his hard, old pride and his obvious grieving; somehow I understood him. Garrell I could not read so well. I saw a mix of things in him that did not sit easy with each other, that, in fact, quarreled and shifted about, so that I could not be sure who I was speaking to. Just as I was thinking that, one of the young men who were Garrell's followers leaned forward and said some words in his ear. He straightened and his expression changed. Looking directly at me, he said, "If you are to live between us in this way, we must come to some understandings. You must not be a corrupting influence on our women. Any Kourmairi woman who leaves her man for your settlement must be honorably returned to us." There were cries of outrage from the Kourmairi women, shouts from the Hadra, and muttered agreement from the men, even those on opposing sides.

I was caught off guard, so flooded with anger as to be rendered speechless. Pell, who had kept her distance from the whole procedure, suddenly sprang into place beside me. With a slight smile and no show of anger at all, she said, "Thank you, Garrell, for pointing out this flaw in our agreements. Pledges of peace have been made, but clearly, we have more to speak of, if we are to be good neighbors. Things have changed with the freeing of Mishghall by the Hadra. Just as the Shokarn can no longer lord it over the Koormir, so men can no longer lord it over their women. Your women must be free to come and go, just as you are. If any of them wishes to live among us, she should be allowed to do so. We could no more return an unwilling woman than you could return a Kourmairi slave to the Shokarn master. I could not, if my life depended on it, force a woman to go back against her will, nor could any Hadra. That must be understood between us if there is ever to be peace here."

Garrell's rage was barely held in check. "Then this is not a valid pledge. I would never have agreed to such a condition."

Lorren was nodding as if accepting the truth of this. "Do you wish to go back on your pledge, Garrell? If so, we must call the women back and begin again."

The look of fury on Garrell's face chilled my heart, but he said quickly, "No, let it stand as it is. Enough of all this talk. I will take my people and go south."

Norn nodded. "And I will take mine and go north up the river. Perhaps when we meet again, we can talk of trading and crops and weather instead of making war on each other."

The two groups began rapidly loading their horses and wagons and moving out. Lorren beckoned to me. I followed him up to the old ruin. From there, we could look down on the scene of departure. We watched for a while in silence, standing so close together I could hear his breathing. I was in a turmoil of feelings: joy that the meeting was finally over and the land safely ours; grief for all the suffering and death that had made this possible. Suddenly Lorren turned to face me. "Well, Tazzil, we have won a great victory today, you and I, and no one has been vanquished. That is the kind of victory I like."

I saw in my mind Garrell's sullen, angry face and was not quite so sure. "Were you not angry at what Garrell's man said of you?"

"Why should I be angry? It was all the truth. Everything that man said was true, only he and I have a different view of it. He sees it as a disgrace. I see it as the lifting of a great burden. It is true that if you count the Zarn as my master, then I am indeed a traitor. I threw away that battle and will fight no other for him. And yes, I have been stripped of rank and uniform and all else the Zarn and his followers think worthwhile. For me, it is a blessing. If only I had my books here. That is the one thing I miss, the one thing I valued from all that. Poor Garrell. He muttered and mumbled and made resistance, and in the end he said what we needed him to say. How can I be angry at him or any of his men? I got exactly what I came for."

I laughed, suddenly understanding. All through the meeting, I had thought that Lorren had no power or control, that he had simply let it follow its own course. Now I understood that he had been the dance master. We had all danced to the steps he had designed. From the very start, he had held to a plan. Every step had moved in us in that direction, though not always in a straight line.

"You will have much clearing to do here," he said, gesturing around with his hand. "It might have been well to ask them to stay and clear up their own rubble, but they are still too new to the ways of peace. They need some time to forget their quarrels."

"And perhaps we can make use of some of it. This, for instance, this would be a fine building, with the walls topped and the roof repaired." Suddenly, I was looking out of a window at a vast, colorful gathering in the meeting field. It was almost like an Essu. There were ships on the water and I could hear the sounds of music and laughter. I could not tell if it was the future I was looking into or the past. In the next moment, I was once again standing beside Lorren in that long-abandoned ruin of stone.

"Lorren, tell me again why you offered us this place. Tell me so I can really comprehend it."

"For many reasons, but to begin with, you must understand that I did not offer it to you. It was not mine to offer. I only asked you to come and see it. In the first place, because the Koormir could not surrender it to each other. No good could come of their being here, only more bloodshed and killing. Neither side could hold it long. They needed a buffer to keep them from doing the work of the Zarn's guards and destroying themselves. A few Wanderers coming and going could not make a lasting peace. And in the second place, because I love this place in ways I cannot explain to you or even to myself. I wanted to see it well settled and even loved. And in the third place, and perhaps most important of all, because I wanted to see the Hadra settled in some safe place where you could flourish and become whatever it is you are meant to be. You have work to do in this world that I barely comprehend and you, yourselves, are only starting to understand."

"And you want to watch."

"If I am allowed to. It is altogether your choice whether or not you wish to be my friend and let me into your lives."

"And if we asked you to leave, would you do so, even though you have made all this possible?"

"Yes, of course. Tazzil, I have no hold on you. I have done what I came to do. There is no price on it. There never was."

I stood staring out at the ocean. The sun was beginning to sink. The day was cooling. The field below us was almost cleared, with only the wispy smoke from a few cookfires to signal all that had happened there. Most of the Kourmairi had already left. In the distance I could see some of the Hadra, exploring their new home. Suddenly my heart ached at the thought of losing Lorren from my life. But I had needed to hear him say he would go if we asked, that we owed him nothing. Once he said it, I knew how much I would miss him, how much I did not want him to leave. I reached out my hand. "Stay and settle near us. It saddens me to think of you gone. I feel that you and I will be friends for the rest of our lives. And Lorren, please, find a way to get your books. We will have need of them here."

Lorren let out a deep sigh. I understood then that he had been holding his breath against what I would say. I smiled at him in the fading light. "So we both had to be ready to give up this place in order to have it," I said aloud. To myself I thought, *No matter what he thinks, the Goddess has been at work here today.*

14

All of the next day was spent exploring this place the Kourmairi had alternately called Zelandria or Indaran, depending on which clan was occupying the territory. We had examined the ruins of the meeting house with thoughts of reconstructing it, clambered over the burnt-out carcasses of boats to go swimming in the bay, and walked out to the end of the long curving spit of land that protected the bay from the thundering surf. Like children, we had waded back and forth across the Escuro, shallow now from summer's dryness, just to be on the other side. Then we had climbed all over the first two hills, making plans for what we would build there. For me, the reality of what we had gained was finally eclipsing the visions in my head.

Late that afternoon, I led the others up the third hill to the lookout rocks, the first place Lorren had shown me. Driven by eagerness and impatience, I went straight up the front rather than taking them by the longer, gentler way that had no view. Pell was right on my heels. "Tazzi, we have to decide what to call this place, now that it is really ours." Her voice was full of excitement, but she was panting from the exertion of struggling up the steep path. Josleen and Hayika groaned, as did several others. "That means at least a three-hour argument," Vestri answered sourly. "At least," Maireth echoed. "Count me out of it," Jhemar said emphatically. "I have heard enough Hadra arguments to last me all my life. They hurt my head. I am willing to call this place by whatever name you all decide." I kept my silence, too filled with joy and wonder to even think of arguing. Jhemar was right. Let them call it whatever they pleased as long as no one thought to take it from us.

We had left our horses below, as there was no room for all of them on that rocky top. Alternately grumbling about the steepness and exclaiming about the view, we reached the top both weary and elated. At that moment, only Hadra were with me. Alyeeta, Olna, and Telakeet had left with Raylia of Indaran to do some healing work. Zheran had seen a long-lost cousin among Norn's clan and gone off to visit with her for a few days. Much to my surprise, Katchia had stayed behind, talking earnestly with Yolande and Bathrani by the ruins of the old meeting hall.

Pell went immediately to the very top and stood looking out, so close to the edge that my stomach clenched and the soles of my feet ached. "Zelindar," she said abruptly. "We can put together their two words, Zelandria and Indaran, and make it ours. Zelindar!" She was nodding, clearly pleased with herself. I could hear other Hadra mumbling the word, trying it out. When I heard Rishka repeating it with no rancor, I knew instantly that it was the right name. The new Hadra city would be Zelindar, perhaps the only time we would ever name something without an argument. *Zelindar,* I whispered softly to myself. The word seemed to echo up from the land below.

Then Pell was stretching out her arms. "Ours! All ours! Three hills, the valleys between them, a river, and an ocean, all ours, a home for star-brats, a final stopping place for this ragged and mismatched collection of thieves, beggars, Witches, and hunted fugitives. Zelindar! Well done, Tazmirrel. You got us here. It was worth every hardship." Then she turned and fixed me with her intent stare. "But now, let me tell you, girl, I, for one, will not travel one more step down that road. If this place does not please you, if it is not good enough, if you want to go on any farther down the coast to settle, then you must go alone. Or, at least, without me."

"No, no, Pell," I said quickly, shaking my head. "I am done with traveling, at least for the moment. This is the place that called to me." In my head, I heard the word *home* echoing like the sound of a great drum.

Tama came up and put her arm through Pell's. There were tears in her eyes. "Is it over? Can we stay? Can we finally make a home together? After all these years, is this the end of running?" Then she pulled on Pell's arm. "And come back from that edge, Pellandria. I could not bear to lose you now to foolishness."

Pell laughed. "The end of running, Tama, I promise you. And no, I do not plan to go tumbling off that edge." She stepped back and put her arms around Tama. "The end of being fugitives, my love. From now on, we are Hadra. We are a power here. We have saved Mishghall, freed the coast from the Zarn's weight, made peace among the Koormir, and claimed a space for ourselves. We can do anything we set our hearts to doing."

Clearly, Pell could still stretch the truth, thief-style. Oh, well, what did it matter? Soon enough, those would be the stories told of us. Probably even now that was the talk. I stepped up on the other side of her and stood staring down, spellbound. Finally, I said, "Can you see it too? The buildings and the flowered terraces and the cobbled walks and the...?"

"And gardens full of summer foods, such as we grew in Darthill?" Ozzet had stepped up beside Tama.

"And fields of grain, there on the plain between the river and the sea," Zenoria added, pointing toward the Escuro.

"Boats," Josleen said with excitement. "Boats filling the bay with their bright sails, so we can go up and down the coast with ease."

Suddenly all of us were standing together at the edge, speaking our dreams. Jhemar talked of shelter for the horses, and Rishka and Zari of having enough grass for them to eat and the peace for them to graze their fill. Kara and Vestri spoke of building a pottery and taking apprentices, to fill the needs of this city we were dreaming into existence. Kara was staring out, speaking as if in a trance, "I will be more than a potter. Shaping bowls and plates is not enough for me anymore. There is something else calling to me, filling my heart, aching to fill my hands. I will make statues of the Goddess for women's houses and for our Central Circle. I will make a huge statue, even finer than the one in Mishghall, when we build our House-of-the-Mother here. I can already feel the clay taking shape under my hands."

Shartel said that when the time came, she would go live among the Koormir of Mishghall to learn metalworking and glassmaking, as she already had some skill at those things from the Muinyairin. Maireth said we should mend the ruin by shore and make it a healing house, I said a meeting house, and Kazouri said both. Ozzet and Mouraine each spoke of boats, on the bay and on the river, and how we must learn to build them.

Kilghari spoke with surprising passion, saying, "I want to build my-self a hut here and live in it all my life. I have had enough of being a wanderer and a fugitive!" Even Hayika joined in. "I want a place that I can always come back to, no matter how far I wander, a place where I am known and welcomed." It was more words than I had ever heard her say that were not spoken in anger. Josleen and Megyair talked of leaving in a few days, as soon as they were rested, to spread the news that we had found a place. They would try to bring back other women. Hopefully they would also bring back badly needed supplies: tools and seed and cloth and food.

As we were on our second or third round of wishes and visions, Pell threw up her hands. "So much work! Just speaking of it all makes me weary. Let us enjoy this last evening of leisure together. Tomorrow is soon enough to start. Then Tazzi is sure to drive us hard and with no mercy." With a deep sigh, she sank to the ground and stretched herself out on her back. Tama sank down beside her. She pulled Pell's head into her lap and began weaving a crown for her from the tiny blue-green flowers that grew all around us on that rocky hilltop.

One by one, the others sat down or stretched out, till I was the last one standing. Kazouri reached over to tug on my leg. "Sit down a moment, Tazzi, and rest yourself. You certainly deserve it. We have the next ten years or more to build this place." Pell and the others added their voices. I sat reluctantly. It was easier than arguing with them. But I stayed close to the edge and turned only halfway around, so I could watch my companions and at the same time look down on that wonderful scene. A slight breeze rippled the blue-green flowers that carpeted the thin soil of our promontory and grew thickly in all the crevices between the rocks. Below us, the waves shimmered and sparkled, golden in the light of the setting sun.

Rishka and Zari had found a soft place in the moss and lay there kissing. Josleen and Megyair were wrapped in each other's arms. Tama had put the little crown of flowers on Pell's head, but Pell quickly put it back on Tama's. "The queen of the Essu. My queen," she said softly, as she reached up to touch Tama's face. Tama leaned over, undid Pell's tunic, and bared her lover's breasts. Gently, she began caressing Pell's lean dark body, which turned slowly and lazily under her hands. This was almost more than I could stand. Not sure if I should watch or look away, I could feel my nipples hardening and the heat rising between my legs. Just then, Kara, who had been sitting back-to-back with Vestri, pulled out her flute and began to play. At first she played songs the rest of us knew. Soon we were all singing with her, caught in the lovely magic of day's end, our voices weaving a spell together on that hilltop. Then, without warning, Kara was playing songs from our childhood, tunes from our village, and then a song she had written just for me.

Suddenly I was torn with longing for everything I had lost: my mother, my sister, my village, my whole childhood, and my lover, Kara, as well. All that had been ripped away from me. I felt grief like a knife blade, while the others lay there, filled with the joy of the moment and unaware of my sorrow. Then the tune changed and as quickly as the grief had come, it was gone. At that moment, sitting at the top of my world and looking down at this beautiful place that was to be our home, I felt happier than ever before in my life. I was surrounded by women who had been my friends and companions through so many dangers, women who were dearer to me than any blood kin could possibly be. Tomorrow we would begin. This final evening was the line between what we had lost and what we would build. For just that moment, all of us were there together at that line.

15

Zelindar! If I had had any idea how hard that first year would be — or perhaps I should say that first ten years — would I have gone in search of it that way? Would I have had the courage or the strength or, indeed, the foolishness? In truth, I had many chances to ask myself why I had been so set on this place when I could easily have stayed and been welcome in Dhashoti's settlement or in half a dozen others up and down the coast. There I could just have done my own work and been like the others; done my own work, no more, no less, and not carried the weight of a new city on my back. But did I have a choice? Did I look for Zelindar or did it seek me out? I had been driven to find it. The place had pulled at me like a magnet, giving me no peace. Perhaps I only did what I had to do, what I was meant to do, from the time I had fled my village.

When women heard that we had found a place to make a Hadra city on the southern coast, they began coming to us from everywhere, just a trickle at first, then more and more, till soon it became a flood of women. Hadra came out of years of hiding: down from the hills, out of secret gathers we had not even known existed, out of the woods, out of caves. They even emerged from tunnels and basements and attics in the cities. They came singly or in small bands, some near dead from starvation, many burned or injured. Often they were as wary and frightened as wild animals and none too friendly. They all had their own tales of terror and pursuit and death, as well as tales of courage and of kindness. Many nights we sat around the fire, telling our stories and listening to each other.

Other Witches came too, some with the bands of Hadra and some from their solitary places in the woods, but all with a hope or a dream of in some way rebuilding or reclaiming the glory of the Witch convents and the lost power of the Witches. Kourmairi women also came to us, women who were not born under the Star and so had no powers but who liked our way of living better than life in the village with their men. Some of them had even been beaten and abused and were running for their lives.

Hardly a day went by without a new influx, sometimes women with useful skills and knowledge but more often women with pressing needs: for healing and food and clothes and shelter and love and much, much, more. At first it was only the twenty or so of us trying to cope with it all. I desperately missed the organizing skills of Renaise and Thalyisi and hoped that some of the other Hadra I knew and trusted would come back with Josleen and Megyair. It was like the scene in Alyeeta's clearing all over again, just as wild and chaotic, but on a far larger scale. And this time, I was the one responsible, having been elected councilor for Zelindar in a sudden, surprise meeting, organized and directed by Pell.

Alyeeta was delighted with that choice. Gloating, she gripped my arm and said in my ear, "I always said, Tazzia, that you were meant for great things. I foresaw it from the first time I met you. I think you should thank me now for insisting that you learn to read and write. You see how much it will be needed? You see how right I was? You should be grateful." Not at all grateful, I shook free of her grip and looked around angrily for Pell.

After the choosing, women all around me were cheering and shouting, crowding close to clap me on the back. Many of them were women I barely knew. They might not have chosen me at all if not for Pell's persuasive speech, full of praise for my "courage and abilities." I found myself grinning and nodding, trying to act pleased, when in truth I was full of fear and wanted only to run and hide. I was also furious with Pell. She was the one who had called the meeting without even consulting me, and, indeed, it was she who had guided the vote.

I had the feeling that Pell had been avoiding me ever since the meeting. When I finally tracked her down, she was hard at work, helping Ozzet fill some barrels. Seeing the look on my face, Ozzet instantly walked away to let us talk. "You did that on purpose," I shouted at Pell. "You made it happen."

"Impossible," she said, laughing. "The Hadra cannot be made to do anything. You know that as well as I do. They only do as they please. They chose you because they thought you best for the work." Even as she said those words, she could hardly contain a little grin.

"No, they cannot be forced, that I know, but they certainly can be guided down one path or another by a skilled leader."

"Well, then that is my last act as leader. I hand it to you, Tazzi. I am done with it now. It is time for you to pick it up. I want no one ever to turn to me again and ask, 'Pell, what is to be done here?' That is yours to say. From now on, Councilor, I will do as I am told." She made a mock bow.

I was angry enough that I would have struck her if I could. Instead, I took a deep breath. "Pell, I am not ready. Help me a little longer. I am afraid."

She shook her head. "No more of that story, Tazzi, I am finished with listening to it. I have heard it too often. You think I was not afraid for all those months of moving us here and there, trying to find safety from the Zarn's fire? You think I was not afraid, knowing that every time I made a wrong choice, it might mean someone's life — and often did? I tell you, I am done with all that now! It is yours! At least you only have peace to deal with, not pursuit and death. Form a council, find good advisors. If you really want my help, I might even be persuaded to be one of them. And remember: you cannot do anything too wrong, for the Hadra cannot be forced to act against their will. Tazzi, I followed you here and helped you organize this one last trip. Now I have nothing left to give. What else can you possibly want of me? WHAT? WHAT!" Those last words exploded with anger.

I threw up my hands, wanting her to stop. "You are right, Pell. Yes, I hear you ... I understand and I accept the..."

But she went on relentlessly, "You knew this was coming. I said I would get us through to safety and then you would have the work of putting it together. I told you over and over that I needed to put this burden down." She glared at me for a moment longer, and then suddenly she was grinning, all her anger gone. Throwing an arm over my shoulder in a comradely way, she said, "Come, Terrazen, you have what you asked for, space for a city. Now you have been elected leader, to do it as you want. You should be overjoyed. Besides, I warned you many times that when peace came, when we had a place to settle, I planned to grow old and fat and lazy, sitting in the sun."

Of course, Pell did no such thing, though I think she did put on a little flesh, a little roundness over her hard frame. Her face even lost some of its tightness, and she no longer moved with that terrible driven haste. Instead, she worked at everything there was to do, building or gathering or clearing, in a steady, easy way, seeing what was needed and moving herself there.

★

For all that first year, I felt as if I never had enough rest or sleep or time. There was always one more thing to do. Somehow the work was forever beyond me. Half the time I was filled with despair at the enormity of what we had undertaken, and the rest of the time I was drunk with a fierce, mad joy for what we were attempting. We were doing it! We were really doing it! We were building our own city! My heart would be filled with excitement. Then, just as quickly, my mood would change. There was no way we could do it fast enough: find enough food, enough shelter, enough horses, enough of everything that was needed for all those pouring in. Some of the Kourmairi women from other settlements even sent us their girl-children when they could not free themselves. At that, I would have drawn the line. How were we to care for children, children who were not even Hadra and who never could be, when we could hardly care for ourselves? But Zheran came forward, saying, "How can you think to turn them away? They are your future. How do you even know if you will have any children of your own?"

I did not have the strength to argue. "Do what you want then, as long as their care is not on my head and they are not in the way."

Zheran had returned from her visit with Norn's people with two little girls to care for. She quickly took charge and organized all the children into a small school that met each morning. Others helped her with the schooling, but much to my surprise, Alyeeta was the first to offer. Together with Ozzet and Olna, they taught and guided the children and found useful tasks for them. And so, in spite of me, these children of strangers became our daughters. Later, I was to be very glad for their presence among us, but at that moment they only seemed like an added burden.

No matter how much there was to do, I tried to find some time each evening to climb to the top of Third Hill. Kara and I would sometimes sit there together, looking out at the view and planning the Zildorn that was to be built at the crest. The word *Zildorn* had come from the Witches: a combination of library, archive, holy place, and healing place; a House-of-the-Mother and much else, besides. This building would be the core and heart of Zelindar, built of the white stone that was native there. Kara talked of archways and sculptures and fountains. She drew pictures of her visions in the dirt and sometimes on paper.

Often Zheran accompanied me on those evening walks. She was always a calming influence. I found myself sharing the troubles of the day with her in a way I could not do with the other Hadra. Sometimes her two little foster daughters would come with us. Zheran would carry Ishnu in her arms. I would put Ursa on my shoulders while she squealed and screamed with delight. Once safely up there, she would clamp her fingers in my "mane" and pretend I was a wild horse to be ridden up the hill.

★

Some of the new Hadra were easy and useful. They found their places among us from the moment they rode in and set down their packs. Others — especially the Shokarn from the cities — were nothing but trouble, much as Nunyair had been. They were accustomed to slaves and servants and thought to find that sort of service among us. Our hard lives did not really suit their pampered tastes — or so they told us so often enough. Some even hoped to resume their old ways now that the danger was over. Of course, among us, there were neither slaves nor servants, not for any price. The only service was what we gave each other, turn and turnabout.

Pell had a sort of patient amusement for everyone, even the Shokarn. She undertook their teaching with rough kindness, but I found their arrogance offensive. I even thought they should be grateful to us. When they tried to hold on to their goods and not put in their share, I would send Kazouri and Katchia after them. There was something about Kazouri's great size that was persuasive, even when she had a smile on her face. When she scowled and her voice roared out like thunder, coins and jewels fell to the ground like rain. She did not have to do that often. Katchia, at her side, would gather up all the treasure. She kept a scrupulous record of everything they collected, though it all went out again, soon enough, for tools and food.

After all the hatred we had endured, perhaps the greatest need among us was for love. If so, I myself could not see it then. During those hectic days, I felt I had no space for love, not for myself nor for others. I, who had once had too many lovers, now resigned myself to none. I accepted that I was to have an empty bed for as long as I was councilor. As to the love others needed, someone else had to supply that. I had none to spare. I was too busy giving orders and directing work. Tamara seemed to take charge of that part of our lives, along with Olna, Cruzia, and Kilghari; greeting the new ones kindly and helping them find their place among us. Indeed, Tama, who had seemed so shy and stood always in Pell's shadow, now became a leader on her own. When she saw me being too rushed for kindness, she would argue forcefully with me, saying, "Without love, Tazzi, none of the rest of this matters. It has no heart."

I was too busy building a city to shelter us all to worry about love. Later, of course, I understood she was right, for what is a city if not its people? People bound by love can make a city wherever they settle. Empty buildings do not make a city. That is what the Kourmairi forgot when they fought with each other over this piece of land. But, of course, I was right too, for without a city to shelter our lives, we could never be the people we needed to become. In the long run, of course, love found its own way to catch up with me, but I will speak of that later.

★

With bright banners flying, Murghanth and Teko and most of their band of Sheezerti rode into the settlement one cool morning at the edge of winter, playing instruments and performing wild tricks on horseback. All work came to an instant halt. Laughing and clapping, everyone rushed to watch. I had forgotten how much joy the Sheezerti brought with them or how much such joy was needed. At the end, Teko stood up on her horse and declared, "A city that is already built can never really be ours. We prefer to live in a city where we can have some say in the building of it. Besides, the Kourmairi are not much better than the Shokarn when it comes to dealing with free women." That was followed by loud cheers. Then the Sheezerti dismounted and were soon swallowed in a mass of women eager to question them.

I had gone back to my work, drawing plans for the Zildorn. Soon I became so absorbed that I forgot the Sheezerti altogether. Suddenly I sensed a presence. Glancing up, I saw Murghanth standing in front of me with her feet wide apart and her arms crossed, looking me up and down. Her dark arms and legs were just as stick thin as they had ever been, and the look from her black eyes was full of challenge. "So, I hear they have made you 'chief' here. Is that true?"

It had already been a hard morning. I had no patience for one of Murghanth's dramas. "Do you have some problem with that?" I asked sharply. I was about to add, *If so, you can go back to the Kourmairi of Mishghall,* when she burst out laughing in that wild way she had.

"None at all, Tazzil. I say it is about time you took charge. I can think of no better chief, and Pell was near worn-out with carrying the weight of it. I am ready to take my place here and do whatever you say, whether it is amusing women or feeding them or lifting rocks to make shelter." Then she hit me lightly on the arm, saying, "Good for you, girl. You found your spot by the sea — and a very beautiful spot, I might add — and got us here safely. Now put me to work."

That night we cleared a big space, and the Sheezerti put on a wonderful new show, with all the women of the settlement clapping and cheering and stamping out the rhythm. Lhiri had ridden in with them. She was very excited to see what a fine place we had found. Though she was prepared to stay, she told me sadly that Nunyair had gone back to Mishghall for the fall and winter. "Building a city in the wilderness is nothing she wants to do. Perhaps she will come later." I had to bite my tongue not to say, *Let her stay where she is. We already have more than enough trouble here.*

"We've separated, at least for now," Lhiri went on, her voice laden with grief. "When I am with her, I go back to being the Kourmairi slave and she to being the Shokarn mistress. It keeps on happening, no matter how we fight it."

I put my arm around her shoulder. "You are better off here with us. Besides, we need you." I was sad for her sadness and so did not say aloud, *You are much better off without that woman,* though I am sure she must have heard it in my mind.

She nodded and rested her head against my shoulder. "It feels as if I have come home at last. Eezore was never my city, nor could the Shokarn ever be my people. I only wish Askarth were here. I wish my mother could have seen all this. She deserved to grow old here with us in this place. Oh, Tazzi, she made my freedom possible with her life. If only she had not turned back..." Suddenly, Lhiri was sobbing out her grief for Askarth in my arms and I was holding her, murmuring what comfort I could against her ear. It was the most kindness I had shown to anyone since coming to Zelindar.

★

Gradually things began to sort themselves out. Part of the meeting house ruin was getting rocked and roofed as shelter for that first winter, and women were also making little shelters from the remnants of old ones. Kara and Vestri found deposits of clay and set up a pottery by the river, working with other potters and even apprenticing women who were not potter-born, something that had never been done before. Ozzet became our seed-gatherer. With Cruzia for company, she went to Kourmairi settlements up and down the coast to talk to farmers, learn about new plants, and gather seeds. Some of us were clearing fields; planting and harvesting crops. Kazouri began making a boat, with the help of two of the Wanderers and several of the new Hadra. Using wool and flax bartered from the Koormir, a few of the Kourmairi women started to weave cloth in a corner of the meeting house, and soon a few Hadra joined them.

Many of us bunked in the half-finished meeting house. For me it seemed an easy thing to do. I had become like a soldier, accustomed to the barracks. For Alyeeta, it was an affront. "Do you really expect me to live among cattle in a cattle pen? Many of those girls do not care. As long as they have a roof over their heads they are satisfied, scratching bugs, snoring, and belching all night. Dirt-children, they know no better. They probably grew up in barns."

I felt as if Alyeeta were deliberately trying to insult me. "Alyeeta, I know you need your own place. I am doing as much as I can..."

"Well, something more will have to be done. When I was mistress of the Witch convent I had my own chambers, separate from the students, as big and fine as any house. At least I could have a little hut of my own here. If that is not possible, then I must leave and go someplace where there is room for me."

"Alyeeta, I promise..."

"Make me no promises, girl. You are riding a hundred different horses at once in a hundred different directions. My little shelter is not at the top of your list, or anyone else's, for that matter."

"Alyeeta, please listen. As soon as I am able I will..." I was speaking to her disappearing back. The words, "...will have to find my own...," floated back to me.

For a short while, I tried desperately to find something suitable for her. And then, I have to admit, just as Alyeeta said, I was off again on my many horses and forgot her need for shelter. In the end, true to her word, Alyeeta found her own, something useful and unexpected, a fair-sized cave chamber in the side of Second Hill, that had little side chambers attached. It even had a small seep-spring at the back corner, like the one in Pell's overhang shelter in the Twisted Forest. The cave entrance was completely hidden by shrubs, so it was only the trickle from the spring that had signaled its location. I think it was Olna who actually found the cave, but Alyeeta did not hesitate to lay claim to it. She was soon removing debris and sweeping it out. When she showed it to me, she was as excited as a child. "It is like a real house, with its own inside water system, a main central room full of light, and little sleeping chambers in semidarkness.

We will rock up the lower part of the front, get glass for the rest, then dig out and rock a pool inside, to catch the spring water for bathing. There will always be a crock of good water on that rock shelf below the mouth of the spring. And then there is the view. From here I can look out and see the bay and the river."

I cautioned her about cold and dampness, but she shook her broom threateningly at me. "How dare you say one word against it. This is so much better than those little rock heaps you call huts. This was made by the hand of the Goddess Herself, and with only a little help from us, it will be the finest dwelling in Zelindar."

Alyeeta was right about her shelter being the finest. Rugs appeared, and then cushions and mats, oil lamps, some little tables, some old trunks for her books. Tapestries, a little worn but nonetheless bright and warm, were soon hanging against the stone walls or being used for privacy at the entrance to the sleep chambers. It turned out that Telakeet and Olna intended to share the "Witch cave" with Alyeeta, at least for that first winter.

I wondered where all these goods were coming from. Did Alyeeta have a hidden stash of treasures somewhere from which the Wanderers were gradually bringing her things each time they came through? Or did she have some direct connection to the Thieves Guild, so that houses in Eezore were being emptied to furnish Alyeeta's cave? "And what if they were," she said sharply when I questioned her. "After all I have lost at their hands, they owe me something in return." I saw I was going to get no answers and decided it was none of my business, so long as she did not bring the Zarn's hounds down on our heads. She found her own "girls" to help rock the lower part of the front. Then, one day, Hereschell himself showed up in a Wanderer wagon with several windows carefully bedded in straw. It was not till much later that I remembered Alyeeta's little stash of coins.

Alyeeta had her house — and with no help from me. At her invitation, I went there one evening for dinner. Ozzet was singing and playing the ferl and Kara was playing the flute. I was urged to bathe in the pool. Olna put in hot rocks from the fire pit. With a groan of pleasure, I lowered my aching body into the pool and lay back in the steaming water. Later, Olna set a table next to me. She brought a bowl of steaming tarmar and a glass of well-fermented parmi-juice. I ate and drank and drowsed and listened to music, feeling as pampered as a lady in a Great-House. Suddenly Alyeeta was shaking my shoulder. I had fallen asleep in the cooling water.

"I see your manners have not improved with age, Tazzia," she said, grinning down at me.

★

With no thought about it, I had gone back to my old habits of sleeping wherever I could find a space when the day ended. Pell tried to talk to me about the terrible stress I was living with, and so did Tama and Olna. I was too busy to listen. I had no time for taking advice, only for giving it. Finally, it was Zheran who rescued me from myself. She had been rebuilding a small hut for herself, as well as for Ishnu and Ursa, her two foster daughters who had been orphaned in the fighting. They were the children of her cousin's dead friend. Her cousin had been taking care of them, but with no man to help and a new home to be built, she had been overwhelmed by the care of her own children, so Zheran had brought the girls back to our settlement.

"These are my children now, since I have lost my boys and they have lost their mother," Zheran told me proudly, putting a protective arm around each of them. She had enlisted Vestri and Murghanth to help raise the stones and fit the window frames. Pleased with her new home and very proud of it, she brought me to see their progress just before the roof went on. "You could share this little shelter with us and have a place to come back to at the end of the day. It would be far better for you than sleeping wherever you can find the room to lay your body down. It is not much to offer, but it is all I have that is really mine."

I shook my head. "What right do I have to this shelter, Zheran? I had no hand in building it."

"Then help me with fitting the poles for the roof and you will have done your part." As Zheran was speaking, the two girls were watching me with large soulful eyes from behind the shelter of her skirt, not sure, after all they had seen in the world, if they should trust me to share their home.

I knew Zheran could easily have found someone else to help with the roof, but somehow I found myself doing as she asked. After that, it seemed easier to have one steady place for my sleep roll than to wander about each night. I moved in with what little I owned, and Zheran began cooking meals for me as well as for the girls. It was nice sometimes to be in the quiet of that little place rather than eating at the noisy campfire. When I tried to thank her, she hushed me. "It is no great thing, Tazzil. I have to cook and make a place for us, anyhow. What is one more? It is no trouble to make a home for you as well, and it warms my heart to see you cared for." So, over my protests and in spite of my pretense that it was not happening, Zheran gradually made a home for me, a place I could come back to when I was weary. But I never really acknowledged that I lived there. And I made it very clear that I would not be a mother to her girls.

After a while, Zheran became my right hand in this settlement that was on its way to becoming the city of Zelindar. She would listen carefully to all my plans and make suggestions. She also made sure I ate and slept and had clothes on my back while my head was filled with visions of the future. I would start a new project, rushing about with all that wild, fierce energy, and she would follow after me, picking up the pieces, seeing that all was accounted for and finished properly.

Sometimes I was embarrassed by all this. It felt as if I had a servant or a secret slave. When I finally protested that she did too much for me, Zheran looked hurt and asked sharply, "Are you going to take this away from me, Tazzil? You promised I would be free to use my skills when I came here. Would you go back on your word?" Then, more gently, she added, "I am only trying to be useful. I see what needs doing and I do it. I need to make some place for myself here." I did not have the heart to protest again, and so I learned to live with my embarrassment.

Not until much later did I understand that in some way Zheran was the wife in my life, much as Yolande was to become Lorren's wife and manage the details of his life. If I had understood, I would not have approved. And yet, how much I needed that help and relied on that quiet steady power. I was burning my life away with wanting to do and do and do. If someone had not fed me and loved me and slowed me down, I would have turned into ashes in my haste. I did not ask this of Zheran, nor would I have. As she said, she simply saw what was needed and did it. Most of the time I was either immensely grateful or too weary to quarrel with the justice of it. And, in spite of this, Zheran herself did not take to our Hadra ways. She did not wear trousers, but a long traditional Kour-mairi skirt; did not cut her hair or shorten her name; did not ride much and never for pleasure, and, I think, never came to trust horses. She spoke quietly, not in that quick, impatient Hadra style. Though she was part of us, she was also apart from us and kept it that way with her quiet dignity and her Kourmairi pride.

★

While we were struggling with our own crude beginnings, Lorren and Yolande were settling near us on another hill and many of the Wanderers were gathering around them. Those two were married in the first warmth of spring. The ceremony was held down by the river and was followed by a big feast. Being a very private person, Yolande might have wished for something smaller and more personal. I knew she had no love for the Hadra and little trust for the Kourmairi, either. Lorren might have preferred that too, but I suppose he thought this a good occasion for peacemaking, for bringing us all together in one big, joyous gathering. Though the year was not yet up, Kourmairi from Zelandria and Indaran had been invited, as well as Wanderers and Hadra.

The women mingled freely, but most of the Kourmairi men from the two camps kept a wary distance from each other, at least at the beginning. Then, as the day wore on and the drink flowed freely, some of the men began drinking and laughing together. By evening, a few were even talking earnestly in small clusters. Weapons had been forbidden and there were no fights. Even so, I was glad for the presence of so many Wanderers. I stayed sober and very watchful the whole time.

Even old Norn came, much to Lorren's delight, and so did his wife, Segna. Norn walked around their settlement, nodding and looking at everything. "Well, Shokarn, you have done good work with this place, in such a short time." Later he mingled with everyone, making toasts and talking trade, listening to the Wanderers' stories of their travels, questioning the Hadra about our progress at Zelindar, and always keeping a watchful eye on the Kourmairi from Indaran. Garrell, on the other hand, was made obvious by his absence, something I could not find it in my heart to regret. Instead, his cousin Ossan came to represent him. Garrell's wife, Friana, was also there, though without her baby, charming us all with her quick smile and kind words.

Spring comes much earlier in the southland than in the north. Indeed, we seemed to have had almost no winter at all, not that I missed it much, especially after the hard winter of the year before. The first spring rains had washed everything clean, and now the sun was blessing us with gentle warmth. There was an extraordinary abundance of birds and flowers. New leaves were beginning to clothe the trees in various shades of green and yellow. The beauty of the day matched the occasion; bright, clear, and near perfect for a wedding. If I shut my eyes, I can still see Yolande as she looked that day, standing by the river, so beautiful in her long blue dress, her arms full of flowers and her red hair rippling in the breeze. She was smiling at Lorren and holding out her hand to him.

That evening, as we sat on the shore, relaxing and listening to music, a small group of Wanderers rode in. There was a cloaked and hooded woman among them who instantly stirred my curiosity. She came to stand by the fire. When she threw back her hood, I saw Shalamith's golden hair shimmering in the firelight. My heart leapt with joy. She had come back to us with the spring. After Shalamith rested for a while, she consented to play her ferl and sing for Lorren and Yolande and their company. For that time, at least, there were no thoughts of old conflicts and hatreds. We all sat late into the night, caught in the spell of the music.

16

Lorren's dream was to set up a semipermanent camp for the Wanderers, as well as a place from which he could observe the Hadra without intruding on our lives. I think he also wanted to watch over our safety. The place he chose to settle was a hill not far inland from the three hills of Zelindar and part of the same range. It had once been called Oshameer by the Kourmairi, but later it came to be called Wanderer Hill, or, more simply, the Hill.

It was a little craggy hill that rose gently from the broad grassy plain where the horses grazed. Lorren and the Wanderers were building a vast gathering hall at the top, overlooking the plain in one direction and looking off toward Zelindar in the other. They were reconstructing what was apparently a Kourmairi ruin from a much earlier time, making it big enough for a Great Gather. All around the sides and going on down the hill were smaller, individual shelters attached to the main hall by tunnels or paths or passageways. The Wanderers seemed to like the idea of having a place of their own as long as it was not too permanent. They wanted a place they could return to but did not have to stay. Often the little huts or shelters were begun by one person, finished by another, and lived in by someone else, or maybe several others in succession. Some of these shelters were no more than small hollows dug into the hillside with their fronts partially rocked up. From a distance they looked like a huge cluster of mushrooms attached to a central core, growing — or rather, pouring — haphazardly down the slope in all directions; many little humps without apparent plan or purpose but with some sort of overall beauty, like a thing of nature that takes on its own particular form from some wordless knowledge.

If a surprise attack were to come from any of the Zarns, it was likely to come from the direction of the plain. It seemed as if Lorren had purposely put himself between us and danger, though he gave me many other reasons, reasons that had to do with convenience and distance or the lay of the land. In truth, I was grateful for that protection, however slight it might be. A constant flow of Wanderers came and went from the Hill. I felt as if they were our eyes and ears, out in the world. The were always gathering: making music and smoking jol; trading horses; sharing gossip and news and stories from everywhere, even the Zarn's cities; bringing supplies; helping with the main building; starting their little shelters; and then vanishing again like smoke on the morning breeze.

I had heard that Hereschell was back in Eezore again, working as a gardener for Lorren's father and being our watcher in that city. He smuggled Lorren's books to him when he could, sending them with whatever Wanderers chanced to be passing through the city. Also, Lorren had put out the word that he was interested in artifacts, natural or otherwise: bones, precious rocks, feathers, and samples of rare wood, as well as implements and shards of pottery from old times, even back to Asharan times. The Wanderers were always bringing back with them little treasures they had found or traded for.

Off one corner of the great hall, Lorren built a little private shelter for himself and Yolande that few were invited to enter. He also built himself a study where others were welcome. It was in this study that he gathered his books and artifacts on shelves that went from the floor clear up to the ceiling. I studied all this with care, wanting to make a place much like it for the Zildorn we Hadra would someday build in Zelindar. No matter how hard I looked or how much time I spent in his study, there was always something more to see, something I had not noticed before.

After that first year or so, as my work at Zelindar began to ease, I found myself more and more often drawn to visiting with Lorren. We had a friendship no one else could understand. Yolande was jealous. It did not take mind-speech to read her distress. Though she treated me with scrupulous politeness, there was always a chill to her manner. I would have preferred anger or directness, anything but her cold, stiff, quiet ways that hurt and left no room for me. Lorren, of course, was always glad to see me and would send Yolande to fetch me some tea. I loved that tea; it reminded me of my village. Yolande made it herself from herbs she gathered. Sometimes I felt contemptuous at how quickly she went to do his bidding for someone she despised. I suppose Yolande was afraid that I wanted to take him away from her. Nothing could have been further from the truth. I wanted him exactly where he was, close by but not in my way.

Of course, I had no sexual interest in Lorren, or, indeed, in any man. Once, in my own way, I even tried to tell her that. Lorren had gone from the room to fetch another book and Yolande had just brought us some tea. I leaned forward and said to her in a low, urgent voice, "Yolande, you have nothing to fear from me. What you and Lorren share, I do not want. What we share, you do not care for, nor do you comprehend. Believe me, I am no threat to you at all." She gave me a cool look from her green eyes, then turned and went out of the room without a word. Clearly, she did not trust me, for she continued to keep a frosty distance between us. Somehow her beauty made the hurt even sharper.

Though Yolande had been born among the Wanderers, where men and women had easy friendships, she had grown up with the Kourmairi. In her Kourmairi world, men and women were not friends. They came together as mates or lived in separate, parallel worlds. Nothing else was considered possible. As for the Hadra, she did not trust or approve of us at all. Our ways were altogether too strange and wild for her. I think she would have been glad to move far away from us, but to her way of thinking, a woman's place is at her husband's side. The man decides where they should live, and so, for Lorren's sake, she tolerated our presence.

Yolande was not the only one who disapproved of our friendship. Alyeeta gave me endless grief on the matter. One morning she caught me on my way to Wanderer Hill, blocked the path, and said in her most cutting manner, "What is it that you find there that you cannot find with us? More books? Better food? Or have you suddenly become a lover of men?"

"Alyeeta, you know perfectly well that is not the case. Now let me by."

"What then...?" She put her hands on her hips. If Telakeet had not called her at that moment, distracting her and so allowing me to slip by, she might have continued to block my way, insisting on an answer I could not give her, since I scarcely understood myself. Rishka echoed Alyeeta's words, saying mockingly, "I see the Hadra are not good enough for you anymore. You had to find yourself a Highborn Shokarn lover. Is he better in bed than we are?" Even Tama asked, "What is there for you, Tazzi, that you cannot find here among your own?" No matter, I was drawn over and over to the Hill, as if by a magnet.

After the weariness and pressures of being councilor in Zelindar, what greater pleasure could there be than to come to Wanderer Hill and sit in Lorren's study, looking at the books and artifacts that crowded the shelves? And what greater pleasure than to talk to him for hours about anything and everything in the world, while staring out over the grassy, horse-dotted plain or enjoying the spicy tea and little round biscuits that Yolande brought us so silently? Lorren was my brother of the mind. No one else talked to me the way he did.

Not that we had no differences between us. He was older, he was a man, he was a Shokarn and a Highborn. All that gave him an easy arrogance of assumptions he was hardly aware of, though in my own bristly way, I lost no chance to point this out to him. Lorren often said that all knowledge could be found between the covers of books. True, much was there, much that I wanted. But I had known many things before I could read or write and had found little of that knowledge between the covers of any books. Once, because I understood some ideas in a book of his, he made the mistake of saying to me, "Tazzil, you have an amazing mind for one who is untrained."

"I have been trained," I snapped. "And by one of the best, one whose knowledge could easily rival yours."

"Please excuse me," he said quickly. "I had meant to offer a compliment, and I see that I offered an insult instead." I looked to see if he mocked me, but his face was very serious. "I only meant untrained in the ways that are familiar to me," he added.

"Even there I have training, for Alyeeta's knowledge is very wide, whereas you, yourself, have no training at all in that other realm."

He threw up his hands. "I stand rebuked, Tazzil. I have no wish to trade insults. I only wished to say in my own clumsy way how much I admire you."

"Well," I conceded grudgingly, "that admiration falls on both sides."

And I, of course, had powers, which was the greatest difference between us. It was something of endless fascination to Lorren, but it also made for envy and a kind of longing. Altogether we were as likely to argue as agree. No matter, I still spent many an afternoon and evening there, thinking I had the best company in the whole world.

Sometimes I brought others there to share those books: Maireth for the information on healing or Ozzet for what she could learn of plants, as she had become our seed-gatherer. Pell came to look at the maps, as she had undertaken to make us some maps on real paper instead of drawing lines with a stick in the dirt. Once I let Ursa, Zheran's foster daughter, come with me because she begged so hard, but she touched everything and asked so many questions that Lorren and I could hardly exchange two words with each other. He answered her with patient kindness, but I never made that error again. Even Alyeeta came to talk with him of books and long-ago times, though she was so rude and abrupt she embarrassed me, and I had to ask her not to come again when I was there. Sometimes it was the Wanderers who came to sit and tell of their adventures in far places or bring offerings for Lorren's collection. All this was well enough, but the times I liked best were when we were alone there, questioning each other intently for information or letting our minds wander on whatever strange and interesting paths they chose to take.

It was on one such afternoon that we planned our trip south together. Full of eagerness, Lorren had been telling me of this wonderful place. "The Wanderers took me there once. Ever since, I have been longing to go back. It is at the far southern tip of Yarmald, where the Escuro flows into the sea. There the river forms a wide swampy delta, rich with life, teeming with more natural specimens than any other place I know. I could show you many things out in the real world, Tazzil, that up till now I have only shown you in books. And I also need some help gathering specimens for my collection. I could even show you the ruins of Bayrhim, the ancient Kourmairi fort-city that sits on the top of a great hill above the swamp."

Suddenly I understood what Lorren had been leading up to. He was asking me to accompany him on this journey. "No, not possible," I said quickly. "I have too much to do here." I was very flattered, but I shook my head emphatically and at once began explaining, objecting, protesting, saying I had no time for such things.

Lorren was patient and persistent. And I, of course, wanted very much to go, so in truth, he had a secret ally. It was only that I felt I had no right to take so much time away from my work. Finally, he won me over by saying, "As councilor of Zelindar, it is important for you to have such knowledge. Think how much it will matter to your people in the future. Only you, Tazzil, there is no other Hadra I would take on such a journey."

"What of Yolande? She will not be pleased."

"I will settle things with Yolande. Not even her great love for me would persuade her to undertake such a journey. She already knows that I am thinking of this trip and planning to ask you to go."

"I will have to bring it before the council and find others to take charge in my place." Even as I said those words, they had a falseness to my ears. I knew the Hadra of the council would be only too glad for me to go. They were constantly urging me to slow down my pace and take some time away.

Now that I could think of this trip as having some official purpose, I felt free to plan in earnest. For the rest of that afternoon, we made notes and lists while we pored over books and charts and maps. Suddenly it was dark, and Yolande was lighting the lamps.

★

I have chronicled the whole trip in an attached account. It details the natural wonders we discovered. It also describes at length the great ruins of Bayrhim, which for me had special meaning as if I had lived there in some other life. Our last view of Bayrhim came as the day was darkening and the ruins were outlined stark and black against a blazing southern sunset. This trip south was one of the great adventures of my life, not because of the risks and dangers but because of the extraordinary beauty of the place and because of Lorren's company. Later, I was to have cause to think on it often and with some pain.

In terms of danger it was an uneventful trip, at least until we were almost home. Then, on that last morning, a storm began to threaten. Jagged flashes of lightning lit the sky, fast followed by the mutterings of thunder. With less than half a day's travel before us, we were riding hard, trying to outrun that storm, when suddenly the whole sky darkened, the wind came up with a roar, and the rain began pelting down on us. "We should climb up to that overhang," Lorren shouted over the din. "There is no shelter here by the road."

The place he pointed to was the lower edge of a bluff partway up the hillside, a long cut in the rock face that seemed high enough to shelter our horses. Looking up at it, my heart sank. The way there was steep and rocky, and there was no path. Also, I felt some other, less tangible uneasiness that I did not share with Lorren. In spite of that, I nodded. It seemed like the only possible refuge and we needed one quickly. We turned off the road and set out, dodging branches and weaving around trees and rocks. Soon we were soaked through. We pushed forward doggedly, our heads bent against the wind. At least we had not far to go, though for the last of it we had to get off the horses and lead them, struggling with them up the steep incline and stumbling over rocks and fallen logs. As soon as we reached the shelter of the cliff, I helped Lorren unstrap the collection packs from Pharoth's back. Then, groaning with weariness, we sank down against the wall of the overhang, not even dealing with our wet clothes.

For a while we sat there in companionable silence, catching our breath, relieved to be out of the worst of the storm. I have no idea how much time went by in that way. As the wind howled and the horses shifted uneasily from foot to foot, I let my mind wander back over scenes of our trip together. When I glanced at Lorren, his head had drooped forward and he appeared to be dozing. My own eyes were getting heavy. As I was about to join him in sleep, the wind shifted sharply and suddenly the rain was driving in on us, full force.

With a curse, Lorren shook himself, jumped to his feet, and shouted, "Stay with the horses, Tazzil, while I go look for better shelter." He was off at a run down the length of the overhang before I could stop him.

"Lorren, wait!" I yelled after him, but my words were lost in the roaring of the wind and the pounding of the rain. Now I was also on my feet and at a loss for what to do. I was reluctant to leave the horses alone in that wild storm, especially Pharoth, with whom I had little mind contact, but I was suddenly very afraid for Lorren. All of my uneasiness was back, not to be ignored this time. As I was going around with this in my mind, frantically trying to decide what to do, Dancer's ears began shifting back and forth. Soon she started dancing on her front feet, becoming more and more agitated. Suddenly she lifted her head and snorted a warning. After that, everything seemed to happen at once. I heard the cry of an Oolanth cat from close by. Almost at the same moment, I heard Lorren's terrified shout. The horses screamed in terror and bolted out into the storm. I found myself running in the opposite direction, running after Lorren, with my heart pounding in my chest, afraid I was already too late.

As I came around the bend, I saw the scene I had been most afraid of. The overhang was wider and higher at that point, with a cave entrance at the back. Lorren was standing almost directly in front of the entrance with his hands thrown up in front of his face. Not thirty feet away, a huge Oolanth was crouching, ready to spring. She was wet from the storm. I had no doubt that her cubs were in that cave. She was trying to get back to them and Lorren was in the way, facing her bare-handed. His knife was back with the pack — not that it would have been of much use against such a creature.

"Lorren," I shouted, as much to get the cat's attention as Lorren's. With a snarl, she swiveled her head around to look at me. I fixed my eyes on hers and tried to make contact. As I touched her mind, the red heat of her rage rocked me on my feet. At the same moment, Lorren called out urgently, "Run for your life, Tazzil! It is already too late for me."

"Lorren, listen to me and do exactly as I say. I cannot waste words." I spoke with great deliberation, never taking my eyes from the cat. "Move slowly and cross in back of me until I am between you and the cat. Walk steadily. Do not run. Go wait for me where we left the horses. I will try to keep her attention and calm her rage."

"Tazzi, I cannot let you..."

"Lorren, for both our sakes, do as I say and DO IT NOW! It is too dangerous for me to talk anymore." I had to trust that Lorren would heed me, for I needed to put all my attention on the cat. She had obviously been ready to spring, but now, confused by my presence, she suddenly found herself with two targets instead of one. Her eyes were flashing back and forth between us and her tail was lashing violently. I could tell Lorren was moving from the way her gaze shifted.

I focused all my powers on trying to reach into her mind with soothing thoughts. She shook her head sharply, as if wanting to clear it, and howled again. Though her howl was not so loud this time, the pain of it rang in my head like a blow. At the same moment, I heard a scatter of rocks behind me. Lorren must have slipped and perhaps fallen.

I dared not turn to look, but kept my eyes fastened on the cat. She seemed a little dazed. Perhaps my pain had turned back on her. Shaking her head several more times, she even rubbed a paw over each ear in turn as if trying to ease some hurt. Her haunches were no longer bunched so tightly. As she did not appear ready to leap at that moment, I thought this to be my chance. I began humming low in my throat, drawing in all the powers I could call on and even summoning the power of others: Alyeeta, Pell, Telakeet. I fastened my eyes on hers. As my hum grew louder, I began swaying slightly on my feet, keeping her attention. She began swaying in response, watching me intently.

Just as I was wondering how I was going to make my escape, I heard mewling from in back of me. One of her cubs must have wandered up to the entrance. At the sound she turned away from me and gave a sharp warning cough. Then, in three magnificent bounds, she passed me and disappeared through the cave entrance. Snatching up the cub as she went, she vanished from the scene as if she had never existed.

With the contact between us broken, I fell to my knees. I felt as if I had thrown my whole weight against a door and pushed on it with all my force, only to have it suddenly fall open. I was in a daze. The center of my being had been sucked out of me. If not for Lorren, I might have stayed on the ground right where I was, numb and mindless. Only the thought of him, waiting for me, not sure if I was alive or dead, forced me to my feet. Shuffling at a long diagonal away from the cave entrance, I reached the back wall of the overhang. Once there, I made my way along it by keeping one hand against the rock for support. In back of me I could hear the mewling of the cubs and the loud purr of the Oolanth cat.

When I came around the curve of the wall, Lorren saw me and leapt to his feet, his expression changing from despair to joy. "Tazzil, are you all right? Did she hurt you? Are you...?"

"...not hurt ... never touched me ... all right..." Actually, I was far from all right. I was so short of breath I could hardly speak. My knees were shaking, my head throbbed painfully, and my stomach was trying to heave itself into my throat. With a groan, I collapsed against the rock and began shivering violently, suddenly aware of how cold and wet I was. Lorren fetched a blanket from his pack and wrapped it around me. Then he sat down next to me and drew me tight against him for warmth. "How can I ever thank you, Tazzil? You saved my life and at great risk to your own."

This seemed a lot of weight for our friendship to bear. I shook my head. "No, Lorren, it was my powers that saved us both. She could not have hurt me. I have to tell you that not all the love in the world would have given me the courage to step between you and an Oolanth cat if I did not have powers. And I should thank you. You were the one who was really brave, for you would have sent me away and faced her alone." I did not mention his foolhardiness in leaving his knife and running down the overhang alone, but I knew it was in his mind.

The storm had abated now to a steady, gentle rain. After a while, my shivering stopped and some heat returned to my body. Warm and safe, I sank into a pleasant lassitude, letting my mind wander out in search of Dancer. She must not have gone too far, for soon I heard the clinking of stones. When I opened my eyes she was standing near us, ears flicking nervously back and forth, unwilling to come any closer. A very distorted horse's-eye view of an Oolanth cat floated into my mind.

"We should leave this place quickly." Lorren spoke with real urgency, but I was reluctant to move. In fact, I could not imagine where I would find the strength to do so.

"Please, Lorren, not until the rain stops. We are safe for now. The cat will not come out and challenge us. She only wanted to reach her cubs and you were standing in her way. They called her in as soon as you were clear of the entrance."

"Have you ever encountered one of the great cats before?"

I nodded. "Many times. When I was a child I used to go up into the hills and play with the cubs, but I knew better than to tell the people of my village. They already thought me strange enough."

The look he gave me then was much like the looks I gave Alyeeta when she did one of her spells, that same combination of admiration, distrust, and discomfort. "Tazzil, are you never afraid?" It was almost an accusation.

"Yes, often, but not in the same ways other humans are. After all, we cannot be physically harmed by another."

Lorren was shaking his head. "What must it be like, never to be compelled by force? I can hardly imagine it. Tell me, how on earth do you keep any sort of order among you if none can be compelled?"

"We have our quarrels and our differences with each other, but we all do what must be done, what we each have the skill and ability to do, for our common need. It is necessary. How else could we live? How else could we have survived this long and outwitted the Zarns? It is also our pride, it is what gives us our place in the world." I shrugged and shook my head. "But it is not true that the Hadra can never be compelled. We cannot be compelled by force, but we can be moved by love or the loss of love, by pride, by pity, by silence or shunning, and in many other ways." I was silent for a moment; then I shook my head again. "In truth, those are only little games of power, not of life and death. The other always has the choice to play or not to play. She can go her own way, though it may cost her heart some pain to do so. Very different from having all your bones broken or your throat slit, being thrown in prison till your spirit cracks and dies, or watching your child or your lover tortured before your eyes and knowing your turn is next. In your world, not playing their game, not doing what they want, means being ready to give up your life or the life of someone you love. What terrible choices. Oh, Lorren, how can you stand it?"

"It is not my world anymore. That is why it was not so hard to leave. I would not trade my life now for all the riches in Eezore. But if not for you and your little black toads, Tazzil, I would never have known there was any other way to live."

I looked at him thoughtfully. "The Shokarn have a lot of power in the world, Lorren. Was it that easy to give it all up?"

"A lot — and none at all. That kind of power is like loneliness itself. How can there ever be any company, when another's words are only an echo of your will? When love is something you can command and others give in fear, how can it really be love? Who would want such a thing? People will say what you want to hear, in fear for their lives, but never what is really in their hearts. That you will never know. It is like a hall of mirrors with only your own reflection in the glass."

I laid my hand over his and we sat in silence until the sun broke through, gold-green on the opposite hill. Then Lorren and I each shouldered a pack and walked to the bottom of the hill, with Dancer following. It took almost an hour of calling and looking and sending out mind-probes to bring Pharoth back to us and much calming and stroking before he would allow Lorren to mount.

★

I stood leaning against Dancer's side in the late-afternoon sun, pleasantly weary from the long ride, almost asleep on my feet. I had been watching Lorren walking his horse to pasture. When he was well out of sight, I turned to leave and was startled to see him standing behind me, only a few feet away. "I just watched you leave. How did you...?"

"I am his brother, Ebron. I did not mean to startle you so."

Now I flushed with embarrassment. It is not easy to approach a Hadra unawares. I must have been more tired than I had realized. There were two Wanderers standing farther back. They were conferring intently with each other, but I had no doubt that they had observed the scene.

As I looked more closely at this man, I saw the differences. For one thing, he was considerably younger. Also, he did not have that tight-drawn look of pain around his eyes that Lorren always had. But he was dressed in rough Wanderer clothes, not fine Shokarn wear. From a distance, I could easily have mistaken him for Lorren again. "You do look very like him. Welcome, Ebron, I know how much he loves you. He spoke of you several times on our trip. It gives me pleasure to meet Lorren's brother." I said all this holding out my hand. I greeted him for Lorren's sake, but my words sounded stiff and false to my own ears. Though he was dressed like a Wanderer and looked like his brother, this man standing here before me in our part of the world was a soldier for the Zarn. "I am Tazzil of the Hadra. How did you get through to us in safety?"

"With those two good Wanderers. They saved my hide several times when I thought surely I was lost." He took my hand in both of his and looked into my eyes. "Tazzil, I am glad to meet you in the flesh. Lorren wrote much of you in the one letter that got through to us, and Hereschell speaks of you often."

"Hereschell," I said sadly, "I wish he would come home. I miss him very much."

"Home? He always says one place is home as much as any another. But he told me to tell you he will be here before winter comes, perhaps in time for the Fall Gather. He say the streets of Eezore are too cold for him in winter. Besides, by then the garden will all be gone."

I looked at this young man more closely. "So Hereschell speaks aloud to you? He does not play the deaf-mute in your presence? You must be..."

"EBRON!" Lorren himself was running up the hill, with Yolande rushing after him. "When Conath came to tell me, I could hardly believe it was really you, here at Wanderer Hill." Ebron opened his arms wide, and Lorren swept him into a fierce hug. They thumped each other on the back in the manner of men. Lorren kissed him on both cheeks and then held his brother away to look at him. "You have grown, little brother. How is it that Father let you come? Did he send a whole troop with you? I am much surprised to see you. He told me I was in such deep disgrace that he no longer considered me part of the family."

"Father is getting older. No matter what he said then, he misses you and was glad for me to come. Besides, you will always be part of my family. When I said I was coming, he offered to send a troop of guards with me. I told him it would only make trouble and cause anger wherever I went, that in fact it might endanger me. He insisted, so I left him a note and slipped out at night with these two friends of Hereschell's, all three of us dressed as beggars. The guards were only too happy to let us out through the gate and so rid the city of some rubbish. The Wanderers had horses waiting on the other side of the wall. We brought more of your endless books in our packs, and so, after many death-defying adventures, here we are."

Lorren put his arm around Yolande, saying, "This is my beloved wife, Yolande, who is willing to share my life here." I saw how Ebron's eyes sparked with interest as he looked at Yolande and took in her beauty. Then Lorren nodded in my direction. "And I see that you have already met Tazzil. She is councilor and headwoman for the Khal Hadera Lossien of Zelindar." Lorren spoke with pride, as if he were introducing some illustrious personage. From his tone, I understood that he was trying to give me stature in his brother's eyes. In spite of that fine title, what Ebron could clearly see in front of him was a scruffy, mud-covered young woman, hardly more than a girl, with the dark skin of the Koormir, something not favored by the Shokarn Uppercaste. I probably looked much like the slaves or serving girls in his father's house.

"Yes, we met. She even mistook me for you and thought you had made a miraculous reappearance at her side." I laughed and Ebron laughed with me, but there was a little frown on his forehead, and an expression of puzzlement around his eyes, so that his handsome face seemed almost at war with itself. He would bear watching, this young man. He would be something to keep an eye on.

Ebron then turned to Yolande, bowed formally, and said, "It is a pleasure and an honor to meet my new sister." With those words, he took her arm, and I was suddenly shut out of that family scene. The three of them walked up the hill together while I mounted Dancer. Exhausted to the core, I turned her toward home, trusting that she would find her own way there.

★

Two days later, a banquet in Ebron's honor was held in the great hall, cooked and organized by the Wanderers. How wonderful to come to something I had no hand in making happen! It almost seemed like a miracle. Huge tables had been set up for the feast. They were covered with platters of steaming food and jugs of drink, and I had not once been to the storeroom to worry or fuss or check on the supplies. Great bunches of wildflowers filled the unfinished hall and swaths of bright fabric had been draped over parts of the stone walls to add more color. In certain places the sky showed through, bright blue and cloudless. Hadra, Wanderers, and even some Kourmairi from the other camps mingled together without rancor for the day. Even Hayika, back from her wandering, had insisted on coming. "I want to meet this new Shokarn 'lordling' for myself," she had said to me with a wink and a grin.

I did not trust her sharp, insulting tongue. "Hayika, you will not..."

"You need not worry about me, Tazzil. I will be politeness itself."

The Witches had also decided to come, though I made Alyeeta promise to watch her words and Olna promise to keep an eye on her.

Ebron was the center of the evening. All eyes were turned on him: telling his stories; laughing and joking and drinking; even flirting outrageously with some of the Kourmairi women. He charmed us all, especially Yolande. I wondered how she reconciled his being a soldier with her views of war, how she could find this man acceptable and the Hadra too strange for her taste when we had never killed anyone and Ebron might have dispatched any number of lives with that ornate sword he wore at his side. As I looked at her moving about the hall in her proud, stately manner, smiling at this one or that one, but with never a friendly look in my direction, I felt that ugly little feeling I now recognized as jealousy.

At some point Ebron stood up, raised his glass of quillof, and made a toast. "To my brother, Lorren, whose fame reaches far and wide." There were cheers in response. Slightly unsteady on his feet, Ebron sat down again abruptly. Waving his empty glass in Lorren's direction, he said in a somewhat slurred voice, "Older brother, you have made quite a reputation for yourself. When we reached the edge of the Zarn's lands and the beginning of Koormir territory, all I had to say was your name and that I was your brother. The Kourmairi escorted us from one settlement to the next, shouting, 'Lorren's brother, Lorren's brother' as if that were something very grand. Your name gave us safe passage. Twice I was even lent a fresh horse. And so I came here more swiftly than I could have imagined, and with very little sleep along the way."

"Why not stay with us, Ebron, now that you are already here?" Yolande spoke quickly, reaching over to cover his hand with hers. There was a plea in her words.

Ebron shook his head. "You know I am on leave and must go back in seven days. But I have only five months left of my guard-bond. After that, I will come back for a longer stay. You may even get tired of seeing my face."

"Is it the end of my duty you are serving out?" Lorren asked, with an edge in his voice. "It is not fair that it should fall on you. How can I let you do that?"

"It is of no matter. It will soon be over and I am glad to see you safely here. Besides, there is nothing you can do one way or the other to change that now."

"Ebron, do not go back to that killing, I beg of you. There is no need. You can stay here with us and find everything you need in this settlement."

"No, Lorren, we have already gone over this territory more than once. I am not ready to lose everything: father, home, city, my mother's memory, my place in the world. I am not ready to be a marked man for the rest of my life, never able to go back. I do not have the courage for it — or the foolishness. I am not you, Lorren. Besides, I left Father with no farewell spoken between us."

Looking at his wide, innocent face, almost as pretty as a girl's, and seeing his boyish charm, I could not imagine this man as a soldier and a killer. Then I thought about the young soldiers, boys, really, who had surrounded Hamiuri's cabin. They would have burned me alive if they could have and with no questions asked. They had surrounded other women with fire. Had Ebron done such things? Could he? I was afraid to look into his mind and afraid to ask. A soldier does what he is commanded to do. A soldier is not a Hadra who cannot be compelled to act against her will.

I wanted to shout at Lorren that he should plead with Ebron not to return to Eezore. No, not plead. As his older brother, I wanted Lorren to order him to stay. How could he possibly let Ebron go back to add to that horror? Then I thought with bitterness, *What does it matter? They will find another one, quick enough, to take his place.* He had not the strength to stand against everything in his life. Not even Lorren had made that choice of his own free will.

"Our poor father," Lorren said suddenly. "He thought he had two fine sons, and look at all the trouble we have caused him."

I was amazed at his tone of compassion. "You are not angry for the way he treated you?"

Lorren shrugged. "Angry? Why should I be angry? My father is not a bad man. He is just a man like any other, one of many such men who do exactly as their fathers have done. He would not know how to think a new thought if his life depended on it, and now I have turned his whole world upside down. Besides, he may have been the one who saved my life."

Ebron's stay among us was for me a mixed blessing. I felt much pain and confusion around this young man who looked so like his brother that sometimes I still mistook them for each other. As Lorren's brother, he was my friend and bound to me in a web of love. As the Zarn's soldier, he was my sworn enemy and a danger to all I loved. His presence reminded me of the smell of burning flesh and of the women who had died in agony in my arms.

Several times he drew me aside, full of puzzlement and curiosity, wanting to talk to me of the Hadra and of our powers and of how we had come to be. I evaded his questions as best I could or gave answers that made us seem stronger and more invincible than we really were. Even talking to him for long seemed unsafe. How did I know if I spoke to the friend or to the foe? They always seemed to be shifting places under his charming, boyish exterior. How did I know what use he would make of my words later, when I, myself, was no longer there to weigh in the balance?

And still we spent many hours together. We rode a few times along the river and even climbed up into the hills one afternoon toward sunset. Looking down at the view of Zelindar and Wanderer Hill, I begged him once again not to go back to Eezore.

"It is only for a short while, Tazzil, a few months at the most. Then I will be free of my duty to the Zarn and can do as I please."

"And how many will you kill in that time, to keep your place in the world?"

"No one, if I am lucky. The captain said I would probably be assigned to guard duty in the city for a while."

I shook my head. "When it comes to it, you will do whatever you are told to do. You would even try to kill me, if those were your orders." Though he shook his head emphatically, I noticed he did not deny my accusation in words. In the end, I was both very sorry and very glad to see him leave.

★

It was Hereschell who brought us the terrible news when he came for the Fall Gather. Ebron had been killed a few weeks before in a border skirmish between the forces of the Zarn of Eezore and the Zarn of Mecktesh. His death had come just two months short of his end of service.

17

Almost a year had passed since Ebron's death. Except for the shock of that news, it had been a wonderfully uneventful year, full of small pleasures and accomplishments. Perhaps things had been going too well for those children of misfortune, the Star-Born. Though we still posted sentries, it was more out of habit now than out of fear. Occasionally we had Kourmairi visitors from Norn's camp, but they were always so courteous and friendly I sometimes suspected this was Norn's way of watching over us. I had almost stopped looking behind me, guarding against an enemy that was now so distant. It had been months since I had sniffed the air for the warning scent of fastfire. I had even grown accustomed to the sounds of peace: women singing, often with Tama and Cruzia taking the lead; Kara and Vestri or some of the Sheezerti playing their flutes; Kazouri's deep, booming voice keeping time to the blows of her mallet; drums around the night fire — our daily music weaving itself through the fabric of our daily lives.

When I heard our sentries sound the alarm, I was on top of Third Hill with Kara and Vestri. We had been making plans for the shape of the city, drawing streets in the dirt with a stick as Pell used to do, only these were streets that did not yet exist and would someday be our own. From that vantage point, we could see Zelindar below us, laid out like a giant map.

We rushed to the edge to look over and saw in the distance what looked to be a group of Norn's men riding in with a man between them, much as the Wanderers had brought Lorren to us that day.

By the time we had run to the bottom, the men were already there and a circle of women had gathered. The one who rode between them was

Rhomar, the man who had been Zheran's husband. A chill went up my back and I shivered. No good could come of that man being here.

It was plain he was very angry. He was trying to shake off the restraining hands of the other men. "I demand to speak to my wife, Zheran, and to Tazzia the Puntyar," he shouted, looking all about as if searching the crowd for our faces.

I pushed my way forward till I stood quite close. "I am here, Rhomar. What do you want of me, and why have you come to disturb our peace this way?"

The look he turned on me was so hot with hate he would have scorched me on the spot if he had the power to do so. "Where is my wife? I will speak when she is here and not before."

"She is not your wife anymore, Rhomar, and she is under no obligation to speak to you."

As I said those words, I saw movement on the other side of the circle and heard Zheran say, "I am here, Rhomar. What do you want with me?"

At the sound of her voice, he whirled about and seemed ready to fling himself from his horse.

Norn's men restrained him, and one of them said, "No violence, that was our agreement. You are not to touch anyone in anger."

"You whore!" Rhomar snarled at her. "Look at this filth you live with." Then he shook his head and took a deep breath as if to get himself under control again. "Your children need you. I have come to take you home and make a decent wife of you again."

I shuddered to think what methods he might use for accomplishing that end. Zheran came no closer; she never took her eyes off him as she spoke. "I am no longer your wife, Rhomar. When I went to Mishghall, you told me not to come back, that our marriage was over. You took away my children. Now I have a new life and other children who need me. My old life with you is over." Though she sounded calm enough, I could see she was trembling.

"Not so fast. I did not come all this way empty-handed and with no cards to play." He pulled something from his pack, then unwrapped it and held it up. With a sick lurch of my stomach, I saw in his hand the account I had so painstakingly written for Alyeeta. I had not seen it since we had left the winter caves. In truth, I had not even looked for it, but had always thought it was packed away safely among Alyeeta's books. Rhomar was taking malicious pleasure from my obvious dismay. He waved the pages at me. "Puntyar, I think this belongs to you. You left this packet in a dark corner of our meeting house. We have done some rebuilding since then. As you can see, it has come to light. Careless of you but very useful for me. Now I have come to trade it for my wife. I have something of yours and you have something of mine. Very simple. This can be quickly done, and I can just as quickly be on my way home with what is mine."

My heart was pounding in my chest. I wanted to leap at his throat. I wanted to beat him into the ground. I could do nothing. My powers kept me a prisoner. Zheran had quickly slipped around the circle till she stood next to me. "Make the trade," she whispered in my ear. "I will find some way to get free of him."

"No," I answered fiercely, gripping her arm in fear. "No! Do not go near him. He is full of violence. Once you are in his hands, he will never let you go again, even if it means keeping you a prisoner, even if it means killing you."

"But all your work, Tazzil."

"Let it go, Zheran. It is not worth your life." All around us, women were shouting at Rhomar in a fury of frustration, while he grinned with pleasure. Kazouri took two strides in his direction, but he raised the packet and shouted, "If anyone tries to get this from me, I will start tearing pages." I saw her stop almost in midstride and stand still with her fists at her sides. Norn's men were conferring with each other. They might have been able to overpower him, but who knew what would have been left of my writing after such a tussle.

We were all trapped in indecision. Twice Zheran tried to go to him, but I held her back, whispering desperately, "Please, Zheran, stay away from him." Finally, I pushed her behind me. When some minutes had passed and she did not come, he said loudly over the uproar, "I am running out of patience. You are all making this more difficult than it needs to be. If my wife is not released to me in another minute, I will begin tearing pages. I will keep on tearing until Zheran comes with me or until there is nothing left to tear."

Suddenly, I heard Alyeeta's voice thundering from the back of the circle, "OUT OF MY WAY!" Instantly, the way parted for her like water, and she was standing in front of Rhomar with a fierce scowl on her face. I had stepped aside, quickly pulling Zheran with me. The hair went up on the back of my neck, and my head began to throb.

"Are you the old Witch who was a friend of Nhokosos?" he asked insolently.

"I am that old Witch," Alyeeta said slowly, giving weight to each word. "He is no longer headman."

"Too bad, he was a good man. Your people could do much worse and probably have."

"Some of us thought him a fool."

"It takes one to know one, Rhomar. Remember, I am also the old Witch who cast a spell on the Zarn's soldiers and sent them fleeing in all directions." Then she reached out her hand. "Now hand me that packet. That account belongs to me. It was written for me, every word and every page. If you destroy any of it, I am the one you will have to reckon with, not Tazzia or Zheran."

"Take care, old Witch. Nhokosos did not end his life well. The same might happen to you." At those words, Ozzet began wailing for her grandfather. It was the first anyone knew of his death.

Alyeeta seemed unmoved. She never took her eyes from Rhomar's face. "Are you really threatening me, here in my own settlement, with all these women around me and Norn's men beside you? You are either a very brave man or an even greater fool than I could have imagined." Her voice was like a knife of ice, not loud, but it cut through to the soul. I shivered again, wishing myself elsewhere.

I could feel Rhomar's anger humming in the air like waves of heat, but Alyeeta's fury was like the winter's cold. It poured from her and made my head ache. The look on her face was the most terrible I had ever seen. Not even when Rishka had first come to us and taunted Alyeeta into a silencing had I seen such a look on her. I wanted to move away, out of her range, but I was frozen to the spot. Everyone else was totally still and silent, staring at those two.

Then Alyeeta said again, "Hand me that packet. It is mine. Do it now, before something happens that you will regret. Then you can leave here safely."

Rhomar gave a roar of rage. "I have had enough of waiting! I warned you! Now I start with the first page."

"HAND ME THAT!"

At that moment, everything happened at once. Rhomar made as if to tear the first page. Alyeeta raised her arms so that her fingers were pointing straight at him. A terrible loud hum came from her throat that made the ground shake under our feet. With a cry Rhomar dropped his trophy and slouched back on the horse, his face twisted in pain. Kazouri leapt forward to retrieve the packet. Alyeeta reached for it. Kazouri looked at me as if for guidance but instead put it in Alyeeta's hand, moving as if with no will of her own. Most of the women had stepped back to escape that blast of sound. I was staggering on my feet, retching and clinging to Zheran. Rhomar slid from his horse and stumbled away, holding his head and groaning. It had all happened as quick as the blink of an eye.

With a nod, Alyeeta slipped the packet into her pouch, then said in her normal voice, "Man of Darthill, I thank you for returning what was mine. Go home now and do not think to come here again, not for any reason whatsoever. Not if you value your worthless life. I will come in the spring to mourn the death of my friend with those of his people who loved him. I hope for your sake you were not the one responsible."

Three of Norn's men went to stop Rhomar's lurching steps and help him back onto his horse. The fourth, Joshan, came to stand in front of me. He was so shaken he could barely speak. "I deeply regret what happened here. We knew the man was full of anger, but we had no idea what he intended. He would have come here anyhow. We met him on the road and tried to dissuade him, but he said he must see his wife, so we thought it better if we came with him. I am so..."

Seeing that he was about to apologize once again, I raised my hands to stop him. "Joshan, this was no fault of yours. It would have been worse without your presence, maybe much worse. We thank you for your kindness and concern. Give our regards to Norn, and say we are grateful for his protection."

Joshan made a slight bow. I did the same in return. Then, without a backward glance, he was on his horse and down the road after the others. I had a feeling he was only too glad to be gone, away from spells and witchings. When I looked around, Alyeeta had vanished. The others were talking excitedly among themselves. Zheran was sobbing wildly, with Olna holding her and the two little girls clinging to her skirt. I was swaying and about to faint when I felt strong arms around me. Teko and Murghanth had come up on either side of me.

They guided me back to the shelter. As we went, Murghanth elaborated in gory detail on what she would have done to Rhomar had her powers not prevented it. She went on in this way until Teko hushed her forcefully. Then she started in on Alyeeta. "That Witch, she is no better than the man. I wish we could have gotten rid of both of them at once, and good riddance to the lot. Her tongue is sharp as a pig-sticker and her spells are enough to make you vomit. I think she has..."

"Please, Murghanth," I struggled to say. "Please stop. Alyeeta has saved us from this and much worse besides. She is my friend..." Much as I wanted to distance myself from Alyeeta at that moment, I could not bear to hear her spoken of so harshly. I was feeling very faint again, though: all I remember after that was Teko saying, "Tazzi is right, Murghanth. Now that is enough," before I slid into darkness.

When I came back to myself again, Zheran was sitting on the bed by me, watching me anxiously by the light of one candle. The girls were asleep on their pallets. My stomach was still lurching about wildly and my head ached and throbbed. With a groan, I raised myself on my elbow.

Zheran touched my face gently with her fingers. "I was afraid for you, Tazzil. Your face was so strange. You looked so ill."

I shook my head and it still rang painfully. "I am not sure which is worse, Rhomar or Alyeeta."

Zheran smiled ruefully. "I have no question which is worse for me. I may appear to speak up bravely when Rhomar is near, but all the time I am shaking inside. Even after all that has passed, that man still has the power to frighten me. Alyeeta..." She shrugged. "You are far more susceptible to Alyeeta than I am."

"Alyeeta," I said slowly, "I love Alyeeta, but she can chill me to my soul. My head still hurts from that hum." I suddenly remembered the look of compulsion on Kazouri's face when she had handed my writing to Alyeeta. It made my stomach clench with nausea.

Zheran was watching me intently, her large dark eyes fixed on my face. "You were ready to sacrifice your writing for my safety," she said softly. There was amazement in her voice that anyone could value her so highly.

"Zheran, it is only words on paper. They came from my head. I could have written them all again. That little pack of paper is certainly not worth your life." Even as I said those words, I knew I would never have written that part of my account again and I was very glad it had been rescued. "But you, Zheran, to save my writing, you were ready to risk your life and put yourself in the hands of the man you fear." She shivered. At that same moment, I shivered too. Struck with wonder at her bravery, I sat up and put my arms around her. "You are safe here with us. I think he will not come back. If he does, we can always send Alyeeta after him."

With a moan, Zheran reached out and clung to me for comfort. I clung to her too, more relieved than I could have imagined that she was still with us. For a while, we held each other in silence. Then I felt her body begin to shake. I thought it was fear until I heard her laughter. Suddenly we were both laughing, remembering together the look on Rhomar's face. "Yes, send Alyeeta after him," she said, choking out the words. "Send Alyeeta after him. She does have her uses, after all."

In a moment or so, she drew away and grew serious. Her eyes on my face made me shiver. I could hardly credit what I was sensing in her mind. When she stroked my cheek again with a featherlight touch, I took her hand and kissed the tips of her fingers. She was struggling for words. "Tazzil, you are so beautiful. I thought so from the first moment I saw you. Do they all tell you that, all your women?"

I shook my head. No one had ever told me before that I was beautiful, not any of my lovers. I had never even thought of myself in that way. In truth, I hardly ever saw my own face and had little concept of my appearance. Aside from that one time in Hamiuri's hut, when I had played with my image in her mirror, I had only caught fleeting glimpses of my reflection in a bowl of water or the surface of a pond. Dhashoti was beautiful and Lhiri and Tama and Yolande and Shalamith. I was just Tazzia, dirt-child, daughter of Nemanthi. Suddenly, in Zheran's eyes, I had become something else.

How could I have lived with this woman for so long and not known what she was feeling? On some level, of course, I must have known. But I was not ready, so I had bought peace with head-blindness. I had blocked her out; closed myself off from her; shut that door as hard as I could. How else could we have done our daily dance of domestic intimacy in that tiny space without all of that intensity exploding in our faces? Now the pretense was gone, stripped away by our moment of shared fear and those few words Zheran had spoken.

I leaned forward and touched my lips to hers, very lightly. I could feel her hesitating, waiting, waiting to see if I was sure. Then an urgent heat rose between us and with it a terrible hunger. It seemed to fill the room and make everything else meaningless. We were both caught in that hunger. Suddenly we had hands all over each other's body, hard and insistent. All the hesitation was gone. We struggled with clothes to reach through to flesh. With a groan, we fell over on the bed together and ripped away the remains of our clothing. I only hope we did not wake the children, but I have to confess that for that moment, we did not even think of them. We were much too busy with each other.

★

I love Alyeeta as much as my own life, yet I must confess there are moments when I cannot bear to be near her. After those times when she displays her powers, I want to be out of sight of her, as far away as possible. For the next few days, even a glimpse of her rounding a corner on the path ahead of me or the flicker of her face across the fire circle was enough to make me turn and go the other way. If I found myself near her cave, my skin would crawl and my steps would quickly take me elsewhere.

One evening, a few days after Rhomar's "visit," Zheran walked in and laid a bundle on the table. I recognized it instantly as my written account. She avoided looking me in the eye and said quickly, "Alyeeta put this in my hand to give to you. She said you have been hiding from her. She told me she read it all and that it is very well written and that you must write the rest as you have promised."

I snatched up the packet and gave a roar of anger. "Never," I shouted, amazed at the depth of my own fury. "Never! Does that Witch think she owns me? That she can order me about this way? I will never set pen to paper again. I will burn my account before I write another word at Alyeeta's command. Why are you running her errands for her like some little slave girl?" I was shocked. I had never shouted at Zheran that way and certainly had never expected to.

To my surprise, instead of cringing, she matched my anger with her own, snatching the package back from me with surprising strength and pressing it to her chest. "No! I forbid it! You will do no such thing! I will not let you. I will guard it with my life and not let you touch it till you have regained your senses. It belongs to the children now, to our daughters. It is their inheritance. Would you take that away from them? I am going to read it to them, a little every day, and you are going to write the rest of it. You can have this again when you are ready to care for it with respect. You were already careless with it, or it would never have fallen into Rhomar's hands and caused such trouble. How could you think to destroy it when I have not even read it yet? I would have risked my life for these pages, and you do not have the sense to value them." Now there was hurt in her voice as well as anger.

I was staring at Zheran in amazement. She was usually so calm and even-tempered, the peace in my life. She stared back so fiercely that I dropped my eyes. "Do whatever you please with it, Zheran," I muttered. "Read it to the children if it pleases you, only do not ask me to write any more. I cannot do that yet."

"Thank you for the book, but I make no promises as to what I will or will not ask."

I saw that the house would not be a place of peace that night and so took my warm shirt from the peg and went to sit by the cookfire. Not even Tama's lovely voice or Kara's flute could soothe my heart or lift my spirits much.

The next morning, I was very contrite for my burst of temper, which really was far more for Alyeeta than for Zheran. I apologized so often that Zheran had to beg me to stop.

"How is it that you know how to read?" I asked, looking intently at this woman who was so full of surprises. "That is not common for Kourmairi girls, not even in Mishghall."

"My father taught me. He was a merchant with a trade route up and down the coast. He even had some dealings with the Zarns' cities. The man had wide knowledge and much curiosity about the world. There were two boys and two girls in our family and he taught us all together, the daughters along with the sons. He said he would not have his girls grow up helpless and ignorant. My sister was restless and resistant, but I read everything I could find, and so my father encouraged me.

"My mother protested, saying there was nothing between the pages of a book that a girl needed to know on her wedding day. And some of the neighbors were scandalized. 'Reading will ruin a girl for marriage,' they told him." Zheran laughed ruefully. "And look at me, ruined indeed. I have left my husband and my children, and I am not even sorry. Perhaps, after all, it was the reading that made me so hard." Then tears welled up in her eyes. "Oh, Tazzi, if I could only see my boys one more time. They probably hate me now. I am sure he tells them terrible things about me. And now think what the stories will be like. No doubt they will grow up to despise their mother and be hard, bitter men like Rhomar."

I came and put my arms around her. "How could your father marry you to such a monster?"

"My father was a kind man and good to us, but he had obligations to Rhomar's family he could not evade."

"Trade goods! We are nothing but trade goods!" I shouted angrily as I turned away and began pacing around the confines of our small hut. "So your father was a good, kind man, but what does it matter? In the end he did as other men do."

Zheran reached for my hand. "And that is why I cannot turn away the children, not any of them. That is why I teach them. That is why I brought back Ishnu and Ursa and made us a home. It will be different for them here. They will have some choice in the shaping of their lives. Here my girls can grow up proud and free, with no chief over them."

★

After I had spent days avoiding her, Alyeeta caught me in the meeting house, where I had gone to consult with Maireth about some herbs. She followed me back out into the sunlight. "Have you done with hiding from me? How long do you think this can go on? All I did was make that man give up the book without laying claim to the woman. I waited, but none of you seemed able to deal with him. What would you have had me do, turn her over to him? After all, she is your *friend*." She made the word *friend* sound poisonous. Suddenly her face softened and changed. "Tazzi, Tazzi, it hurts when you hide away from me. Do you know how much I love you?" That terrible look of pain came into her face, the betrayal she felt so deeply when I did not trust her, when I distanced myself from her power.

That look tore at my heart, touching me, as always, in ways her anger never could. "Oh, Alyeeta, why do you do this to me?" Everything in me melted and I felt myself about to cry.

Her face changed again and she snapped sharply, "No! Why do you do this to *me*? That is the real question." Nothing in her voice reflected the grief that had been in her face only moments before. "I have been searching for you everywhere to tell you how pleased I am with your account, how well you write for an unschooled girl."

It was amazing how skilled Alyeeta was in wrapping an insult in a compliment. "Thank you, Alyeeta, but I am done with writing, no matter how you flatter me. There is too much else that takes my time here. And if you had really wanted to find me, I am in our little house most evenings after dark when I am not by the campfire."

"Oh, yes, living with your Kourmairi *wife* and her two foster daughters. Perhaps I did not want to intrude on your domestic bliss. How was I to know if I would find welcome there." The way Alyeeta said the word *wife,* it sounded like a curse or an insult. "Yes, and that *wife* of yours was the cause of all the trouble and disruption. If not for her, that man would never have come here. Besides, she has come between us."

I was about to rush to Zheran's defense and protest the utter unfairness of all this when I suddenly realized that Alyeeta was jealous, that it was jealousy that lay behind her words.

"Yes, I am jealous and not proud of it, either," she snapped, as if she had picked the thought out of my head. "Look what you have done, look what you have brought me to. And now you have crossed that boundary. No use denying it, I know you are lovers as well as housemates."

"How did you...?"

"What an idiot. Are you going to ask me how I know when it is written plain as words on your face, in your eyes, in the way your body moves? Do you take me for a fool?"

"Alyeeta, it was only that one time, because we were both so frightened, and we held each other, and so it happened. But Zheran is not like that. She is not that way. Her passion does not lie with women."

"What sort of garbage is that? You are the fool. Have you never seen how she looks at you? She would lay down her life for your sake. Look how she has made a home for you. I think she came to Mishghall with us because of you."

I threw up my hands. "Alyeeta, wait..."

"No, you listen now, girl, and listen well. This is the truth I am telling you. There will be many more times between you. That was only the beginning. She is the great love of your life and she will be the last. The others were only an introduction, a beginning, even me, Tazzia, even me, much as I hate to admit it."

"Alyeeta," I hissed in annoyance, narrowing my eyes at her. Though she appeared to speak in earnest, I thought this only some new inventive torment to plague me with.

"This is no jest, Tazzia. I know that is hard to believe, since I so often mock and tease and say cutting and malicious things, but believe me, at this moment I speak the truth as I know it. This is the woman you will love for the rest of your life. For your sake, I will try to curb my spiteful tongue, not an easy thing to do after all these years. And she is not so bad, really. She will love you and take good care of you. For that I should be grateful. Besides, I am an old woman; what claims can I make on you?"

As Alyeeta said those words, I really looked at her. I could see how she had changed since we had first met in Hamishair. This was no longer the sturdy woman of middle years who had mocked and challenged us at the entrance to her hut. There were all the signs of sudden age, clear before my eyes. My stomach clenched in fear and I wondered what this meant for the future. How could I not have noticed what was right before my eyes?

★

As for the book, Zheran kept it in her care. I did not write in it for several more years. There were many things I would do for those two women I loved so much, but not even for them could I make myself pick up that burden again, at least not yet.

18

Children!? That was fast becoming the most heated question among us. We had found a safe place for the Hadra to live, but how were we to go on? Who would take our places as we grew older? Who would live in this wonderful city we were building? And if we were to have children, how was this to happen? And when? And would those children have our powers? It seemed as if we were all taking sides over this; our many discussions kept turning into quarrels. I was as troubled by these questions as anyone. I was also very sure we were not yet ready for children. There was too much still to be done. I wanted us to wait. How could we care for children in this unfinished place? How could we care for children when we could hardly care for ourselves?

Though I certainly did not count myself among them, I understood that many of the Hadra had a longing for children deep in their bodies as well as in their spirits. For them, children were more important than buildings, and they were getting older every day, feeling time slipping by. After all, we were still women, even if we were Hadra. If we had been ordinary village girls, we would have had three or four little ones by now. Lhiri and Kilghari and Ozzet and several others spoke to me of having babies. Of all of them, it was Tama whose pain I felt most keenly. She frequently came to sit in our house on the pretext of a visit, but it was mostly to be with the children. Zheran often gathered the other foundlings there, along with her own two. Then Tama would sit at our little table, drinking tea and holding one of them in her lap. With her eyes full of longing, she would say, "I wish I could have a little girl like you. Maybe the Mother will send me one soon."

Of Zheran's two, it was Ishnu, the youngest, who loved to be fussed over. She was gentle and compliant and very fond of Tama, clamoring to sit on her knee or braid her hair or try on her beads. Ursa, on the other hand, was as likely to be scrambling to the top of the newly completed meeting house walls as to be sitting at home being held. Though I myself could not fully comprehend it, still I could feel Tama's persistent hunger. Yet, at that time in my life, I could not even imagine wanting a child of my own. It seemed as if I already had a hundred hundred children, all clamoring for my care and attention.

Zheran was the one that Tama came to talk with, because Zheran, with her own terrible loss, could best understand. Finally, Tama came to see me one day while I was on Third Hill, directing some building on the Zildorn. I knew instantly what the subject was to be. "Tama, I have no time at this moment," I said quickly, hoping to escape. "We can talk later. I need to go now and confer with Jhemar about the new horses."

"No, Tazzil, not this time," she said in a determined way, blocking my path. "You cannot avoid this anymore. Jhemar can wait. I am at least as important as new horses."

I threw up my hands. "Well, Tama, have your say, though I already know where the subject lies and have no better answers than before."

"But I do. Tazzia, you have to call a meeting of the council. Ozzet and I and some of the other Hadra who want children will be there to speak. A way has to be found before we do something desperate or foolish or both. Time is passing fast for us. Soon it may be too late. We have been meeting among ourselves, and we think we have a good plan. Now all we need is your agreement and that of council."

It came as a surprise that this had been happening without my knowledge. I felt somewhat hurt at not being consulted. Tama easily read my thoughts. "You have been much too busy making buildings to pay attention to such things. You think it unimportant, but in the end, this may matter more to the Hadra than all the rocks you can put together." Though she said it mildly enough, still I understood that I had been rebuked. I had no choice but to call a meeting of the council. I knew Tama would not go away quietly and let me be.

As chosen leader of the Hadra, I had immense power — or none at all — depending on whether or not the Hadra wished to follow. When we had arrived in Zelindar, a leader had been needed to give direction to this venture and to hold things together at the center. Being chosen, I, in turn, had chosen a council that I thought could help me make wise decisions

— if such a thing is possible in the face of so many unknowns. We did not make laws, of course, for the Hadra cannot enforce laws on each other. Instead, we made agreements, sometimes only after long hours of talking. But if the Hadra did not like my way of doing and wished to follow another course, they could gather together and choose a different leader, who in turn would chose a new council. After all, I had no army at my command to enforce my will and certainly wanted none. But sometimes the very idea of such a change frightened me. I really thought I was the best one for this piece of work, at least at that moment. Also, I had so many things I still wanted to do. Nevertheless, there were times when I would gladly have handed over the leadership to almost anyone.

Still, in those first years, the only real challenge had come from Nothra, who was angry that I had blocked her way about some small thing I cannot now recall. Eyes blazing, she had come with three of her Sheezerti friends to face me down. "Nothra," I told her, "if you want another leader, either go where it pleases you better or gather the women of Zelindar, tell them your grievances, and choose from among you someone who suits your needs. Until that time I am councilor here, and you will do as I say."

"We will see about that. I have many friends here. You may not be councilor long." With that, Nothra had turned on her heel and marched off. I thought she was going to carry out her threat. It was one of those days when I might well have welcomed it. Instead, she went to the ocean to cool her anger. Later she came to find me and apologize. Tama, I knew, would not give up so easily.

We were thirteen altogether, twelve on the council and myself as Councilor. I had chosen six that I knew well and trusted: Pell, Rishka, Lhiri, Maireth, Kilghari, and Murghanth. Jhemar had refused, saying it would be too painful, with her empathic sensitivity, to sit with everyone's angry thoughts buzzing in her head. "I much prefer the company of horses, thank you," she told me with a laugh. I had also asked Kazouri, but she turned me down, saying, "Please, Tazzi, ask another. I have little patience with all that talk and am not much good at it. Set me some task where I can use my body and I will gladly do it for you." So I had chosen Murghanth in her stead, which I occasionally had the chance to regret. Murghanth had a sharp tongue and a biting wit. She sometimes brought the whole meeting to a halt with her explosive anger. Nonetheless, I valued her honesty and clear insights. As for the other six, I had asked the women I did not know so well to choose them from among themselves.

Now the full council, along with Tama's group, had all gathered in the Central Circle. Many others on both sides of the question had come to watch and add their voices. Though the circle looked gay and festive, with banks of bright flowers everywhere, the spirit of the meeting was tense and somber. With Tama as their leader, at least twenty Hadra were there to speak for having children. Murghanth was already in one of her moods. "Brats! One more time! Why do you waste our lives with this, Tama? I will only say again what I have said before: we are not ready."

It was Ozzet who spoke up this time instead of Tama, saying firmly, "We want to be heard today by the whole council, not by each of you, one at a time. We have a plan to put forth, and we have given it much thought."

Murghanth seemed ready to burst out again when Kilghari, who agreed with Tama, held up her hand. "Please, Murghanth, we have come together in council meeting for this purpose, so let us at least hear what they have to say."

"What new thing can they possibly say that we have not heard before?"

"If you would only shut your mouth for long enough, stick-woman, you might find out," one of Tama's companions yelled angrily. It was Nothra, the same Sheezerti who had challenged me that day last fall. She seemed equally ready to take on Murghanth.

Murghanth whirled on her. "Belly-of-a-dog!" she shouted back. "Is that any way to talk to someone who sits on the council, especially another Sheezerti?" At that, the council meeting disintegrated into chaos, with Hadra all shouting at each other. We would, no doubt, have come to blows if such a thing were possible among us. As it was, it took a while for Pell, myself, and Kilghari to restore some order and longer still for there to be enough quiet for Tama to speak.

Tama stood very straight before us, while the rest of us, having finally been silenced, sat in a semicircle to listen. "Sisters, Councilor, Hadra of the council, thank you for hearing us. We have talked much among ourselves. We have tried to look at all the questions and find some solution. It has not been easy, but waiting any longer is simply not an answer. After considering everything, we came to the idea of inviting those men who are willing, Wanderer and Kourmairi both, to attend our fall Essu. In that way we are in our own place, with the safety of Zelindar around us, and cannot come to harm. Those of us intending to make babies can come together with the men under cover of darkness so that no man can lay claim to the child and no Hadra can make any claim on the man."

With those words the meeting erupted again. Tama was barely able to finish her speech before the storm broke. Murghanth was on her feet, screaming, "Is that what we have come to, a bunch of whores in the night with no shame at all? Will you carry a little pouch for the coins? How can you think to bring this filth here into our own city?" Many angry voices were shouting back at Tama, though Murghanth's was still the loudest. Finally Murghanth burst out, "I will not stay and listen to this garbage any longer!" Before storming off, she threatened, "If this happens, the Essu will have to take place without the Sheezerti. We will not disgrace ourselves by performing there."

After Murghanth's fiery exit, the meeting went on with less turmoil, but now there was a flood of questions. Kilghari asked, "What if they are boys? Will they stay here among us or go to the Kourmairi to be raised?" And Shartel asked, "Do we choose these men or do they choose themselves?" And Rishka added, "What if we think some of them unsuitable?" Then Lhiri raised her voice: "Since these children will have no fathers, will they at least have a second mother or will we all be their mothers?" Altogether far more questions were raised than answered. After much talk and no decision, we finally ended that meeting by planning the next one.

Following a month of meeting and talking and arguing and meeting yet again one more time, we finally let Tama and Ozzet and the others have their way, not because we liked their plan but because we finally understood that all the other alternatives were so much worse. Murghanth stormed off for the last time, shouting, "Let someone else take my place on this council of fools!" But she did not fight the decision anymore, and we did not argue with her departure.

And so, that fall, for the first time, we invited the Wanderers and Kourmairi who were our neighbors to come to our Essu. There were horse races and foot races and boat races, along with games of chance and games of skill. Cookfires burned day and night. The Kourmairi brought food to share, and together we feasted on the plenty of our harvest. Zelindar echoed with the sound of men's voices. Never before had Hadra wrestled with Wanderers and Kourmairi. We Hadra even drank some yors and quillof, something we did not usually allow ourselves. The Muinyairin did a show of trick riding, changing horses at a run to the shouts of the watchers. Then a group of Wanderers did a performance of mime and music that gained them thunderous applause. Finally, not to be outdone, the Sheezerti, with Murghanth in the lead, appeared in all their finery and entertained us with their best performance ever. Later, when I questioned her, Murghanth answered tartly, "I have a right to change my mind. Besides, we could not let the Wanderers best us in that way."

Under all the merriment and rivalry, another energy was humming, an energy that seemed both full of threat and full of promise. When it grew dark, fires were started and torches lit. I went with Pell to get Tama ready for this new and frightening adventure, this stranger in the dark. In the end, she must go to meet with him alone. My hands shook. Pell tried to joke, but she stumbled over her words. Tama kept saying soothing, reassuring things, yet she could not look Pell in the eye. Finally, we had bathed Tama and rubbed her with scented oil, put flowers in her hair, kissed her, and hugged her tightly. Pell was holding her when the drums began to play. "Stay with me, Tama, please," she pleaded. "Not this year, at least wait a year. By then I will be ready. How can I bear to let you go to some man or men I do not even know?" Never before had I heard Pell beg for anything.

Tama was shaking her head. "Pell, we have argued all this a hundred times or more and you swore you would let me go when the time came. You know I would not choose to hurt you, but I do what I must from my own heart." Tama gave her a last, hard kiss. Then Pell released her and turned away. Without another word, Tama vanished, naked, into the darkness.

I stood for a while keeping Pell silent company, until she turned to me and said ruefully, "Well, she certainly has a lot of courage, that one. I cannot imagine going out to join with some strange man in the dark. In truth, I cannot imagine joining with men at all, at any time of day or night or for any purpose whatsoever. I would rather face the Zarn's guards armed with fastfire any day. Come, let us go drink some more quillof together so we can get through these next few hours." She slipped her arm through mine, and we went off to find the barrel of quillof Norn had donated to the festivities. The rest of that evening was all a drunken blur to me, and the fierce headache of the next morning was something I had no wish to repeat.

★

By the next spring, it seemed that everywhere I looked I saw swollen bellies parading themselves around. Because of our powers, most of the Hadra had known very soon whether or not they had conceived. Tama told me that the man had been gentle and respectful and Ozzet said much the same, but I had not much interest in their talk of the "Gimling," as these ritualized matings came to be called. It was already clear to me that it would be repeated again in the fall. Most of those who tried were carrying new life and now others were eager to try. Pell had more than resigned herself to being a co-mother. She was bursting with pride now, as if she herself had fathered this child, instead of some shadow-man lurking in the darkness. She often rested her hand on Tama's distended belly with a pleased little smile on her face. Even Murghanth had come around in her thinking, for several among the Sheezerti were pregnant, including Nothra. Now Murghanth was full of talk of how the little ones would become part of the troupe and give it new life. But she did not come back to sit on council and we did not ask her to. Teko had taken her place, and that was fine with me.

With the coming invasion of babies, we were short of midwives, and so, reluctantly, I took up my old occupation and taught others the skill as well. It fell my lot, with Zheran assisting, to be there for the birth of Tama's baby. Pell was pacing around, as nervous and useless as any new father. She alternated between being afraid to look and putting herself right in our way. "Pell," I finally told her in exasperation, "either stay behind Tama and help Zheran rub her back or I must order you to leave the room and stay away until you are called." To my surprise, she did as she was told and gave us no further trouble.

When the head crowned with its thatch of dark hair, a rush of joy opened up my heart. I saw the new one through a blur of tears as I reached out to catch her and ease her passage from her mother's body. In all those years of fire and blood and violence and fear, I had forgotten the simple miracle of helping new life into the world. All shiny with blood and mucus, the baby's long black hair stood up in spikes. Her dark eyes glanced around as if she could already focus on our faces, and her small red hands opened and closed, grabbing eagerly at life. We laid her at her mother's breast and Tama groaned with pleasure. I suppose she was not much different from any other new baby, though at that moment she looked astonishingly beautiful to me. When her mouth found the nipple, Tama groaned again. For a moment everyone in the room fell silent to concentrate on the sound of sucking.

Soon the babies were coming one after the other. I was often awakened in the dark of night, as babies seem to like that time best for making their first appearance in the world. If the birth was in the daytime, Ishnu would follow me there. At first I tried to discourage her, as I did not want to be burdened with the child, but she would sneak back when I was not watching. I would suddenly see her little face peering out intently from among the women. She was very persistent. After a while, it seemed easier to let her help with small chores than to try to send her away. After all, she was not much younger than I had been when Old Tolgath had begun my training, and she soon proved to be quick and attentive.

At first, Ishnu had been afraid that Tama would lose interest in her now that Tama had her own child. Instead, Ishnu became a little second mother. She was as likely to be with Pell and Tama and the new baby as at home with Zheran.

When these birthings were finally over, one of our most pressing questions had been answered. Among the Hadra, all the babies were female. Apparently, that was another of our Hadra powers.

★

Yolande came to visit with us now, something she had never done before the babies were born. And some of the new mothers went to visit her at the Hill. Some even went to show Lorren their babies, sitting amidst his books and artifacts, proudly displaying their wriggly, noisy bundles. I suppose I should have been glad of this and in a way, of course, I was. This was finally the peace I had wanted for so long between Yolande and the Hadra. Though she did not become my friend, at least Yolande began to talk to me as if I were simply another woman. Perhaps, now that she saw me as a midwife, I was no longer a dangerous monster in her eyes.

One morning, when she was on her way to visit with Tama and the baby, she sought me out. "Tazzil, it seems I have judged you Hadra wrongly, or harshly, and I would like to make amends. Perhaps I can do so now, by helping to care for these new children." I knew Yolande had lost her only child in the fighting and Lorren had confided in me that they had tried for a baby of their own with no success.

"Yolande, we are very grateful for your help. As there are few mothers or aunts or grandmothers here among us to share their wisdom, we need someone to guide us through."

She smiled and there was no ice in it this time. "I needed to start a new life. If I had stayed among the Kourmairi, everything would have reminded me of the man I loved and lost, of my child who was killed. I would have grown hard and bitter, full of grief and thoughts of vengeance.

Here, I can forget. I can see something new being born and be a part of it as well. I can really put my love where it is valued. Maybe I can even help to mend some of the terrible harm that has been done."

I thought again of how very beautiful she was. Now, when she looked at me, her green eyes had compassion in them instead of coldness. Yes, I was glad enough to have peace between us, but when I went to visit with Lorren, it felt as if my sanctuary had been invaded by babies, the sound and the smell and the sight of them.

19

This visit from Friana was very different from all the others, that much I could tell at a glance. Ozzet had come running to fetch me. I had been with Maireth and Katchia in the new storeroom that was attached to the common kitchen. We were sorting through supplies when I thought I heard my name being called. Then Ozzet burst in on us, saying breathlessly, "Tazzil, come quickly! Friana! Trouble! Come quickly!" I dropped what I was holding and rushed out after her, with the other two close on my heels.

Trouble indeed, that was plain enough to see. Even at a distance I could tell from how Friana's horse stood: legs apart, head down, sides heaving. Friana would never have ridden her horse to exhaustion that way for amusement. When I came closer, I saw the dark purple stain of a bruise across her cheek, the swollen eye, and the cut, puffy lips. With her arm bent at a strange angle, she held her little girl in front of her on the winded horse. Clearly, the child was terrified. Friana had her new baby cradled in a shawl that was tied to her back. Yes, trouble! It looked like a whole lot of trouble to me.

In the six or so years since the Hadra had occupied Zelindar, Friana had come to visit several times, though we had not seen her since the new baby was born. She always came with other Kourmairi women from her settlement, laughing and chatting gaily with everyone, stopping to gossip with the Kourmairi women who lived among us, bringing things to trade or exchanging small gifts. Her little girl Marklishia — Markla to us — was a real favorite in the settlement and often came with her mother, though I had never again seen the boy who had been a baby in Friana's arms at that fateful meeting.

This was not the first time I had seen marks on Friana's face or arms. Before, when we asked, she had usually laughed it off, blaming her clumsiness or some little household accident, though, of course, we all knew well enough who was to blame and she knew we knew. When she spoke of Garrell, she always said he was a kind, good man under his rough exterior. I had my doubts. I wondered why she defended him so and why, each time, she returned to him. This time I did not think she would be going back. I felt the chill wind of foreknowing go up my back.

Other women had already gathered. They were trying to coax Markla from Friana's arms so that Friana could dismount, but Markla was sobbing wildly and clinging tightly to her mother. Friana was shaking her head, saying to them, "No, wait for Tazzil. She must give me an answer." As soon as she saw me, she called out in a voice full of desperation, "Tazzil, can you help me? Tell me if I can stay. I cannot go back, I would kill myself first, and I am afraid to go to Sierran's for fear it will give Garrell an excuse to begin the killing again. Only tell me if I can stay here before I get off this poor horse." Many voices were answering her all at once, calling out, "Stay with us, Friana." "Of course we want you here." "You and the children are always welcome among us." But Friana kept her eyes fixed on me. "What do you say, Tazzil? You are leader here. What do you say?"

"Yes, of course you can stay. You will be safe here. We will see to it." Even as I gave my quick assurance, I felt that chill again and shivered.

"Garrell will come after me. He will come here, you must know that."

"Whatever Garrell does, he cannot take you away from us against your will." Friana groaned and slid from the horse as if she had been holding herself up by sheer will. Ozzet caught Markla in her arms. Kazouri and Shartel caught Friana and cushioned her fall. They lowered her down gently, keeping the baby from harm. Tama untied the shawl with care. She lifted the baby tenderly to hold against her chest. It seemed strange that the baby had slept through it all. Her head lolled awkwardly and I wondered if she had been drugged to make escape possible.

We made an odd little procession. Ozzet carried Markla to the meeting house. Pell and Kazouri carried Friana, while Zheran and I rushed ahead to make a pallet for her. Tama followed with the baby. Other women came trailing after us, to help or to look. They stayed hovering in the doorway.

When we got Friana settled, we tucked the baby in beside her. "Rest now," I whispered, gently brushing the hair back from her injured face. "I will be back in a while. Time enough to talk of all this later, after you have had some sleep."

"No!" she said fiercely, gripping my wrist with surprising strength. "Stay! We must talk now, Tazzil. Later may be too late. I have not come all this way to lose everything for a little sleep. Prop me up so I can talk." Even as she spoke, she struggled to sit up again. I helped her, and other women quickly brought pillows to support her back. Her voice was raspy and forced. Every word was clearly an effort, but she went on. "The first thing is the children. If anything happens to me, keep them and protect them. He wants them dead, at least the little one. And if Garrell and I both die, then take them to Sierran. She is like a sister to me and will raise them as her own. But not if he is still alive. That would put Sierran and her family in grave danger."

She gave a deep sigh and shut her eyes as if she were done. I was going to ease her down, but she opened her eyes again and fastened me with her stare. "Not yet, Tazzil. I am not finished yet. I must say it all and you must listen. This is important. Garrell is a very angry man and his anger grows worse all the time. In his head, many things have gotten mixed up together. He blames all of you, as well as me, for what he sees as his defeat. He feels Zelindar was stolen from our people by Lorren's trickery and Norn's treachery. He thinks he could have won the land for good with one more fight because Norn was getting too old to hold on. But Norn and Lorren and the Wanderers and especially the 'dirty filthy Hadra' all conspired to cheat him out of his victory, a victory he believes was rightly his. He also thinks the women among his people betrayed him and that I, his wife, led this betrayal. This is what he thinks when he is very drunk on yors. When he is sober, he knows I love him and have stood by him. But now he is drunk and bitter more often than not. His own people are turning against him. There is even talk of choosing a new leader, one who is less warlike, less filled with violence. He takes this as one more sign of betrayal and cannot see his own part in it.

"He was the one who wanted this new baby. I would have been happy with two. Our lives are still too hard. There is still too much to do and build and plant for us to be able to support many children, but he wanted another son. For him, that would have been a sign of favor from the gods. It would have restored his pride. And he was sure it would have secured his place as leader far into the future.

"When the baby was a girl, he was furious. He stayed drunk for a week. He did not even want to see her. He refused to hold her, shouting angrily, 'How do I even know it is mine? I said I wanted a boy and look what you gave me. How do I know you did not lie down with some other man?' All my assurances were meaningless to him. We have not even had a naming for her. Then he said he wanted to try again right away for a boy-child, that we should make another baby. When I said I could not care for more than three children, he said he could fix that by doing away with the baby. As luck would have it, she was not with me at that moment or he surely would have killed her. I cried and pleaded with him. He got furious, saying I loved this ugly baby more than I loved him. Then he beat me, as you can see. Finally, he threw me down on the floor and left the house, nailing the doors shut to make me his prisoner. As he went he shouted, 'I am going to find those girls and deal with them now. No man needs two girl-children in his life.'

"Of course, everyone had heard him, for he was shouting very loudly. They hid the children from his vengeance. Luckily for us, he was too drunk to search for long. When he fell asleep in the street, my sister came to free me. She brought me my children and a horse and sent me on my way. I left Amrald. He will come to no harm from his father, but the other two are in danger. The baby he would surely kill. She represents all his troubles. Even Markla is not safe with him. He has no love for her and has beaten her before for answering him in her own way. I have no doubt that he would kill me, too, if he had the chance, now that I have run away from him and am making myself free of his will. In this mood he is a very dangerous man. Everything serves to fuel his anger. I will not go back. Truly, I would kill myself first. If we cannot stay here, perhaps we could take refuge in some other Kourmairi settlement or perhaps among the Hadra farther up the coast."

"Oh, Friana, we would never send you away. We are pledged to your safety. You and the children will find a home among us. That was part of the agreement with the Kourmairi. I always wondered why you did not come sooner, why you stayed so long with that man. It was clear long before this that he was mistreating you."

"How can I tell it so you can understand?" She was shaking her head and tears were shining in her eyes. "We were children together. We shared our dreams. He was my first lover and I was his. When his father was killed he became chief. I was so proud of him, but I was afraid for him too. He was so young, too young for all the weight life thrust on his shoulders. Also, he was very bitter and hurt because of his father's death. I was not just his lover and his wife, I was his best friend as well, the one he trusted with his innermost secrets, with his real self. When he started getting violent, I understood that it was the pressure driving him. And each time he was so sorry and so ashamed. How could I abandon him to his shame?

"I thought things would be better with peace, but they only got worse. He was so young. He wanted so much to win for his people. Instead, we had to leave, and the despised Hadra got to live where we should have been, here on his father's land — at least that is how he sees it. He feels he has failed, been made a fool of, because Lorren outtalked him. Now he is a bitter, lost man who has turned his anger on the one person who loved him above all else. And now, of course, I have done as he said; I, too, have betrayed him." She began coughing and could not go on. Tears were running down her face unheeded. It was very painful to see her weeping for a man who wished to kill her children and would most likely kill her too if he had the chance.

"Now sleep," I said, trying to ease her down. "It is time for you to sleep and gain back your strength. Your daughters are safe here with us." Carefully I brushed away her tears with my sleeve. This time she let herself be lowered down, but before she shut her eyes, she tugged on my hand to draw me close. "Be careful, Tazzil, be very careful. He is an extremely dangerous man and he is sure to come here looking for me." Then she closed her eyes, her breathing changed, and she was gone from consciousness. When I straightened up, I found myself looking straight into Alyeeta's eyes. She had witnessed the whole scene and was now watching me with a strange expression on her face. She shook her head at me, then turned away without a word and slipped out of the meeting house.

Olna settled by the mat with her hand over Friana's heart, watching while the exhausted woman slept. Shartel and Kazouri guarded the door. Zheran sat with Markla in her lap while Tama ran to get some food for the child. I went to make sure the horse had been cared for and to see about doubling the watch. I also sent messengers to Lorren and to Norn and another messenger to warn the Wanderers and to say we wanted to consult with them.

That night we called a meeting to explain what had happened, not just a council meeting but a meeting of the whole settlement of Zelindar. Most of the Hadra and all the Kourmairi women among us spoke in favor of offering Friana shelter. Many said they would take turns guarding and helping her. Only Rishka had some angry words to say. "There are more and more draiga every day, wanting to shelter in our city, and this one comes with a whole bag of troubles. I have no doubt that she will cause far more grief than she is worth."

With that, Alyeeta stood up and said quietly, "I think we have no choice but to take her in. Nonetheless, we should have some wariness of a woman who lies to us about her man's violence and who still grieves for him." Her words were fair and well chosen and, for Alyeeta, very moderate. Even so, they threw a chill of foreboding over the meeting.

In the next few days, Lorren as well as several other Wanderers came to confer with us. There was tension and wariness all through the settlement. I had no doubt that Friana was right: Garrell was likely a very dangerous man. I also had no doubt that sooner or later he would come to Zelindar to claim her, in spite of our agreements with the Koormir. All of us were watchful in a way we had not been for years. Yet in the end, when he came, it was not to Zelindar but to Wanderer Hill. Perhaps he thought to find more sympathy there.

Five days after Friana had taken refuge with us, the Wanderer Ormorth came looking for me. He was a big man given to few words. "Garrell is at Wanderer Hill, demanding to be heard. Lorren asked for you to come as quickly as you can." It would have taken too long to find Dancer. I called out to Pell and Rishka to follow as fast as they could and climbed on behind Ormorth on his large, bony horse. It was like riding on Crusher again. I was glad we were going no farther than Wanderer Hill.

Already I could hear word going out through the settlement that Garrell had come. Friana was standing in the doorway as we rode by, holding onto the door frame and still looking very frail and shaky. "What is it, Tazzil? I heard all the commotion. Is it Garrell? Is he here?"

"Yes, it is Garrell, but fortunately he came to Wanderer Hill instead of here. Possibly he thought that Lorren, as a man, could understand, whereas the Hadra would all be against him. You are still very weak. You do not need to come and face him. We can speak for you. Perhaps, if all goes well, you will not need to see him at all."

She nodded and gave me a feeble little wave. "Good luck with him, Tazzil. He will not make it easy. Remember what I said. He is a very dangerous man."

We went as fast as we could with two people on that big awkward mount. Ormorth offered no comments and I asked no questions, wanting only to be there soon to end the misery of the ride. As I came rushing into the room, I heard Lorren say, "We will not begin until Tazzil is here." From the tone of his voice, I thought it was probably not the first time he had said those words.

The huge meeting hall was packed with Wanderers. They must have been gathering for days. Benches lined the back of the hall; in one corner there was a raised platform on which Lorren, Garrell, Yolande, and Bathrani were seated. Except for those last two, I think I was the only woman in the room, but it was hard to tell, for among the Wanderers men and women dress much alike. When Garrell saw me enter, he said hastily, "She is here. Now we can begin."

"No," I answered quickly. "Not until Pell and Rishka are here. I do not want to be the only Hadra present." There was a strained silence after that until Pell and Rishka rushed into the room, flushed and breathless. Then Lorren nodded and said to Garrell in a strangely formal way, "You may now proceed."

Garrell had been seated. With those words he jumped to his feet, looked all around the room, took a commanding pose, and began holding forth as if he had prepared a speech for his followers. "I have come here to speak of my wife, Friana, and to ask you, Lorren, for some help in this matter. This woman has left home, gone from her husband's side, abandoned one child, stolen the other two, run to hide with the Hadra — and all for no reason. I have no doubt these Hadra women had some hand in it. Perhaps they have been plotting it all this time. They may not be above stealing the children of others. Someone among them may even have been her secret lover and taught her all their filthy tricks. Or perhaps she was lured there by their promises of an easy, lustful life. If they are willing to steal away a man's wife, they would no doubt stop at nothing, not even—"

"Not true! None of that is true! Not one word!" I shouted. I was seething with anger and shaken by the terrible injustice of his words.

"Quiet, Tazzil, wait, you will have your turn. Let the man speak. Let him finish what he has to say."

"But ... But..." The words were pressing against my lips, wanting to burst out. I could not believe Lorren was silencing me in this way. It seemed as if he were siding with Garrell. I could feel Rishka's rage on one side of me, ready to boil over. Pell, on the other side, took my arm in a tight grip and said in my ear, "Patience, Tazzi, it will all come round. You must trust Lorren. He has his ways and this is his place. Just wait a little while and see how it turns."

Encouraged by my being silenced, Garrell went on, "I have been a good husband, given her children and a home, and now she has repaid me with this ingratitude. I believe she has been schooled by the Hadra, who hate men. They have turned her mind against me. I have come to seek justice here for the harm done to me. That is all I ask for." He gave a slight nod of his head, as if to indicate that he was done.

"Lies! All lies!" a voice shouted from the back. "How dare you come before all these people and tell such lies?" Garrell gasped. All heads turned. It was Friana, standing on a bench at the back of the room. Her fists were raised. She was shaking them at Garrell. Made strong and beautiful by the flame of anger, she looked totally different from the wan and feeble woman I had left such a short time before. There were no tears now. It was as if anger had burned all that away. She must have come with Kazouri, who was standing next to her, large and protective.

Garrell lunged as if to go at Friana, but was restrained by his own men, who had leapt up on the platform. Several Wanderers moved instantly to stand in front of him. Garrell's face was blotched with anger and his scar was throbbing vividly. "Silence! As your husband, I order you to be quiet. I order you! Who are you to come here and contradict me? I will teach you obedience soon enough."

"Garrell, you will sit down. You will order no one to do anything right now," Lorren said forcefully. "This is Wanderer space and you are a guest here. You have had your say and we have all listened politely. Now it is Friana's turn to speak and to be heard. If you cannot abide by that, then you may leave now, but you cannot disrupt this gathering with your outbursts."

"She is only a woman. Why would you listen to her stories? She will lie if—"

"Silence!" Ormorth roared.

"Sit down now or leave," Lorren added. "There is to be no violence here and no threat of violence." Garrell's two companions almost pushed him into a chair. Then they stood on either side of him, each with a hand on his shoulder, as if to prevent him from leaping up again.

Friana went on as if she had not been interrupted. "I am still weak, trying to recover from the beating you gave me, yet I knew I had to come here to speak for myself. I knew that no one else could do that for me. How can you lie about me that way when I am the one who loved you and stood by you all those years; I am the one who bore your children and suffered your blows. I even lied to other women when they questioned me about my cuts and bruises, because I could not bear to shame you in their eyes. You were my husband; I would have stayed with you all my life. But when you threatened to kill our baby, I knew it was time to leave. I had no other choice."

"I did not mean it. I was drunk," Garrell called out, struggling to rise again against the restraining hands of his companions. "I never would have harmed our child. Never!"

Lorren said sharply, "I tell you again, man, keep your peace. Later you may have another chance to speak."

At the same moment, Friana said, "Not so. Drunken men kill as well as sober ones. A baby is a fragile thing that can easily be broken. It cannot be mended like a beaten wife. 'Sorry' will not bring a baby back to life again." Then she turned her gaze on Lorren. "Now I would like to come forward and face this man and look him in the eye while I speak the truth of my life with him, or at least the truth as I have lived it. This is the only time I will ever tell my story to so many, and these are likely the last words Garrell will hear from me."

Lorren nodded. "Find your own place to speak from, Friana."

Friana walked slowly to the front of the room, with all eyes on her and the way parting before her. Kazouri stayed close by her side. Friana stopped near Garrell, though far enough back so he could not reach her with one leap. At the same time, Bathrani left her seat on the platform and slipped quickly through the crowd to stand on the other side of Friana. Now I could sit back and listen. It was Garrell's turn to be choking on unspoken words.

"I want you to be able to see me clearly, Garrell, so that you know I speak my own words and my own truth and am under no compulsion from another. This is not the Hadra who speak through me, nor is it the Wanderers. This is Friana speaking, the woman who was your wife for so many years. Even now, I bear the marks of your fists on my face and on my body. I want you to also see those clearly, so you cannot pretend that beating did not happen. The story I tell is not something I learned from the Hadra or the Witches. It is what I learned from my own life; it is written on my own body."

Occasionally stumbling over the words, Friana told her story slowly and thoughtfully, chronicling all those unspoken years of blows and abuse. We listened in silence. Sometimes she faltered. Sometimes she shook so that she could barely stand, but when anyone reached out a hand to steady her, she brushed them away. At the end of it she said, "There, it is finished, it has all been said. It never needs to be said again." She made a slight nod to us all and added, "Thank you for hearing me. No one has ever heard me before, never in all that time. I told no one." Then to Garrell she said softly, "I am sorry, Garrell, that it came to this. I wish it could have been different between us. I grieve for your pain. I tried so hard. I really loved you once. All that is over now." As Friana turned to leave, she stumbled suddenly and would have fallen if Kazouri had not grabbed her arm. Bathrani moved quickly to steady her from the other side. Friana left the room supported between them.

Garrell stared after her for a moment in amazed silence. Then he found his voice. "Lorren, are you going to let her leave that way? Are you really going to let her take away my children? Are you going to send me home without my wife and my children?"

Up till then, Yolande had watched everything and had not said a word. Suddenly she stood up, her red hair flaming brightly in the evening light, her green eyes flashing. She pointed her finger at Garrell and shouted, "I want that man out of my house! I am done with patience! I am done with listening! This house is my home as well as Lorren's, and I cannot stand the sight of that man's face anymore. I do not want to hear his voice ever again. It brings back all those years of war and death and misery. It reminds me of losing my man and my child, of being driven out of my home. It was Garrell who wanted to keep fighting and fighting until we all were dead. Get him out now, before he says another word."

Lorren was shaking his head, looking back and forth between Yolande and Garrell. "Man, did you hear nothing at all today? Have you understood none of this? I cannot make Friana come back to you, nor would I wish to. It is you who have driven her away with your own hands. In fact, it is not in my power to make Friana do anything at all. I have no army and no guards to do my bidding. If I am leader here, it is by consent or because others like my advice or my ways, but Wanderers cannot be compelled against their will and they will never compel another's will. It is against their code, against the Cerroi. As to your children, a man who is violent forfeits his right to his children. Children have their own rights. Now Yolande has said she wants you gone from here, and I must honor her wishes, as she so seldom makes them known. You have two of your own men with you. Perhaps Ormorth, Jallen, and Marth will also consent to escort you home." Then he bowed slightly. "There is something to be learned from this day, Garrell, if you can open your heart to it."

By now Garrell had struggled to his feet. His eyes were wild as he swung his head around, glaring at us all. Then he fastened his glare on Lorren. "You will regret this, Lorren the traitor, you and that woman of yours, you will be sorry for this day, I promise you that. All the misfortune in my life has been because of you. You took my father's land by trickery and now you have taken away my wife and children. You will be sorry. You will wish—"

"Go now!" Yolande thundered in a voice full of pain and fury. "NOW!"

Lorren's voice cut through the air like ice. "Out of our house! Never come back here again, Garrell, unless there is some common danger and you have been granted permission. Never come back to Wanderer Hill or Zelindar or anywhere nearby, and never try to see Friana again. That is final and absolute. Now leave!"

"On to your horse now," Ormorth commanded, forcefully taking hold of Garrell's arm. "We have a long ride ahead."

I stood watching Garrell leave, shaking my head until Rishka leaned over and said in my ear, "I think I have heard enough philosophical drivel today to last me all my life. Personally, if I could, I would take that man out and hang him. And maybe even that would be too kind."

I laughed and felt some of the tension drain away. "Ah yes, Rishka, you always were a fountain of kindness. I remember that from when we first met."

"Those were the days, eh? Well, I think I have been getting soft ever since. But in truth, what possible excuse is there for leaving a man like that alive after what he has done? He is not worth one hair on her head. And you know what the worst of it is? The worst of it is that he thinks he has the right. And the rest of the worst is that she grieves for him."

"He could change, Rishka. Maybe he learned something today."

She gave a bark of bitterly laughter. "Oh, I have no doubt he could change, but for better or for worse? What will he have to do to his next wife to prove he is a man? Chain her to the bed? Break her legs? Cut off her hands? Yes, I have no doubt he could change, but tell me, Tazzi, did he seem to you like a better man when he left? Do you think he opened his heart to Lorren's little homilies? I say he is a dangerous creature and not much addicted to the truth. The fact of it is, we would be better off with him dead, all of us. Instead, he is free to go home with his heart full of hate and make more trouble." With that, she slipped her arm through mine. "Come on, Councilor. Let me give you a ride home on Lightfoot's back. Your ride has already left, going in another direction."

There were still so many things I wanted to talk to Lorren about. There were even questions I wanted to ask Yolande, if she would consent to answer me. But not on this day. This day had already held more than one day's worth of happenings. I squeezed Rishka's arm and followed her out of the shelter.

The day was already turning toward evening. We rode home in silence, each in our own thoughts, though I was glad for the contact of Rishka's body against mine. Her words kept going through my head. I knew she was right. We would all be better off with Garrell dead. And yet, I felt some perverse crack of pity in my heart for the man, perhaps the same pity I had felt for Rishka when she had first come to us so full of rage and hate.

20

A year later, old Norn died in the early spring. His death came after a hard, three-month battle with coughing-sickness that no cure seemed able to touch, neither Kourmairi medicine nor Witch healings, nor anything else that was tried. A day or so later, his old wife, Segna, died too. It was as if she had only been waiting for him. Their double funeral brought many of us together, Hadra and Kourmairi and Wanderer. A Kourmairi delegation even came from Indaran to pay their respects. It was led by Garrell's cousin, Ossan, the new chief who had been chosen in his place. Garrell's absence did not surprise me. I certainly did not miss him. No doubt Lorren and Yolande were equally relieved not to see him there.

Standing by the funeral pyre, I was amazed at the sense of grief and loss I felt for this man had I barely known. It was as if something very fine had gone out of the world. Though I had spoken to Norn only a few times, still I had felt his protective presence watching over us all those years as we were struggling to build Zelindar. He must have known he was dying, for he had summoned me only a month before to meet the new headman, wanting, I suppose, to ensure continued peace and friendship between our peoples.

Lomaire had seemed to me as different from Norn as possible, though I sensed a strong mutual respect between them. A much younger man, he struck me as shrewd, hardheaded, practical, and fair, altogether not a bad combination for leading the Kourmairi settlement of Zelandria forward into a new era. I liked the man, yet I did not think I would ever feel the affection for him that I felt for Norn. He held out his hand to me while looking me up and down as if to take my measure. "So this is the Hadra chief. I regret I was not here for your other visits, Tazzil. And I am very glad for this chance to meet you at last." There was a slight tone of mockery or challenge in his voice. In his head I could hear him thinking, *But she is only a girl. How can she possibly have done all those things?*

I took his hand, pressed it hard, and smiled boldly into his face. "True, I am only a girl, but I am also a Hadra leader. Though we may all look like girls to you, every Hadra has done as much or more than all those stories that are told of us. Do not be fooled, Lomaire, appearances can be very deceiving."

Norn chuckled into his hand. For a moment, Lomaire stared at me, totally taken aback. Then he threw back his head and laughed. "So you can read minds, just as they say. Well, I consider myself warned. I will not think to cheat you in a trade and will do my best to keep on your good side. I can see you would make a fine ally and a formidable enemy."

"Exactly right," I answered with a nod. "A good plan. Much better an ally than an enemy."

Norn was looking very pleased. "I told you she would be something to reckon with. You have met your match and more here, Lomaire." Then he reached for a hand from each of us and pressed them together. "See that you both deal fairly and honorably with each other in the years to come. I have not much time left in this world. I am an old warrior and my kind is not needed here anymore. It is up to you now to make the new way." Suddenly he began coughing, a deep, wracking cough that shook his whole body. Segna rushed in to scold us for keeping him up so long. Then, turning her anxiety on Norn, she asked sharply, "How can you ever hope to get well if you let people take up so much of your time?" She shooed us out and was already fussing over him as we left. That was the last time I saw Norn alive.

★

I happened to be present when Lomaire and Ossan first met. Lomaire and I had been standing together, talking of Norn's death, when Ossan walked up to us. I was the one who introduced them to each other. Though they were polite enough, there was an instant tension in the air. They reminded me of two rams taking each other's measure, pawing the ground and eager to butt heads. Lomaire bowed slightly and said in that same ironic tone he had used with me, "And so, Ossan, we meet without a blade between us, you, the new chief of the Indaran settlement and I, the new headman at

Zelandria. I met your father once when our people were still enemies. I am glad to meet you now, when there is peace between our people. And I grieve that it is Norn's death that brings us here together. Let us hope there will be some happier occasion for us to meet again."

"I, too, grieve for him, though he was once my enemy. He was a bold warrior, a good leader, and an honorable man. And I also hope there will be happier times for our people all to gather."

Under this stiff, restrained talk there were some very different thoughts at work. From Ossan's mind I heard, *This man is lucky we meet in peace. He does not look as if he could hold his own with a sword. At least Norn was a fighter. This one is nothing but a merchant.*

At the very same moment, Lomaire was thinking, *Ossan is not very secure in his chiefdom. I make him uneasy, and he wishes he had his sword in hand to make him my equal. Then he would feel more like a man.*

I almost erupted in laughter; it was a hard struggle to continue making this pretense of polite conversation. Lomaire must have seen the little smile that twitched at the corner of my mouth. Suddenly he gave Ossan a brotherly pat on the shoulder. "Be careful, Ossan; this one has the gift of reading minds. From me, you have nothing to fear on that count. I would not know if you meant to run me through with your sword in the next minute, but she knows all your thoughts and how they differ from your spoken words. Of course she knows mine as well, so we are equal in that."

Ossan flushed and so did I. Lomaire had caught us both off guard and leveled us both with one well-aimed blow. I had to take a moment to catch my breath before I answered, "Well, Lomaire, as you said of me, you would make a formidable enemy. I would much rather have you for a friend. Ossan, I trust we shall meet again in better times. Now if you will both excuse me, I need to go see to the horses." The only thing I needed to see to was mending my pride and getting myself extricated from there as quickly as possible. Lomaire needed no gift of mind-sight to know that. As I walked away quickly, I heard them laughing together.

★

At the funeral pyre, Nanyia rose to speak for her grandmother, Segna. She shared childhood memories of her and even sang some songs that Segna had taught her when Nanyia was still a girl. As Nanyia stepped down, her face was wet with tears, but she shook away the hands that reached out with comfort and walked off by herself. Then Lomaire stood up to speak for Norn. This man who spoke with such passion seemed very different from the Lomaire that Norn had introduced to me or the one who had just bested me so cleverly with his words. The grief in his voice sounded real and very deep. "I mourn this man with my whole heart. I grieve for him as if he had been my own father. And, indeed, he has been a father to all of us, leading us through a hard, bloody time and into a time of peace. He is at rest now, and we must continue to build our settlement in his memory, a settlement he would be proud of if..."

As I was far from the platform, the rest of Lomaire's words were lost to me, drowned out by the wailing and chanting for the dead. After a while, I went even farther away, to be alone with my own thoughts and feelings. If I could have chosen anyone in the whole world as my grandfather, I think I would have chosen Norn. Later, when we each came up to speak our own words for the dead and add our sticks to the funeral pyre, that is what I said. Before that, of course, I had to make my formal speech as Hadra councilor.

The funeral rites were to go on all week, but some of us left after only three days, feeling we were needed at home. I rode back with Alyeeta, Lorren, Yolande, Pell, and Hereschell, an interesting combination, to be sure. At first, we shared our memories of Norn. Then, for most of the way, we talked of all that had happened in our lives since that fateful meeting at the river between the Kourmairi and the Hadra. Finally, Lorren and Hereschell began talking of Ebron's death and whether they could have prevented it. I felt a terrible sense of foreboding. Yolande looked strangely agitated, almost ill. At last, she had to ask them to stop. We all reached home in a very somber mood.

★

More than a year had gone by since our first crop of babies was born. In spite of my terrible predictions, they were all thriving, and Zelindar had not collapsed under the weight of this added burden. I myself was trying to learn how to live with the noise and disruption of children at every meeting and on every project. Now other women were swollen with child from last fall's Essu. In the rush and busyness of our lives, we had not yet held a naming and welcoming ceremony for the ones already born from the first Gimling. It was well past time.

Finally, it was decided at council that we would do a single ritual for all the new children. Tama, Ozzet, and Kilghari spoke for planning it. One morning, a month or so after Norn's death, mothers took their children down to the bay by the first light of dawn. I was with Pell and Tama as they made their preparations to go. Tama and Ishnu were fussing about, looking for last-minute things and putting them all in a basket while Pell held the child awkwardly in her arms. Laisha alternately cooed and struggled for freedom. Pell was shaking her head. "Tell me, Tazzi, did you ever think when we were forcing open the gates of Eezore or fleeing the Zarn's fastfire that it would end like this, with you as councilor of a Hadra city and me as a nursemaid to a wet and wriggly child?"

Without looking up from what she was doing, Tama said almost sharply, "Pell, if it is too hard to hold her, put her down for Ishnu to mind." By then, Laisha had struggled free of Pell's grip and was toddling unsteadily out the door with Ishnu in pursuit.

Pell shrugged and shook her head. "I try, but I am not much good at it. Tell me, Tazzi, what am I to this child? a father? an extra mother? an uncle? Maybe when she is older, I can be her big sister and teach her to ride and swim and tumble. Right now, I am all thumbs."

I had to laugh at the look of perplexed helplessness on Pell's face, especially when I thought of all the deadly perils she had faced with nothing more than her wits and her little thief-knife.

"Poor Pellandria," Tama said, giving her a quick hug and a kiss on the cheek. "Defeated and outwitted by a baby." Then Tama was out the door, rushing after the children. Ishnu had already caught Laisha up in her strong, skinny arms. Pell sighed as she took up the basket. She set off and I followed. We were soon joined by much of the population of Zelindar, flowing down to the bay together in the early-morning light.

Most of the beach had been cleared. Those boat carcasses that still remained had been hung with garlands of flowers and ribbons. Banners were flying from poles stuck in the sand. Even the boats in the bay were brightly decked. Zheran had come to join us, companionably slipping her arm through mine. She was beaming with pride at Ishnu and Laisha.

I looked around at all of us. We were quite a sight, all dressed in our best and brightest clothes for this ritual. Even Yolande was there, wearing a long, sea green dress that rippled in the wind and was almost the same color as the waves. Hugging the children, laughing and talking with the Hadra, she seemed very much at ease among us. I suppose being surrounded by a horde of little creatures made the Hadra seem less threatening to her, more like "normal women."

Suddenly Zheran loosened my arm with a gasp of fear and began running toward the shore. Looking in that direction, I saw Ursa, arms outstretched, balancing on the pointed prow of a boat that was bobbing up and down in the bay, appearing and disappearing as it headed for shore through fairly rough waves. With a cry I headed after Zheran, pushing my way through the crowd with as much speed as I could manage. Zheran reached the edge of the water just as the boat bumped the shore, its prow crunching into the sand. With a shout of laughter, Ursa tumbled into Zheran's arms, babbling excitedly, "They let me row! I almost fell in! I want to build a boat!"

Zheran immediately set to scolding Ursa for her recklessness and every Hadra in the boat for allowing it. Next, she turned to me. By then I had run up, flushed and panting. "What am I to do with her, Tazzil? She is such a constant worry. I am always afraid for her life. What makes her so wild? She is much more like a Hadra than a Kourmairi."

I shook my head. "Let her be, Zheran. I hate to see you worry so. She is agile enough and smart enough to keep herself safe. Besides, she is already a strong swimmer." So often I found myself caught between anger at the child for causing her mother so much grief and admiration for her free, wild spirit that I had no wish to tame. In exasperation I turned to scold Ursa next, but she had already taken advantage of this exchange to dash off and disappear into the crowd.

Mouraine, whose boat it was, had been watching the whole scene. Now she was laughing herself silly. When I glared at her, she shrugged and said with a grin, "No way would I have a baby if that is what they turn into. Boats are so much easier to handle, even in the worst of weather."

"Babies turn into women like you, born to plague the rest of us," I snapped at her. Now, thoroughly aggravated with Zheran and Ursa and Mouraine and most of all with myself for my bad temper, I trudged up the shore to join the other Hadra on the beach. Zheran had already gone to look for Ursa.

When the early-morning sun first showed its glowing rim over the hills of Zelindar, touching the waves with gold, that was the signal for the ritual to begin. Each mother stepped forward with her child in her arms and walked to the edge of the water. If she had a companion, that woman went with her. The rest of us drew back silently to watch. Tama went first, holding Laisha high and facing the sea. "Goddess, Mother of us all, here before You is Your child Laisha, daughter of Tamaraine and Pellandria, granddaughter of Ansoniya and Charaindru..." Tama named her mother and Pell's mother and then their mothers and their mothers' mothers, going as far back as she was able. "Mother, we name her Laisha in Your sight and hold her up to ask for Your blessing. Goddess, may You guide and protect her in this life. May she follow in Your ways. Blessed be." Tama scooped up some water from the sea to sprinkle over the child's head and in the palms of her hands. Not at all cowed by this solemn occasion, Laisha crowed with delight and tried to grab her mother's hair.

Next, Tama turned to face us. "Before you who are the women of my family and my city, we name this child Laisha. We trust she will grow up among you loved and accepted and will find her place here in Zelindar. May you also guide and protect her in this life. Laisha," she said again. This time the women answered. *Laisha, Laisha, Laisha* echoed up and down the shore.

Then the next woman held up her child and said her words, and then the next and the next, until all were done. I felt myself being relentlessly seduced into accepting this invasion of noisy little beings in our lives. When this formal part was over, there was some singing, followed by a simple breakfast of nuts, fruit, and bread, laid out on blankets on the beach. Afterward, there were games and races organized for the older children like Ishnu and Ursa, as well as wrestling and tumbling contests. Ursa won an embarrassing amount of times and made sure we noticed, while Ishnu did not win at all and hardly seemed to care.

At the end of these festivities, we all wound our way together in a long procession to the Central Circle, for Kara had announced a "surprise." There, among the terraces of bright flowers, sat a stone platform with a large, mysterious, veiled object on it. I knew it had not been there the day before. It must have been carried and set in place in the night with the greatest care for secrecy. Kara and Vestri went up on either side of this strange object while Yolande came forward to say some words about the courage of young women choosing to have babies under such circumstances. Luckily for me, it was not a long speech, for I was quite out of patience with all this talk of babies. Also, I was burning with curiosity about this hidden object. When Yolande finished, she gave a slight nod of her head. Kara and Vestri undid the cord and drew back the cloth. The surprise was suddenly revealed as a larger-than-life clay statue of a seated woman, with a girl-child standing boldly on her shoulders. The child's arms were raised in a gesture of triumph. A moment of hushed silence was quickly followed by a chorus of exclamations and then a deafening thunder of applause.

Kara had been making smaller sculptures for a while but nothing on this grand a scale. Later, I went up to congratulate her. When I hugged her, she was still shivering with excitement. "We did it! We did it! We kept it a secret. Vestri and all the apprentices helped me in the making of it. We brought it here in the dark of night." Women were crowding around to touch and caress the wonderful clay figures. Many were bringing flowers to lay at the mother's feet. Someone had woven a wreath of flowers for each of their heads.

I felt suddenly humble and deeply touched. Tears stung my eyes. This was surely the finest work I had ever seen. "Thank you, Kara, you have given Zelindar a central heart." Before I left, I heard Yolande asking Kara if she would shape a sculpture for Wanderer Hill. Kara blushed and nodded, looking very pleased. I felt full of pride for her. She had certainly come a far way from being the girl who was just a maker of plates and jugs for her family's trade. Her life was happening just as she had wished that first day in Zelindar so many years ago, that day when we had all stood together at the top of Third Hill, looking down and sharing our hopes.

Later, after Ishnu went off with Tama and Pell, and Ursa disappeared again — no doubt to more mischief — Zheran and I went home alone. As we were walking companionably together, arm in arm, she said, thoughtfully and with some sadness, "I wonder if my daughters will ever find such acceptance here."

Without a thought, I answered, "One will, but in her own time and in her own way. The other will not want it." I had no idea where those words had come from, yet instantly I knew them to be true. Zheran nodded without question, as if she really had her answer. I was feeling very loving toward her at that moment and glad we were alone together after all the excitement of the morning. Besides feeling weary, a strange sort of peaceful acceptance had come over me: for babies, for children, for mothers, for lovers, for whatever else came into my life.

Alyeeta, of course, had been right about us. After a while, Zheran and I had indeed become lovers, but in a quiet way. This was not the youthful passion I had shared with Kara or the hard sexuality that I had known with Pell or that strange bond that had tied me to Alyeeta. Certainly this had none of the wild madness that Rishka had brought into my life. With Zheran I shared a gentle, quiet loving that filled my soul with much-needed peace, gave some steadiness to my life, and made me humbly grateful.

Now, with the house empty of children, we took off our ritual clothes, set them aside with care, and lay down together for a moment of rest.

Feeling loving and contented, I reached over and drew Zheran's body against mine. She gave a deep sigh of pleasure and snuggled into me. Gently, almost playfully, I nibbled on the back of her neck. Then, with sudden urgency, those nibbles turned into sharp little bites.

Both of us had talked of how tired we were, how much we needed to rest. Instead, I found myself needing to touch, to reach out, to be close. Almost without volition, my hands began traveling over the soft familiar roundness of her body: over her breasts, her belly, her thighs. Sensuously unresistant, I could feel her opening herself to me in a way she was seldom able to when the girls were home, even when they were sleeping.

Soon she was moving catlike against my caresses and giving little moans of pleasure. Heat rose between us. Moaning in response, I found myself sinking deeper and deeper into the familiar comfort of her warmth while waves of desire burned along my nerves. As my hands moved down her body, Zheran groaned and parted her legs slightly. My fingers slipped into her wet fullness. With another groan, she turned a little, opening her legs wider and arching her back, spreading herself out under my hands. Following that invitation, my finger began moving faster and faster. I was feeling the echo of her pleasure as an ache of desire deep in my own body, a rising heat between my legs. Responding to the rocking of her body and the urgency of her moans, I slipped another finger inside and then a third. She was opening still more under the pressure of my fingers, her body calling to my hand, pushing against it, hungry and needful. I pressed harder, pushing back against her need.

Suddenly the resistance was gone and my whole hand slipped inside her. I gave a gasp of surprise at finding myself enveloped in deep, wet warmth, a living cave that closed around my wrist. Awed and startled, I moved my hand slightly. With a wild cry of pleasure, she clamped her legs around my arm and rode my hand until her whole body shuddered in release. As my cry echoed hers, she sank hard fingers into my hair and grabbed me against her in a bone-crushing embrace. Then, for a while, we lay still and silent that way, bodies pressed tight together, heart beating against heart, breath ragged, my hand still inside her.

Finally I whispered in her ear, "Zheran, you have to give me back my hand." With a sigh she released me. I drew back a little to look at her. "Woman, you are certainly full of surprises. That has never happened to me before with anyone." I was amazed that this reserved, dignified woman could suddenly be so wild and full of passion.

She gave me a quick, sharp look, an expression that had both blame and heat in it. "Or with me either, Tazzil, you may be sure of that."

Later, Zheran fell asleep in my arms. I lay awake a long time. Watching her sleep, there was such a feeling of tenderness in my heart, I found myself wishing that nothing more eventful than that day's happenings would ever again occur in our lives.

21

The advance of the Shokarn army was no secret. Such a large force could not move through the land undetected. First, Kourmairi from the east rode in to warn us. Then came the Wanderers who had been tracking and observing the army's movements. Next, our own sentries found the guards and began following them in our direction, reporting back to us in relays. From all reports, the Shokarn were avoiding Kourmairi settlements and, indeed, whenever possible, any contact at all with the Kourmairi. It seemed clear that Zelindar and Wanderer Hill were the targets of this incursion.

When they were less than half a day's ride away, we Hadra would have known with no warning from anyone. We each had our own inner warning systems hammering away at us, signaling the approach of some large, hostile force. My head throbbed constantly and my chest ached. Many of the other Hadra complained of the impact. Jhemar, especially, felt assaulted.

Already there had been meetings, discussions, and even some arguments among us. Some of the Kourmairi and even some of the Wanderers spoke for attacking the Shokarn before they came any closer, as we were many times their number, which our sentries had reported at fewer than four hundred and probably closer to three. "We will have to fight them sooner or later. Why not do it as far from our homes as possible?" That was the question many were asking.

The Hadra, of course, could not fight in that manner, and Lorren was totally opposed to the inevitable bloodshed that would follow. He argued for a very different course, saying, "Let me go and speak with them under a flag of safe conduct. I think I can persuade them to go back. Who would know better what to say to a captain of the guards? They may be soldiers, but after all, they are still just men and not so different from ourselves."

Yolande, with none of her usual calm demeanor, cried and pleaded with him to change his mind. "I am begging you, my husband. Please, Lorren, if you have ever loved me, do not go. It will likely mean your death." The rest of us joined her, calling out, "No, Lorren, they will surely kill you." "Lorren, you will only be throwing your life away." "Whatever you say to them, Lorren, we will still have to fight." There were even some mutterings of suspicion among the Kourmairi concerning Lorren's loyalty. "What do we really know of this man? Why should we follow him? Perhaps he is still the Zarn's agent and is planning to leave us open to attack." Through all of it, Lorren was adamant. "I have to do this. Of what use is all my work here if it only ends in slaughter?"

By late afternoon, the enemy appeared as tiny black dots across the width of the plain. We were all assembled at Wanderer Hill, Wanderer and Hadra and Kourmairi from both settlements. There were even some Kourmairi from north and east of us and some Hadra from other settlements. I had been dismayed and angry to see Garrell among the Kourmairi from Indaran. The talk was that Ossan was gravely ill from eating poisoned food and so Garrell had come in his place. Because of our common danger and at Garrell's insistence, Lorren had reluctantly granted him permission to be there among us, in spite of Yolande's strong objections.

Lomaire was also there, probably because he thought he should be, but he looked uneasy and out of place. He would have been far more comfortable, I suppose, if a vast caravan of merchants were advancing on us rather than a hostile army. At least he had the good sense to stay out of the way and let some of the other men of Zelandria take charge. A few of our people, Lomaire among them, stayed at the top of Wanderer Hill to keep watch on what was happening, but most of us, many hundred strong, went to gather at the base of the hill where the flatlands began. Our extra horses had already been taken off to the side, clearing the space between us and the Shokarn army. The Koormir and the Wanderers were armed with whatever they could find in preparation for an attack: swords, pitchforks, pikes. The Hadra were interspersed among them. We were massed as if for battle, though we had finally agreed to let Lorren try his plan first. We agreed partly because he had been so insistent but also because we really had nothing better to offer. Even Yolande had fallen silent.

The Shokarn finally came in sight late in the day. Lorren rode forward with those we had agreed would accompany him: Ormorth and Turin from among the Wanderers; Garrell and two others from Indaran; three men I did not know from Zelandria. Of the Hadra, Pell, Rishka, and myself rode beside him. As we approached the Shokarn, an angry buzz rose in back of us from among our ranks. The noise grew louder and louder, until Lorren finally signaled for silence. It was then that I noticed a Kourmairi among the Shokarn. Rhomar, the man who had been Zheran's husband, was riding with them as if he were their guide.

As they got closer I could see the Shokarn captain conferring intently with Rhomar. The captain seemed confused and angry. We may not have been as Rhomar had led him to expect. Meanwhile, we continued riding forward at a slow, steady pace. Lorren rode in the middle, bearing a huge yellow banner for safe-speaking. When we were within hearing range, Lorren called out, "Captain Perthan, on your honor, I claim the shelter of a Shokarn truce so we may talk."

"Lorren the traitor, we were once friends when you served the Zarn, but you can no longer lay claim to my friendship. You have dishonored your Shokarn name and can claim nothing of us." Nonetheless, the captain raised his hand for his troops to stop. Then he rode forward several more steps before he himself stopped. When Rhomar made a move to accompany him, he was ordered to stay back. *That, at least, is a beginning,* I thought. *Perhaps something good will come of Lorren's plan after all.*

Lorren spoke very calmly. "I ask that you and I both dismount, Captain, and that we meet in the middle to confer. My people are somewhat outarmed, but yours, as you can see, are far outnumbered. Perthan, please, you cannot win this encounter. Few of you will even get home alive. But many of my own people will also die unnecessarily. I want to avoid that if at all possible."

"I will give you till the departing sun touches the tallest tree on that hill to say your piece, Lorren the traitor, that is all. Then we will do what we were sent here to do. You must not expect me to go back to Eezore in disgrace as you did. I have no plans to live as an outcast and be a penniless Wanderer all my life." After those words, they both rode forward slowly till they were about twenty feet apart. Then Lorren raised his hand, slid from his horse, and took a few more steps. He planted the flag of truce by driving the sharpened end of the pole into the ground. After that, he stepped back again with a slight bow. The yellow flag flapped between them like a strange sort of boundary. "First of all, Captain, why have you come here into our peaceful country with this force of men?"

"A country that harbors the Hadra is not a peaceful country. The Hadra are all enemies of the Zarn and any who shelter them are his enemies as well. By befriending them, you have declared war on the Zarn himself. He plans to see you all punished as traitors." While the captain recited those harsh words as if they had been committed to memory, he kept glancing nervously at our large number.

"The Hadra cannot help who they are," Lorren answered. "They were born with powers. They did not choose them and could not put them aside even if they wished to, but they are no threat to the Zarn." He spoke in a clear, steady voice that seemed to hold no anger. "You can see that they have gone as far from him as possible. Why have you followed us here when all we want is peace?"

"The Hadra are all outlaws, as are many of the Wanderers. As you well know, the Hadra even fought against the Zarn's guards in Mishghall, something he will never forgive. And you, Lorren, you are an escaped prisoner. I have orders to burn out this nest of traitors and to bring you back alive to stand trial in Eezore as an example for others." At this, there was an uproar from the watchers, followed by a thunderous response from the guards. When Lorren and the captain had succeeded in bringing silence again, Lorren asked calmly, "And if I agreed to go back peacefully with you to Eezore, would you turn away from here and leave these folk in peace?"

Now the Wanderers were shouting, "No! No! We will fight for you, Lorren! We will not let you go!" Over this noise I heard Rhomar shouting, "Do not listen. Do not trust him. He is the leader of their army, he is the one. Without him their defense will quickly fail and fall apart. Kill him and they will lose all their will to fight." He looked as if he could barely restrain himself. At his words, I signaled to Pell and Rishka. Quickly we started riding forward. At the same moment, Rhomar suddenly dashed from the ranks of guards and began charging straight at Lorren with his sword drawn. Urging Dancer into a gallop, I cut in front of Lorren from one side just as Pell and Rishka came in from the other.

We were not an instant too soon. Howling with rage, Rhomar was upon us, ready to cut down an unarmed man. Instead, he met with three Hadra, crashed against our wall of power, and fell from his horse with his own bloody sword in his chest. It all happened so fast that Lorren had no chance to step back. All of us were spattered with Rhomar's blood, and the captain himself was thrown down by Rhomar's fleeing horse.

Now the fighting will begin, I thought. My heart was pounding with fear. Rishka and Pell rushed to help the captain to his feet so his men could see he was unharmed, while I kept my body in front of Lorren to shield him from another assault. The Shokarn troops seemed ready to break rank and attack at any moment, even without an order from their leader. I was watching so intently for danger from that direction that I was unaware of danger in back of us until I heard the shouts. By the time I turned, it was already too late. Garrell had ridden at Lorren, thrown himself off his horse onto Lorren's back, and stabbed him three times before his own men could grab his arms and stop him.

Yolande wailed from the top of the Hill, a loud, terrible cry of grief and anguish. As if that had been a signal, those who had been watchers at the top came roaring down the hill, riding full speed. They joined those waiting at the bottom and suddenly all the Kourmairi and Wanderers, howling and screaming with rage, were charging straight at the Shokarn troops. The Shokarn, leaderless and vastly outnumbered, turned and fled. The battle that Lorren would have given his life to avoid was suddenly in motion all around us. All we could do now was try to shelter his body until the mass of riders had passed. He was still breathing, but there was blood bubbling between his lips.

Yolande had quickly ridden up to us. With a cry she threw herself off her horse. In an instant, she was at Lorren's side. Taking hold of his hand, she pleaded, "Stay with us, Lorren. Alyeeta will mend you. Trust us. We will take you home."

Lorren was shaking his head. It was plainly a struggle for him to speak. "Too late, my love ... Just as well ... So sorry ... Loved you so much ... Take care of her, Tazzil ... Good friend..." He groaned and his head slumped back. The bubbling of blood turned into a flow. He gave a last few gasps and then was still.

"Do something, Alyeeta! Help him! All of you! Why are you just standing there?" Yolande jumped up, grabbed Alyeeta's shoulders, and began shaking her. Gently, Pell and I took hold of Yolande's arms from either side to restrain her.

Alyeeta was shaking her head. "It is too late, child. I would have tried anything possible to save him, but the damage was already done." Alyeeta, who never cried, had tears in her eyes.

"No! No! No!" Yolande was shouting, struggling in our arms.

The captain had fallen nearby, trampled by the rushing horses. His body looked broken and he was groaning in pain. With a yell, Yolande broke free of our grip, snatched up Perthan's sword, and rushed over to him. Carried by the force of her fury, she stabbed him through the heart, driving the sword straight down and covering herself with blood. Then she stumbled back to Lorren and threw herself down on his body, screaming and beating the ground with her fists. "I told you not to go! I told you! I told you! Oh, Lorren, why did you have to leave me?"

The rush of the battle had already moved past us. Lorren was dead, Rhomar was dead, the captain was dead, and there were other bodies lying on the ground beyond them. Yolande was sobbing in Bathrani's arms. Ormorth took down the truce flag and hacked the pole in two with the captain's bloody sword. Then we bound the flag to the two pieces of pole, making a litter of that bright, hopeful yellow flag to carry Lorren's body home. Yolande got to her feet with Bathrani's help. At that moment, Garrell's two companions came forward, dragging Garrell between them, bound with rope. They had been watching the scene intently. "Lady, do you want us to kill him now or do you want to cut his throat yourself?"

Yolande glanced down at her bloody hands and tried to wipe them on her bloody skirt. Next, she looked Garrell full in the face with a long, silent stare. Then she turned away and said to the men, "No, keep him a prisoner. Let him stand trial before all our people. Let him answer for what he has done here." She stood very straight at that moment. Her eyes were dry now. She spoke with an icy calm that was even more frightening than her rage had been.

We shifted Lorren's body onto the cloth. As soon as we lifted him, his blood made a sea of orange-red on that yellow cloth. Together we made our way slowly up the Hill, carrying Lorren home. Ormorth and two other Wanderers took the weight of the pole on one side, while Pell, Rishka, and myself went on the other. Yolande went alongside with a hand on his body. She was stately and dignified again, with no sign of the fierce rage that had just killed a man, though I could feel it simmering just under her surface cold. Though her hands and clothes were covered with blood, she took no notice of it. When others tried to take her arm to give support, she shook them off.

No one rode. Everyone walked slowly behind us. The mourning dirge started from in back of us and swept forward, suddenly making Lorren's death very real. It had all happened so fast that it was hard to comprehend. Now, with that sound, I suddenly understood that Lorren was not wounded. We were not really taking him home. He would not be healed. He would never sit up again or speak or smile or share his study with me. He was really dead. The rest of us were caught in the dirge and added our own voices. Only Yolande remained silent, her silence ringing louder in my ears than the chant itself. In the distance, I could still hear the sounds of battle. The sun was setting now over Wanderer Hill, in a bank of blood red clouds.

★

The altar in the meeting hall at Wanderer Hill had been cleared, and Lorren's body had been laid out there, covered with flowers and aromatic leaves. The Wanderers took turns loyally standing watch over him. Ormorth, his craggy face all twisted with grief, was the first to stand at Lorren's head, while Conath, crying openly, stood at his feet.

The funeral seemed endless. Though the funeral pyre was lit on the third evening, the mourning and commemoration went on for weeks afterward, with people coming from as far away as Mishghall and even Eezore. The Koormir of Indaran and Zelandria were there in peace. Many Kourmairi came from settlements still farther away. Some even came from Darthill. Hadra arrived from the coastal settlements to grieve with us for our loss, and many stayed to see what we were building at Zelindar. Wanderers returned from wherever they had been traveling when the awful message had caught up with them. Hereschell had already been on his way home. Now, though his own grief was crushing, he was prepared to stay and help in whatever way he could.

The funeral taught me much about Lorren that I had not known when he was alive. He was my friend, and I had my own terrible loss to deal with. Now I also saw how much he meant to others, in ways I could not have imagined. So many stories were told of him. All throughout Yarmald, he had stood for hope and change. He had been a guard captain and trained killer who had become a man of peace; a Highborn who gladly let go of all he owned and shared what he had; a Shokarn who treated Wanderers and Kourmairi and Hadra as equals; a soldier who felt grief and guilt and pain for everyone he had ever harmed; a man of factual learning who had opened his mind and heart to the learning that only Witches and Star-Born could teach. He had made possible a home for the Wanderers and a place for the Hadra to live in peace. Even the Witches had found a refuge because of him. The Kourmairi from both settlements had ended their deadly little war under his guidance. He had touched and transformed all our lives. As I watched and listened to all this, I felt numb with grief and disbelief. Some part of my mind was still unable to accept the reality of what had happened.

★

It was not till after the funeral was over that the trial began. Garrell had been held prisoner all this time by his own people. From his appearance, he had been badly beaten and scarcely fed at all. When he was brought into the hall, he looked about, dazed and bewildered. This was clearly not the end of the drama as he had envisioned it.

The proceedings lasted two days, two days that seemed endless to me. As councilor for the Hadra, out of respect for Yolande, out of my deep love for Lorren, and for a dozen other reasons, it was necessary for me to attend. But if it were just up to me, if I had had the choice, I would not have set foot in that place. Once there, I could not sit still for long. Sometimes I paced at the back of the hall and sometimes I had to go out for air. I felt as if the breath were being sucked out of me.

The trial was convened at Wanderer Hill in the great hall. This time the hall felt dark and somber. There were no banners and bright flowers to grace the stark stone walls. A platform for speakers had been set up in the corner again and Hereschell had been chosen to preside. The Kourmairi of Indaran had wished to hold the trial in their own settlement. Perhaps they had wanted to show how harsh they could be to one of their own who had broken his pledge. After all, Garrell had disgraced them all by going against his word. But Yolande had insisted on it being held at the Hill. Hereschell had given her his backing. Because of her loss and the Kourmairi's terrible debt to her, she had her way. Yolande said almost nothing during those two days, until it was her own turn to speak. She sat very still and pale the whole time, listening intently to every word, her eyes sometimes fixed on the speaker and sometimes on Garrell.

With all the heated feelings in that constantly shifting crowd, Hereschell often had to struggle to keep order. Ossan was the first to speak. His words were tight and his body stiff, almost rigid, with barely suppressed fury. "It was no sudden impulsive anger that caused Lorren's death. That man," he said, pointing at Garrell as if he could not bear to say his name, "that man has been planning betrayal and vengeance for a long time. His first visit to Darthill was over a year ago. That was probably when he started plotting this treachery with Rhomar, cursed-be-his-name!

"I have no doubt that my own poisoning was part of his plot. I met with that man to share some food and drink and talk on the night before those of us from Indaran were to set out for Wanderer Hill. I had said he could not come, and he was trying to change my mind. Later, I was so sick I almost died. The next morning he rode off with our people, telling them I had appointed him to go in my place. I cannot prove his was the poisoner's hand, but I know it in my heart as surely as I know the sun will rise each morning. It was days before I could stand on my own feet again. It is only by Her mercy that I am here today or, for that matter, that any of us are here. He deliberately brought the Shokarn army down on our heads. He could have gotten us all killed." At those words, the crowd exploded in shouts of agreement and loud angry curses. Ossan sat down abruptly. He still looked weak and ill.

After that, there was an outpouring of words. Many of Garrell's own people spoke against him, especially the men, trying to distance themselves as much as possible from his guilt. Several of them recounted the violent and inflammatory things he had said to them and assured us of their own total innocence in all this. "I told him that he was mistaken. I said over and over that Lorren was a great man and a great leader who had finally brought peace to the Koormir, but he would not listen. Even after he was no longer headman, he still wanted us to follow him into all kinds of dangerous mischief. I knew he was not a sound man, but I had no idea he contemplated murder or that he thought of bringing in the Shokarn guards."

I heard many versions of these words in those two days. The Kourmairi spoke hour after hour in this vein, each trying very hard to make as much space as possible between the speaker and "that man" with his loathsome deeds. The rest of us added our own litany of accusations. Poor Garrell, he had unintentionally brought us all together by uniting us against him.

Aside from this self-serving talk, the most important information to surface was that Garrell had taken that first trip to Darthill not long after the incident with Friana. He had returned several more times. It was no accident that Rhomar thought Lorren to be our war leader. Garrell must have enflamed his mind with such absurd ideas. When Garrell finally spoke for himself, he was both defiant and bewildered, not yet able to comprehend what great wrong he had done. He even spoke freely of conspiring with Rhomar. "I had hoped the guards would fight the Wanderers and the Hadra, leaving Zelindar open to my people. Then we could reclaim what was rightfully ours, all that had been stolen away by that man's trickery."

Even after all his people had said, somehow Garrell still managed to see himself as a misunderstood hero and leader, a brave and clever man ridding the world of traitors like Lorren who stood in the way of his grand plans. He had pictured driving out the Hadra and the Wanderers and leading his people to victory — over the small inconvenience of piles of dead bodies. Hereschell kept having to call for silence over the crowd's indignant buzz. When Hereschell questioned Garrell about breaking his sword-oath, Garrell answered scornfully, "That had no meaning. It was not even my own sword I swore on, just one taken at random from the pile." He went on, with righteous anger, to tell how Lorren and Yolande had personally done him wrong. "They lured away my wife and little children, turned them over to the Hadra for their use, judged against me, and sent me home bereft."

Rishka, standing next to me, kept saying, "Liar, liar, liar," like an angry little chant, but I shook my head. I thought something far more disturbing was happening here. The man was not a liar. He believed his own words, all of them, no matter how preposterous they sounded to the rest of us. His mind was held captive by bitterness. His thoughts had been shaped by it. When Pell, on the other side of me, began echoing Rishka by also chanting, "Liar, liar," I snapped impatiently, "Well, Pell, you are not so fond of the truth yourself."

At that, Pell answered indignantly, "I may tell stories, but I never lie." I smiled then, for the first and only time during that trial. How could I hope to explain to either of them that I was in an anguish of pity for this man who pictured himself as a noble and heroic leader and appeared to others only as a treacherous murderer and a fool?

While Garrell defended himself during the trial, Yolande sat very straight, listening to his every word. She said not one word in response. In the end, when she rose to speak for herself, she was painfully brief. First, she looked all around in silence, as if trying to gather her words. Finally she shook her head. "All ruined, his life and Lorren's and mine. I have listened and listened, waiting for my time to speak, thinking I had so much to say — but what does any of it matter now? All ruined. The person that mattered most to me in the world is dead. Garrell has had his revenge and destroyed his own life as well. Nothing that you do to this man will bring Lorren back. And what can I possibly say that will change in any way what has happened here?" With that, she sat down again, that in her eyes were a man's to do. She looked out of her cool green eyes at a world where the sun had suddenly been extinguished and became more like the Hadra all the time with what she could do and undertake. Yet, I think she still saw us as strange creatures, not proper women, for, in her world, there were men and they did things in a certain way and there were women and they did things in a different way. We Hadra were some deviant thing outside that system, though she herself became more like us with each passing day.

22

Now that Rhomar was dead, Ozzet had decided to go back to Darthill for a visit. She longed to see her grandmother and mother and sisters again. Most of all, she missed her father. Also, she felt the need to mourn properly for her grandfather, Nhokosos, and to solve the mystery of his death. She would do a seed-search for us as well. She even spoke of trying to find us a boat in Darthill and returning by way of the Escuro River, exploring its banks to see what grew there and staying at settlements along the way. Several of her Hadra friends were planning to go with her. It sounded to me like a fine adventure and probably very valuable to us as well. I even felt a little pull of longing for the freedom of the road. But I had no time for such things at that moment, not with the new Zildorn rising at the top of Third Hill.

Since Alyeeta had spoken of going back to Darthill to mourn for Nhokosos, Ozzet asked if she wanted to accompany them. Alyeeta was quick to refuse. "No, thank you. I am much too old for such a trip. Since my pony, Gandolair, has died, there is no horse I trust. As for boats, they are even worse than horses. Take my respects to your family. I leave it to you to mourn for my old friend and discover if it was treachery that killed him. Come back and tell me everything, Ozzet."

Ozzet also asked Zheran if she wanted to go back with her, but Zheran shook her head. "No, the children need me here. Besides, all that is over now. Rhomar has poisoned Darthill for me. If my sons want to see me, they will have to come in this direction. I will send them a message with you, though who knows if they will want to hear from me after all their father has said. Perhaps they even blame me for his death."

then as she was later, seeming so carefree, laughing with such ease when she came to visit, and, still later, with the dark stain of that bruise across her cheek. She had also followed her fate and made her own choices. What did I know or understand of such a life and how could I judge? I disentangled my hand from hers and stood up slowly. "I will do anything for you that I can, Friana, but Garrell has put himself beyond my help." As I walked away from the sound of her crying, my heart was tearing with pity. At that moment, being human did not seem like an easy thing.

I should have hated this man for killing the friend I loved. I should have felt avenged as I saw him walk off, naked and dazed, into whatever exile he would find, or, more likely, into his own slow, lonely death. Instead, I found myself sick with pity. I had to ask myself what I might have done and who I might have killed when I had been so filled with bitterness, if my powers had not prevented me. Now I was filled with pity instead, pity for everyone: for Yolande and Ormorth; for Friana and Garrell and their children; for Rishka, who had been so bitter and so angry herself; for Alyeeta with her terrible losses; and, of course, for Lorren, and even for myself, though no more and no less than for the others. Who could I find to talk to in my grief and confusion who would understand all of it?

With Yolande I could share my grief for Lorren, but I dared not whisper a word of kindness for Garrell. With Friana I could share my feelings about Garrell, but she would plead with me to change what could not be changed. Certainly I could not talk with Pell or Rishka, who both thought we should have killed Garrell outright; nor with Alyeeta, who said she would have gladly strung him up herself. Even Zheran felt no mercy for Garrell; he was too much like Rhomar. And none of them really understood my feelings for Lorren.

Finally I went looking for Olna. We sat together in the shade of some trees while I poured out my heart to her. She listened to me for a long time with her quiet kindness. At last she said softly, "Now you understand what I meant so long ago when I told you there were only two choices left for me in the world: love or hate. Now you can see why I chose love, a hard choice but the only one I could make. It was not made without a lot of pain." Then she stood up suddenly and held out her hand to me. "Come with me, Tazzia, I have something to show you."

Without question I followed her. We went in silence, going by smaller and smaller paths that wound upward, until we scrambled out onto a small rock ledge high above the water. The way we had just come was well concealed from sight by vines and brush. This must have been one of Olna's secret little places that she was sharing with me out of love.

"This is where I come to think when the world grows too perplexing. No one can find me here. I sit looking out at the sea and letting the Mother take away my pain. If you have more to say, Tazzia, I would be glad to listen, as it is also a good place for talking." Deeply touched by her offer, I shook my head. Instead, we sat there together a long time in silence, watching the rise and fall of the waves, rhythmic and ceaseless, like the breathing of some giant being.

★

For those next few months, Lorren was often on my mind. No matter what else I was doing, thoughts of him would intrude unexpectedly. Full of eagerness, I would suddenly think of something to tell him or show him, only to remember with a sinking heart. Then I would relive his death one more time. I kept wondering why he had put himself directly in harm's way. It was hard to think there had been no intention in it. Anyone could have seen this might happen. Could Lorren have walked into his death so unawares or had it been his wish in some secret inner place? Had he grown weary of hauling along all his old guilts, all his pain over what he had done in the past? It was a suspicion I never shared with Yolande. She had pain enough of her own to deal with without thinking that Lorren had walked knowingly to his death, that he had left her on purpose.

Such a loss, such a waste. It was madness for the Shokarn to have thought Lorren our war chief; Lorren who only wanted peace, who would never have lorded power over anyone that way. He was not that kind of leader. Besides, the Wanderers would never have allowed it. How painfully ironic that the battle had been won and the Shokarn defeated in the name of a man of peace.

O Lorren! Where are you now? I had been so sure we would be friends all our lives. I knew he would not willingly have left this place, nor would I, and so I thought we would grow old together, sharing the memories of near a lifetime, being friends and neighbors and something more, something for which there is scant example between men and women, passionate companions of the mind. My grief and loss were terrible. I could scarcely imagine what Yolande must be feeling. Yet even our shared loss did not break the final boundary between us — at least, not at first.

After Lorren's death, Yolande became the undisputed leader of the Hill, doing many of those things her husband had once done, those things suddenly putting her head in her hands. Bathrani went to put her arms around Yolande, and I felt a sharp stab of pain in my chest, as if a knife blade had twisted there.

After the trial was over and everyone had had their say, Yolande rose one last time. "I want nothing to do with the sentencing. I only wanted the truth to be spoken here and the truth to be heard." We Hadra said the same and so did the Wanderers. It was left to the Kourmairi leaders of both settlements to decide, and that took most of the next day. The rest of us milled about Wanderer Hill, not part of making the decision and yet unable to go home till we had heard it.

Hereschell came up to me and laid an arm over my shoulder. "This has not been easy to listen to, Tazzi, not for those of us who loved Lorren as we did." Then he shook his head. "Poor Garrell. Poor fool, poor, poor fool. He even deluded himself into believing he was doing something good for his people. He knows nothing of the Cerroi. I am very glad it was the Wanderers who fostered me and not the Kourmairi. I myself could have been that man if I had been raised on such a diet of bitterness and hate."

"So could I," I said softly, "but my powers would not let me. I could almost feel sorry for him, even after all the damage he has done. Tell me, Hereschell, is that too strange?"

He shook his head. "What else could one feel? He has lost everything, even his soul. And he still has no comprehension of what he did."

I nodded. As we were speaking, I had been looking out from Wanderer Hill over the hills of Zelindar toward the sea. "There is so much here along this southern coast with which to make a good life. There is as much as any of us need, as much as we could possibly desire. How did he manage to shut his eyes to all of it?" Even as I said those words, my heart ached with pity.

In the afternoon a gong was rung. We all rushed to fill the hall again. Such a large crowd had assembled that many were left outside, straining to listen and to see in through the doors and windows. A loud, expectant hum of voices filled the room. Hereschell raised his hands for silence. But it was Ossan who finally rose to speak those words: *"Naked exile!"*

I could feel the shock run through the room. Now the sound rose from a hum to a roar. The Kourmairi consider such a sentence worse than death, worse even than hanging. The person is sent out with nothing but his bare skin. No Kourmairi is to help him in any way: no healing, no food, no water, no clothes, no shelter. They cannot even speak with him. If they do anything to even acknowledge his existence, they will suffer the same sentence. It had not been only Lorren's murder that had weighed in the decision but also Garrell's betrayal of his own people, his treachery in conspiring to bring Shokarn troops among us.

It would have been kinder to slit his throat, much kinder. From now on, he was a marked man, his forehead tattooed for all to see. If he ever came back to Indaran or Zelandria or if he was sighted anywhere along this southern coast by the men of those settlements, he could be killed on sight.

Over the uproar I suddenly heard Friana cry out across the crowded hall, "No! No! No!" Her voice rose in a terrible wail. I saw Hereschell and Bathrani rush to her, but I was trapped where I was. By the time I was able to struggle through the crush, they had carried her outside and laid her down on some sort of mat under a tree. I dropped to my knees beside her and she grabbed my hand. "Thank the Goddess you are here. Talk to them, Tazzil; make them change. They will listen to you. It is the madness in him that made him do such a terrible thing, and now he is to be punished for it. Oh, what will become of him? It is a walking death. It would have been more merciful to kill him outright. If not for the children, I would go with him and share his exile."

"You would be exiled too, branded as he will be, cut off from all the rest of us."

"Part of me will be exiled with him anyway. How can I sleep at night, thinking of him wandering alone with no clothes and no weapons? How can I ever have any peace during the day? And I feel some terrible responsibility for what happened. If I had not come here, if I had stayed with him, none of this would have happened."

"And your little girls would both be dead and likely you would be dead as well. No, Friana, you did what you had to do."

Hereschell came to squat at my side. "Garrell had his own fate to follow and his own choices to make, and so, no doubt, did Lorren. You were only the excuse, Friana, you were not the cause."

"It will be my torture, my sentence, to think of him every day, out there, suffering. It would be easier to share it with him, but my children need me. They have already suffered enough." She turned to Bathrani, appealing to her. "No one understands, we were children together, we grew up sharing our dreams. He is a piece of me and I of him. My heart will go into exile with him."

I had a sudden flash of that lovely young woman with her baby in her arms, defying her angry young husband in order to end the killing. And

For the next few days, I was hardly home at all. Besides being involved with the preparations for Ozzet's trip, I was making trade deals with the Wanderers and organizing the replanting of several storm-damaged fields. Finally, Zheran caught hold of me when both the girls were out of the house. She actually blocked my way before I could rush off again. "I need to talk to you, Tazzil, if you can stand still long enough to listen." She was annoyed, but there was also a note of desperation in her voice.

Though I knew it was not fair to Zheran, keeping busy was one of my ways of dealing with the terrible pain of Lorren's death. I sat down immediately. "I am here and listening. What is troubling you, Zheran?"

"It is Ursa. What should I tell her, Tazzil? She wants to go north with Ozzet and her friends. She is much too young to leave, and besides, she does not have their powers of protection. But she is so relentlessly insistent. She gives me no peace about it."

"You are the one who is really her mother, not me. You are the one who should decide."

"But what if you thought of her as yours, what would you say then? Tell me, is she not too young?"

"I doubt if you really want to hear my answer, Zheran."

"Of course I do. Why else would I ask you?"

I shrugged, feeling trapped and wary. "She will soon have her first-bloods. She will be thirteen years this summer. If it were mine to decide, I would bless her and let her go. She is old enough to go out and take some risks in the world."

At those words, Zheran gave a wailing cry such as Kourmairi women give for the dead. Then she sat rocking herself with her head in her hands. "You do not care for her, you never did. If you loved her, you would not think of sending her out into such dangers. How do you know she will come back alive? Maybe I will never see her again. I have already lost one family. How can I bear to lose another?"

"Zheran, you were not much older when you married and had your first child. You yourself left your own family and went to live in a new place, among strangers."

"But I did not choose to go. I had no choice. She is the one wanting to leave, insisting on it. I would never have sent her away. Never!"

I threw up my hands. "Zheran, it is yours to decide. There is no need to ask me when you only want to argue. Do what you think best."

"What!? You will not even fight for her? Her freedom does not matter to you? You will let her mother's crazy fears cripple her life? You would argue better for any other girl in Zelindar, perhaps any other girl in all Yarmald."

Now I was seething with anger. "Well, just tell me the right answer, Zheran, so I will know what to say. Whichever way I speak, I am under attack. The wind blows in both directions. I think I am safer out of this house."

I could barely hold my temper. I had my hand on the door latch when she caught my arm. "Wait, Tazzil, I am sorry. It is just that I am so confused and so afraid for her. I think I must be a little mad with it. I thought they would grow up and marry and live near me in safety. Ishnu will, but not Ursa. She is a wild one, more like a Hadra. How did she get so wild living in my house? She really is more like your daughter. Look how she rides."

Yes, I thought, *and how she stands, how she carries herself, how she climbs to the top of everything, how she looks out at the world with a pride that is almost arrogance. Why was I not more of a mother to this child when I had the chance?* It was other women who had taught her to swim and to read and to ride, because I thought I had no time. I was always busy, and now it was too late. Now she was leaving, and the only gift I could give to make up for my absence was to argue for her freedom. I was shaking my head. "Zheran, Ursa has her own wild nature, shaped by the Mother. She needs to be true to her nature, just as you need to be true to yours."

At my words, Zheran gave another wail of grief. I went to put my arms around her and held her against me in silence. When she was a little calmer, I whispered softly in her ear, "Sometimes it is better to give consent when the bird will fly anyway. That way, she goes with your blessing instead of your curse. That way, there are not bitter feelings on both sides." *And not the terrible crushing guilt if something happens and bad words are the last words ever spoken, words that come back to poison the air.* I did not say that part aloud to Zheran. She wept for a while in my arms. Then we went together to find Ursa.

★

I think that was the longest summer of my life, and perhaps the hardest as well. Everywhere I went I saw Zheran's reproachful eyes, though, in truth, she did not reproach me with words. She had been right. Ozzet and the others did not come back. It seemed that Ursa was lost out in the world, just as Zheran had feared. For a while we kept up hope, but when

"Alyeeta!" I shouted in exasperation, jumping to my feet. "How can you be so contrary? In all the years I have loved you, have I ever told you how absolutely impossible you are?"

"Often, though perhaps not as many times as you have thought it."

"No, hardly as many." I leaned over and put my hand on her mouth to silence her. Then, as I bent to nibble on her ear, I slipped my other hand over her breast and gently pinched her nipple.

When she tried to pull away from me, I freed her mouth and took hold of her wrist in a firm grip. The moment she could speak again, she said disdainfully, "I feel her standing over us, giving us permission like children told they can go and play."

"Do you remember, once long ago, how you tied my hands to the bedpost? Perhaps I should do that to you now and cover your mouth as well."

Alyeeta struggled harder in my grip. "No, no, Tazzia, I am too old for that kind of play. Love me gently this last time or let me be."

"Good, then come inside," I answered, tugging on her wrist. "We do not need to make a display of ourselves out here for all of Zelindar to see."

"Since when has that ever stopped you?" Alyeeta asked mockingly. Nonetheless, she yielded to my tug and came with me.

The cave chamber was warm from the sun. A brightly patterned rug covered a large part of the hard-packed dirt floor. There was a fire in the fire pit and several rocks glowed red at the center of it. I looked about suspiciously. "There is no one else here?"

"No, we are all alone. I was about to bathe before you appeared." She lit a smudge pot of sweet-herb, and the pungent aroma quickly filled the chamber. By moving a rock, she diverted the flow of fresh cold water away from the pool. Then, with a forked, green stick, she rolled one of the glowing rocks into it. Instantly, there was a loud hiss and a thick cloud of steam rose from the water. She immediately followed this with two more rocks. When I rushed to help her, she brushed me aside. "I can manage well enough in my own home. I have been doing it for a long time without your help. Now take off your clothes."

"Are you sure no one...?"

"I will put a circle of protection around us."

The windows had instantly fogged over. Steam hung in the air like mist, obscuring the rest of the cave from sight. The ferns surrounding the upper side of the pool bobbed gently in the warm air, and the moss covering the rocks gleamed with moisture. My senses were dizzied by the aroma of sweet-herb. The whole place seemed filled with magic. Almost as if under a spell, I slipped free of my clothes, pulled out the cooling rocks, and slid my naked body into the warm water. I found myself groaning with pleasure as my dark hair floated out around my head like seaweed.

Instantly, Alyeeta's hands were on me, hard and demanding, traveling over my breasts and my belly and down between my legs. Then her body slid in next to mine. "If this is to be the last time, then I want as much of you as I can get," she growled fiercely in my ear. Gripping my hair with one hand, she kissed me deeply. With her mouth on mine and her leg pressing itself insistently between my legs, I quickly surrendered to Alyeeta and the water, greedily taking in all the pleasures of that moment.

Afterward, we rolled out, wet and steamy, onto the rug. Now it was my turn to be the lover. She had asked me to be gentle this last time, and I was, moving my fingers very slowly over the contours of her body, exploring and saying good-bye with the same touch, feeling the grief and the pleasure all mingled together, remembering through our bodies all we had shared. I wanted to recall every detail of this body under my hands. *This is the last time I will ever touch her here and here and here in this spot, the last time my mouth will cover hers, the last time my fingers will enter this place, the last time I will hear her cry out with passion, the last time, the last time...* Those words kept going through my head. Drawing it out as long as possible, I moved with sensuous slowness, as if floating in a trance or in a deep, slow dream.

When our loving was finally over, Alyeeta put me out the door as if she had been the one to make the decision. "I am getting much too old for this sort of thing. Look at the gray hairs, the wrinkles. My hands have even started to shake. For shame! You are abusing an old woman with your desires." I wanted to protest that she looked no older than when I had first met her. So it had seemed during those weeks of loving. But now, as I looked closely, I saw that what she said was indeed true.

Walking back down the hill, I was filled with grief and loss. At the same time, I felt incredibly relieved to be out from under Alyeeta's spell. Clearly, I had been caught in her web those past few weeks. Truth be told, I was really very glad that Zheran had finally laid claim to me and called me home.

wondered if Zheran was woman enough to keep you or if you would miss Alyeeta's loving after a while and come back for another taste of it. After all, we Witches know something of that art."

Stung by that, I answered more sharply than I meant to, "It is because of Ursa. I was the one who said she should go. And now she is probably dead somewhere out there. It is too hard to stay home with Zheran and watch her grieve. When I am there, she does not even notice my presence. Besides, it is all my fault."

"Oh, Ursa," Alyeeta said contemptuously, with a dismissive wave of her hand. "Never fear, Ursa will show up again, like a bad coin." Suddenly, she grabbed my arm and spun me about, shaking me and shouting in my face, "Do you really feel she is dead, Tazzia? Do you feel it? Do you?"

I shut my eyes and dropped into my deepest self. After a while I shook my head. When I pictured Ursa, I could not feel her death. Perhaps I even felt a little candle flicker of life from that direction.

"Fool, you would know if she were dead. She is still alive somewhere, while you are making yourself mad with grief. But if that is the only reason you are here with me, you may as well go home to your *wife.*"

"I am here because I love you, Alyeeta."

"Tell me no lies, girl, you are here because you need me to sop up your grief and your guilt." In spite of her sharp retort, Alyeeta did not send me away.

Though I did not keep it a secret from Zheran, neither did I tell her directly. Perhaps it was Alyeeta's barely concealed look of triumph that gave us away. Zheran stopped me one day when I came to get some article of clothing from her house. "Tazzil, I cannot tell you how to live your life, or who to be with, or when to share your body or your loving, but I can speak for myself and say what I can and cannot live with. I know that you had several lovers before me, all at the same time. That may be the Hadra way or your way, and I do not fault you for that. For me, I know I cannot abide it. It would cause me too much grief and uncertainty. I would rather live alone. Then, when I am able, I could learn to be your friend, rather than your lover. This may be the hardest thing I have ever said to you, Tazzil, but you must choose. I cannot welcome you home from another woman's bed. It hurts my spirit and my pride too much; in the end, it will destroy my love for you."

I felt torn apart and began twisting my shirt in an agony of guilt and confusion. "Oh, Zheran, how can I close her out after all this time?"

"Do what you must, Tazzil, out of your deepest heart. I will say again, I am not speaking of what you should do but only of what I can and cannot live with, from my own truest nature."

Suddenly I was flooded with despair. I saw the future before me cold and loveless with Zheran gone out of my life. "No, you are the one I want to spend my life with. Alyeeta herself even said you were the one great love of my life. I think she has only been toying with me in her way or perhaps toying with us both. I will tell her it has to end." Now I was shaken with the grief of loss from the other direction. How was I to do this thing?

"If that is really your decision, go tell her and be with her one last time. Then you will truly know which path to take."

"Zheran, I already know."

"Go! Then I will be sure and so will you and so will Alyeeta."

Alyeeta was full of mockery when I went to talk with her. I found her sitting in the sun in front of her cave and sank down beside her. As I spoke, she set down the book she had been studying to stare at me with contempt. "So," she said scornfully, "you are going to become like a married woman, as bound and tied as if to a man?"

"Come, Alyeeta, before this summer we had not been lovers for years, you and I."

"Had not and cannot are two very different horses."

"Alyeeta, I am happy with Zheran, happier than I have ever been in my life. Be glad for my happiness."

"I am glad, so glad that if I were younger I would beat the drum and dance for joy in the Central Circle. But take care with happiness. It is dangerous. It can drug you to sleep. Are you so happy that you would allow her to bind you hand and foot? Does this happiness give her the right to tell you what to do?"

"No, Alyeeta, but she does have the right to say what she can and cannot live with for herself."

"Then let us be lovers one last time if we must seal this forever."

"She said you would ask that."

"Oh, and what did she say about it? Is she willing? Will she allow it?"

"That it would be a loving ending. That she is willing this one last time."

"And so we have her agreement? How nice! In that case perhaps I do not want this."

two months went by and then another with no word of them, hope became harder to hold onto. Josleen and Megyair had gone north to track them down but could find no trace of them after Darthill. Hereschell and some of the Wanderers had gone in search of them along the river and had also come back with nothing.

I went through my days with a terrible weight on my heart. Ishnu was painfully kind and courteous to us both and very helpful with the younger children. Sometimes Zheran and I clung together, our passion strangely rekindled by loss and despair. At other times, we barely spoke for days, and I found other places to be besides the little hut that rebuked me with its silence. I think it was all the harder for Zheran because she had never totally approved of her oldest girl. Now she regretted any harsh or critical words she might have spoken. My burden of guilt felt crushing at times. At other times, I felt angry with Ursa for having been so insistent. *You could be here among us, going about your days alive and well, and your mother and I would still be happy,* I would tell her reproachfully in my head.

It was during that terrible time that Yolande and I finally became friends. We shared our losses with each other. The differences between us did not seem so great after all. Had they ever really mattered all that much? When I talked to her of Ursa, she grieved with me as only a mother could who has lost her own daughter. With Yolande I talked of Lorren as I could with no one else. Who else had known him so well? For her it was the same. Who could better understand what she had lost? And who else knew those little pieces of Lorren's life that she did not? I was only too glad to share with her whatever I knew, if only for the sake of hearing his name spoken aloud. We often sat together in his study. She would shake her head and say sadly, "I thought he would be here beside me all my life. Instead, he was just on loan for that little piece of time. I suppose I should be grateful even for that, but it is very hard. Now I regret every cross word I ever spoke to him and every unkind thing I ever did."

Yolande had changed; something in her had shifted. Needing to know everything Lorren had known, to find him again through his books, she learned, with Alyeeta's help and mine, how to read and to write. Armed with that knowledge, she went searching in those pages for the part of him she had ignored when he was beside her in the flesh. Having decided to continue his work at Wanderer Hill, she spent much of her time adding to the library and the collection, supervising the building, planning for the future. She even learned to row a boat, to chop wood, to build a shelter. I would see her striding about in pants. She had given up long skirts, at least during the day, saying they hampered her too much.

Once, she came to see me on some matter of mutual security, much as if she were another Councilor. She sat across the table from me, her cool green eyes on my face, looking me right in the eye as she never used to do. After we had concluded our business, she said with a shrug, "I am no longer a real woman. For his sake, I do those things no proper woman should do. Now I am more like you and can better understand you and no longer feel quite so strange in your presence." Then she shrugged again. "And what does it matter, anyhow? There will never again be a man in my life. Now all that is left for me is to carry on his work in whatever way I am able to."

Would that really be the truth of her life? Whether in skirts or trousers, Yolande was still very beautiful. Though she seemed unaware of their glances, I saw the way men looked at her, especially Hereschell. I wondered if she noticed how his eyes followed her with a look of hunger and longing, but I kept my peace on it. It was all too soon. Instead, I reached across and very gently laid my hand over hers, not knowing if she would allow it. "We both loved him," I said softly. "We both loved him in our own very different ways. It should make for some closeness between us."

I thought she would draw back. I saw her face tighten and harden. But then something in her began to crack. Shaking her head, she said in a voice full of barely controlled grief, "Oh, Tazzil, it is so hard ... I would gladly have taken my own life when he was killed. It is only for the children's sake I did not do so. There has been enough death in their young lives. But sometimes I wish..." Then suddenly she was crying, sobbing wildly. I, who had been the stranger and the enemy and the rival, got up and went to put my arms around her. She laid her head against my breast and we cried together for that man who had meant so much to both of us.

★

More and more often now, I went to stay with Alyeeta. She offered me the comfort of her ear and her bed and her arms. It was in that way that we became lovers again. She poured her loving out on me. Out of guilt and grief and need, I succumbed. Though it had been several years since we had been together in that way, I sank easily into the pleasure and the comfort of it. Alyeeta, for her part, could not resist gloating a little. "I

★

First I heard the sound of bells and horns, then Kazouri's voice shouting from the riverside, "Ozzet is back! Ozzet is back with a new boat!" *Boat, boat, boat, boat* echoed back from the bluffs along the river. I ran full speed toward the sound, my heart pounding with fear and hope. When I got there, several women, some of them strangers to me, were already busy unloading heaps of bales and baskets onto the shore. It was a big boat, brightly painted in bold patterns, and piled high with goods. To my eyes this was a strange-looking craft, wide and shallow, very different in design from the narrow, deep-hulled boats of our southern coast. Ozzet was standing in the bow, commanding the scene with a loud voice, and more Hadra were rushing forward to help.

Of the women disembarking and the women crowding around them, I had eyes for only one. Ursa was already on the shore. She turned to face me, her expression a strange mixture of defiance and hopeful pleading. She looked as if she had grown two inches and filled out: she had breasts, she had hips, the muscles rippled under her skin.

"Look how strong I am now," she said, raising her arms and flexing her muscles to show me. "When there was no wind, we paddled, and where the water was shallow, we hauled the boat. I even helped to build her. Most of the designs painted on her sides are mine. We built the boat ourselves, from the beginning. That was what took us so long. They taught us how in a settlement north of Darthill, a different style from how the Kourmairi build boats here. We wanted to bring her home as a surprise. Now we can teach other women here how to do it. Were you worried? Are you glad to see me back?" She said all this very fast, her words tumbling over one another, as if to stop me from speaking. I was about to say, *Ursa, we thought you were dead,* when she looked straight into my eyes and asked, "Are you proud of me, Mother?" Her eyes were flashing and her fists were raised to make her muscles leap. She had never called me "Mother" before, not in all the years I had lived in her mother's house. Now she was laying claim to me and, at the same time, putting all her vulnerable young self out there before me: making a challenge and taking a terrible, heartbreaking risk.

Suddenly there were tears in my eyes. I wanted to hug her and hold her safe and close, but I sensed that was not what was wanted. "Very proud, my daughter," I said solemnly. "My heart is filled with pride. You have become a fine, strong woman while you were away, and you have brought us home a splendid boat, beautifully painted. Very, very proud, my Ursa."

Every word was true. Then I could not resist adding, "But you worried us both, especially Zheran. She was terrified that you were injured somewhere or perhaps even dead. Indeed, we thought you were all dead. She grieved for you ... You should have sent us word..."

"That was not so easy to do. We were in some danger and so had to stay hidden. Besides, we wanted the new boat to be a surprise. Anyhow, mothers are supposed to worry. If you do not worry your mother, you are being too tame. That is what Nhari says." She made a slight nod of her head in the direction of the young stranger who was watching intently from several paces away.

Those were cruel words. I wanted to shake her. I wanted to scold her for her callousness. Then I realized it was just her youth speaking, and I really did not want to scold her for anything at all. I was too glad to see her safely home. Instead, I shouted, "Ursa!" and grabbed her in a giant hug. For a moment or so, she hugged me back like a child, though the crush of her arms was anything but childlike. Then she disentangled herself with dignity and said quite formally, "I have brought back something for you, Tazzil. It is on very poor paper, but that was all I could find in Darthill." From the pouch at her waist she drew out a pack of papers, bound together at one edge with cord. On the cover, large curling letters said, *"An account of our boat journey down the Escuro River, with maps and pictures, as recorded by Ursalynde of Zelindar."*

"It is not quite the same quality as yours, but I thought it might please you, nonetheless." With sudden shyness, she looked down at the ground, and two red dots of color appeared on her cheeks.

I took the account from her hands and glanced through the pages. There were maps, descriptions of the landscape, detailed drawings of plants and flowers, and accounts of events for each day, all meticulously recorded. I stared at it, speechless with admiration. My daughter had done this amazing piece of work, this child who was always being scolded for her wildness, who could never sit still for her lessons.

"Have you nothing to say, Tazzil?" It was Zheran's voice, almost at my elbow. Neither of us had noticed her approach through the crush of other women. I flushed with surprise and said quickly, "It is too wonderful for words. I was just wondering how our little break-neck managed to grow up so suddenly into this tall, strong, learned young woman. This account will have an honored place in the Zildorn for many to read in years to come. It will give us an incentive to finally get the building finished. Such fine work must have a home..." Now that I could speak

23

The morning after Ursa's return, the four of us were sitting around the eating table in our little hut, looking at maps and drawings and listening to Ursa tell stories of her trip. Zheran was glowing with pride. Ishnu was leaning forward, her attention fastened on every word, listening to her older sister with a rapt admiration only slightly tinged with envy. I looked around at their faces and thought, *This is my family...*

After all my losses, I had a family and a home again. Why had it taken me so long to recognize that? And now it would not last much longer. The girls were growing up. They would soon be gone. I had wasted the time resenting them, when I could have been loving them. What a fool I had been. Then, suddenly, I thought of my mother and sister, and the pain of missing them rushed through me again. All gone now, my other life, all swept away. Suddenly, I was flooded with waves of grief and joy following one upon the other, grief for what I had lost and joy for these three who meant so much to me.

Ursa had taken off the binding cords and spread the pages out on the table so we could see many things at once. "Here," she said, speaking with new authority and pointing to a place on a long map made up of several pieces of paper fastened together. "Right here you can see a wide bend in the Escuro River. The Koormir have made a great Essu ground at that spot. The Kourmairi come together from many settlements for the Essu, and even some Hadra come from these settlements here and here. And in this place, a wild river from the mountains rushes down into the Escuro and forms a little lake. Down below that, the land is flat and the river spreads out into broad swamplands, stretching as far as the eyes can see. That part of the Escuro meanders and has many streams and estuaries, so it is not always easy to follow. The birds and the plants — everything is different there. I tried to capture them as best I could." As she was speaking, she spread out pages of brightly colored pictures on the table. "We spent weeks in those swamps, exploring, mapping, sometimes getting lost. There were creatures such as I could not have imagined. Look at this one with the long spiky tail and this one with the crest and fangs. Once, Ozzet even had to rescue me from the jaws of a..." Ursa caught the look of horror on her mother's face. She stopped in midsentence and put her hand over Zheran's. "Oh, Mother, I am so sorry for the grief I caused you. I did not think ... One day just flowed into the next ... It was all so new ... The truth of it is I forgot anything else existed except what was happening right in front of me at that moment. Please try to forgive my selfishness."

Zheran's smile of pride and pleasure could have lit up the night sky. "All that is forgiven and forgotten. I am only glad to have you safely home again. Besides, a child who does not worry her mother is too tame."

Now Ursa bowed her head and flushed with embarrassment. "I had no idea you heard my careless words."

"It is of no matter now. And besides, you were right." After that, there was a moment of silence. On impulse, I reached out and took Ursa's hand on one side of me and Ishnu's on the other. Zheran did the same on her side, so that we were all four linked in a circle. Then Zheran said softly, "Thank You, Mother. Out of all the chaos of these times, You brought us together in this place." I let those words sink into my heart, giving thanks inwardly. The silence stretched on and on, filling me with peace, until Ishnu suddenly broke through it, saying angrily, "Mother, it is time you found me a husband. I am tired of being the child of the house."

Zheran bristled instantly. "Impossible, ridiculous, you are much too young," she burst out. "It is not time yet. There is no way to..."

While Zheran went on protesting, Ursa looked at her sister in surprise. "Why would you not want to find your own husband? I never plan to marry, but if I did, I would certainly insist on choosing the man myself."

"Of course you would. You have made yourself over into a Hadra. But I have not. I am still a Kourmairi like my mother, and I will go by their ways."

Ganthor and his people. I think Nhari is so brave. I wish she could leave with us and come to live in Zelindar. Then I think I would be less lonely there.

★

Things have moved very fast since I wrote those last words, and I have not been able to get back to my account for several days. We are now in the settlement of Bonathaire, north of Darthill. The people here are very friendly to us. They are willing to keep our presence among them secret. On our last day in Darthill, Ozzet's mother summoned us into their little hut. She had her sister guard the door to make sure we were not overheard. "You are all in danger," she told us in a fierce whisper, "especially if you take Nhari with you. And you must take her. She would not survive here long once you were gone. You have said you are going to Mishghall tomorrow. I have heard that some of those men plan to attack you before you get there and leave you for dead. I know you have powers, but you will have two with you who are unprotected, and who knows what manner of harm they plan. They will expect you on the road west to Mishghall in the morning. I suggest you leave tonight. Go north and head for the settlement of Bonathaire. I have friends there. If this seems a good plan to you, some of the women will get food prepared in secret and have your horses ready. You can slip out in the dead of night and be gone long before they think to look for you."

Ozzet threw her arms around her mother. "Come with us, all of you, all my family. We can make a good life together there in the south. It is beautiful and there is an abundance of everything."

Her mother pulled free and shook her head. "Think what you are asking, child. There is your grandmother, who is too old to travel, and your sister Selvayne, who is pregnant and almost at term, and your other sister, who has two small children. Besides, they each have husbands, who in turn have families of their own here. And you know your father would never leave. No, this is where I will live out my life. Go now while you have the chance, so I only have to weep for your departure and not for your death."

★

We rode for three nights and slept hidden during the day with sentries posted. I am glad to be in Bonathaire, but the ride here was a torture for me. I wish I could say I am as brave and resourceful as the Hadra.

276

Instead, I rode in fear the whole way. All the memories of the war between our people were rekindled: people screaming; bodies in the street; our father being killed and then our mother; being left alone with Ishnu in the middle of all that horror until Dhurnathi found us. I said nothing of my feelings, but, of course, the Hadra knew. Ozzet kept close to give me comfort. She tried to get me to talk of my fears, but I shook my head and kept my mouth closed on the ugliness of the past. Perhaps someday I will find a way to speak of it all.

As soon as we got here, we started building a boat with the help of the Kourmairi. It will be a fine, big boat, big enough for all of us. Two others besides Nhari left Darthill with us. They are nice enough, but it is Nhari who is my real friend. Never in my life have I had such a friend. We are closer than sisters. In fact... This was followed by another part that said, "Too personal" next to it. This time it was crossed out well enough to be completely illegible. *So,* I thought, *our daughter is growing up...*

This personal part, in turn, was followed by a description of their stay in Bonathaire. I fell asleep reading about the building of the boat and dreamt a terrifying dream. I was seventeen again. It was my first year with the Hadra. We were trying to escape from fastfire and the Zarn's guards. The only way to flee was by boat, but we could not build one fast enough or well enough. We knew they were coming. We could feel them advancing on us. Yet, every time we jumped into the boat to leave, it sprang a leak and began to sink. I groaned aloud and woke in a sweat, thrashing about. Zheran wrapped me in her arms and I fell asleep again, held safely in her loving embrace.

again, I was running on at the mouth, unable to stop, but Zheran had already turned away. She was paying no more attention to me. Her eyes were on Ursa with such a mixture of hurt and pride it made me want to cry.

"Hello, Mother," Ursa said, almost shyly. "I am very sorry for all the pain and worry I caused you." She seemed truly contrite, with none of the callous arrogance she had expressed just moments before.

"None of that matters now. You are home safe," Zheran said, reaching out her arms. This time Ursa let herself be folded into an embrace without pulling away. Nhari was watching this scene, looking lost and lonely. I reached out my hand to her. "Please forgive our poor manners, Nhari. Welcome to Zelindar."

★

Later that evening, we held a joyful celebration for the safe return of our voyagers. Songs were sung around a huge fire, and afterward the travelers told stories of their adventures. Ozzet began the tale, then others leapt in eagerly to add their part. Ursa was at my side. She had sought me out deliberately, crossing the circle to sit next to me, with Nhari following after her. When her companions from the trip looked in her direction, Ursa shook her head shyly, and when I tried to question her, she answered each time that it was all written in her account. I finally understood that she was eager for me to read it right away.

As I was weary, I stayed only a short while. Then I stole away from the festivities to read a little by candlelight and satisfy my curiosity. The first few pages of Ursa's account were a description of the preparations and the departure. The part that caught my eye — or rather my heart — was the part she had crossed out. She had written "Too personal" next to it and even drawn a design of leaves and flowers over the spot, but most of the words were still quite legible.

There are eight of us setting out. I am the youngest, but no one reminds me of that. Ozzet treats me with respect, like an equal, as do the others. She expects me to take part in all the decisions and do my full share of the work, not always easy, as the Hadra have their powers to help them and are sometimes hard to keep up with. Still, I am determined to prove my worth. Sometimes, at home, it is hard to know where I stand. One mother fusses over me as if I were still a helpless child, and the other ignores me completely. Even in Zelindar itself, it is hard to know where or how I fit into the fabric of things. What are we, we who were born to the Koormir but have grown up among the Hadra? We do not have Hadra powers, yet are we not their daughters just the same? That gave my heart a little twist as I read it — and likely, it was meant to.

The next several pages covered the trip to Darthill: the scenery, the vegetation, the people they encountered on the way, the creatures they saw. It was all interesting and well written but not what I was looking for. The part about Darthill was what grabbed my attention: *Finally we are here at the settlement of Darthill, our destination, the place we have been riding toward for days. I should feel happy and relieved. Instead, I wish us back on the road. I think the others feel the same, even Ozzet, though she has not said it in so many words.*

Though most of the women and some of the men of Darthill treat us warmly and seem glad to see us, still there is an undercurrent of fear and suspicion here. Because of what Rhomar said, Ozzet is looking into her grandfather's death. We went to see the swinging bridge that stands high over the river. This is where he is supposed to have fallen to his death. It is hard to imagine how a man who was familiar with that bridge for so many years and even helped to build it could have fallen by accident. The hair went up on the back of my neck when I stood there looking down.

Ganthor, who is now headman of the village, was a friend of Rhomar's. He watches us suspiciously and even follows us about when he thinks we cannot see him. He and his followers blame us for Rhomar's death and miss no opportunity to say something rude or insulting. Rhomar's two sons also give us strange looks and refuse to speak to us, as though we are somehow to blame for what happened to their father. They tore up Zheran's message and threw the pieces to the wind, though I noticed that they read it first.

I think the other Kourmairi of Darthill are afraid of Ganthor's follow-ers, as they do not speak up in our defense. Ozzet says her grandfather would not have been so cowardly, but, of course, that may be why he is dead. To add to the tension, there is a girl here named Nhari who is two years my senior. She is not married and does not plan to be, having already turned down two suitors. She says she wants to be like the Hadra and follows them around whenever she can.

The second suitor is the son of the headman. Ganthor was extremely angered by her refusal and keeps threatening to make a real woman of her, by which, I suppose, he means to force her to his will. Naturally, Nhari's mother is very frightened by these threats. She has asked Ozzet to watch out for Nhari. This, of course, does not make us more beloved by

"I have not made myself over into anything," Ursa answered indignantly. "I am who I always was, only more so, whatever that makes me. And even if I was born among them, the Koormir have no claim on me. Besides, look what they did to our lives with their ways."

By then Ishnu was ignoring her sister and looking defiantly at me. "Have you nothing to add to this scolding, Tazzil, now that you have finally decided at this late time to become my other mother?"

I could not have been more surprised. I had never before heard a rude word out of her mouth. It seemed that the good child had become the bad one overnight. The magic moment was broken. Now all our attention, for better or worse, was focused on Ishnu. Ursa's maps and stories were forgotten. I took a deep breath and answered mildly, with none of Zheran's charge, "If you are asking what I think, Ishnu, I must say I agree with your mother. It is too early to make a decision you will have to live with the rest of your life. And I also agree with your sister that you should make your own choice. What if your mother finds you a suitable husband and you have a wonderful wedding, and then a few years down the road, when you are a little older, you find the man who is your true mate and you fall in love? By then you will already have a family, and nothing but grief will come of it for everyone: for you, for the children, for both men. Better to wait awhile and live a little before you bind yourself for life to another person." I saw she was about to interrupt me and held up my hand. "But I know the young have their own ways, and you will no doubt do as you please, just as I did. You know that I give no orders here and never have. I only ask that you give some thought to what we are saying."

Ishnu jumped to her feet. "Maybe I will start right now looking for this husband, this true mate who is waiting somewhere for me. Or is Ursa the only one free to travel about?" She looked around defiantly at us all, as if waiting to be stopped.

There was a stricken look on Zheran's face. She was struggling to speak. I was afraid that whatever she said would only throw fuel on the fire, so I jumped quickly into the gap. "Ishnu, you have a whole life ahead of you, full of love and adventure and joy and pain. Ursa's little moment of glory can take none of that away from you. Do not destroy it for yourself."

Now she turned on Zheran, and there was a quaver in her voice. "When Ursa was gone, when you thought she was dead, you forgot all about me. You were grieving so much for her, I did not even exist for you. And now that you have her home again, I have no place anymore. I want my own home and..." Suddenly Ishnu was crying like a little girl. Zheran grabbed her in a hug and began whispering endearments in her ear. Then Ursa hugged her too, and after a moment, I wrapped my arms around all three of them. Muffled by her sobs, I heard Ishnu saying in a little-girl voice, "Ursa, Big Sister, I did not mean to spoil your homecoming. It was only that I felt so lost and worthless."

Only minutes later, Ursa and Ishnu were making plans for some sort of boat trip. Soon after that, Nhari was standing in the doorway, looking a little uncertain of her welcome. We had just drawn her into the family circle when a group of Hadra appeared at the door. For a change, they were not looking for me but for Ursa, wanting to hear about the trip and see her account with its maps and pictures. Ishnu was glued to her side, helping tell the story with great enthusiasm, while Nhari stood shyly at her shoulder, adding a few words now and then. I reached over, took Zheran's hand, and drew her out of the house. "Come on, old woman, it is time for us to be gone from here."

★

That next year or so was a time of relative peace and prosperity for Zelindar, and so for me as well. There were no more raids from Eezore. My grief for Lorren was easing with time, and Yolande had become part of our lives. As our harvests were good, we traded food for goods with the folk of Wanderer Hill. We also traded with Wanderers who were passing through. Hadra came to visit us from other settlements, bringing news of peace up and down the coast.

In the city itself, we were building new shelters and enlarging old ones, paving streets, and shaping more terraces for growing vegetables and flowers. Visiting Hadra or Wanderers sometimes brought us little saplings from far places; we were planting them all through the city. We were also building more and more boats. Kourmairi men from Indaran taught us the skill of cutting and shaping the beautiful white rock that was so plentiful here, and so our Zildorn was almost finished. With the help of Vestri and the others, Kara had made a huge statue of the Goddess to stand in front of the Zildorn at the very top of Third Hill. Life in Zelindar was beginning to have some shape and pattern that was predictable. And I was finally learning to be grateful for the powers I had so often cursed. It was with the aid of our Kersh, as we came to call our powers, that we were able to lift rocks and logs to shape our city.

forehead and down each of my cheeks. I had been marked and claimed. It was as if I were being initiated into the future. I could feel the blood-marks puckering to dryness on my face. I resisted wiping them away. Instead, I gave a quick nod of my head and for a moment stared straight into her eyes.

When I stepped down, Ursa moved to the front of the platform. Her four companions came forward and took off her cloak, revealing a red tunic. The edges of it were ripped into long red streamers that shivered in the breeze. Her arms and legs were also heavily patterned with red, whether paint or blood I could not tell. She bowed deeply in all four directions. Then she raised her head to look at the Hadra.

"First, I want to thank all the women who raised me and taught me and had their patience tested at my hands. I particularly want to thank my four mothers: Nyaran, my birthmother, the woman who gave me life and died in the war trying to protect me; Dhurnathi, my mother's friend, who rescued me from starvation and became my mother for as long as she could manage; Zheran, who adopted me, raised me with love, and shared her home with me; and Tazzil, who showed me by example what a woman of will and courage can do in this world. Then I want to thank all of you who have made a place for me in your lives. In some way, you are all my mothers."

All this was said quite formally. Then she bowed again. This time when she raised her eyes, she looked around at us all in a challenging and defiant manner and took another step forward. When she spoke, her words were full of passion and fierceness. Her voice came loud and bold, reaching for the farthest watchers on the slope. "I am not a Kourmairi who has fostered among you and will now be sent back tamely to marry and live among the Koormir. I am a Neshtair. I may not have Hadra powers, but I have Hadra spirit. On this day I speak not just for myself, but for all of us, for all the young women, almost thirty strong, who have fostered here among you and think of Zelindar as our home. We are the Neshtair. You have taken a name for yourselves, and so have we. Neshtair! It is a Muinyairin word for those who are adopted into the tribe, only in this case it is we who have adopted you.

"Some of your fosterlings may go home to a Kourmairi settlement. For us, this is our home. We have no other. You must either accept us or put us out to wander." She stopped and bowed her head again. There was a long moment of stunned silence. All I could hear were the sounds of the sea and the snapping of banners. Then Hayika gave her wild cry, Kazouri roared her approval, and suddenly all the Hadra on the hillside were on their feet, stamping, clapping, and cheering.

It was done, it was over. Ursa had risked everything in that bold way she had, and she had won. Zheran came to stand beside me. I put my arms around her waist and whispered in her ear, "She is quite a girl, our daughter, our little Neshtair." I wondered where Rishka was at that moment and what she was thinking.

When the uproar died down, Ursa flashed us all a bright smile and added, "Besides, you need us. We are the bridge between you and your new, little ones. It is not natural for there to be no one between in age, no aunts, no older sisters. They need someone to look up to and follow after and pester with questions, and you need our help in raising them." She swept us with a look of triumph. Then her four companions came forward again. In a few quick motions, they stripped off her short tunic.

Suddenly Ursa was standing naked before us, dressed only in a fierce design of red paint or blood. There was a collective intake of breath from those watching. Zheran gasped and turned her face against my shoulder to avert her eyes. "Tazzil, how could she do such a thing? It is disgraceful. I am so ashamed. In Darthill she would be punished with a beating or worse."

"Then thank the Goddess this is not Darthill. Here, no one will beat her. In fact, the Hadra love it. She has won their hearts. Now watch what comes next and leave all that shame in the past, where it belongs."

The other four stripped down to short red tunics and began to dance with Ursa, slapping hands, stamping feet, turning together and then apart. They started slowly, but soon were moving faster and faster, creating their own music with their hands and feet until they were all a whirling blur of red.

Pell came up in back of me. "By the Goddess, Tazzi, were we ever so young? It exhausts me just to watch them. If we wanted to refuse them a place here, I believe they would wear us down with their energy. We would be forced to say yes just to make them stop."

Teko had come up on the other side of me. "I believe the Sheezerti will adopt some of these Neshtair into their troupes, for the sake of new blood, so to speak."

Pell laughed appreciatively, and I saw that Zheran had turned to watch again. "How did she learn all that? How can she move so swiftly? Oh, Tazzil, it seems just yesterday that she was a frightened little girl hiding behind my skirts. How did this all happen so fast?"

reached out to you. At least these young ones have better manners — far better."

"Aiyeee, what has happened to Hayika? I thought at least she would understand. I always thought that sooner or later the Kourmairi women would go back to their own people, or at least, most of them would. You, of course, might not want that, as you have taken up with one of them. I believed the same of these fosterlings. Now they tell us they want to stay with us the rest of their lives. Do we have no choice?"

"There is no use talking to you, Rishka," I said, turning away in disgust. "Your head is hard as a post and your heart is hard as stone."

"You should call a council meeting and see what the others say," she shouted after me as I walked off. "Maybe they are not all so full of kindness and mercy, either."

I did as she said and called a meeting, but Rishka was wrong. It was one of our shortest meetings, and Rishka found herself alone in her opinion. That did nothing to sweeten her mood.

Now that the council had agreed these young women were a permanent part of our lives, we needed some more formal way of acknowledging their presence among us. I conferred with Hayika and Kilghari and Olna. I talked at length to Ursa. We all agreed that her first-bloods would probably be the best occasion for such a ceremony. Though we helped, in the end, it was mostly the young women themselves who made the preparations and organized the day. They had chosen a place near the sea, where the gently rising bank could provide seating for most of Zelindar, built a raised platform of logs and planks on the beach, and set out some log seating for the closest watchers.

Everything was red! The Central Circle of Zelindar was decked with red streamers, ribbons, and banners. Kara's statue of mother and daughter was surrounded by huge bunches of red flowers that almost obscured it. The platform on the beach was covered with a red cloth and flanked by poles with more red banners, flapping and snapping in the sharp sea breeze. The young women had on robes or shirts or tunics of red, and Ursa herself was in a long red cloak with her face in shadow.

After the watchers had all been seated — something Kazouri and I attended to — Ursa's companions wound their way down the beach toward us in a colorful procession. Some of them played music, leading the slow ceremonial walk to the raised platform where I was already standing. Ursa herself went between four young women who had already had their first-bloods that spring. This little procession was at once solemn and festive and gay. It was also very beautiful, with the sea sparkling blue-green and silver behind them and all that red cloth rippling in the wind. Watching, I felt the sting of tears in my eyes.

When they stopped at the edge of the platform, I reached out for Ursa's hand and drew her up. Then she was standing silently beside me, with the hood still partially covering her face. Looking around at the Hadra assembled on the hillside, I felt a little shiver of nervous excitement. Women were leaning forward, all waiting expectantly for this surprise performance which most of them had not had any part in creating.

Zheran was standing nearby, watching intently. Not all our words had persuaded her to share that platform with us. I looked to her now, suddenly wanting reassurance. She smiled, and I saw her give Ursa a little nod of encouragement. I took a deep breath and glanced at Ursa. Suddenly the words flowed with ease. "Ursalynde of Zelandria and Zelindar, I welcome you as a woman into this circle of women. The red thread of your bloods binds us together. It also binds you to the past as well as to the future, to generations of women who have bled and nurtured life." At my first words, Ursa had thrown back her hood. A murmur of surprise rose from the watchers; her face was smeared with red in a bold, stark pattern.

I went on, gaining the power of my words and speaking louder. "Though you were born of another woman's body in a place far from my village, still you are truly my daughter, the only one I will ever have. I welcome you now as a woman into my family, my tribe, my people. May you live among us and prosper. May you find here all the love and shelter and encouragement that you need to blossom into your truest self. May you have the children of the body that I never had, if that is your wish. May they grow up among us and always feel at home here. May your life be tied to ours by bonds of love and blood and shared experience."

Luckily for me, Ishnu was off visiting her former foster mother at the moment. Perhaps she was looking for that elusive husband. I was glad she was not there to hear me speak. My words might have been hurtful and seemed like a betrayal. She had also been my foster child, and I had loved her too, in my own neglectful way, but in truth, it was Ursa who was really my daughter.

I took Ursa's red-marked face in both hands and kissed her on the forehead. She stepped back and thrust her fingers between her legs. Then, with a quick sudden motion of her red fingers, she made a line across my

★

It was that next spring — the spring after the boat trip — when Ursa finally had her first-bloods. Kilghari had told her about the Muinyairin first-bloods rites, those rites by which girls were accepted as women into the Muinyairin tribes. All that winter, Ursa had been organizing the young women who were like her, those who were too young to be Hadra but who had no wish to be Kourmairi anymore. She had asked me to do a first-bloods ritual for her that would also be an acceptance ritual for the rest of them.

Besides Nhari, there were four others of that age who had come back on the boat with Ozzet and more than twenty who had fostered among us or come to us later on their own. At Ursa's insistence, Kazouri had finally agreed to train them in self-defense and unarmed combat. Kazouri had been resistant at first, but in the end, she had been delighted to put her skills to use again. Kara, Cruzia, and even Shalamith had been induced to teach what music they knew on the flute, the ferl, and the kerril. Even the Sheezerti had been prevailed upon to teach some of their precious acrobatic tricks.

I could not have been more surprised when Hayika took up with these young women on one of her infrequent visits to Zelindar. She decided to stay for a while and train them in the Muinyairin style of riding. Hayika seemed to enjoy these wild young women who were so ripe for training and also so hungry for attention. Much to my amusement, I would often see them following her about, imitating her ways and her style and even her manner of walking. "For draiga they are not so bad," she said to me admiringly one day, as the whole troupe of them swept by us, riding fast and trading horses on the run. It was hard not to be alarmed. I suppose my days of wild riding were behind me. I was very glad Zheran was not there to witness this, and at the same time, my heart swelled with pride. That daughter of ours was a thing to watch.

Most of the Hadra admired these young women, especially those among us who had been Muinyairin. Rishka was the exception. She had nothing but sour words for them. Ursa did not complain: it was not her way. It was Nhari who drew me aside, hurt and puzzled. "Why is Rishka always so angry? Why does she hate us so? What have we ever done to her? Everything she says to us is intentionally rude and hurtful." Those were almost the same questions that Dorca had asked in despair all those many years back, shortly after we had freed her from Eezore.

I shrugged and shook my head. "That one has never been very easy to understand, but I will speak with her."

Now Nhari looked startled and put a restraining hand on my arm. "Oh, no, please, do not use my name. It would only make matters worse — much worse." I gave her my assurance and went to look for Rishka. Her unkindness made me very angry. In some way it also hurt me deeply. These young women who had no name and no place in the world were trying so hard to make a life for themselves among us.

I found Rishka easily enough, but when I tried to talk to her, she gave me a sullen and resentful glare. "They are not one thing or another. They are no longer Kourmairi and can never be Hadra. Of what use are they to us or anyone?"

"Perhaps they are something new in the world, just as we are. I see them as not so different from ourselves a few years back, when we were trying to find some safe place to put our lives."

"This is different. They are not under a death edict. They can go back to the villages they came from. Their people are settled now."

"Those are no longer their people. They have lived with us too long, or they came here because they could not fit themselves into the Kourmairi mold anymore. Rishka, why do you resent them so? Can we not accept them here and make a place for them among us? Do you remember how Hayika once said that we, the Kourmairi and the Shokarn, would never accept the Muinyairin? Yet look at us now. We have a name and are becoming a people. In spite of our differences, we are building a city together. How is this any different? These are the children of the future. How can we send them back to a place that is no longer theirs? Be a little merciful, old friend. Show a little kindness."

"Mercy! Mercy! What do we need with more mercy?" she burst out angrily. "Next, you will be even more merciful and want to invite Kourmairi men — or better yet, Shokarn guards — to come live among us."

I shook my head. "Sometimes I think you have no generosity in your heart."

"Sometimes I have no heart. Who was ever generous with me?"

I could hear the raw pain under her anger, but my own anger got the best of me. "We were, Rishka, all of us! Alyeeta may have silenced you, but she never spoke for throwing you back out where you came from. We took you in when you were like an Oolanth cub, all claws and fangs, spitting and snarling in every direction, and clawing at every hand that

Then she was shaking her head. "But naked ... How can she? ... I would never..."

When the dance stopped, they were all panting hard. Ursa was sweating so profusely that the red on her body ran like rivers of blood. They all bowed to a thunder of applause. Then Ursa jumped down, exhausted, into Nhari's arms and was enveloped in a hug. When she began to shiver, Nhari wrapped her in her cloak. Before they went to find seats, Ursa turned to look at me with a triumphant grin. "Well, Mother, do you think we Neshtair know how to put on a good show? There is more to come, too."

"Well done, Daughter," I said with an answering grin. "You have amazed me once again." As I was already weary, I decided I would find a seat for watching in comfort whatever was to follow. Ursa was not participating in the next part. With Kazouri standing at the side and cheering them on, the Neshtair put on a spirited display of self-defense and unarmed combat. I was absorbed in watching when I saw motion out of the corner of my eye. I turned to see Rishka approaching me. She caught my eye and sauntered deliberately in my direction. We had not exchanged a word since she had blasted me with her rage at the council meeting. I was still very angry and had no desire to speak to her at that moment. I certainly had no wish to renew our conflict in the midst of Ursa's celebration.

No doubt she knew my feelings. Nonetheless, she came and sat next to me on the log, leaning forward so I could not ignore her. I was about to make some biting remark when she surprised me by saying, "These Neshtair might almost be bearable after all. If only they had powers, they could easily be mistaken for Hadra. One has to admire their courage and their skill and most especially their tenacity — particularly that little stepdaughter of yours, Ursa. You have taught her well, Tazzil."

I turned to face her. "Thank you, Rishka, I am glad you are finally able to see her true worth, but give me no credit for who she has become. She is her own fine person. I am afraid that I contributed far more neglect than influence to her growth."

"Come now, Tazzi, I think you can take some credit. You do not have to be her tutor to be her example. She is more like you than you know. And I am sorry for my bitter, angry words. There is still some old monster of ugliness that lives inside. Sometimes it insists on speaking for me in words that come back to shame me later. And then my pride rises up and makes it doubly hard for me to admit my fault. Forgive me, Terrazen."

"Forgiven," I said softly. "But later you must tell them what you said to me. They think you hate them all, and it hurts their brave young hearts." She nodded, and I put my hand on her arm, very glad for some peace between us. She flashed me a quick, crooked little smile and then turned her attention back to the action. In that way, sitting side by side, we watched the rest of the performance together in silence. After that, there was a show of acrobatics, with some of the Sheezerti joining in. Then the platform was cleared away for a wild display of trick horseback riding on the beach, followed by feasting and campfires down by the shore. Pell found me again, and again we commiserated with each other on how we were almost getting too old for such a day.

★

That fall, a small group of riders appeared: two women carrying children on their horses, two boys sharing a smaller horse, and two men who kept themselves somewhat apart. I noticed them from a distance and thought them to be Wanderers hoping to shelter with us for a while or perhaps needing directions to Wanderer Hill. I gave it no thought until Zari came to look for me, saying the women would speak to Tazmirrel and to no other. It had been a long time since anyone had called for me by that name. I gave a little shiver and followed her back down the hill, my head suddenly filled with ghosts.

As I drew closer, I saw an old woman, drawn and haggard, and a younger woman who looked hard and angry. The older one was staring at me as if she thought she knew me. Then, suddenly, I saw my mother and Ghira. The older woman was calling out, "Tazzia, is that really you?"

"Mother!" I shouted, running to her. She handed the baby to the older boy, slid from her horse, and fell into my arms. For a moment we both talked at once: "I never thought..." "Is it really..." "Afraid you were dead..." "So glad..." At last we were both able to draw back a little and look at each other. We had both aged and changed. We had each been through a lifetime of experiences since we had last seen each other. It was hard to take my eyes from her face.

Finally I thought to look around for Ghira, eager to greet her too. She was standing near me, but when her eyes met mine, it was with a hostile stare. Though she held out her hand, she did not embrace me. "Greetings, Sister," she said coolly. "It has been a long time. When you fled Nemanthi I never thought to see you again. You have found yourself a good place here."

She even read my account. Zheran had brought it out, saying that she thought I could be trusted with it now. It was my mother, with Zheran's help, who finally convinced me to begin writing on it again.

One morning, thirty or so Hadra, organized by Kazouri, appeared at our house and began cutting and stacking rocks for an addition, so that my mother and the babies would have space that winter. It was very much needed, and, I must admit, I was most grateful. Our family had grown. Now our daughters had a grandmother and babies to play with. Though Ursa was often gone on the boat with Nhari and Ozzet and Cruzia, this was still her home, and, of course, Nhari had moved in with us. Now that I was finally taking time to write the rest of my account, I needed the space to do it.

Sometimes on those winter days when we sat by the fire, Yolande would come and join us. When Yolande and Zheran and my mother and some of the other Kourmairi women got to talking together, I often felt like the outsider among them. Then I would go to find some Hadra company. Or I would climb up to the cave to sit with Alyeeta and the other Witches, who had all come together in Alyeeta's house for the winter.

Though we were very close at that time, Alyeeta and I never became lovers again. I think that would have stopped even if Zheran had not spoken to me that day. That part of our connection was over. More exactly, that part of Alyeeta's life was over. It was her mind, or rather her spirit, that occupied her now, not her body.

I think we were both saying good-bye to each other that winter. At some moment, Alyeeta took my face between her hands and looked deep into my eyes. "We are very different at the core, you and I, Tazzia. Witch and Hadra are more different than you understand. Our Witch magic is in our spells. Your power is in absolute truth. You are not even able to lie. We create illusion. You go to the deepest layer of reality. You *are* your power, and you were born to it. You need no spells, no words, and no learning. You only have to tap into what lies at your core. Sometimes you only have to exist; that is enough. I have envied you for it and hated you for it and loved you for it all these years." She kissed me on the forehead and I saw her lips quiver. Then she pushed me away roughly and turned the talk to other things.

24

That next spring, two young men found their way to us with the help and guidance of some Wanderers. The older of the two I would have known as Zheran's son even if no word had been spoken; Morkel's resemblance to his mother was that strong. The younger one, Arnath, unfortunately reminded me of his father, glaring at everyone and everything in that same sullen and superior way. Zheran, of course, was delighted to have them with her at last and so could overlook a great deal of folly. I, on the other hand, found it hard to suddenly be dealing with an angry young man in the only home I had. Ursa and Nhari more or less ignored them, but it made my stomach turn to watch the way Ishnu fussed over them both. The difference was that Morkel returned her attentions with kindness and a warm smile, while Arnath grunted or grumbled, scowling no matter what was done for him.

That Arnath! He filled the house with his gloomy, truculent presence. Whenever I came in, I felt as if I were stumbling over him, even if his feet were not out in the passageway, which they often were. He was sneeringly critical — even contemptuous — of everything in Zelindar. Of course, I had been to Darthill and knew that things there were not so grand; knew, in fact, that Zelindar was far superior in many ways. But I kept my silence and tried not to respond to his bait, otherwise we would have been at it day and night.

Zheran loved having them with her and was as proud as an Oolanth cat with her cubs. She would look from one to the other of them and burst out, "So hard to believe! I thought I would never see you again. And now you are really here under my roof..."

Friana had been listening to all this. "Ghira, you can ride with me back to my settlement. The man I was married to is dead. I have nothing left to fear now, and my son is still living there. These women have been kind and loving to me, taken me in and sheltered me through a dangerous time, but this is not my place, either. Maybe it is time to go home now to my own people. You can come with me and take your chances there."

"A fine, generous offer, but what am I to do with all these children?"

"Take the older two," Friana suggested. "Take the boys with you and leave the girls with your mother, if she is willing, or perhaps with the other women here."

My mother, Nairenyati, said she would be pleased to keep the girls. Ishnu was quick to add, "I would be glad to help you with them." She had been leaning over my shoulder, listening intently to everything that was being said. Instantly she made herself into a little mother for the girls, setting the baby, Bethlee, on her hip and taking Bonisha by the hand.

I was shaking my head with amazement, still trying to put it all together. "And what about my brother? Where is Kerris? Did he die with Jortho fighting the Shokarn?"

My mother looked embarrassed and confused, but Ghira spoke up with no shame at all. "Gone to Eezore to join the Thieves Guild. He left after the earlier raids; said he was going to Eezore to see the city that had plagued our lives. He planned to join the Guild there. They had already approached him at the market in Koormir, because he made such good knives. They also had observed a few displays of his light fingers. He said if the Zarns were going to come so far to raid our villages, then he would take some misery back to Eezore, where the trouble came from, and earn his living at the same time. We heard from him a few times. He sent us some goods and some coins when times were hard, but since we fled westward, there has been no word. He probably thinks us dead."

"If he is still living, I can get word to him," I said. "Pell has connections with the Thieves Guild." Ghira shrugged, as if it did not matter to her one way or the other, but I saw my mother's face light up. I nodded my reassurance. "We will tell Pell, and the Wanderers can take back word."

In the end, Ghira stayed only a few days with us before she was on her way again. I wished her luck and sent her off with some provisions and a second horse. But, in truth, I was not sorry to see her go. Friana I would miss, though what she said was true — she was not one of us and never could be.

My mother, who was renamed Renya among us, became an instant favorite with the women of Zelindar, Hadra and Kourmairi both. She seemed quite content to stay where she was, saying, "I have seen enough of men in this lifetime. If I want to see more, I can visit Wanderer Hill or the Kourmairi settlement of Indaran, where Ghira has gone. I do not have to live with them."

Four days after my mother came to visit, I resigned as councilor and asked Kilghari to take my place. Kilghari agreed, but only if I would replace her on the council. The women of Zelindar approved of my choice. Finally, in my thirtieth year, I was free to set down my burden. Zheran was overjoyed. She had been after me for some time to do this. I needed the rest. I needed to step back and not be held responsible for everything — or, perhaps, not hold myself responsible for all of it. And in truth, I was exhausted to the core, deeply weary, much as Pell had been. I thought the change would be good for Zelindar as well. I had pushed and driven and argued and insisted, all necessary at the beginning. Perhaps now it was time for a gentler hand on the reins. The choosing was easy and almost unanimous.

Suddenly I was free. FREE! On those lovely fall days, I took long walks with my mother on the beach, catching up on all that had happened in our lives since our disastrous parting so many years before. After a while, that drawn, gray look left her and some color came back into her face. Every day she looked younger and walked straighter. Sometimes the babies came with us. My mother would carry one, while I took the other on my hip or back.

Sometimes Ishnu came with us, tending to the little ones and basking in my mother's kindly love and approval, and sometimes Zheran accompanied us, leaving other women in charge of the children. Zheran and my mother formed an easy friendship. Other Hadra, Pell or Lhiri or Tama, might join us part of the way, wanting to get to know my mother better. Kara often sought her out so they could talk of Nemanthi and the past. Altogether, I think those were the happiest days of my life since childhood, happy except for the terrible loss and grief of Lorren's death that lay under everything else in my life. So many times I found myself wishing my mother could have met him.

After a while, my mother became part of Zelindar, as if she had always lived there. She organized the care of our new little ones so their mothers could be free for part of the day, and Ishnu became her assistant. She learned to read from Alyeeta, whom she admired but never really trusted.

I wanted to hug her too, but it was clear she would not let me. "Welcome to Zelindar," I said as warmly as I could, in spite of her frosty stare. "Come sit in the Central Circle and we will get you food and drink and some blankets to lay down the little ones."

Women were quickly gathering from all over. I was shouting joyously, "My mother and sister! My mother and sister and babies, they have found me! They are here! My mother and sister..." I went on in this way until Ghira said dryly, "I think they must all have heard you by now."

As soon as the children were settled and there was food and drink all around, for the Wanderer men as well as for my family, I asked for their stories. My mother spoke of the journey and how kind the Wanderers had been, but my sister was silent until I finally asked, "How is it with you, Ghira? Are you married? Where is the father of these children? Did he come with you?"

"No to all of it, and I am no better than what you see," she answered with a bitter edge to her voice. "In the end I married Jortho, the man you stabbed. No one else would have me, as I was your sister. They were afraid I might carry some taint of that strangeness of yours. He wanted you, but he made do with me, instead. He was not always kind, but he was a hard worker and gave me two fine children.

"The Shokarn troops swept through our village a few times after you left, looking for star-brats. They did some damage and killed a few people. After that, they left us in peace for a while. Then, a year or so later, things got more serious. The Shokarn came back and destroyed Nemanthi totally, burnt it to the ground, because they thought we had harbored traitors. What a joke, as if we were not all traitors by then. Who could be a Kourmairi and be loyal to the Zarn? Jortho was killed at the beginning of the fighting, and so we had fled to a settlement closer to the coast where Father had some cousins. We had already left before the soldiers came and demolished our village, but some who escaped told us later of the slaughter. They killed everyone they could lay their hands on. There is no one left there. Nothing remains of Nemanthi, nothing remains standing. Even the stones have been overthrown and buried."

I looked at the younger children. "They are not Jortho's, then? Is that your second husband?" I asked, glancing at one of the men.

"That one is Kairzen, a Wanderer who agreed to be our guide here, and the other is his friend. There was no second husband. No one in the cousins' village wanted a wife who was already used and had two children. Besides, who knew, I might be a Witch or something worse. In their eyes, I was tainted by being your sister. The other two are the children of chance. Those men may not have wanted me for a wife, but that does not mean they left me in peace."

My mother interrupted her story, saying, "I would have come to look for you sooner, Daughter. There were Wanderers who spoke of a Tazzil or a Tazzi, though never a Tazzia; still, I thought it might be you. They even offered to guide us here, but your father forbade it. He even forbade my sending you a message, for fear you might come yourself. He said that..." Suddenly she stopped, stumbling over her words, but I could hear in her head, *She has already made more than trouble enough for her family. Why should we look for her now that she is finally out of our lives?* "But now he is dead," she continued quickly. "He died of a failed heart, and I was free to come and look for you. Oh, Tazmirrel, I am so glad to see you alive."

"I did not come to look for you," Ghira said quickly, "but for a husband. Here, they are not so afraid of the Star-Born, and so that will not stand in my way. I hear these Koormir have fought against each other and there have been many deaths. Perhaps there is some man looking for a wife to care for his children, a man who will not care too much about my reputation and will not mind a few extra little ones. I am still a young woman and very tired of being alone."

"We are called Hadra now. That is how we speak of ourselves and that is what our friends call us." It was hard to recognize my sweet little sister in this bitter and hardened young woman who glared at me as if I were the source of all her troubles. I may well have been, but it certainly was not through any intention of mine. I reached out my hand, saying, "Ghira, neither of our lives has been easy, but the Zarn's armies are at fault for that, not the Hadra."

"Easy for you to say," she answered, drawing back. "Look at you here, the chosen leader, with a house and a family, love and respect, and a whole city rising around you. What do I have? Four fatherless children, an old mother who is dependent on me, and no place to lay my head down."

"We will make a place for you here, Ghira, and for the children too. You will never have to run again."

"An easy offer to make. How can I stay here with two boy-children? Besides, I have no wish to live in a place that is all women. What kind of a life is that? It is not natural. It might please you and the other Puntyar like you, but I need a man in my life."

291

Though I took pleasure in Zheran's pleasure, this invasion put an end to my writing. In my secret heart I hoped her sons would soon be on their way, now that they had re-established contact — or at least that her younger son would find some other place to perch himself. I was very glad at the moment that Zheran did not have the Hadra gift of reading minds. My thoughts would have been exceedingly hurtful. But, of course, her mind was not on me or my thoughts. Ursa and I did not have to read each other's minds. A shared look across the table would do when Arnath was being particularly obnoxious.

I think it was Zheran's guilt for abandoning her children that made her overlook such boorish behavior, but when Arnath said, for at least the tenth time, "In Darthill it is better than Zelindar because...," I wished I did not have Hadra powers and could simply smash the chair over his head as he deserved. Of course, I would not have done that to Zheran's son. Instead, I left the house once again, seeking refuge for the day with Pell and Tama. At other times, when he was too much for me, I would stroll down the beach, or climb up to the Zildorn to see how the building was progressing. After all, it was spring. There were many places for escape.

What gave me some hope was that Arnath talked constantly of leaving as soon as he could persuade his brother to go. For me, it could not be soon enough. In that, at least, we were on the same side. Then it happened. It was like an explosion among us. Suddenly, Morkel and Ishnu looked at each other in that certain way and fell in love. After that, they had eyes only for each other — nothing else mattered. When I saw the despairing look on Arnath's face, I could almost sympathize. He was no more eager to stay than I was to have him there.

Now every time I came into the hut, I felt as if I were intruding, stumbling over love — or perhaps suffocating on it. The air was thick with it, making it hard to breathe. It filled all the space. Before, with Arnath, it had been ill humor that crowded the space, and now it was an excess of affection. I am not sure which was worse. Zheran and my mother, Renya, added their cloying enthusiasm. I had to remind myself to be as happy for Ishnu with her love as I was for Ursa with hers, though at least Ursa had shown the good sense to take some of her passion elsewhere. Morkel was a fine young man, there was no denying that. And he clearly had a central place in Zheran's heart. She was so happy to see her children together, she could hardly contain herself. Perhaps I was jealous. My mother was taken up with the babies and Zheran with the young people, and now they were even talking of a wedding. There seemed no place for me there.

It was almost by default that I took up with Arnath: he seemed to feel even more displaced than I did. After a while, he stopped complaining so loudly and being so disdainful about everything. He kept saying he was only waiting for his brother to be done so they could leave together, but he knew as well as I did that his brother was not leaving anytime soon, if ever. I sensed that he himself was not much more comfortable in Darthill than he was in Zelindar. After a while, I saw that his nastiness was only a cover for all the pain and confusion of his life: his father's violent death and everything that surrounded it; his mother's desertion and this strange, incomprehensible, new life of hers.

"Why? Why did she leave us? I thought she was happy at home. And to live like this, in a crowded little hut. We had a fine house, one of the best in the village. What else did she need? She could have had anything, whatever she asked for."

Anything but herself, I thought sadly, but I did not try to explain. It was too soon for him to hear such things. With one excuse or another, we took long rides together while he talked out his grief and bewilderment. Sometimes I tried gently to explain, especially when I felt the questions were real and not full of accusations. Mostly I just let him go on and on. Finally, I ran out of errands to invent as an excuse for riding out. When I tried to get him to come to Wanderer Hill with me, he refused, saying, "That woman will not want to see the son of the man responsible for her husband's death." At last, on the pretext of needing to talk to Lomaire about some trade, I told Arnath I was riding to the Kourmairi settlement of Zelandria. I asked him to accompany me, saying I might need his help.

He talked the whole way, pouring out his heart. He even told me that he had known his father planned to kill Lorren and had conspired with Garrell to do so. After some subtle probing, I got him to admit that he was really afraid of going home. He did not trust the men who had been his father's friends. They were the ones who had supported Rhomar in his vengeful plot and probably also the ones who had disposed of Nhokosos.

In spite of myself, my heart was beginning to warm to this boy who had been like a thorn in my side. Still, there were things he needed to hear. When we were approaching the village, I dropped back to ride next to him. "You cannot be as contemptuous of Zelandria as you have been of Zelindar. Lomaire is a proud man. He is proud of what has been done here in so short a time and will take offense at insults." I had the momentary

★

Summer passed into fall. I sensed the baby long before any bulge showed. Too young, too young, my heart cried out, but that is the way with Kourmairi women, and certainly my little foster daughter Ishnu had been given every chance to make her choices. I wondered if she herself knew. I could feel the new life every time I came near her, could feel its little spirit reaching out into the world. Inspired by Ghira's wedding, Ishnu and Morkel were talking about a wedding in the spring. They were waiting that long at Zheran's insistence. I thought it might well be after the fact, after the baby. How would Ishnu react? Like a Hadra or a Kourmairi? Did she already know and was she keeping quiet with her secret? I could sense nothing from Zheran. It hurt to keep secrets from her or from my mother, but I did not want to be the one to say. Ursa gave me knowing glances that told me she already knew. That girl was becoming more like a Hadra every day.

After years of wandering about, not knowing where I was going to put my head down each night, I suddenly found myself as caught up in domestic concerns as any village wife. On top of everything else, Yolande and Hereschell were talking about the possibility of marrying, though she had said many times after Lorren's death that she would never marry again. Perhaps, with Arnath added to this, we could have a rash of spring weddings, culminating in a huge, week-long celebration. Lomaire had promised both young men a share of land at Zelandria, though, in truth, some land should have gone to the young women as well. Ishnu should have gotten the share that would rightfully have belonged to her parents, and Jeelia, also, should have her own plot. I was determined to speak to Lomaire on the matter, but in the end, other things intervened to take my attention.

★

I thought that my life had reached a place of peace at last. I thought it was now time to reap the harvest of all I had struggled so hard to plant. Then, on a cold midwinter day, Olna came to fetch me, saying Alyeeta had sent her. I felt a rush of fear, but Olna would say nothing more. I already knew it was useless to try reading her mind. Olna turned and rushed off while I hurried after her.

Alyeeta was lying in her bed, surrounded by the other Witches. She turned to look at me. The moment her eyes met mine, I knew. "I am dying, Child," she said in a low voice. "And I needed to see you one last time."

I was thirty then and had been the councilor of Zelindar for many years. Only Alyeeta could have called me "Child" that way. My heart stopped like a stone in my breast. I knew beyond any doubt that she spoke the truth. That did not stop my despairing protest. I threw myself down beside her bed. "Oh, Alyeeta, do not tell me that, not so soon after Lorren's death."

She was shaking her head. "Child, it is not a thing I tell you or do not tell you. It is a fact. I will not wake up in the morning. I know it. Witches always know when they are about to die. I have far, far overstayed my time here, mostly for your sake. And now that time is up. There is nothing left of me, only a hollow husk. Tazzil, you must hear this and accept it and understand it, because this time there is no way around it."

"Oh, Alyeeta, Alyeeta, please, I cannot bear it!"

"Crying and begging will avail you nothing. It is time to say good-bye. Tazzil, please, out of our long time together, do just this one thing without an argument."

"But it is your *life* we are speaking of..."

"Yes, my life. Mine to choose, and I am at the end of it. No matter how much we may love one another in this world, we are really here for ourselves. If we are here only for others, we become a hollow, empty thing, the walking dead. I stayed for you, long after I was already weary of living. It has been very entertaining. I would not have missed it for the world. I am incredibly lucky for this friendship. We both are. But now it is over."

"But I wanted to finish the Zildorn for you and put your books there in a safe and honored place and finish my own account for you and put it there too. Alyeeta, there are so many things I still want to do for you."

"Then do them for me. Do them in my name. But if you have ever loved me, Tazzia, then in human kindness do not try to make me wait here any longer. Carve my name over the entryway if it pleases you, but do not ask me to stay with these tired bones in this weary flesh. The Mother calls me elsewhere."

It was plain to see that she was weary to the bone, to the soul. I knew it was the truth that she had stayed so long because of me, and I wondered again how old she really was, wondered if she would tell me now, but of course I did not ask. Already the grieving had set in on me. When she saw the look on my face, she reached out her hand. "Child, I have loved you long and well, better than anyone else in my life. I have given you as much of myself as I could. Do not spend your time crying for me. You have

★

Ghira and Lomaire had a fine wedding, the finest I have ever seen. It was much finer even than Yolande and Lorren's, but I liked it less. For my taste, there an excess of everything, especially drink. My sister loved it. For her it was a vindication, a grand public acceptance after all the slights she had suffered and the shame she had endured. I could tell that my mother was very pleased to see my sister so well settled.

For Ghira's sake, I tried to be happy; for myself, I was less so. After much urging, I finally drank some brew, and so I went about for the rest of the day with my Hadra powers all muddled and my head throbbing. Of course I knew better. I had been fool enough to let myself get challenged by Lomaire. Poor man, he was much confused by the Hadra, never knowing whether to treat us with the courtesy and condescension he reserved for women or with the bluff hardiness he shared with men. He was a good man. He was a good friend and staunch ally to Zelindar, and he truly loved my sister, but after spending three nights under his roof, I felt like an Oolanth cat about to explode with rage. The idea of sharing his bed was beyond comprehension. Ghira, however, appeared to be flourishing. She was almost like a girl again, gay and lighthearted and very pretty.

People came from everywhere. Many of the Hadra came from Zelindar, accompanied by my mother and Zheran and some of the other Kourmairi women. Kourmairi from Indaran mingled easily with the folk of Zelandria. Friana seemed particularly pleased for Ghira, as if she had arranged the whole thing herself — which I suspect she had. This time, when Ossan and Lomaire met, they appeared to be friendly and at ease with each other. Hereschell and Yolande were there, along with the others from Wanderer Hill. Those two seemed very much together. Indeed, I had never seen Hereschell look that way at any woman; Yolande appeared to be returning his loving glances. Whenever I happened to catch sight of Arnath, he had some young woman clinging to his arm. He grinned and waved when he caught my eye.

It was a hot day. We spent our time between the feasting tables and the river, where there was much splashing and shouting and running in and out of the water. For me, most of the day passed in confusion. I did not know how to deal with being a Hadra and a Kourmairi at the same time. It felt as if the different parts of my life were colliding, rather than merging. Perhaps that was the real secret of why I was fool enough to drink.

What I preferred to the wedding itself was the dinner we had the night before, a dinner for family and close friends. A big plank table had been set up under the gobal tree in Lomaire's yard, and torches had been stuck in the ground for light. What an amazing meal! It was amazing for me because in some ways it was so very ordinary. We all sat around the table together as a family. Besides some friends and relatives of Lomaire, there were: my mother; my sister and her future husband with her four children and his four children; my lover with her two sons and our two daughters, one of each betrothed to the other. Our other daughter had brought her young lover, and Zheran's other son had one of the prettiest girls I had ever seen sitting roguishly on his lap for much of the meal. I kept looking at all of them together there. It was so normal, so ordinary. This was something I never thought to have again in my life, and it made me want to cry. I thought briefly of my father. Then I thought of my brother Kerris, and wondered if any of the Wanderers had been able to find him in Eezore. I even had a moment of missing him, but soon I was caught by the wonderful aromas of the food and fell to eating with a good appetite. Ghira and the other women had done well.

There was a strangely dressed man sitting close to the end of the table, talking intently with Lomaire. We had not yet been introduced. I assumed him to be one of Lomaire's friends. There was something familiar in the man's manner, if not his appearance, but every time I glanced in his direction, he looked away. Finally, during a lull in the flow of talk, he stood up and raised his glass to make a toast. "To Tazmirrel, a woman who has withstood all the hardships life could throw at her and emerged victorious." Recognition hit me like a hammer. "Kerris," I whispered in amazement. Then I shouted, "Kerris!" and leapt to my feet. With no regard for the glass in his hand, I ran to him and threw myself into his arms, forgetting in that one moment all the bitterness that lay between us.

After that, we had little to say to each other, though I was very glad to know Kerris was still alive and well somewhere in the world. My mother, of course, was overjoyed. As soon as the dinner was over, she took him by the arm and led him about, proudly introducing him to everyone as her son. Before he left Zelandria, I watched Kerris working out some complicated dealings with Lomaire and Hereschell and Pell. Regardless of my feelings, I could see Kerris was back in my life — and not just because of my mother.

pleasure of seeing him flush with embarrassment at the thought of all his mean words to us. Then, just as quickly, I was ashamed of my own meanness.

When we got to Lomaire's house, who should I find sitting in the yard under a huge gobal tree but my sister Ghira? As I introduced Arnath, she rose to greet me with a big smile and even a hug. She seemed genuinely glad to see me. This was very different from our last meeting. She even filled three mugs of water from a crock, offered us some fruit from a big wooden bowl, and invited us to join her on the bench. When she sat down again, a little girl came running up and climbed into her lap. It seemed as if the child had done it so often she did not have to ask. "His children are wonderfully kind. See, they love me already, especially little Nanomi." She spoke quickly and hugged the child to her as if for protection against any judgments I might make. "Friana brought me here for a visit and I have been here ever since. Lomaire and I are planning to marry at midsummer and invite everyone from both settlements, and Wanderer Hill and Zelindar, as well. Will you come?"

"Of course I will come. Nothing could keep me away." I knew Lomaire had lost his first wife in the fighting, leaving him with two small children. His second wife had died in childbirth after her second baby. There was no doubt he was looking for a mother for his children. But when he came striding into the yard a few minutes later, I saw the look of lust and love that passed between them and knew this was not just a match of convenience.

There were more excited greetings and a flurry of plans. Then I chanced to glance at Arnath and see his hurt, sullen look. His face was all closed down with pain, an outsider once again. Quickly I introduced him as Zheran's son, but that may have been no better. When Ghira rose, saying, "I need to go to the well for more water," I said quickly, "Arnath can help you with that." He shot me an angry, accusing look, but he went anyhow.

As soon as he was out of earshot, I told Lomaire as quickly as I could of Arnath's predicament. Lomaire nodded while I talked. When they came back, carrying the full water pail between them, Lomaire hardly waited for them to set it down before he said, "I know you are planning to ride home soon, young man, but I have much work to do here before the wedding and I am terribly shorthanded. Everyone is busy elsewhere. I wonder if you could spare me a week or so of time before you leave. I promise I will reward you well. I would not think to ask, except we are all family of a sort here and I am close to being desperate."

I saw the spark of hope in Arnath's eyes, though he answered with restraint, "I would be pleased to stay and help you, perhaps for even longer than a week, if my brother is not yet ready to leave."

Before my departure, Ghira filled a little sack with sweets for our mother and entrusted it to me. "Will you take her a message for me, Tazzia? Tell her I love her and miss her and that I am very happy here. Tell her I will come to visit soon, to see her as well as the little ones." I promised to take her message and refrained from saying that the little ones were doing very well without her. Not till I was mounted and ready to go did she say one word to me of what had passed between us the last time we met. Then she looked up at me with a plea in her eyes. "I hope I am still your sister, in spite of all my harsh words. I allowed the unhappiness of these last few years to turn to bitterness. I am happy with this man. There is love here. I feel more like my old self every day."

I nodded. I understood about bitterness. "You will always be my sister, Ghira. I rejoice in your happiness and wish you well and am very glad to have you back in my life. I have grieved for you, Sister."

"And I for you." For just a moment, she pressed her cheek against my knee, then she straightened abruptly. "Come back soon, Tazzia, and be sure to come for the wedding. It will be very fine. It is not every day that the headman gets married."

Before I left, I reached for Arnath's hand and looked straight into his eyes. "Is this well with you? Is this what you want? If not, you have only to say. You do not have to stay."

For just a moment there was the flash of a smile not so different from his brother's. It was the first time I had ever seen him smile. "I believe it is what we both want, Tazzil of Zelindar. It gets me out from under your feet and gives me some work to do that matters. In Zelindar there is nothing for a man to do. Women do it all. Tell my mother I am needed here. Tell her I will see her soon."

When I finally rode off, there were already several Kourmairi girls hanging around Lomaire's gate, giggling and looking at Arnath with curiosity. I hoped one of them would find a way to soften the heart of that confused and lonely boy. Riding home alone, I felt more lighthearted than I had in weeks. I was very excited to be bringing my mother such good news from Ghira, and I hoped Zheran would not be too upset with my creative meddling.

much else to do. And never reproach yourself for anything between us. You have been friend and lover to me. You were the daughter I never had, the student I could entrust with my knowledge. You gave me reason to live, and hope and joy and pride besides. We have built something here together that in some measure has made up for what the Zarns destroyed. I was a recluse in the forest, close to madness, living alone with my books and my pony, when you came into my life and gave me an excuse for joining the world again. It has been a grand adventure. Good-bye, Tazzia. Goddess bless you and watch over you. As it must be. No more words now. Just give me your hand." Even as she was speaking those last words, her voice was fading to a whisper.

I stopped protesting, put my hand in hers, and sank into silence. The other Witches sat down around us. For a long time, there was no sound in the cave but our breathing, Alyeeta's slightly labored. From beyond the cave came the muffled sounds of Zelindar, and from beyond that, the endless sighing of the sea. All that seemed to be in another world. Alyeeta — my mother, lover, friend, teacher, and guide — was going out of my life. Before dusk, her hand suddenly tightened on mine in a convulsive grip. Her whole body tensed and shook for a moment, then, with a groan and a great sigh, her breathing stopped. It was over. Alyeeta was gone.

The pain was so sharp it felt as if someone had stabbed me in the chest with a jagged knife. By custom I should have sat quietly by the body, keeping it company, at least for that night. Instead, I leapt to my feet and ran out of the cave, wailing. In my rush, I passed a blur of startled faces. I saw Zheran's, but I did not stop. I had to run and keep running. That strange sound kept pouring from my mouth. When I found Dancer, I rode off on her without a word to anyone, going up into the hills, away from Zelindar. I kept going for a long time, not eating, hardly sleeping, stopping only because Dancer needed to stop. It was several days before I turned back, riding slowly toward home with a heavy heart. First I went to the top of Third Hill, needing to re-enter gradually and hoping no one else would be there. I was in luck. The almost-finished Zildorn and the hilltop around it were deserted.

Carved into the archway over the Zildorn entrance by a skilled hand, probably Vestri's, I saw the names *Alyeeta ... Aisha ... Arimaine*. It had been done Witch style, with her mother's name and then her grand-mother's after hers. Below the names were the words *Witch ... Warrior ... Wisewoman*. Under that it said, *She was mother to the Hadra and taught us to survive.* Nearby, on a rock platform, was the statue of the

Goddess that Kara had been working on for so long. The words *For Alyeeta* were carved in the base, and the statue was surrounded with little offerings and flowers. Moving as if in a trance, I picked some flowers from between the rocks, twined their stems together, and laid them with the other offerings.

Seeing those carved words gave her death an absolute finality. Now, at last, I was able to cry. The flowers and the offerings swam in my tears, a blur of bright colors. I was too late, too late to prepare the body or join in the ritual or say my words at the funeral fire. I am not proud of my impulse to run and will not defend it here. And I am very glad that I was not still councilor of Zelindar at the time. I can only say that the impulse was stronger than I was. I could not stay still with my grief, though now it had caught up with me anyhow. I am grateful that at least I had been there to say good-bye to the living, even if I had run away from the dead. Oh, Alyeeta! It would take a whole book to explain those few carved words over the entrance.

And what did I really know of Alyeeta's life, before our life became her life? Suddenly, I needed to talk to the Witches, Olna in particular. I was not ready yet to face Zheran or the Hadra. Trying to stay out of sight, I took a back pathway to the cave, one known to few besides the Witches. The instant I came around the last bend, I knew. All gone! Even the glass had been taken away. The rocks of the front wall were thrown down and scattered. With my heart pounding, I climbed over the rubble and stepped into the cave. Everything was gone: the cushions, the oil lamps, the rugs, the books. Even the little dam on the bathing pool had been broken, and the water was flowing freely again. The space was back to being a cave, with almost no sign of ever having been a home. All that remained of Alyeeta was the water jug by the spring, the one Kara had made for her with Alyeeta's name painted on it. Feeling numb and bewildered, I went to pick up the jug and sat down on a rock ledge, cradling it in my arms.

That is how Pell found me. I looked up at the sound of her feet on the loose rocks, but I could find no words of greeting. "I have been watching for you, Tazzi. I thought you might come here first." She stood waiting until I gave a slight nod. Then she came and sat by me on the ledge, not speaking, not touching me, just giving comfort by her silent presence.

Finally, with a deep sigh, I set down the jug and turned to look at her. "So, Alyeeta is really dead. Pell, where are the Witches? I need to speak to Olna, and to Shalamith, too."

Pell shook her head. "All gone, all the Witches."

cilor of Zelindar, they consider me a sort of repository of knowledge. Also, they think it was all some great adventure that we shared, and they feel left out. Little do they know the terrible pains and hardships of those times. Well, I have grown weary of telling those tales over and over. Let them read it here.

Enough of all this. The story that I had to tell is finished now. No, not finished. It will never be finished. Not as long as there are Hadra left alive in the world. But let them tell their own tales. My part of this story is done. I will no longer put pen to paper in this manner, nor will I ever be councilor again — I value my health and my sanity too much to be talked down that road once more.

It is time for me to rest now, to look every day at the view, the beauty that the Goddess has created, and to enjoy what we ourselves have built here. It is time to read all the books that Lorren left us in his library. I have no wish to rush about anymore the way I once did, no wish to build and fix and make and do. Let others do that now.

Sometimes I walk in the woods, gathering herbs, remembering that once, as a child, I was a Witch and a healer. Now that I move more slowly and listen with care, some of my healing powers have come back to me, a good thing, since so many little ones among us are in need of them. There are moments now when I even feel myself reconnecting with the little girl of my childhood village, the one who talked to birds and animals and walked far into the forest where others feared to go, the one who petted the bull and turned aside a wolf with a basket of eggs. Sometimes I think that child is waiting there for me at the end of my life, waiting with her innocence and her untried powers.

Often I go to visit with Yolande, or she comes here. We, who were once almost enemies, are now the best of friends. We walk about together on the shore and talk of all that has passed; or we share our memories of Lorren and Hereschell; or we do not talk at all, sitting side by side, remembering in silence. Zheran joins us when she can, but she walks with a cane now, and her eyesight is worsening rapidly. Ursa and Nhari visit almost daily to make sure we have what we need, and Pell and Tama and their brood of daughters and granddaughters are often with us.

But why am I maundering on and on? Now it is time to pass it on to the young ones. There is only one thing I need to say at the end of all this: Take care, Daughters! It is not over yet. The Hadra have gathered and become a people. Zelindar is a fine settlement, on its way to being a city. We have more settlements to the north, and some forming south of us. I have lived to see all this accomplished, and I feel I could die happy. But I hear rumors. Those of our sisters who are spies in the Zarns' cities say there is talk of invasion. I do not think they will leave us in peace. No matter how much they have, they must have more. They fear our powers and our influence among the Kourmairi. They must move soon, before we are any stronger.

If they all gathered against us, I fear for our survival. I am old now. Perhaps I will die knowing only what is won and not be forced to see it lost again. But to the younger Hadra who have grown up with the peace and beauty of this place and take it for granted, I must leave a warning. Daughters, the Zarns are not finished with us. We sit here like a bright jewel on the coast, tempting them by our very existence. You must hold yourselves prepared. Do not expect this peace to last forever. As Olna so often said, "Those who cannot be controlled are a threat to those who must control." The peace and power we have was dearly bought and paid for and must be guarded. It may not last. The Zarns will not take our success lightly, for it challenges their power. Sooner or later, they will have to make their move. Take care, and be ready!

As it must be,
Tazmirrel of Nemanthi
Tazzil of Zelindar

EPILOGUE

I have just finished rereading the last few pages of this account. Sitting here in the Zildorn, I am suddenly flooded with memories. Even now — some twenty years later — Alyeeta's death brings tears to my eyes, though by now the pain is dull, softened by time. I have kept faith with her as best I could. I have seen to the building of a Zildorn that safely holds all of her books and all of our stories and has room for whatever other knowledge we may gather. I have put together my notes of our past as she asked me to. She cannot ask more from me.

In honor of the twentieth anniversary of Alyeeta's death, this whole book has been recopied in Ursa's clear, careful hand. Her fine drawings decorate the edges of many of the pages, and her pictures help to tell the tales. It pleases me to see that she has made a work of art out of my rough scribbles. Ursa has asked me to write a few words here at the end. I would be glad to, but Goddess, what am I to say that has not already been said?

The first part of my account I wrote when I was very young and all those things had just occurred. I have made only a few small changes, and those only for the sake of clarity. This last part, which I have simply called *The Hadra*, I wrote afterward, looking back, trying hard to remember everything just as it was — not an easy task, believe me. Some I even wrote after Alyeeta's death. Of course, I would not have written any of this if Alyeeta had not urged me to.

I wrote about that time because I was there at the very beginning, before we even had a name. Perhaps I also wrote because the telling helped to free me from it all. Sometimes the younger Hadra come to me now, wanting to know how it was back then. Because I was First Coun-

"What do you mean, gone? Where are they? I have to see Olna, I have to talk to her."

She shook her head again. "They all left as soon as the funeral fire had been lit and they had said their words for Alyeeta. They did not keep her company through the night or even wait for us to speak. They seemed in a great hurry to be away from here. I know nothing of where they went, only that they were looking for an Asharan asking place."

"They took everything with them?" I asked, gesturing around the empty cave.

"They took nothing. Everything went either to the Zildorn or to the meeting house, according to Alyeeta's wishes. I think they did not expect to live very long. Oh, Tazzi, they looked so old, even Olna. I have never seen living women who looked so old." Pell shuddered and turned away, but I caught the picture from her mind.

"Did they leave nothing for me, no word?"

"Olna left you a message."

"Where is it?" I asked eagerly. "Give it to me."

Pell opened her empty hands. "It was only a few words, nothing that needed to be written. All she said was 'Tell Tazzia to remember her choices.' That was her whole message."

★

When I finally went home to Zheran, I was sad and silent, my head full of ghosts. I was very glad to find her alone. As I came up to our shelter, I saw her stooped over in her little garden with her hands in the dirt, surrounded by the bright ordinary magic of the flowers and vegetables that grew so abundantly for her. Suddenly, my heart was filled with love. Zheran straightened instantly, wiping her hands on her skirt. "Welcome home, Tazzil," she said softly, opening her arms to me. I walked slowly into her embrace, and we held each other a long time without speaking. At last Zheran stepped back to look in my face. "Tazzil...?"

"Alyeeta is gone, Zheran. Perhaps in some way that is a relief for you."

Zheran shook her head. "No, I am very sorry she is dead. In truth, I often did not understand her or trust her. Sometimes I did not even like her. But I always trusted her love for you, and I trusted her intentions for this place. We worked together teaching the children, and in the process, she became my teacher. There was much I learned from her. I admired her and sometimes even envied her, and I shall miss her very much. Come, I have something to show you."

She took my hand and led me around to the side of the shelter. There I saw a little sapling standing bravely in the freshly dug earth. "A parmi tree. I planted it for her. In years to come, we will eat parmi-fruit and remember Alyeeta and tell stories of her life among us. That is how the people of Darthill fill the space that is left by death." Hand in hand, we stood in silence, looking at those little gray twigs that were both a commemoration for the dead and a promise of new life.

Finally, as if at a signal, we both turned and went inside. Suddenly I realized how exhausted and hungry I was. With a groan, I sank down on the bench and rested my head on the table, while Zheran made me a cup of tea and something to eat. When she came to sit across the table from me, she was very contrite. "Oh, Tazzil, if I had only known what it meant to you, I would never have asked you to sever your connection with her in that way."

"Zheran, what we severed at that time needed to be severed. We stopped being lovers with our bodies. That was all a tease, a game, a challenge, something that amused Alyeeta. It was time for that to end. The real connection between us was never severed. We have always been lovers in our spirits. No, no, not the right word. What can I say? She was..." I shrugged and stopped speaking, feeling betrayed by words. Then, with a struggle, I tried again. "I want to say she was the rock in my life, but how can you say that of someone so moody, so changeable, so unpredictable, so mocking, so capable of cruelty as well as love? No, she held my life in the palms of her hands all these years, keeping me safe. And she stayed here for me, lending me her strength until she had none left, and then even longer. Now she is gone, and we have our own lives to live."

I reached out to Zheran and took her hand in mine. We sat that way in silence for a while, looking at each other across the table. Then, with great deliberation, she freed her hand from mine, stood up, took a packet from the highest shelf, and laid it on the table. It was my account lying in front of me. "Finish it, Tazzil. It is the one last thing you can do for her."

URSA'S ACCOUNT

These are my words for Tazzil, set down more than ten years after her own. The Hadra have asked me to write something in her honor, here at the end of her account — not an easy thing for me to do, under the circumstances. My heart is full of pain and loss and — yes — confusion. I cannot write empty words of praise. I can write only the truth as I know it from my own heart and my own life.

Three days ago, my fourth mother died. To others she was Tazzil of Zelindar, founder of this city and First Councilor of the Hadra. To me she was Fourth Mother, the reluctant one, the woman I also knew as Tazzi or Tazzia. If my third mother, Zheran, were still alive, perhaps they would have asked her to write this instead of me, but she is already gone.

Tazzil was the woman who was my mother's lover and, in some ways, her husband as well, for my mother chose to be the wife. I knew Tazzil as the woman who *stayed* in our house but did not really *live* there because she was too busy and had too much else to do. I admired her, as others did. How could I not? But I also longed for her to really be my mother: to teach me to ride; to talk to me about what she was doing; to take me with her sometimes; to even remember I existed. Other girls thought it must be exciting to live with the councilor and be at the center of everything, a sort of honor. In truth, it was very lonely.

Though I loved Zheran, I was not like her and knew it from the beginning. In spirit, I was Tazzil's daughter. It was Tazzil I was like, and it was her attention I craved. Is that not the nature of humans, to hunger always for what we cannot have? I would have given anything for her to notice me and be as proud of me as I was of her.

Other books of interest from
ALYSON PUBLICATIONS

AMNESTY, by Louise A. Blum, $20.00, cloth. Maura Jaeger has hidden herself in the hills of rural Pennsylvania, teaching English at a small state college and rigorously avoiding all relationships. When her father dies, she must return to the small town where she grew up, confronting ghosts at every turn: her beloved brother Colin, whose tour of duty in Vietnam changed him forever; the town that shunned her family when her brother Zach fled to Canada to dodge the draft; the lovers who left her behind; and the family that has exiled her for her lesbianism. Forced to re-examine the childhood that she has fought so hard to forget, Maura must grant herself amnesty, and begin to live life on her own terms.

THE FEMME MYSTIQUE, edited by Lesléa Newman, $12.00, paper. A fascinating and insightful look at the world of femme identity within the lesbian community, written by femmes, former femmes, femme wanna-bes, femme admirers, and, of course, femme fatales. Through poetry, essays, short fiction, and photography, *The Femme Mystique* explores what it means to be a femme and a lesbian in a society that often trivializes the feminine.

THE WANDERGROUND, by Sally Miller Gearhart, $9.00, paper. These absorbing, imaginative stories tell of a future women's culture, created in harmony with the natural world. The women depicted combine the control of mind and matter with a sensuous adherence to their own realities and history.

DAUGHTERS OF KHATON, by Merril Mushroom, $8.00, paper. A team of space explorers searches the galaxy for unpopulated planets suitable for human colonization. Their ship accidentally lands on Khaton, a beautiful land of perfectly balanced light, color, fragrance, and flowers that is populated only by lesbians.

HAPPY ENDINGS ARE ALL ALIKE, by Sandra Scoppettone, $7.00, paper. It was their last summer before college, and Jaret and Peggy were in love. But as Jaret said, "It always seems as if when something great happens, then something lousy happens soon after." Soon her worst fears turned into brute reality.

LEAVE A LIGHT ON FOR ME, by Jean Swallow, $10.00, paper. Morgan is a computer instructor who doesn't understand what exactly has happened to her long-term relationship with Georgia, nor what exactly is happening to her own body when she stands near Elizabeth. Georgia, forced into exile from both the South and the alcoholic family she loves *and* hates, doesn't understand why, after six years of recovery, she still hasn't found her way home. And Elizabeth, the rich and beautiful doctor, doesn't understand why she can't keep a girlfriend. But Bernice, who watches and waits, understands a lot by just being herself. Together, this engaging foursome moves from a difficult past into a passionate and hopeful future.

CHOICES, by Nancy Toder, $9.00, paper. Lesbian love can bring joy and passion; it can also bring conflicts. In this straightforward, sensitive novel, Nancy Toder conveys the fear and confusion of a woman coming to terms with her sexual and emotional attraction to other women.

WORLDS APART, edited by Camilla Decarnin, Eric Garber, and Lyn Paleo, $6.00, paper. Adventure, romance, excitement — and perhaps some genuine alternatives for our future — highlight this startling collection of lesbian and gay science-fiction writing. The authors of these stories explore issues of sexuality and gender relations in the context of futuristic societies, showing us our possible alternatives. The results are sometimes hilarious and sometimes disturbing.

BUTCH, by Jay Rayn, $8.00, paper. Michaeline "Mike" Landetti doesn't have a word for what she is, but from the beginning of memory she has played ball with the boys and fallen in love with the girls. Jay Rayn has written a moving story about growing up butch and learning to make your way in a less-than-accepting world. First published by Free Women Press.

BUTCH II, by Jay Rayn, $9.00, paper. Mike is back! Beginning where *Butch* ended, *Butch II* continues to lure the reader into Michaeline Landetti's life with its poignancy and bitter truths. After returning from Chile, where she learns about oppression she's never known, Mike's sense of outrage drives her into an angry fight for social justice. But even in the midst of all this, Mike hasn't given up looking for "Ms. Right" — and it's this need for love that steers Mike toward her final heartbreak.

Watch for the next installment in
Diana Rivers's Hadra series:

THE RED LINE OF YARMALD

The Hadra have found refuge in Zelindar, the city they built by the sea, but what is to stop the Zarns from invading Yarmald to re-establish their power on the coast? This is the story of three women whose lives intertwine to transform their world: Noya, the young woman chosen to be councilor for Zelindar in a time of war; Amairi, the Shokarn Highborn who escapes her husband's violence to become a Wanderer; and Jolaina, the Kourmairi peasant girl who becomes the Zarna's lover and adviser, then a warrior, when her mistress is betrayed and overthrown.

...while enjoying the other books in the series:

JOURNEY TO ZELINDAR
The personal account of Sair of Semasi

by Diana Rivers • $10.00, paper

Sair grows up as the pampered daughter of an upper-caste family in a patriarchal city-state, but her life is forever changed by a brutal gang rape. Abandoned and left for dead, she makes her way to the ocean to kill herself. There she is rescued by the Hadra, wild riding-women who accept her into their culture. *Journey to Zelindar* is Sair's own tale of her adventures among the Hadra, who ride their horses by consent, speak mind-to-mind with each other, and are all lovers of women.

★ "Spun from the same magic thread as Sally Gearhart's *Wanderground.* You'll ride bareback across the Red Line into a Goddess land of mindspeak and sensual ecstasies and unforgettable women — who have no word for celibacy." —Noretta Koertge

★ "So engrossing you'll find yourself losing sight of reality. One can only hope that there are many more to come." —*Our Own Community Press*